THE HARVEST

Books by Scott Nicholson

THE RED CHURCH

THE HARVEST

Published by Pinnacle Books

THE HARVEST

Scott Nicholson

PINNACLE BOOKS
Kensington Publishing Corp.

PINNACLE BOOKS are published by

Kensington Publishing Corp.
850 Third Avenue
New York, NY 10022

Pinnacle and the P logo Reg. U.S. Pat. & TM Off.

ISBN 0-7394-3736-4

Printed in the United States of America

For Brian, an all-around good seed.

Prologue: Monday

It fell from the heavens.

The object cut a hot, green-yellow slice through the dark belly of the atmosphere and shot to earth under the cover of twilight clouds.

It rammed into the worn granite of the Appalachian mountainside, plowing into the ground and throwing bits of rock and shredded fern and stump dust into the air. Steam rose from its scalded shell and joined the night fog. The thing inside the shell rested, wounded from the impact and weary from its journey across galaxies.

It would heal. It always had.

The rain began, clattering across the metallic skin. An orifice opened, dripping sulfuric meringue, and a trembling tendril tested the air. Then it drooped to the ground and probed the soil, verifying that its instinct had not failed.

Bacteria. Protozoa. Amino acids. Life.

Food.

Chapter One

Tamara Leon ran across the parking lot with rain pounding her head and shoulders. She hadn't brought her umbrella today, and she cursed herself for the oversight. The fierce winds of a Southern Appalachian spring often reduced umbrellas to rags and twisted metal anyway. Still, it would have given her a meager talisman against the rain gods if nothing else.

She rammed the key into the door lock of her Toyota sedan and worked the handle, then slid into the driver's seat as rain drummed the roof. Tamara slammed the door and caught her breath, her leather satchel spotted with water. She looked at herself in the rearview mirror to see if the Gloomies were hiding in her eyes.

Nope, only eyes.

She wiped a clear circle on the fogged window with the sleeve of her coat. The brick buildings of Westridge University stood clean, square, and solid around the perimeter of the parking lot. The college had all the personality of a tweedy, pipe-smoking administrator. Not a hint of controversy roamed those halls, except when Tamara cut loose with one of her more spectacular psychology theories.

She started the car to let the heat circulate before she started the long drive up the mountain. The rain continued to pelt down like liquid ball bearings. At least it wasn't snowing. Then the half-hour drive could easily stretch into two or three hours. She pulled out of the parking lot, the windshield wipers beating sheets of water off the glass.

Tamara slid a tape into the cassette deck, *Wild Planet* by the B-52's, and killed the miles by singing along with Cindy and Kate, making up harmony parts as the duo wailed away in the high registers. Drivers passing her, seeing her bobbing up and down in her seat and shaking her head from side to side, probably took her for a drunk. But she was doing a great job of closing down, putting the workday behind her.

This was *her* time. She wasn't Dr. Leon and she wasn't "Mommy" or "honey," as she would be in a half hour. And time away from home meant a delay in defending herself from Robert's increasingly cruel taunts. She could pretend, at least for another evening, that home was a happy place.

She often wondered if her whole life had been role-playing. Little tomboy, teenage jock, valedictorian of her college class, wife, professor, mother, unheralded backup singer for the B-52's. Everything but Daddy's little girl. The one thing she would have liked to have been, but had never gotten the chance.

And it was all her fault.

Freud would say she had some kind of penis fixation—*everything* was, with him—and Jung would say she was responding to some ancestral instinct that compelled her to wear masks. But to Tamara, it was because of her Gloomies, the bad things she felt and saw and heard before they ever happened.

Nuts, every one of us, she thought, tossing back her damp hair and cackling like a demented witch in a bad TV movie. Studying psychology made you wonder if you were crazy, and teaching it removed all doubt.

The miles whirred by under her wet tires, and soon she hit the outskirts of Windshake. She drove past a stucco-sided motel that hugged the edge of a cliff. A plastic black bear stood by the motel office, its paws raised against the rain. It wore a black T-shirt that said John 3:16 in white letters. Most days, she could look out over the valleys below and see a 180-degree panorama. But today she saw only a mist that covered the mountains like a gray wool blanket. She had just crossed the county line when the first whispering of Gloomies echoed in the caves of her skull.

Shhhh, they seemed to say, as if calming her, hushing her, lulling her into dropping her defenses. But her defenses were rock solid, the Great Wall of China against Mongol hordes. Gloomies didn't exist. Hadn't Robert told her that a dozen times, each reminder more terse and insistent than the one before?

She passed a boarded fruit stand that huddled under a red gap of hill. Through the chicken wire that had been strung across the front of the store, shelves of honey jars caught the last feeble daylight and reflected back like golden eyes. Rubber tomahawks and long burgundy ears of Indian corn hung from the rafters. A life-sized hillbilly doll, corncob pipe tucked into the black bush of its beard, sat in a rocker under an awning, its stitched face fixed on the highway.

Hillbillies and barn dances, church socials and knitting bees. Cow pastures and cornfields. Burley tobacco warehouses and craft shops. Windshake wasn't a melting pot, it was a big black kettle where you dipped your slaughtered hogs.

The quaint attraction of small-town life had worn off in a couple of months. Quite a change from Chapel Hill. That community had a real international flavor and was an energetic wellspring of ideas. There, people gathered in coffeehouses and bars and discussed Sartre and Pollock, Camus and Marxism. Here, they drank liquor from Dixie cups in the Moose Lodge parking lot and talked about hubcaps. She wasn't sure which of the two lifestyles was the most compelling.

The sibilant noise wended through the alleys of her head again: *Shhhhh.*

No. She wasn't hearing telepathic signals. The Gloomies could keep to themselves. *Because they aren't real, are they?*

Tamara cranked the stereo another notch, and Fred Schneider talk-chanted his way through an amphetamine-fueled tune about a girl from Planet Claire. She took the narrow fork into their neighborhood, a cluster of small houses at the foot of the slopes. The closer she got to the driveway, the tighter her stomach clenched, her body anticipating another showdown. What would it be tonight, cold indifference or hot rage?

Think happy thoughts.

At least Robert had a job here and the family was relatively secure. She was lucky to have a position at Westridge. Even if she had given up her assistantship at the University of North Carolina, where she'd been a rising star in the psychology department.

Don't think about it, she told herself. *You know good and well that Robert wanted to stay, wanted you to develop your career.*

But she'd watched his face grow longer and older as he came home jobless every day, tired from delivering aircheck tapes to Piedmont radio stations, worn out from filling up program directors' voicemail boxes, pissed off at the media whiz kids who wouldn't recognize talent even if it came from Walter Cronkite's golden pipes.

She'd decided that, for his self-esteem and their mutual happiness, they'd be better off moving here, where Robert had been offered an air shift. It meant a cut in pay for Tamara and not much of a boost in overall household income. But her sacrifice had been repaid with sullen resentment, and the gulf between them had only widened when her disturbed sleep and headaches began.

Because she had been stupid enough to share her suspicions with him, that the strange set of sensations she'd nicknamed the Gloomies were back.

The invisible voice came again, louder, more drawn out this time: *Shhhhuuu.*

As if the Gloomies were trying out a new tongue, breaking it in, forming a forgotten language or else a word not yet learned.

She turned into their driveway and pushed the nagging thought-sound from her mind. Happy, happy thoughts. The house was neat, cedar-planked and stained clear, with red-wood trim. No garage, but they had three bedrooms and two baths. An ordinary home where nothing bad could happen.

And we can have it paid off in, oh, thirty-nine years or so.

Tamara was suddenly struck with a vision of herself as an old woman, bones bent from more than seven decades of holding themselves up. Her lying on the plaid couch and fill-ing the air with the stench of decaying flesh. Robert gone somewhere, off to another marriage to a woman who didn't have imagination, who didn't "hear voices." Cats. She would need lots of cats, the cliché of the crazy old dowager.

She shuddered and looked through the window into the lighted kitchen. Her heart leaped with joy and she broke into a smile, the thoughts of her own mortality falling from her like blossoms from a storm-struck peach tree.

Kevin and Ginger sat at the table, bent over their school-books. Kevin looked so much like his father, with his thin nose, curly hair, and quick brown eyes. Ginger was a minia-ture replica of Tamara. Ginger had blonde hair, too, but it was slightly more reddish than her mother's. She had the turned-out ears as well, and her straight hair was tucked be-hind them. But the ears were not unflattering, as much as Tamara had hated her own worst feature. In fact, Ginger's ears complemented her wide expressive face. And her lips were plump and curvy, the kind some man would be falling all over himself to kiss one day.

There you go again with that "future" nonsense. Better enjoy what you have, because it can all be taken away in the blink of an eye.

Like her father had been taken.

Because she had ignored the voice of the Gloomies.

Happy, happy thoughts, damn it.

She honked, waved, jumped from the car, and ran to the front door, the rain tapping out its tireless rhythm on her head and shoulders. The kids met her just inside the house, ducking under her wet trench coat for a hug.

"Hello, my cuties," she said. "What did we learn at school today?"

Kevin hopped up and down. "I made three homers in kickball. We had to play in the gym because of the rain, and all you had to do for a homer was, like, kick it into the bleachers. I rocked their little world, dude."

Kevin wagged his index fingers as if they were six-shooters, then blew the imaginary gun smoke from his fingertips and returned the weapons to their holsters.

"Uh—okay, dude. What about you, pumpkin?" She stroked Ginger's soft hair.

Ginger looked up and flashed her mother a bright green smile. "I ate a crayon."

"My goodness. You get in the bathroom and brush your teeth right this minute."

"Sorry, Mommy," Ginger said, but Tamara could tell she wasn't. And Tamara had to wait until Ginger was down the hall before she could allow herself to laugh into her hand.

"Has Daddy called?" she asked Kevin.

"Not since we got off the bus."

Tamara looked at the clock. Twenty past five. Robert's shift ended at two, and his production work usually took only a couple of hours at the most. Still, she shouldn't worry. He was a big boy. He would be here.

He wouldn't die on her. Not like—

She caught herself. *There you go again. What kind of a downer are you on, girl? Dancing with the Gloomies again. Well, it's a morbid kind of day, what with this dreary weather.*

And thinking about the past doesn't do a thing to cheer you up.

"Hon, would you bring some kindling from the laundry room?" she said to Kevin. "I'll build a nice fire and make us a round of hot chocolate."

Kevin whooped in anticipation of a good sugar buzz and skated across the oak floor in his stockinged feet.

Tamara put the kettle on to boil and was rummaging in the cabinets when the whispers returned.

Shu-shaaa.

Soft as a snake burrowing in the crevices of her mind.

"No," she said, slamming the cabinet closed. She had heard *nothing*. Because Gloomies weren't real.

Especially not this one, the strange sibilant phrase that chilled her bones and carried doom as if it were a typhoid wind.

Even when Robert pulled into the driveway ten minutes later, Tamara still hadn't shaken the sense of foreboding. She'd always been sensitive. *Too* sensitive, her sisters had constantly reminded her. Always letting little things bother her, a sixth sense for the negative. She wondered if she might be suffering from a touch of depression.

Yeah, right. And probably schizophrenia with delusions of grandeur. With a dose of bipolar disorder thrown in on the side.

Nope, I'm just plain old crazy. Crazy, I can live with. And look on the bright side. At least your hubby didn't die today. Even if sometimes you can't stand him.

But she was going to give it a try. Happy, happy thoughts. For the kids. For him. For herself.

"You look like you had a rough day," she said as Robert elbowed through the door, arms loaded with radio copy, cassette tapes, and damp manila envelopes.

"Hundred percent chance," Robert said. He leaned forward to kiss her. "But the sun's breaking through the clouds."

Happy thoughts indeed. "Hmmm. Another kiss like that, and I could get a sunburn."

He winked. "Later, when it's dark."

"Is that your forecast?"

"No, honey, that is a guarantee." He dumped his work onto the sofa and sat down. He was already lost in Robertville, studying some advertising circulars.

Tamara knocked on the table. "Hello? Aren't you going to ask about my day?"

"Yeah. Can you believe it? Hardware store wants to do a special campaign for Blossomfest." He hummed an uneven jingle, then said in his radio voice, "'Spring has sprung and Windshake is blooming, time for scrubbing, mopping, and brooming.' Catchy, huh?"

"My day was fine. I proved that ESP doesn't exist."

"Huh?"

"My husband can't read my mind because he can't even read my lips."

"Sorry." Robert put his papers away, went to her, and massaged her neck. "I'd be afraid to read your mind. But I can read your body like a book. Every single page."

He rubbed lower, then stopped when Kevin came into the room with a load of firewood.

"More Gloomies?" Robert whispered to her.

She looked away and nodded. This was one of those times she wished her constitution enabled her to lie. His hands dropped from her shoulders, the room grew ten degrees cooler, and household chores suddenly seemed intensely interesting.

Tamara and Kevin sipped hot chocolate and built the fire while Robert started supper. After the meal, Tamara sat at the kitchen table with a stack of student papers she had to grade. But her attention wandered and her gaze kept returning to the window. The world outside was harsh, gray, and ugly. The rain ran down the glass in silver streaks, not merrily but angrily, as if it would like to come inside and make itself at home.

As if it were thin fingers scratching, scratching, scratching, searching for a fissure.

And the sound the water made: *shu-shaaa, shu-shaaa.*

She turned her chair around so that she faced the wall and put the weather out of her mind. A storm in Windshake was more the rule than the exception, especially at this time of year. She told herself that all was well, her family was safe and snug and soon to be tucked in.

Happy, happy, happy.

But still the Gloomies swirled in her head and heart. The soft whispers played all evening and followed her into a restless sleep, crowding the three-foot gap of ice between her husband's flesh and her own.

Chapter Two

Ralph Bumgarner shook the mason jar and held it up where the sunshine broke through the bare limbs of the oak trees. Ralph hardly had much of a face. He was mostly ears and teeth and nose, his head just an excuse to hold up a Red Man cap. He squinted like a scientist studying a test tube as he shook the jar again. Bubbles rose in the jar and clung to the glass at the surface of the liquid.

"Frog eyes, same as always," Don Oscar Moody said. "And it'll burn a blue flame if you light it. That's how you can tell a good batch."

"A man's got to be careful these days. Now, it's nothing personal, because I've been buying off you for six years. But everybody makes mistakes."

"Hey, I got *pride*." Don Oscar pounded himself in the chest twice with his thumb. His friends told him he looked like Mister Magoo, because he was round-headed and bald with a bulbous nose. So what if the veins in his face had blossomed and broken from a lifetime of taste-testing his product? He'd never put much stock in looks anyway, and at least he had Ralph beat all to hell in that department. "Family's been doing this for generations."

"And you do it proud," Ralph said, shaking the jar

again. "But a fellow hears stories. People going blind and such."

Don Oscar stomped his boot into the mud. *Beggars ought not be choosers.* "Now, you just come here and look," he said, grabbing Ralph by the shoulder.

He led Ralph into the springhouse. The building's stone base was covered with thick green moss, and the slat-board siding was dark with rot. The two men blinked as their eyes adjusted to the weak light that spilled through the doorway. A sweet fog of fermenting corn mash crowded the room.

The springhouse had been built into the side of the hill. A stone reservoir was set high into the back bank, and a wooden chute carried water into the room, spilling silver dribbles from gaps in the planks. The earthen floor, soggy from the leaks, was a marsh of boot prints. A row of wooden-staved barrels lined one side of the springhouse.

At the center of the room sat a large contraption that looked like a stripped-down washing machine crossed with a UFO, plugs and coils sprouting from its metal body like hot copper worms. The coils wound into the channeled stream, and clear liquid dripped from the mouth of the pipe into a glass gallon jar at the far side of the room. A fire flickered under the rig, casting low shadows against the walls. The end of the pipe belched a puff of steam.

"Thing of beauty," Don Oscar said, beaming like a father whose son had just been elected to office. "Ain't an ounce of lead in that still."

Which wasn't true. Don Oscar had used lead solder to secure the pipe joints. But compared to the poison that a lot of his competitors brewed up using car radiators as condensers, Don Oscar practically deserved a seal of approval from the FDA.

Don Oscar pointed to the black corners of the springhouse ceiling. "And here's my latest little addition to the business. I done divided up the stovepipe into four, so the smoke gets spread out a mite better. Them Feds got helio-copters nowadays. Two of the pipes go into the bank about twenty yards and come out under a laurel thicket. It's a bitch to clear the ash out of those pipes every few months, but the smoke'll never give me away."

Ralph nodded in admiration, his Andy Griffith ears cutting a faint breeze in the air. "Feds are out hunting for dope these days, now that the hippies finally wised up enough to plant the shit out in the wilderness."

Don Oscar winced at the mention of his other competitors. "I smoked that stuff once, even thought about getting into it myself. Hear the money's real good. But who the hell wants to deal with a bunch of stinking hippies?"

"Well, they say a man's got to change with the times." Ralph flicked his tongue beneath his beaver teeth, his small eyes shining in the darkness. "But I'm a believer in tradition myself."

"Amen to that, brother." Don Oscar took a mason jar from the shelf that ran under a boarded-up window. Ralph didn't disguise his desperation as Don Oscar's hand tightened around the lid.

"Let me show you something," Don Oscar said. Ralph let his stringy muscles sag in disappointment. Don Oscar led him over to one of the barrels. As he did, a low rumble rolled through the mountains, shaking the springhouse walls.

"Thunderstorm sure moved in fast," Ralph said. "And me on foot."

"That ain't no thunder. Them boys are dynamiting over on Sugarfoot again. Gonna knock that whole blamed mountain down to gravel if they keep it up."

Don Oscar lifted the plywood lid off the nearest barrel, then let it drop back down. A cloying stench clubbed the air of the room.

Better not let Ralph see THAT, Don Oscar thought. *Damned possum crawling in there and dying like that. Hell, it'll cook out. At least it died happy.*

He moved to the next barrel and pulled off the lid, then stood aside so that Ralph could see.

"Looks like either runny tar or soupy cow shit," said Ralph.

"That there's prime wort, my friend. That's what gets cooked down to make that joy juice you like so much."

"What the hell did you show me that for?" Ralph said, drawing back and crinkling his rodent face.

"So you'd appreciate the product. And not bitch about the price. Now, if you want to get messed up—and I don't mean stoned, I mean *stone*, like a rock, where you can't hardly move your arms and legs—then you dip your tin cup into this and take a gulp."

Ralph leaned closer, hesitant, looking into the murk of the fermenting mash as if divining the future in its surface.

"It's all science, see," Don Oscar said, loquacious from the sampling he'd done. "Convert sugar to ethanol, distill to stouten and purify, slow-cook to perfection or else you get it too watery. Yep, I could write a book on this stuff."

Ralph looked like he didn't give a rat's ass about the how or even the why of grain alcohol. Right now he seemed worried about the *when*. The first faint tremors worked through his limbs and sweat oozed from the pores of his sallow skin. Ralph needed a drink soon or he'd go into spasms right there on the muddy floor of the cookhouse.

But when you're buying on credit, especially unreliable credit, you better rein in your horses and bite your tongue and nod at all the right times, Don Oscar thought. *I'm calling all the shots here. Hey, that's pretty damn funny, all the SHOTS here, ha-ha.*

Ralph pointed to something, a pale powdery thread that branched out like a tree root down the side of the barrel into the wort. "What the hell's that?"

Don Oscar bent down and looked, pressing his soft belly against the rim of the barrel. "Some kind of fungus or dry rot, I reckon. Won't hurt nothing. It all comes out in the wash."

"Dry rot when it's so wet in here?"

Don Oscar reached into the barrel and touched the tendril. It squirmed spongily and crumbled. Don Oscar rubbed his fingers together, spilling motes of green and white dust onto the surface of the wort.

"Smells funny," Don Oscar said, whiffing like a maitre d' checking a vintage.

"Whatever you say, buddy. Can I have my jar now? You know how I get the shakes."

Don Oscar knew perfectly well how Ralph got the shakes. That was why he was making Ralph wait. There wasn't a lot of entertainment out in the sticks, especially here on the back side of Bear Claw twenty miles from nowhere in either direction. "When can you pay?"

Ralph's eyes were dark as salamanders. "Got my disability coming at the first of the month, same as usual."

"And what's my guarantee you won't blow it all on that factory beer at the Moose Lodge before I get mine?" Don Oscar rubbed his fingers against his flannel shirt. That mold or whatever it was had made his hand itch.

"I promise, Don Oscar."

Don Oscar smiled to himself in secret pleasure. He didn't care much if Ralph paid or not. He ran a healthy small business, with low overhead and tax-free profit. He allowed himself a helping of mountain generosity. "Here you go, Ralphie."

Ralph grabbed at Don Oscar's hand, prying the bootlegger's fingers away, then held the jar to his chest as he ran for the door, slipping on the dark, damp floor.

Took it like a chipmunk grabbing an acorn. Don Oscar watched from the springhouse as Ralph struggled with the lid and tipped the jar bottom to the sky. Ralph's Red Man cap nearly slid off, but the adjustable strip stuck to his collar. The bill of the ball cap jutted cockeyed toward the treetops. Some of the liquor streaked down Ralph's stubbled chin and wet his shirt as he gulped.

Ralph wiped his mouth with his jacket sleeve and headed into the woods. Don Oscar watched until Ralph disappeared among the pale saplings and gray-mottled trunks of the oaks. He listened to Ralph's feet kicking up dead leaves for another minute, until the sound grew fainter and blended with the warbling of Carolina wrens and the chattering of squirrels.

Don Oscar checked the pressure gauge on the still and added some hickory kindling to the fire. The batch would hold for the evening. His hand itched like crazy now, and a headache was coming on like a thunderstorm riding fast clouds. Maybe he'd better get to the house and lay down, let Genevieve make him a hot bowl of soup and maybe take a Goody's powder.

He closed and locked the springhouse door and headed down the trail to the house. By the time he was halfway home, his head felt as if it had been crushed between two boulders and his mind was playing tricks on him. The trees seemed way too green, and the new March growth shivered without a wind. Maybe that last batch had been a bit too powerful.

Genevieve Moody looked up from her quilting and out the window to see if her husband had finished his business deal. She didn't trust Ralph Bumgarner a bit. But Donnie could take care of things. He always had, and he'd sold to rougher folks than Ralph.

It was the tail end of winter, the trees deader than four o'clock and hardly any blooms to speak of, but still the fresh smell of jack pine rosin came through the screen door. The woods were going to bust with green any day now, with scrappy black clouds pushing another storm. It was God dipping His waterspout to tend His garden, priming it for another spring.

That last stitch is a mite loose, but after all it's a quilt. It's the wrinkles and loose threads and whatnot that gives them character. And the handmade look sells so good down at the antique shop.

Maybe she'd give this quilt away instead of selling it. To

Eula Mae or one of the Mull kids, Lord only knew they needed all the help they could get. And it's not like she needed the money, what with Donnie doing so good.

Okay, now, Mister Needle, don't jump at my old fingers like that. A body'd think you lived off my blood the way you act.

She didn't see Donnie yet. Ralph might have been trying to pull a fast one, make a horse trade, though Ralph was plumb out of horses. Ralph had big ears, and mountain lore held that was a sign of a long and enduring lover, but she didn't see how any woman could ever stand to put him to the test. This was one of those times she didn't like Donnie's being a moonshiner. Because of the company it drew.

But, she had to admit, she liked store-bought groceries and the new Wagoneer and not having to keep up pole beans and yellow squash like her sisters. Donnie had promised a satellite dish come summer. And he was right proud of his work.

"Family tradition," he called it, and his cheeks got all puffy and cute when he smiled.

Well, family is family, after all, and I'll stand by my man come heck or high water.

Maybe the apple didn't fall far from the tree, and maybe one bad apple spoiled the whole bunch, and maybe the worm turned, but Donnie had never lifted a hand against her. She knew for a fact none of her sisters could say the same about *their* good-for-nothing husbands.

And Donnie got respect. His customers came from all walks, not just the down-and-outers like Ralph and his kind. Chief Crosley was kept greased up and shut up with a monthly case and Chester Mull was regular as prunes and oatmeal. Half the Moose Lodge were customers. Even some of them snooty Lion's Clubbers weren't above a little illegal pleasure. And that old preacher, not Blevins, but the one before him, Hardwick, paid a call every Monday come rain or shine.

She had time for her hobbies and when she wanted a weaving loom, Donnie ran right out and bought one without batting an eye, two thousand dollars just like that. It sat over there in the corner with dusty strings hanging from it like cobwebs but Donnie hadn't ever said an unkind word about her not using it anymore. She took another glance out the window, at the sky going thick as flies on molasses.

No Donnie.

She let her attention wander from the quilt in her lap to the kitchen. It was cluttered with cookbooks, recipes, and enamelware, bought by Donnie so she could finally win the chow-chow contest at the festival. He'd even bought her a Cuisinart.

"It's *science*," he'd told her. "Not luck or old mountain secrets, else Elvira Oswig wouldn't be getting the blue ribbon year after year. She got the system down, is all."

Blossomfest was coming up this weekend and that last batch of chow-chow was going to win for her. Donnie had said wasn't no judge on Earth going to be able to pass up this year's Moody entry.

And here he came now, wobbling down the trail like he'd taken too many samples and holding his head like it was a broken bucket leaking water.

Lordy, girl, get your old bones up and help him into his chair, 'cause you know he works hard for you and never once asks for thanks, only a little hanky-panky once in a while, but they ALL do that. And anyway, that don't take much time at all, and if it keeps Donnie home, then I'm glad to oblige.

She put aside her needle and scraps. Her husband stumbled up the steps, feet dragging as if his boots were filled with creek mud.

"Hey, honey, are you feeling okay?" she asked, standing and brushing the threads from her lap.

To tell the truth, he looked like heck warmed over and he was nodding, but that didn't mean nothing because he hated to complain. He put his arms around her, but his eyes were only partly open, the whites showing like sick moons.

"Here, maybe I better put you to bed, Donnie."

He leaned on her, heavy, like he wanted some hanky-panky, but it was the afternoon and they hadn't done it in the daylight since she was barely off her Daddy's knee and, besides, his breath smelled like a crock of sauerkraut that had turned.

"You got the fever?" she asked. "Looks like you're having some kind of spell, took ill with something."

Why wouldn't he look at her?

"Honey?"

She tried to back away, but his arms were strong and his face pressed closer. The rims of his eyes were swollen and tinged with green, the color of rotted watermelons.

"Say something," she said. "And you may as well stop trying to kiss me until you get that dead skunk out of your mouth and—"

She finally figured out what was bothering her, besides the smell and his strange eyes. His mouth on hers caused no stir of wind.

Lordy, that ain't right, and you got to get away because he ain't breathing and why don't your legs work and he still wants that kiss and his tongue feels like cold slimy snakeskin and why don't your legs work and what's he putting in your mouth that's slithery and oh my Lord now you can't breathe and this ain't real but you can't breathe that sure is real and something's wrong in your bones and guts and God let my lungs work, girl, this must be what it's like to die only why does it hurt so much and now you'll never get that blue ribbon and we're all sauerkraut and what is this shhhhh oh Lordy Jesus I can't feel my heartbeat and the whole world's gone green and white and green and white 'cause this must be what they call your life flashing before your eyes flashing before your flashing

Chapter Three

A black cloud crawled across the sky, scrubbing the top of Bear Claw as it headed east. Little gray dots of cumulus followed in its trail like deformed cows bound for pasture. At sunrise, the clouds had been spread as thin as apple butter. In the few hours since, they had clumped up like they meant business. And this time of year, *raining* was the sky's main piece of business.

Chester Mull rubbed the knots of his hands together, hoping the friction would melt the arthritis away. March in the high country was always miserable. The cold and damp weather alternated with brief bursts of sunshine to keep his joints in constant agony, one moment shrunk tighter than fiddle strings and the next looser than Eula Mae Pritcher's morals. Now his aching bones told him that the daily thunderstorm was right on schedule.

Static electricity prickled the wiry gray hairs on the back of his hands. He looked out across the yard at the blue banty hens scratching in the dirt. They wouldn't have sense enough to get out of the rain, and Chester was damned if he was going to go down and shoo them into the barn. He was happy right where he was, with his bony hind end parked in the roped-together bottom of his rocking chair.

A concussion sounded over the mountain, echoing off the granite slopes and stinging Chester's ears. Those boys were blasting away over on Sugarfoot again, chiseling that mountain apart one piece at a time. A wonder the whole damned peak hadn't slid down already, the way they stoked the dynamite. Well, that was the price of progress. He only wished they'd do their progressing a few hundred miles closer to the flatlands.

He turned his head and shot a brown stream of tobacco off the side of the porch. The arc came up a little short, the juice hitting on one of the warped pine planks and quivering in the dust before beginning the slow job of making a permanent stain.

"Damn Days O' Work never did make a good hockwad," he muttered to the air. He had started talking to himself about six years ago, a few months after Hattie had left him to join the Lord. But he made good company, even if he did say so himself. And there was nobody around to disagree with that opinion. Plus, this way, he didn't have to worry about no back sass.

Chester scratched the red gorkle of his neck, the neck that Hattie had always said looked like a turkey's. He mashed his gums together, trying to squeeze a little more nicotine out of his chaw. A dark line of saliva trickled down one side of his mouth, adding yet another color to his possum-hide beard. He reached down and scratched his ragged redbone hound, Boomer, behind the ears and looked out over his farm like a king surveying his castle keep.

The barn was almost ready to give up the ghost. Johnny and Sylvester, his good-for-nothing younguns, had propped long locust poles against the side of the barn where it sagged toward the ground. The rusty tin roof had buckled under the strain of gravity, and there were gaps in it big enough to drop a hay bale through. Chester didn't really mind, because he sure as hell wasn't going to chase no cows around over these hills and put them up of a night. He'd culled his herd down to a half dozen last spring, then sold them at the auction house down in Windshake.

As far as he knew, the only thing that lived in the barn now were the rats, because the pointy-nosed bastards never seemed to get tired of moldy corn. The chickens were just as likely to roost up on the porch rails, and the bats had been driven out by the winter sleet that played Ping-Pong with their radar. So, as far as Chester cared, the whole thing could fall over. DeWalt, the California Yankee who lived over the ridge, had already offered to buy the barn for its wormy chestnut beams and planks.

The toolshed had already collapsed, squatting down in the side yard like a bullfrog with a rump full of wet bugs. An old horse-drawn hay rake quietly flaked away at the back of the shed, its tines curving into the brown turf. The barnyard spread out into stubbled pasture, broken here and there by slack barbed wire strung between gray posts. Johnson grass and saw briars covered what used to be the potato patch, and locust sprigs and blackberry thickets had crept down from the forest slopes to lay claim to the hay fields.

The Mull family had once owned land as far as the eye could see, both sides of Bear Claw and a big chunk of Antler Ridge, plus a pie-shaped wedge of Brushy Fork where the headwaters of the Little Hawk River sprang from between the cracks of mossy rocks. The acreage had been chopped up and married off until each branch of the family was now down to a few hundred acres. Chester had inherited a prime spot here in the valley, but his outlands were all granite cliffs and crags bristling with jack pine. He had been lucky to palm a piece of it off on DeWalt.

Chester chuckled at DeWalt's bid to become a country boy. Some tobacco juice slid down the wrong way and caused him to cough. His lungs caught fire as they worked like bellows to push out the bad air. Thinking about DeWalt always made him laugh, but even a good belly laugh wasn't worth this kind of pain. When he recovered, and his scrawny head had stopped bobbing like an apple on the seat of a moving hay wagon, he ratched his throat clear and spat out the offending gob.

His thoughts returned to DeWalt, but this time he was more careful with his chaw. Chester had sold the darned fool twenty acres of rock face, so straight up and down that from an airplane the lot looked barely the size of a football field. DeWalt had given him ninety thousand dollars in California Yankee money, but it spent just as good up here in North Carolina. Better, in fact.

Used to be, Chester had to squeeze his old sack of bones behind the wheel of his '57 Ford pickup every Sunday and drive around the snaky logging roads to the head of Cane Creek. There, in a springhouse tucked between the crotch of two streams, Don Oscar Moody cooked up the clearest moonshine in Pickett County. Don Oscar's joy juice went down smoother than antifreeze and ran on through without messing around in the liver too much. At twelve dollars a quart, Chester figured his pleasure came to a couple of bucks an hour. That was cheaper than the medicine a lot of his old acquaintances were on, and a damn sight more fun.

Chester usually loaded up a cardboard box in the back of his pickup at about the time that Preacher Blevins was wrapping up his sermon down at Windshake Baptist. Don Oscar always greased Chester up with a couple of swigs of free samples just so the ride home wouldn't be so bumpy.

"Shock absorbers," Don Oscar called them. Once Chester had laid a tire down in the eroded rut of that old red road after a few too many samples. When the Ford had sunk up to its round fender, he'd had to walk in with his armful of lead-heavy shine. But ever since that DeWalt deal, Don Oscar had started coming to *him*.

Thinking of moonshine made Chester thirsty. He squinted up into the sky, trying to place the sun's position in the smear of clouds.

"Close enough to noon, I reckon," he said, trying to lift

his trembling varicose flesh off the rocking chair. One of the chair runners pinched Boomer's tail and the hound yelped.

"You old blessid fool, you'd think by now you'd keep your ass end out from under there." Chester smoothed the mange on the dog's wrinkled forehead. Boomer looked up at him with sad, droopy eyes that had chunks of sleep crust tucked in the corners.

Chester stood on quivering legs and hooked his thumbs under the straps of his blue jean overalls. He looked out on the tops of the Blue Ridge Mountains that bucked and swooped all around the horizon. When he was a boy, he'd been able to see clear to Tennessee from right here on the porch. Now he could barely see forty miles on a good day, and sometimes at night he couldn't even make out the little pinpricks of orange and blue light that marked Windshake about twenty miles below.

It was because of pollution that the visibility was poor, DeWalt had told him. Industrial grime churned out of smokestacks in Cleveland and Pittsburgh came to roost here in the eastern highlands.

DeWalt seemed angry when he said that, but Chester didn't really give a rat's ass either way. The scenic beauty of the mountains had brought people like DeWalt here, people who had made a mint as lawyers and doctors and manufacturers in the hellholes of California, New York, and Florida. Those same people gobbled up that big-city money like a fat boy slamming doughnuts at a church social, then locked the city in the rearview mirror when they had a big enough pile. The way Chester saw it, they all had a hand in the pollution, because when you got right down to it, everybody used disposable razors and bought fast-food burgers in Styrofoam containers and hauled their asses around in huge smog machines.

The mountains weren't all that hot to look at, anyway. Not anymore. Over on Sugarfoot, a twenty-story condominium complex rose above the ridge, looking sort of unreal, like something Hollywood dreamed up for one of its outer space picture shows. Below the condo, a gang of bulldozers had gouged a ski slope into the side of the mountain. Thanks to snowblowers, the white strip of slope still zigzagged down the side of the hill even though the last freeze had been three weeks ago.

Most of the prime peaks had summer homes strewn across them. The ones that hadn't been heavily developed were scarred by the bleached bones of balsam that the acid rain had killed off. The blasting crews had been going at it hard and heavy, too, knocking red holes in the mountainsides. And those big silvery slabs of granite weren't all that eye-catching to Chester.

"A little bit of heaven," the postcards said, the ones they sold in the stores along the interstate, on racks right next to the straw hats and Confederate-flag key chains. If this was heaven, the Good Lord had gotten something bass-ackward, in Chester's opinion.

But he was as eager as the next man to get his hands on some California Yankee green, and he didn't care if it had passed through one of them drug-lord bank accounts to get to him or not. It was simple economics in Chester's opinion. He'd worked that old cornfield out there for nigh on sixty years, starting when he was seven, when his dad had first handed him a hoe and told him to get used to the feel of it. And what did he have to show for it?

Knotted-up fingers and a bad back. Sure, it had provided food for the Mull family and their animals, but he could sell the damned field and buy canned corn and Saran-wrapped steak down at the Sav-a-Ton for the next two hundred years. All that talk about farming being God's work was just so much horseshit. If idle hands were the devil's playground, let the bastard play.

The sky was darker now and the wind was mashing the clouds together like lumps of rotten potatoes. The mountains grew shadowy, their features lost. Chester reached into his mouth, plucked out his chaw, and laid it on the porch rail.

Looked like one of old Boomer's turds, Hattie always said, but she'd been big on snuff herself and hadn't had much room to talk.

The first drops of rain fell on the tin roof of the porch. The rain sounded like a mess of elves working away with shoe hammers. DeWalt said it was a relaxing sound, and liked to sit here on the porch during rainy afternoons. But Chester thought a man might as well have marbles rolling around inside his skull. Chester watched the drops bounce off the Ford's black hood. Rivulets of red clay ran down the twin dirt tracks of the driveway. He'd be going nowhere today if this kept up.

But that was just fine with Chester. That meant nobody would be out to bother *him,* either. That slack-eyed Johnny Mack wouldn't be trying to hit him up for liquor money and Sylvester wouldn't be wanting to take him squirrel hunting. And DeWalt, even though he had a shiny four-wheel drive, didn't like getting his two-hundred-dollar boots muddy. DeWalt liked to keep his things just the way they looked in the catalog.

"About time for a little liquid lunch, Boomer," Chester said. Boomer looked up, thumped his tail a couple of times, and farted.

"You're entitled to your opinion," Chester said.

The rain began falling in thick silver sheets, and Chester could barely see across the yard. But at the edge of the forest, about two miles up the slope, that weird green stuff was still glowing. Sure as hell wasn't foxfire, the glow-in-the-dark fungus that freaked out city folk. The glow had been there a couple of days now, but Chester hadn't yet mustered the energy to walk out and check on it.

Now that he thought about it, the glowing had started right after the last rain. Maybe it was a sign of spring or something. He'd have to ask DeWalt about it. DeWalt seemed to have a lot of book-learning. He liked to read up on mountain folklore and such.

But, hell, in all those damned stories Chester had to listen to growing up, sitting on the plank edge of Grandpappy's knee, he'd never heard anything about shiny green stuff. Sure, the old lady with the lamp that haunted the Brushy Fork bridge, the scarecrow boy in the barn, the panther that screamed like a woman while it followed the wagon in from the fields—he'd heard all those. But nothing about no green stuff.

Of course, they didn't pass on stories like they used to. Chester's dad had tried to get him to carry on the oral tradition, but Chester didn't see the point. They had picture shows in Windshake, and now almost everybody in these parts had a television. Who wanted to sit around and listen to a toothless old geezer flapping his jowls?

Chester stretched and his spine popped. His joints were tightening up on him for sure. He forgot all about the shiny green stuff. It was time for some good old Southern self-medication. He lifted the latch on his gray-planked cabin door and went inside.

The alien stretched its tendrils into the soil, edging its way deeper into the cave. It found a quiet, moist place between two large rocks. Its slick effluence coated the granite surrounding it, and its cells mutated to mimic those of the humus and loam that coated the skin of this new world. Since emerging from its seed, the alien had probed the exotic chemical soup around it, drawing nourishment, assimilating the structural order of the strange biosystem, fulfilling the necessities of survival.

A native life form slid from a crevice, this one far more complex than the bacteria that had provided the alien sustenance in the wake of its impact. The life form was as cool as the air, sluggish, and emanated a primitive intelligence. The life form slithered into contact with one of the alien's tendrils, exhaling in pain as its nervous system fused with that of the alien's. The life form writhed as its metabolism slowed, then it fell still and its warmth faded.

The alien tried to comprehend the sound that had fallen from the life form's forked tongue.

Shhh.

Shu-shaaa.

A symbol.

A sound, a fluctuation in air pressure, a varying system of vibrations. The alien tried the symbol again, experimenting, seeking to give it meaning.

Shu-shaaa.

Chapter Four

The creek was up, ripping a brown, swollen seam in the twisting gully. Muddy water frothed over huge gray stones, the currents carving fresh wounds of erosion in the creek banks. Twigs and leaves torpedoed past on the water's surface, nature's detritus swept downhill. The creek, like the steadily falling rain, obeyed the relentless gravity that had been inflicted upon the universe.

Gravity pressed upon Herbert Webster DeWalt, III, and had been pressing on him for fifty-six years. Gravity had loosened his skin from his skull, causing visible but unremarkable wrinkles to line his forehead. The unending work of physics had caused his cheeks to sag a bit, and when he turned his head, the meat beneath his molars quivered slightly. The spinning hands of the clock had marked him. There were silvery streaks through his brunette hair, except for two patches at his temples that had gone completely white. But none of those ruinous, tireless forces of nature had touched his eyes.

DeWalt's eyes were still clear and true. He could tell a hawk from a buzzard at four hundred yards and could read the small print on the bottom of his mutual fund statements without eyeglasses. His eyes still shone with curiosity and still glittered with false optimism. His eyes saw things as they were, and DeWalt had learned that his eyes never lied to him.

And his eyes were telling him that the water had a greenish tint to it. Even the rain was tinged with irradiant green. DeWalt stood in the window of his custom-built cabin, watching as the storm tongue-lashed the mountains. He bit down on the stem of his pipe and sucked, even though the ashes in the bowl were long cold.

In his three years in the Appalachians, he'd studied the weather closely, had made it one of the foundations of his latest lifestyle. And he knew even less now than when he'd started. The sudden snows that could swoop in anytime between October and May, the ever-shifting winds that brought arctic air masses or tropical hurricane blow-bys with equal ambivalence, the temperatures that could fluctuate thirty degrees in a day—all these he had observed and grown accustomed to.

But green rain?

He crossed his arms over his insulated vest, holding one elbow as his other hand toyed with his pipe. He leaned back in his easy chair and looked at the leather tips of his L.L. Bean boots. He was a *faux* mountain man, and he knew it. Behind him, covering two walls of the living room, were books on Appalachian folklore and history. He'd read most of them. But he wondered if this little mountain getaway was just another of his passing fancies.

"A man of the earth," they'd called him, back when he was making his fortune off the land. He hadn't been a real estate genius, simply knew how to work hard and be lucky at exactly the same time. He'd been just another longhaired college dropout, hanging loose at a commune in San Bernardino and exploring the philosophy of sex, drugs, and rock 'n' roll. But that got old fast as some of those beautiful people crashed and burned and saw spiders crawling on their skin. DeWalt's head was too square to really buy into the whole hippie business, anyway. Nothing on this earth was free, especially love.

The Summer of Love faded into the Autumn of Indifference, and then the Winter of World-Weariness set in. When the commune broke up in the early seventies, DeWalt borrowed the money to buy the huge tract of land, using his father's outdoor advertising business as collateral. He kept on buying as the disillusioned started giving up on California as the gateway to nirvana, as they packed up for the New Mexico deserts and Alaska and Oregon. He divided his original tract into lots and made a small fortune selling out to the new professionals who were starting to flock in because of the West Coast's budding technology scene.

He spent a half-dozen years in real estate, and his pile had grown. It was easy money, and fun, at least at first. It was a mental puzzle, a little math game that was more invigorating than the tedious psychedelic journey that had preceded. DeWalt turned an obscene profit, but that, too, grew boring.

It was then that he had started his odyssey. Trying to find himself, as he called it. Getting away from it all. Going to wherever *it* might be.

A year sailing abroad, through the Mediterranean, the Bahamas, the Marshall Islands, meeting week-long friends and one-night lovers, drinking piña colodas and screwdrivers by the quart. One day he had staggered ashore in Naples, Italy. On impulse, he caught a cab to Rome, then on to Vatican City. Looking for God, he'd thought. Staring at those ancient stone buildings that housed the holy. And seeing only the piazza streaked with pigeon shit.

Back to the States, where he'd developed an interest in trains. He built a miniature railway around his mansion in Bakersfield, complete with a steam locomotive and red caboose. He started a steam engine museum and collected and restored old boxcars and locomotives. After five years of that, he woke up one morning wondering what he'd been doing with his life now that it was half over. He sold his house and the train collection, making money even as he was dumping them.

Off to Pennsylvania Dutch country, where he bought a farm and stocked it with Arabian horses. The collector bug bit again, only this time it was horse-drawn vehicles that captured his fancy. Buggies, surreys, stagecoaches, and sleighs filled his huge Gothic barn, and it was all he could do to keep the horses exercised with weekly outings. He'd enjoyed those years, the smell of dogwoods and manure, the wind carrying the scent of meadows across the yard, the unhurried pace of his days.

But again he grew restless, tense from too much relaxation. He still felt as if he were missing something. Perhaps if he had a wife. So he tried that. Two months of heaven followed by two years of hell, and DeWalt was cured of monogamy for the rest of his life. Soon he divorced the farm as well, and spent a half decade in the steel and concrete towers of New York City, dabbling in publishing, playing the sophisticated Man About Town, philanthropist, and patron of the arts. Then the skyscrapers and the press of people had started suffocating him, and again he had to run.

Here to the mountains. The peaceful, back-to-nature scenery mixed with good folksy folks. Except he had learned that people were people, no matter what corner of the world you walked. People had flaws. People were human. And wherever he went, there he was, alone yet unable to find himself.

But, at least, here in his cabin, he had some sense of being at home. Good land, a stream out front to fly-fish in, a nice stack of locust logs crackling away in the fireplace, a little garden spot where he grew golf-ball-sized tomatoes, a telephone that rarely rang more than once a day. Yes, he had it all.

Even green rain.

He scratched a kitchen match against a hearthstone and lit his pipe. He'd read about foxfire, even found some of it, but foxfire shone like a faded glow-in-the-dark toy. A luminant fungus. Basically just rotten wood, when you came right down to it.

Acid rain wasn't just a theory anymore. It was a fact. Sulfur levels in precipitation had risen exponentially in the last few years. You didn't have to be a scientist to stand on a peak and pass judgment on the haze that covered the low-lying valleys. You didn't have to be a botanist to know something was killing the balsam trees, something recent and constant that stripped the branches bare and left jagged wooden skeletons.

But acid rain is colorless and subtle. This stuff is knocking on the skin of the earth like pellets of antifreeze.

DeWalt looked out the window again. The sun had given up trying to break through the clouds and had slid on over to another side of the earth where its prospects might be better. Darkness fell as heavily as the rain. DeWalt couldn't see the radiance anymore, but he could hear the angry roar of the flooded creek and the ticking of the raindrops on the shake shingles of the roof. He felt as if his cabin were under assault.

Nothing for it but to wait it out. Seems all he ever did was wait, wait for this or that to end, wait for something better to come along, wait for something to rekindle his passion for living. DeWalt sat with his face toward the fire, feeling like the bitter old man he thought he'd never be.

He didn't have to do anything with his remaining years. He had found Success, at least the most coveted aspect of it. He could sit here and grow old and wormy and tarred and toothless and never lift another finger. And that was the most terrifying thing DeWalt had ever experienced.

Financially, he was set for life. Even in the wanderlust of his middle years he'd always managed to sock it away, hand it over to bald men in double-breasted suits who knew how to mate money, to put it out to stud like DeWalt had done with his prized Arabians. And those men, the top of their heads gleaming more brightly than their eyes ever did, mailed him statements every month.

And the bottom line was always larger than the previous month's.

But money wasn't enough, even twenty-million, four-hundred-and-some-odd-thousand dollars of it. And he'd come to the same contradiction over and over. Nothing on this earth was free, yet money didn't buy the things you really wanted.

Money couldn't buy happiness. Couldn't buy contentment. Couldn't buy religion. Couldn't buy love. Money could rent it for a hell of a long time, but he always found out in the end that it belonged to someone else, that it could never be his.

He had seen something in the faces of people, some odd light that he had never seen in the bathroom mirror. Couples on honeymoon in the streets of Rome, oblivious to the insane traffic and carbon monoxide, eyes locked onto each other's. Children on playgrounds in littered parks, laughing and running and shouting at the sky just for the joy of it. Families leaving church on Sunday afternoon, their smiles dull but somehow beatific, as if they had just been told secrets that would never find their way to DeWalt's ears.

Even the old mountain people of Windshake, their hands worn and crippled, their few teeth ochred and rotted and resembling dead bumblebees in their sagging mouths, had an inner peace that baffled DeWalt. They had seen nothing but hard times, had watched while the wind punched over their corn, while disease swept through their cattle, while late frosts crept under the cover of darkness and took the blossoms from their orchards like evil lords despoiling snow-white virgins.

Yet they still rose with the sun in the morning, went out with their hoes and their ramshackle tractors and their milk buckets and got on with their chores. They pushed their carts down the aisles of the grocery store with that same determination, suffused with a kind of grim dignity. They even walked down the narrow Main Street sidewalks with that same gait, as if they had found enlightenment while loading sacks of feed or shelling peas or canning blackberry preserves.

Maybe it was an inbred trait. The population had been raiding the same gene pool for centuries, like drawing water from a communal well. Look at old Chester Mull. Never saw him depressed. Of course, you rarely saw him sober, either, but there was more to it than that. Maybe it was a kinship with the soil, some connection to the spirit of nature that seemed to fill these mountains with energy, like electricity that had jumped its wires.

Whatever it was, DeWalt was a little bit jealous. He wasn't a petty man and he wasn't a miser. He'd always sliced off a chunk of his money pie to spread among charities. He hadn't been as visibly generous since moving to Windshake because he'd sensed resentment among the locals when he had tried.

"We do for ourselves," their eyes seemed to say. So he couldn't buy his way into this cozy little club that the Mulls and Bumgarners and Turnbills and Easleys and Moodys belonged to.

But neither could they join his club. The Royal Order of the Bleeding Hearts. Membership, one, with DeWalt as its founder, chairman, secretary, and treasurer.

Will the meeting now come to order?

The minutes of our last meeting are the same as the hundreds before that and exactly the same as the ones from this meeting. We'll scratch our balls and yawn and feel sorry for ourselves. I yield the floor.

But what of the green rain?

Fuggingwhat?

Green rain, sir. Precipitation imbued with luminous color of the primary variety.

Brother DeWalt, perhaps your hallucinations are the result of the handful of acid trips you took during the Summer of Love. Flashback city, man, where all the streets run the wrong way.

I resent the implications, sir. Recreational chemistry experiments have no connection with natural phenomena.

Is it not all chemistry, Mr. DeWalt? Is it not all action and reaction, Oh Loyal Lodge Brother? Matter and energy, although the former doesn't and you have none of the latter? Pardon me for my outburst. Now I shall shut up and sit down and scratch my balls and grow old quietly.

Thank you. That concludes this meeting of the Royal Order of the Bleeding Hearts.

The firelight threw an amber glow across the room, casting shadows on the log walls that flickered like shy ghosts, here one second, gone the next. A stray spark sputtered and hissed like a rocket, then died against the mesh of the fire screen. DeWalt watched the spark fade to gray. It clung to the screen, inert and burned up, a flake of ash, which was exactly how DeWalt felt.

Nettie Hartbarger glanced up from the Bible, sneaking a peek at the handsome man across the table.

"Will you read some more scripture for me?" Bill Lemly asked in his deep, quiet voice. "It makes more sense when you say it. It sounds like poetry."

Bill clutched a Sprite in his big-knuckled hands. He looked at Nettie with his soft brown eyes and smiled. She was in the middle of St. Luke, Chapter Four. Maybe that wasn't the best verse of choice for spinning a web of seduction.

She read: "And Jesus being full of the Holy Ghost, returned from the Jordan, and was led by the spirit into the desert for the space of forty days, and was tempted by the devil. And he ate nothing in those days, and when they were ended, he was hungry."

She looked up again, and Bill was nodding gently as if transfixed by the rhythm of the scriptures. Or maybe he had been listening to the rain bouncing off her apartment roof.

Nettie continued: "And the devil said to him, 'If thou be the Son of God, say to this stone that it may be made bread.' And Jesus answered him, 'It is written that man liveth not by bread alone, but by every word of God.'

"And the devil led him into a high mountain, and shewed him all the kingdoms of the world in a moment of time, and he said to Him, 'To Thee will I give all this power, and the glory of them, for to me they are delivered, and to whom I will, I give them. If thou therefore wilt adore before me, all shall be thine.' "

Nettie was thinking that she wouldn't mind if Bill would adore her. And all of the kingdoms of her flesh would most definitely be *his*.

Bill hunched forward, hands under the table, jaw clenched as if he, too, were looking out over the devil's vistas of gold and marble. He appeared to be in a state of rapture. Nettie took a sip of her soft drink. She would have loved a glass of wine, but was afraid Bill would disapprove. She swallowed and continued.

"And Jesus answering said to him, 'It is written, thou shalt adore the Lord thy God, and him only shalt thou serve.' And the devil brought him to Jerusalem and set him on a pinnacle of the temple, and he said to him, 'If thou be the Son of God, cast thyself from hence. For it is written, that he hath given his angels charge over thee, that they keep thee, and that in their hands they shall bear thee up, lest perhaps thou dash thy foot against a stone.' "

Nettie wished that she were an angel. Not like the one she was going to be when she went to heaven, but one here on Earth, so Bill would love her. She knew her hair was dark and angels were supposed to be blond. And she was petite, not buxom and curvy. No wonder Bill hadn't made a pass at her, even after four months of dating.

She glanced at him and caught him looking away and frowning in self-reproach. He must have been chastising himself for going out with such a homely girl. Maybe she was a mercy case, and Bill was being nice to her out of a sense of Christian duty. She finished the chapter and closed her Bible. She put her hands out halfway across the table, hoping he would take hold of them. Bill still looked lost in thought.

"Would you like to watch some television?" she asked, hoping she didn't sound desperate.

At least if they were on the couch together, he couldn't avoid touching her. And that would not be bad at all, being close to his warm, strong body, smelling his subtle masculine aftershave and maybe just a teeny hint of sweat. And maybe she could get up the nerve to lean her head oh so lightly on his shoulder until his breath was on her cheek.

And she was thinking "couch," when she really wanted "bed," when she really wanted him to stand up and carry her in his arms and lay her gently on her clean white bedspread and lean over her with his lips and hair and hands all over—

Bill stood, making the chair squeak on the linoleum in his haste. "I'm afraid I have to go, Nettie," he said, hands clasped in front of him like a Quaker. "Got a few phone calls to make."

She looked down at the tabletop, hoping her disappointment didn't show.

"But your reading was pretty. I thank you so much." He started for the door.

"Bill?" she said, and he turned.

Ask me out again, ask me out again, she was thinking. *It doesn't have to be once a week.*

"Yes, Nettie?"

"See you in church."

Bill nodded and smiled, then ducked through the doorway into the rainy night.

In bed, Tamara rolled over and felt Robert stir. He grunted and yawned, and she reached for him.

"Hey," he whispered in the dark.

"We need to talk," she said.

"Great. Just when I was dreaming about a guest spot on 'Larry King Live.'"

"Tough day, huh?"

"Lousy. Patterson's just about unbearable. The great Oompah Loompah strikes again. And that same crappy music over and over."

"At least it's radio work."

"Well, I'm getting a little too old to try and figure out what I want to be when I grow up. And it looks like the big time is just going to pass Bobby Lee right on by."

He'd referred to his on-air handle, which meant that he was stuck inside himself again, dwelling on his own problems, and wouldn't have any room in his soul for Tamara's. For their *mutual* problems. "Now, Robert, we've been over this a hundred times already. Stick with what you like."

Tamara rubbed Robert's hairy chest and snuggled against his shoulder. "Besides, you're not getting older, you're just getting better. You'll make it one day, just wait and see."

Robert's hand dropped to her belly and caressed its way up to her breasts. She felt a small stir under her skin and her pulse accelerated. But the Gloomies hovered in the back of her mind like old ghosts, ghosts of her father and half-buried memories, and bad things yet to crawl from the shadows.

"Robert, I don't think—"

She gasped in involuntary arousal. Then the Gloomies crested and crashed like a tidal wave, sweeping the shores of her mind.

Shu-shaaa.

She took Robert's hand from her chest and held it. "I'm sorry, I'm just not in the mood tonight."

Robert puffed like a schoolboy who had been denied a toy. "What's wrong?"

"The Gloomies. You know."

She felt him tense in anger and then relax. *Oh, just her "head stuff,"* he was probably thinking. *Nothing serious.*

"Honey, that was so many years ago," he finally said. "You've got to stop blaming yourself."

"I can't help it."

Robert sighed and then was quiet as the rain drummed off the roof, its fury seeming to diminish along with their passion. Tamara looked out the window, trying to give her anxiety a shape in the darkness.

In a few minutes, Robert was snoring but Tamara was more wide-awake than before. She was worried that she would have the dream again, the one where her family was swallowed by . . . by . . . she wasn't sure what.

She only knew that she was alone with the Gloomies. And she could tell they were ready to dance the night away.

Chapter Five

The eyes were everywhere. Always the eyes. White eyes, white faces.

James Washington Wallace eased down the sidewalk, hunching his back and trying to draw his head inside his body like a turtle. His hands were in his pockets, and his Washington Wizards cap was pulled all the way down to his brow. Now if he could only do away with the lower part of his face, not an inch of black skin would show. The light rain fell on his shoulders, but he endured quietly. Lord knows, he'd learned how to endure.

He hated Windshake. Maybe it was because he was one of only three African-Americans living here.

African-Americans, hell. We's NIGGERS here. May as well call a spade a spade.

So what if he had a masters degree in Library Science? Did he honestly expect that these lily-white rednecks would let him touch their books? Work right there in a public place where their little girls went on Saturday mornings to watch G-rated videos? Where he might even drink from the same water fountain as the white folks?

He stepped on the wet sidewalk cracks as he purposefully watched his feet, measuring the distance between the next pair of shoes ahead so that he could veer to the side and avoid having to make eye contact. He didn't look into the paned-glass storefronts, either, because he could guarantee that he'd see a couple of good old boys with their arms folded, staring at him. Then he would see their mouths move, and he didn't have to be a lip-reader to know they were sharing a racist joke.

Come on, James. Don't be so paranoid.

But he had a right to be. He didn't know what was worse, the open hatred of the inbred, cornfed illiterates, or the sidelong glances of the well-to-do tourists. It was no secret that most of them retired here or vacationed here because of the low crime rate. And in their minds, low crime rate equaled no niggers.

If only he were back in D.C. He'd had a decent job at the Smithsonian, a government gig that actually served a purpose. He'd worked in the paper archives section, preserving and cataloging historical documents. There was nothing like an old brown piece of paper covered with sloppy words inked from the tip of a quill pen. Great words from great men.

Sure, most of them had been white. But in James's mind, you couldn't turn the tide of history. Those dustwigs had it right on the money. Ben Franklin, Thomas Jefferson, and George Washington (who may have been a distant relative, according to family legend, hence James's middle name) had been farsighted and wise. Take the Constitution, for example. Damn thing had stood the test of time, that's for sure. Even if most of the people who drafted it had held slaves, freedom had to start somewhere.

Aunt Mayzie liked to tell him about the "good old days" of the civil rights movement. How the brothers and sisters had taken over the buses in Birmingham or the lunch counters in Greensboro, or marched through the streets while the Klan and sometimes the cops pelted them with rocks and rotten fruit. And now she kept asking James why he didn't get into the African Pride movement.

"Roots are important," she'd say, hissing through the gaps in her teeth. "Used to be, we were kings and queens. That's where civilization began, you know. The dark heart of Africa."

Well, if we were so damned almighty, why'd we let the Dutch and English waltz in and round us up like cattle?

But he couldn't say that to Aunt Mayzie. Diabetes had cost her a foot and probably a good dozen years of the tail end of her life. And her heart was a ticking time bomb. May as well let her have her illusions. She was just sitting around under her brightly colored shawl watching reruns of "The Jeffersons" until her Lord called, anyway.

And when she died, he'd am-the-fucking-scray out of Dodge. He had a mission here, but he wasn't whole-heartedly enthusiastic about it. His mother was the one who had talked him into moving to Windshake to take care of Aunt Mayzie in her final years. Mom had won the argument before it had even started. As she said, *We takes care of our own, James.*

He'd driven up to Windshake in his black Honda Accord, growing increasingly worried as the towns got smaller and smaller. By the time he'd begun climbing the thin road up into the Appalachian mountains, he'd had serious misgivings. But there was no turning back, no way he could ever look his mother in the eyes again if he disappointed her now.

So he'd settled in with Aunt Mayzie, taking a cramped back room in her little slate-sided house. He'd even gotten a job, which was where he was heading now. He glanced at his watch. Ten minutes early, just as he always was.

He pushed open the door of Buddy's Grill and ducked in, shaking the rain off his shoulders. Buddy stood at the chipped counter in a white T-shirt that squeezed rings in the red meat above his biceps. Buddy wasn't wearing his dentures. His lips flopped around, the same way his pancakes flopped when his spatula worked them over on the stainless steel surface of the grill.

James was always amazed that the customers didn't get grossed out by the loose-jowled cook. But everyone seemed to love him. In fact, he was practically a local institution. Last year, a national travel magazine had featured Buddy's Grill as a "must visit" and had rated it four thumbs-up out of five. Local color had a lot of value in the rural South, James decided. In fact, color was damn near everything.

He nodded to Buddy, who raised a spatula in greeting, flipping drops of black grease across the newspaper that was spread across the counter. Mollie, the frizzy-haired day waitress, smiled at him and turned back to her ashtray. James went to the back and strapped on a dirty apron and took up his position at the Hobart. The little can-shaped dishwasher was practically his best friend these days. He'd even named it "The Tin Man." At least back here he was safe from the white eyes.

But not from the white voices.

They'd sit with their fat white asses perched on the vinyl stools that lined the counter, eating and talking and soaking up free refills of coffee. He'd endured the "Martin Luther Coon Day" jokes during the last half of January, and when President's Day had rolled around, they'd even knocked Abraham Lincoln for "freeing the niggers."

James was well educated and had seen a bit of the world. He knew racism was a universal truth, even up north. But he'd never seen people so vicious, so burning with blind hatred. They hadn't torched any crosses on Aunt Mayzie's lawn, but they'd shot a lot of arrows with their eyes and launched missiles with their words.

Well, if it was any consolation, the bastards would die young from arteriosclerosis. He couldn't believe the way those rednecks packed away the sausage and eggs. As if that wasn't bad enough, they had to have gravy to dip their biscuits in. Buddy's gravy was dangerous stuff, death gray with pools of fat congealed across the top. Cholesterol heaven.

He hadn't yet decided if Buddy was a racist. Sure, Buddy had given him a job and probably had endured a lot of ribbing from his customers over it. Buddy was up-front about everything, but he made good and damned sure that James was "out-back."

"Minimum wage plus a quarter," Buddy had told him on his first day. The words had flopped out between the droopy skin of his jaws as his tongue tried vainly to enunciate the *t*'s against his bare gums. "Never gonna move up, never get a raise. Take it or leave it."

James had taken it. He had no false pride. Lots of true pride, the kind that gave him self-confidence that one day he'd make a mark on the world. But he also knew how to let it hibernate, to keep it buried away deep inside, where no white eyes could see.

They called him a monkey. He'd be a damn monkey, all right. In fact, he'd be *three* monkeys. Hear no evil, see no evil, speak no evil.

And one day Windshake would be a distant memory, maybe a chapter in his autobiography. He wasn't exactly wishing that Aunt Mayzie would pass on for any selfish reasons. He accepted that the Lord moved in His own good time. But he often found himself praying for the Lord to get His white ass on down here and take her home. In His infinite wisdom, of course. To ease her suffering, you see.

James loaded a rack of dishes and started the Hobart. He walked to the back door where the food service trucks unloaded. He always helped the drivers carry the cases of products inside, even though it wasn't in his job description. He found that if he worked twice as hard as any other living human, then even a white boss would be satisfied, if grudgingly.

There were no trucks in the back lot. It was raining steadily now. He looked down the back streets of Windshake at the garbage-strewn alleys whose pictures somehow never made it into the pages of *Southern Living*. An old railroad track ran parallel to the one-lane road, a crisscross of creosote timbers and rust red metal sleeping on a bed of gray gravel.

Two teenage boys were leaning against a brick wall, shielded from the rain by a droopy awning. They passed a joint back and forth, giggling and wiping their noses. One of them turned away, and James could see the steam from the boy's piss curling up the side of the wall. Suddenly a bolt of lightning flashed across the sky, followed almost immediately by a whiplash of thunder. The boy who had been taking a leak jumped a foot up in the air, and his buzz buddy started laughing so hard it looked like *he* might piss, too, only before he even got his pants down. They were still scuffling in stoned horseplay when James went back inside the grill.

Must be nice to just stand around anywhere and smoke a good joint, James thought. But there was no way in hell he was going to be caught holding. A black man in a new Honda Accord drew enough attention in this town. People probably assumed he was a drug dealer, bringing big-city crack to the elementary schools of Pickett County. He hadn't been pulled over by the Man yet, but the local cops always did a double-take as he passed, as if to say, "Just make a wrong move, boy, and we'll be on your ass like a fly on shit."

Besides, James had given up dope in graduate school. Any fool could make the Dean's List in a four-year school, stoned or otherwise. But he'd found out that if you had dreams, if you wanted to be Somebody, then you had to get your act together. And you couldn't get your act together if you were staring at the ceiling fan and grooving on its synchronicity with the cosmos.

James pulled a rack of bone white plates from the Hobart. "You got them nice and clean, Mr. Tin Man," he said in his low bass. "Practically pristine. Unsullied. Spotless."

He held a plate to the light and looked into it. He was almost startled by the reflection that filled the round bottom of the plate. He rarely looked in the mirror, because he hated to see his dark face staring back at him. But this fool he was looking at now was a little different from that one. This fool was one uptight, paranoid prima donna who had to take everything so seriously. His eyes were dark and bottomless and alive, but he knew how to shut them down like the iris of a camera, how to make them blank and unreadable. He tilted the plate to make his reflection distort.

"'The eye sees not itself but by reflection,'" he said, remembering Shakespeare's line from some literature class. "Whatever the hell that means."

Buddy called from the grill, saying they needed some plates up front, and not yesterday, either.

James picked up a clean stack and put them on the service ledge where Mollie could pick them up.

"Yazzah, mazzah," he muttered under his breath.

The alien snatched the faint vibration out of the air, testing it, tasting it.

Maz-zaaa.

Another symbol. It added it to the *shu-shaaa*, this planet's original symbol. The *maz-zaaa* had been less distinct, as if radiated from a distant constellation. Perhaps it had no meaning. Perhaps none of this planet's life forms were intelligent enough to combine multiple symbols. Perhaps this planet had nothing to offer besides its nutrients.

Now that the alien had grown comfortable in the cave, roots spreading through the forest and siphoning energy, it allowed a moment to open its pulsing center to the strange world that surrounded it.

The oxygen mixture swirled through the vegetation above and a soft hydrogen-oxygen mixture pelted the skin of the planet. Static electricity caused the alien's tendrils to tingle. A small creature raced across the soil, its passage echoing through the alien's cave. The vibrations were almost painful, and the alien slipped back into a state of rest, focusing on that strange symbol *shu-shaaa*.

Chapter Six

It was turning out to be one of those nightmare shifts. First, the printer had gone berserk and started eating the AP feed so he couldn't read the weather copy, and then Melvin Patterson, the station GM, had popped into the studio to chew his rear about skipping around in the playlist. Now this squeaky birdbrain was calling in to report some green lights. Robert Leon, known to WRNC's listening audience as "Bobby Lee," let out a sigh and pressed the phone more tightly to his ear.

"I haven't heard anything about it, ma'am," he said, wondering why in the hell she had called the radio station. Didn't she have any friends, for God's sake?

"Ain't you got no other reports of 'em?" The voice on the other end of the phone screeched like fingernails across a blackboard. "Up around Bear Claw?"

"Not that I know of. You may want to try the local authorities, ma'am."

Robert looked at the countdown cue on the Denon CD player. Twelve more seconds of Mariah Carey trying to shatter glass. He rubbed his forehead.

"But they's *lights*, don't you see?" the caller said. "Up in the woods. Might be one of them UFO's I been hearing about."

Why would an intelligent alien species want to land in Windshake? Robert slid a CD into the second player.

"Maybe you ought to videotape it and send it in to 'Unsolved Mysteries,' " he said. "Listen, I've got to go. Bye, now, and thanks for listening to WRNC."

He hung up the phone and flipped the mic switch over at the same time. He drew air down into his abdomen, the way he had learned in college, then belted out in his artificially cheery baritone.

"That was 'Dream Lover' by Mariah Carey."

And I hope you were smart enough to turn your radio off before she really got rolling.

"It's fourteen minutes after eleven and forty-one degrees in the High Country under cloudy skies. Bobby Lee here sharing your day with you."

Only because I can't find a better job.

"You're listening to AM 1220, WRNC, your source for local news and sports."

Because all our sponsors ARE the news or else their sons play on the high school football team.

"Coming up after the break, I'll have a look at the weather."

Let the radio crap on your head for three more minutes just so I can tell you what you would already know if you had enough sense to look out the window. And I'm really being a flaming asswipe today, so I'll shut up now.

Robert punched the button on the cart player. Sav-a-Ton was having a sale on spareribs. The cart machine held three spots that fired off in sequence, so Robert had time to leave the control room and catch a couple of drags off a cigarette. He swung open the back door and stood under the small awning, watching the weeds wilt in the gravel parking lot.

Betty Turnbill, the station secretary, stepped out beside him.

"Mornin', Bobby." She batted her false eyelashes. "Mind if I join you?"

"It's a free country," Robert said, sucking smoke into his lungs. Betty tucked a cigarette between her rose-painted lips and leaned forward, expecting a light. Her red bouffant wiggled slightly as she shook her shoulders. It was the first time Robert had ever seen her hair actually move. Well, except for that one time, but it had been dark then. And he was positive he'd be reminded of *that* for the rest of his career at WRNC.

Robert fumbled in his pockets and drew out a Bic and put fire to the end of Betty's Virginia Slim. She puffed, making caves in her hollow jaws, and exhaled a curling gray pillar of smoke. Robert looked at her. Her hazel irises clashed miserably with her aqua eye shadow, and the blush on her cheekbones looked as if it had been applied with a putty knife. She drew the cigarette away from her mouth and Robert saw tiny clumps of lipstick hanging from the butt. The sight made the coffee in his stomach gurgle and roil.

She jutted her tiny chin toward him and smiled. She was trying to flirt, but her face was contorted into a mask that was more come-on-get-real than come-hither. The aroma of her Elizabeth Taylor perfume hung around the doorway despite the brisk wind. Robert guessed the fragrance was probably heavier than air, and didn't drift away so much as sag to the ground.

"Got to go," he muttered, flipping his half-finished cigarette into a mud puddle. "Melvin would scream bloody murder if we had a second of dead air."

"Bye, Bobby. Come up and see me sometime."

Mae West in Minnie Pearl's body. No, thank you, darlin'. Once was one time too many.

Robert rushed into the studio just as the tag on the last commercial trailed away. He slipped on the headphones and opened the mic.

"And Billy Buck Dodge-Jeep-Chrysler would like to congratulate Edna Massey for winning this month's gingerbread bake-off," Robert said, settling into the control room's swivel chair. "Well, the weather word for today is *rain*, and I'd say fifty percent chance is as good a guess as any, starting this afternoon and tapering off around midnight. Highs will be in the fifties and lows in the upper thirties."

He started the CD player and finished speaking over the instrumental opening bars of "Hotel California." "Up next, it's the Eagles on AM 1220, WRNC."

Robert leaned back in the chair and put his hands behind his head. He'd bounced around a half-dozen little AM stations in his fifteen-year career, but this one had to be the runt of the litter. You were supposed to get better and better jobs as you gained experience in your field, especially when you were talented. But other than that brief spot on an FM Country morning show, he'd been about as hot a property as a broken Ninja Turtle doll.

"A Ham-It-Up Breakfast," the FM show had been called. That dip into big-market FM had lasted about two months, and his show had been slowly climbing up the Charlotte ratings charts. He'd had Garth Brooks and Jeff Foxworthy on as guests, and seemed primed to make a run at syndication. He knew it was his break, his one shot that would bring him everything he deserved. But the station was sold out from under him, or rather, over his head, and converted to a conservative talk format faster than he could say "hallelujah." Instead of the wit and wisdom of Bobby Lee, the listening audience was treated to the bombast of Rush Limbaugh and Reverend Floyd Hardwick. The damnedest blow of all had been the fact that the station's ratings had doubled within the week.

He'd lucked into a midday drive-time job and bounced around a little, and now here he was again, right back where he'd been ten years ago. But at least he was eating, he thought, as he patted the basketball that had somehow grown in his stomach over the course of his middle age. And being an announcer beat the heck out of working for a living. He only hoped Tamara was happy with his latest career move.

The Eagles were winding down, and Elton John was in and cued, ready to tell everybody why they called it the blues. As if old Eltie knew, with his stretch limousines and Kensington estate.

But we all have our own battles to fight, Robert thought. Rock stars had their share of worries, too. Like whether to wear a feather boa with the leopard-skin tux, for one thing. For another, they probably had to be on a first-name basis with their accountants. Accountants were almost as boring as psych researchers.

Robert fired off the Elton John song without an intro and walked up front to get another cup of coffee. He peeked around the corner and saw Melvin Patterson sitting behind his mahogany desk. Patterson was always bitching about how the station was about to go under, but his desk and cream-colored leather chair must have cost a few hundred reps of that Billy Buck Dodge-Jeep-Chrysler spot. Betty's desk was by the front door, and she had her back to him. Despite himself, his eyes fell to her bottom. Her rump was spread out like a water balloon, quivery yet shapeless at the same time.

Robert filled his cup and went back to the studio. He turned down the monitor speakers so he wouldn't have to absorb any more adult contemporary rhythms than he'd already been bombarded with. He was sure that they caused cancer, or at least made you lose your hair and start voting Republican. But he didn't care if the manager told him to play the greatest hits of Boxcar Willie over and over, as long as the numbers added up on the paycheck every Friday morning.

He killed the next half hour with meatless banter and hits from Whitney Houston, Madonna, Michael English, and Lionel Richie. Before he knew it, it was two minutes until noon and Dennis Thorne, WRNC's answer to Walter Cronkite, or at least Les Nessman, but slightly taller than both, was standing behind him ready to take over the chair for the twelve-o'clock news.

"What's your lead, Dennis?" Robert asked him.

Dennis smoothed his gel-thick black hair as if he were going in front of a camera. "Chemical spill at Bryson's Feed Supply."

"Damn, man, you got some hard-hitting stuff today. Did you check with Melvin?"

"Check? What for?"

"Bryson's been a sponsor since you were sticking boogers under the desk in journalism school, my friend. I don't think that will pass the censors."

"It's okay. It was the delivery driver's fault. She was filling in, wasn't very experienced. She forgot to latch the back of the trailer and a couple of barrels of pesticide bounced around in the parking lot as she was pulling away. Some experimental stuff called Acrobat M-Z, supposed to kill blue mold on tobacco."

"Emergency Response team situation?"

"Yeah. They just hosed the stuff into the ditch."

"Maybe we'll get some weird mutant life forms to go with the green lights."

"Green lights?" Dennis adjusted his tie as Robert got up and gave him the chair.

"Long story," Robert said, waving to the sound console. "It's all yours, guy. I'm going to catch me a smoke break."

Dennis waved him away and spread his news copy out on the desk. As the "On Air" sign lit up, Robert went out back. The rain had started, a soft trickle. A spasm of lightning lashed across the murk of the horizon; a couple of seconds later it was followed by a booming bass line of thunder.

Robert worked his way through a Camel Light. Tamara would soon be heading down the mountain for her afternoon classes. He shouldn't have been such a jerk last night. But she was driving him crazy lately. At first her little premonitions had been cute and quirky, because she was quick to search for rational explanations based on her knowledge of psychology. But lately she had become obsessed, taking them seriously, growing distracted and distant.

Gloomies. What a bunch of crap.

Still, her skin had felt wonderful last night. He should have kept his mouth shut and his hands busy and maybe—

Robert's pulse sped up. Then he heard Betty's brittle laughter erupt from the far end of the building and his mood crash-landed like the Hindenburg, only without the climactic explosion.

For the hundredth time, he cursed himself for his moment of weakness, the one blotch on his marital record. It had occurred at the station Christmas party three months ago. Tamara had to give a final exam to her night class and hadn't been able to make it, so Robert endured the party alone, chumming around with people he already saw too much of at work. They stood around the catered buffet spread trying to make conversation over the roast beef and rye, but shoptalk seemed to be the only thing they had in common.

After Melvin and his frosty-haired trophy wife left, Jack Ashley, the morning man, brought a couple of bottles of Wild Turkey from under the seat of his truck and started them around the room. Robert hadn't been much of a drinker since becoming a family man, but he thought a few sips might keep him from dying of boredom. He had intended to have only enough to get himself warm faced, because he knew what would happen if he got the old ball rolling.

Warm faced came and went, and then he was starting to get a little thick lipped. *Drink just enough to chuck up that clam dip,* he'd told himself, *then you've had enough.* But the clam dip stayed down, and so did a good pint of eighty-proof whiskey. For the first time, he noticed what great senses of humor the WRNC staff had. Rick Dixon, the college student running the board that night, probably would have motivated a lot of little old ladies to call in and complain to Patterson about the crude jokes that filled the airwaves of Pickett

County. Fortunately, most of their listening audience beat the sun to bed every night.

Somewhere along the way to getting wobbly headed, damned if Betty Turnbill didn't start looking *good*. If Robert squinted just a little bit, she resembled a younger, if slightly seedier, Reba McIntyre. And those wrinkles in her pink wool sweater just might have been breasts, and there could have been a real smile beneath her painted one. She corralled him in a corner after most of the staff had left, her whiskey-and-Cheez Whiz breath on his neck and her hands roving over his ample flesh. And the next thing he knew, they were in the backseat of his car, bumping like a couple of awkward high schoolers. More than once, if he remembered correctly, but he couldn't be sure.

He'd driven home at three in the morning with a fuzzy tongue and his clothes smelling like a French whorehouse. Tamara was already in bed, snoring gently. He peeked into the kids' rooms. Kevin had been fast asleep under the glow-in-the-dark stars stuck on his ceiling and Ginger was somewhere in the middle of a pile of stuffed bears and aardvarks and frogs. He crept into the bathroom and took a shower, trying to wash Betty's raw scent off his skin. By the time he'd lathered up, he'd almost convinced himself the night had never happened. But then he looked down at the traitorous piece of meat dangling between his legs and knew that he'd lost something he'd never regain.

Now Betty was always flirting with him, teasing him about that night, and jokingly threatening to tell Tamara.

Damn her, Robert thought, chain firing another cigarette before the first had sizzled out. And dee-double-damn himself. He had promised himself that he'd never stray again, and, so far, he'd been as true as an encyclopedia. But sometimes he wondered if his little inner demon, as the rednecks liked to say about the South, was going to rise again.

But maybe it was all Tamara's fault. If she hadn't been

going on about those damned Gloomies all the time, driving him nuts, not understanding the pressure he was under—

He blew smoke into the hallway as he made his way back to the studio. Through the monitor speakers, he heard Dennis heading into the break with a whimsical feature about the woolly worm's weather predictions. The official woolly worm had two dark rings at the end of its body, heralding two more weeks of snowy weather. Dennis told the audience that the woolly worm was eighty-three percent accurate, which beat the predictions of the National Weather Service all to hell.

They've even broken mountain folklore down to a scientific formula, Robert thought. *Mysterious green lights and Gloomies, maybe everybody wants to believe in magic. So why the hell can't I?*

Robert looked through the large plate glass into the control room. Dennis held up two fingers. Two minutes left before the wrap-up. Time enough to check the entertainment wire.

Patterson was in the hall, blocking it with his chubby elbows angled out at his sides, the requisite scowl on his face.

Christ, why didn't he ditch those acrylic sweater vests? They make him look even more like one of Willy Wonka's Oompah Loompahs than usual.

"You were late again, Robert," Patterson said in the gravelly voice the old ladies in WRNC's audience swooned over. At least those who didn't know him personally.

"Yeah. Couldn't find the car keys this morning. Won't happen again."

"Better not. By the way, we've got a remote this weekend for Blossomfest, and I'm volunteering the on-air staff to emcee it. So don't make any plans."

"Fine," Robert said, aching for the cup of coffee that was waiting in the storeroom that passed for a lounge. "You're the boss."

He sidestepped to the right, and Patterson yielded, letting

him pass. Patterson's scowl drifted into a smug smile, an expression Robert wouldn't mind feeding to him with a shovel one day.

"One more thing," Patterson said to his back. "You've got to re-cut that Petty Pleasures spot. Dawn Petty called and said the voiceover wasn't exciting enough."

Exciting, hell. How do you work up a good phlegmball of enthusiasm over a craft and knickknack shop? What did she want, Dick Vitale on uppers, telling the world what a "special, special place" it was?

"Aye-aye, Commander. I'll get right on it." Robert turned the corner and Betty was standing there, batting her thick waxy eyelashes.

"When you going to get right on *this?*" she whispered, jutting her chest at him.

"Not now, Betty," he said. *In fact, not ever again.*

He hoped.

When Dennis turned the console back over to Robert, the mic smelled of cologne and breath mints. It was time to read the daily obituaries. Robert had a healthy respect for the dead, especially because he didn't want to be among their number. But for some reason, reading the daily obituaries always made him want to snicker.

Perhaps it was due to trying to maintain the appropriate blend of gravity and pep. Maybe it was because of the odd local names. It could be because of his off-beat sense of humor. Or maybe it was what Tamara called his "inappropriate emotional response disorder." Whatever it was, he sometimes had to flip the mic off for a second to cover his snickers.

He opened the folder and looked at the name of the first dearly departed. It was Dooley R. Klutz.

Robert felt as if he could really use a drink.

Chapter Seven

Sylvester Mull cradled his .30-06 in the crook of his left elbow, his trigger hand gripping the wooden stock. He ducked under a low pine branch, one of the few scraps of greenery in the mountains this time of year. He was hunting out of season and wore brown camouflage coveralls, but still felt as exposed as a peacock in a turkey pen. The damned deer seemed to be getting smarter and smarter, or maybe he was just getting dumber.

Last year, he'd only bagged a couple of bucks, a four-pointer and a six-pointer. Not even worth hanging those scraggly-assed sets of horns on the wall down at the Moose Lodge. But he didn't hunt for the glory of it, like a lot of those beer-bellied Moosers did. He liked to put meat on the table cheap, or free if possible. Of course, they weren't exactly giving away ammunition these days, what with them damn liberals putting the pressure on the gun industry.

But hunting was only half the reason he lurked in the woods. The joy was in getting away out here on the back side of Bear Claw, where the car exhaust didn't burn your eyes and the only noise was the northwest wind tangling with the treetops.

Blow on, wind, he thought to himself, *just push the ass end of winter right on out of these parts.*

The last snows had been late and deep. It might only be his imagination, but he couldn't remember the weather ever being so bad. Seemed to have gotten worse over the last few years. And them damned geniuses on the news kept on about global warming when any fool could plainly tell it was getting *colder*.

Used to be, by this time of the year, red buds would be hanging on the tips of the oak and hickory trees and the briars would have little sprigs of bright green leaves up and down their spines. But today, everything was the color of mud and barn stalls, dreary from the rainstorm that had hit the mountains last night. The wind had pushed the storm away, though another sprinkle had started around noon. The first stubborn flowers had poked through the dead leaves, bloodroot, trout lilies, and slim, pale stalks of chickweed. In the protected hollows, mist hung like gunsmoke over a battlefield. The mist was easy to hide in, and maybe, if he was lucky, a buck or doe might just pass right under his nose.

Sylvester had built this stand last fall, when the hunting season had about petered out. Dead pine branches stacked against each other, a few logs strung together with twine to hold the mess up, and a little leaf-covered tarp tied overhead to keep him dry. With his brown clothes and hair, he blended with the environment. And he ought to, as many years as he'd hoofed through these woods trying to rustle up some meat. He didn't wear one of those flaming orange hats that they sold in the sporting goods section down at the Kmart.

That was one of the dumbest things Sylvester had ever heard of. Might as well carry a neon sign that said, *Hey, deer, come over here and get blown to hell.* Prevented accidents, they said. Well, if a fellow couldn't tell a man from an animal, he had no business in the woods with a gun anyway.

People didn't start off small, the way they should. Sylvester

had been out here when he was eight years old, carrying a
.410 shotgun with the safety on, staring at the ground behind
his daddy Chester's boot heels, wondering why the old bastard had drug him out of a warm, quilted bed into the frosty
morning. Then Daddy had pointed out a fat gray squirrel
running across the limb of a poplar tree. Didn't say a word,
just tapped Sylvester on the shoulder, aimed his long gun at
the sky, then suddenly, *Ba-boom,* and the squirrel was spinning through the air, scattering the red drops of its blood.

Sylvester ran after his daddy, and they stood over the
small gray animal. Its tiny chest rose and fell in frantic gasps
and the faded pink nostrils flared as it drew its final breaths.

"Bastards will bite you," Chester had said, raising the butt
of his rifle over the squirrel's head. "Make sure they're dead
before you pick 'em up."

The squirrel gave a final shiver and lay still. Chester bent
over and picked it up by the tail. He held it in front of
Sylvester's face and spun it slowly around. A dozen dark
holes pocked the white tufts of its chest. Chester dropped it
in the pocket of his coat as if it were an old glove. Then he
slid back the bolt of his shotgun and the spent shell kicked
out. Bitter blue smoke curled from the open chamber as
Chester slid a fresh shell into place. He closed the gun with
a metallic click, then looked Sylvester in the eye and gave
him a bloodshot wink.

"That's some good eating, boy," his daddy said, but Sylvester
had been sick to his stomach, had almost laid his sausage-
gravy-and-biscuit breakfast onto the forest floor. But he
swallowed instead, the acid gurgling back into his stomach.
Damned if he was going to puke in front of the old man.

Chester shot two more that day, and even let Sylvester
have a crack at a third. Sylvester had seen the small moving
ball of fur scurrying around the bark of a sycamore like a
stripe up a barber's pole. He'd pointed and fired, closing his
eyes even as his finger tightened over the trigger, and the

roar pushed his eardrums inward and the gun's recoil sat him on his hind end. He'd opened his eyes, blinking at the sky, disoriented.

His daddy was laughing so hard Sylvester thought his scrawny ribs might crack. Sylvester turned his head and saw the squirrel, branches bending under its weight as it put distance between itself and the noises of death. The .410 was a few feet away from Sylvester, lying across an old yellow stump.

He'd rolled to his knees, then stood up shakily. Chester, still hooting like a crazy owl, slapped him on the back so hard that Sylvester almost fell over again. Then Chester pulled a bottle of clear liquid from one of his coat pockets and handed it to Sylvester.

"Reckon you're a man now, except for the 'gettin' laid' part," Chester said, his chuckles squeezing out between his bare gums.

Sylvester thought it was water in the jar, and he sure was thirsty, what with almost being sick and all. He turned up the bottle and had a mouthful halfway to his gut when he noticed something wasn't right. His nose burned and fire ripped across his tongue and throat, as hot as hell's front door. He tried to squirt the gasoline-tasting stuff out of his mouth, but some had already passed the point of no return and was already gnawing a hole in his stomach. Then he really *was* sick, spewing moss-colored vomit all over his boots.

Chester erupted into fresh laughter, his guffaws echoing across the sloped mountain valleys, sending every bit of game for a dozen square miles scurrying for their knotholes and dens. And Sylvester was sure that if he'd had a shell left in the .410, he'd have pointed it at the open black maw of the old bastard's face and shredded him a new blowhole.

They walked the three miles back home, Sylvester with his head drooping, swearing he'd never touch a gun again, much less go out in the woods with his daddy. And he sure as hell was never going to touch that mean water again.

But the next week, he'd been back out there, and he'd pegged himself a fat squirrel. At the sight of his first kill on the ground, its gray intestines spilling from its belly, he'd felt as high as a Georgia pine. He scooped it up and hefted its weight, a double palmful of good meat. He didn't even mind the black beads of the squirrel's eyes trapped open by sudden death. He tucked the animal inside his shirt and carried it home, feeling its warmth fade as it stiffened.

And his daddy had grinned like a rotten jack-o'-lantern, his lips creasing almost up to the tips of his big leathery ears.

"It's in the blood, boy," Chester said, helping himself to a swig from his jar to celebrate. Then he wiped his mouth with the back of his shirt sleeve and offered the bottle to Sylvester. His brother, Johnny Mack, had looked on, jealousy smoldering in his dark eyes. Johnny Mack was two years older than Sylvester and had never shot anything but a crippled possum cornered in the henhouse where it had been stealing the chicken's eggs.

Sylvester had refused the liquor, and never did answer the call of the bottle that cried out in his blood, but he sure as hell was hooked on hunting. Hooked right now, half his mind wandering but the other half sharp as a sentry's. Because hunting was timeless, the past pretty much like the present, whether in season or out. He could just as easily have been a brainless caveman waiting to spear a hairy elephant or a space alien with a zapper ray-gun, like in the movies. The hunter and the hunted, that's what it all came down to.

Sylvester crouched in the stand, his feet hot in his boots, and listened to the forest. Nothing but wind and the soft splash of the rain, but that was okay. Plenty of time to think. A bad day of hunting beat the hell out of the best day of work. He'd called in sick down at Bryson's Feed where he drove a delivery truck, and it wasn't the first time he'd skipped to go after deer or pheasant or squirrels.

Hell, he *had* been sick, in a way. Sick of that yackitty-assed wife of his, Peggy, and those snot-nosed brats she'd laid on him, those brats who sat on their sorry asses all day staring bug eyed at them video games. All crowded in the nasty trailer that Peggy was too lazy to clean. Who wouldn't want to escape from that?

He didn't escape in beer the way most of his fellow Moosers did, even though the thought was mighty tempting. He only had to look around on a Friday night at those sad-eyed middle-aged losers to remind himself how fast it all went away. Their last good years were draining through their livers, the alcohol fogging their fat heads and blurring their eyesight. He wasn't even sure why he had joined the Lodge. Probably because you had to own a necktie to get into the Lion's Club.

Most of his friends belonged to the Lodge. Billy Ray Silas, for one. They'd gone hunting and fishing together for the last twenty years, and once every six months they packed up and headed to the top of Blackstone Mountain for a week-long camping trip. Of course, they spent three days of pump 'n' pay at a whorehouse in Titusville before they even unloaded the truck. But Sylvester always brought something back, a good twenty-inch rainbow trout or a ten-point buck, and, once, a black bear.

And when he returned, his lips chapped from the wind, Peggy would be all lovey-dovey and they'd actually get along for a few weeks, doing the horizontal hoedown at least every other night. But that was before he'd found out about Jimmy Morris, his loyal Lodge brother. Seems Jimmy had been wearing out his bedsheets whenever Sylvester was gone, riding his wife before Sylvester's truck exhaust had even dissolved over the driveway. And Peggy must have felt guilty, because after his camping trips, she had been doing all kinds of imaginative bedroom sports. Or maybe Jimmy had just taught an old dog some new tricks.

To hell with them both.

Sylvester felt the comforting weight of the .30-06 across his arm. A good gun was all a body needed, a long, true-blue barrel and a worn woodstock. And some deep forest, which was getting harder to find since all the old local families had started selling off their land. Even his old man had peddled off pieces of the Mull birthright. The old farmstead had gone to seed, and if Sylvester ever did inherit a chunk of acreage, it would take years of work to get it yielding again.

Besides, Chester was never going to die at this rate. All that damned moonshine must have mummified the bastard, because he didn't seem to be slowing down any. Chester didn't lift a finger around the farm, but he still managed to get down to the Sav-a-Ton and load up on TV dinners and chewing tobacco. The last time Sylvester had visited him, a few weeks back when a late winter snowstorm had melted down enough for the farm road to be passable, the old man had been curled up under a blanket, his dog at his feet, and a jar of rotgut at his elbow, as happy as a rooster in a henhouse.

A twig snapped in the distance, jerking Sylvester out of his reverie. His senses sharpened as if his ears had telescoped out and were swiveling back and forth like secret-agent radar dishes. Leaves shuffled somewhere to his left, about a hundred yards away, just over a ridge.

Must be a big son of a bitch, judging from the racket.

Sylvester peered at the edges of a laurel thicket. A deer couldn't get through there, the branches were too knotted together. And the top end of the ridge was too steep. Even a mountain buck couldn't climb those granite boulders that jutted from the earth like gray teeth, especially with rain still soaking the loam beneath the leaves.

So it would have to come around the lower end of the laurel thicket, and Sylvester had a clear line of sight to the spot where it would most likely emerge. Now it was an enemy, as surely as the Japs or Injuns were in a John Wayne movie. It wanted to keep its meat attached to the bones, but Sylvester wanted to field dress it and slice it into steaks. It would die before it even knew it was hunted.

The back of Sylvester's neck tingled and sweat popped out around his scalp line. It wasn't a nervous sweat. Sylvester was locked in. This was his reason to roll out of bed in the morning, his dope, his religion. He had something to kill.

Sylvester wasn't complicated enough to try to understand why he gained so much pleasure from hunting. An anthropologist might have chalked it up to some primordial survival instinct still swirling in the genes at the base of the human backbone, even after all these millennia. A psychologist might have decreed that Sylvester was still trying to measure up against the judgments of a harsh father figure. A Mooser would have said that killing was more fun than a fart in an elevator. But Sylvester was untroubled by the many facets of the equation. Because the equation was simple: the hunter versus the hunted.

He pressed the gunstock against his cheek and pulled back the safety. It slid smoothly and easily, loose from years of being lovingly oiled. Sylvester aimed down the barrel to the tiny wingtip of the sight, then lined the gun up with the spot where the footfalls were headed. He breathed shallowly to hush the roar of his own blood in his ears and to steady his hands.

He saw movement through the drizzle, a quiver of laurel branch, and his finger grew taut on the trigger. He knew the exact degree of pressure he could apply before the hammer fell, and he was halfway there. Then his eyes saw a spot of brown, a more reddish brown than the surrounding dead leaves and tree trunks. His finger notched to about three-quarters.

Another step, Sylvester said to himself, *just show me the white fur target on your chest, and I'll park your ass in the deep freezer back home.*

And suddenly the animal stepped into the clearing, and Sylvester's finger was squeezing out the last millimeters of the trigger's resistance when he saw that it wasn't a buck that had lurched between the trees.

In that same micro-second, although it seemed to stretch out so long it felt like minutes, Sylvester pushed up with his left hand as the roar of the igniting charge filled his ears. Sylvester's mind collected several observations in that slow-motion instant: the smell of the gunpowder, harsh and cloying; the slight kick of the gun butt against his shoulder, like that of a baby jackass; the mist lifting as if someone had sucked it up with a king-sized vacuum cleaner; and the sound of the bullet whistling through the treetops overhead, carving a slice in the sky before digging into the mountainside somewhere hundreds of yards away.

The sweat was back on his scalp line, and this time it *was* nervous sweat. He'd almost shot somebody.

He leaned his rifle against the stand and looked at the figure that stumbled between the trees. Whoever it was didn't seem to have heard the shot. Sylvester's hands trembled. He looked down at them as if they were someone else's.

He stepped from the stand and looked down the ridge. The figure staggered and fell.

Sweet holy hell. I didn't shoot the son of a bitch, did I?

Tears of panic tried to collect in the corners of his eyes, but he blinked them away. He ran toward the fallen heap of flesh, hopping down the ridge, slipping on the rotten rug of leaves. They'd lock him up, sure as hell. Never give him another hunting license. Kick him out of the Lodge, maybe.

The huddled form was rising, wobbly but still alive. "Praise to Thee," Sylvester muttered to the wet gray sky, not really giving a good goddamn whether or not anybody was up there to hear him.

He saw that it was a man he'd almost shot, a short man whose dark hair hung in wet mop strings. His back was to Sylvester, but he looked familiar. Those square ears jutting out from under a red ball cap gave him away as surely as if he'd handed Sylvester a picture ID.

"Ralph," Sylvester hollered, reaching to touch the man on the shoulder.

Ralph Bumgarner was as dumb as a hitching post, but even *he* knew better than to stagger around in the woods in a deerskin jacket. With a white wool collar to boot. *Must be drunker than a sailor on shore leave.*

"I almost shot you, you crazy fool," Sylvester said, and suddenly his words flew back down his throat.

Because Ralph had turned.

Because Ralph's eyes were glowing green, the color of lime Jell-O, but shiny, as if a Coleman lantern was burning inside the cavity of his skull.

Because Ralph's face was ashen, pale, and dead, his flesh bulging against his skin like white mud in a Ziplock baggie.

Because Ralph planted his hands on Sylvester's shoulders and pulled him closer, and Sylvester's bones felt as if they had turned to Jell-O themselves, because he couldn't run.

Because Ralph opened his mouth as if he were going to plant a big soul kiss, and Sylvester got the feeling that there was a lot more to it than homosexual attraction.

Because Ralph's breath was maggoty and putrid, blowing from the black swamp of his gums, promising a French that was a hundred times ranker than the ones he'd gotten from the Titusville whores.

Because Ralph's tongue was in his mouth, slick as a slug but with the scaly texture of a dead trout, and a flood of cold slime gushed into Sylvester's throat.

Because the slime was changing him, joining and separating his cells, breaking him down, altering his metabolism.

Because Sylvester felt himself dying but had a feeling that simply dying and getting it over with would have been the best thing that ever happened.

Because now he was dead.

And ready to hunt.

Chapter Eight

James rolled out of bed, uncoiling like a rusty spring.

His six-foot-three-inch body had fought another losing round with the five-foot-eight-inch mattress. High sunlight burned through the curtains. He dressed and went to check on his aunt. She was watching television.

On the screen, Oprah Winfrey was chatting with Richard Simmons. Richard actually had on a suit and tie instead of his pastel tank top and peppermint shorts, and the audience was uncomfortably quiet. They didn't know what to make of his new, dry-cleaned image. They preferred the sweaty, chipper aerobics machine they had come to know and love.

"How are you feeling today, Aunt Mayzie?" James asked, rubbing the back of his neck.

"I'm fine, honey." Her voice was rich and ancient, the kind that smoothed troubled waters. "Ain't so weak today, and I had a bowl of oatmeal and a banana."

"Why didn't you let me get breakfast for you?"

" 'Cause I didn't want to wait 'til I was nothing but skin and bones. I believe you could sleep right through Joshua blowing his trumpet."

James looked sheepishly at Aunt Mayzie. Her right leg, or rather the scarred stump of it below her knee, was propped on a vinyl settee. A crutch leaned against the table beside her recliner, and her empty bowl sat on the sofa, flakes of oatmeal congealing around its rim. She held a coffee mug in her creased hands.

"You didn't put sugar in that, did you?" James asked.

"No, Mister Boss Man. Between you and that Dr. Wheatley, I'm guaranteed not to have another ounce of joy in this world."

"But I'll bet it's not decaf."

"Now, the caffeine gets the old heart ticking of a morning. Ain't no harm in it. Plus, if it kills me, it'll kill me off slow, and something else is bound to get me before then."

In James's opinion, the most dangerous harm was the slow, silent kind. Like the poison of racism. It wasn't the gaptoothed redneck poking his shotgun out the window of his Chevy pickup, it was the white-collar white saying *Sorry, but your—er—qualifications don't suit our needs at this time.*

James ran his dark hand over the peeling paint of the doorjamb. He wondered if this would be a good time to suggest that Aunt Mayzie consider moving into a good northern assisted-care home, one of those clean places with a satellite dish and a sauna and a fitness gym. Northerners weren't totally open-minded, but at least they'd freed their niggers once upon a time without having a gun held to their heads. But she'd never leave here, and he knew why, from the stories Momma had told him.

Mayzie and her husband moved to Windshake forty years ago, fresh from between the honeymoon sheets, to take jobs at the new sock factory. Had settled in this house, filled it with love and a baby and linen curtains. But the baby had died of what they now called Sudden Infant Death Syndrome, only back then they called it "baby just up and died." Uncle Theodore had followed their baby to heaven three years later in a factory accident, when the cotton press had grabbed his sleeve and pulled him into its iron jaws.

Mayzie had gotten some money from the factory, enough to pay off the house. Black lives were cheap, especially back then, but housing was cheap in those days as well. So Aunt Mayzie had kept working at the factory and tending her marigold beds and became a local fixture as the "town nigger." The Civil Rights turmoil bypassed Windshake, as had most everything else. Then her diabetes had taken a turn for the worse and she had retired to her little house with her television set, tabby cat, and the ghost of her right foot.

Now she was a part of the house. She *was* the house. The framing studs were her bones, the rafters her ribs, the slate siding tiles her skin. Her nerves were lined on the shelf, in a collection of animal salt shakers and miniature teapots. Her lungs were the screen doors, opened during the summer to let in the mountain breeze. Her eyes were the windows, watching as the forsythia bloomed and bluejays scrapped and dandelions filled the cracks in the sidewalk and Old Man Thompson doddered by to deliver her mail. And her heart was the photograph on the mantel, a cracked black-and-white portrait of a smiling young Theo holding a round-cheeked infant.

"Looks like the rain has done passed on," Aunt Mayzie said, looking out the window over her corner of Windshake. "And look yonder, the crocuses are starting to poke up."

"Maybe spring's finally getting here. It sure took its own sweet time. Hard to believe this is the South. I thought it was supposed to be scorching down here."

"The mountains is a land unto itself. And the bad makes you appreciate the good. It's going to be the kind of day makes you forget all that snow."

"Yes, ma'am." James watched the wind press against the stubby balsam shrubs that lined the walkway. "Maybe we can go for a walk after I get off work."

"Walk, nothing. I got an appointment with Dr. Wheatley today. I ain't got to walk nowhere when I got to walk *somewhere*."

"You didn't tell me."

"I most certainly did. Last night. But you had your eyes

glued on that basketball game like they was giving away money."

"Georgetown was playing, Aunt Mayzie. I've got to keep up with my old school. But what's this appointment for? Something wrong?"

"Just a checkup, is all. Anyways, my appointment's at three o'clock and I know you can't get off work. And I don't even want you to ask. I done fine for myself for thirty years, and I hope to do for at least a few more, the Good Lord willing."

Yes, but for most of those years, you had two good feet and one strong heart, James thought. *And you can't use my Honda because you never learned how to drive. Always a walker, you were. A mile to the factory, half mile to the Sav-a-Ton, two miles to church. Three miles to catch the Greyhound for the annual family visit. Miles and miles put on those wide black feet, their experience now halved.*

"Let me set you up with a cab, then." James put his hands on his hips. He felt ridiculous trying to stare down the woman who could stare down his own mother.

"Ain't setting foot in a car with that fool Maynard. Keeps a bottle under the seat and a cinder block on the gas pedal. No, I reckon a little stretch ain't gonna do me no harm."

James pictured Aunt Mayzie crutching down the sidewalk, wearing the purple velour coat James had gotten her for Christmas, a diaphanous red scarf knotted under her chin. Nodding to the white folks, stopping once in a while to rest her armpits, wearing the submissive smile that had hardened on her face like lava turned to obsidian.

"It's only a few blocks, James. Now you go on and don't worry about me. You're going to be late for work."

James glanced at his Timex. He'd have to run, and he hated to sweat. The steam from the Tin Man was bad enough. He had to be cool. Not like one of those shuffling gangsta stereotypes that populated the rap videos. No, cool like Frederick Douglass and George Washington Carver and Colin Powell.

"You sure you'll be okay?" James asked, his dark brow crinkling.

"I ain't helpless yet, James, even if you seem in an awful hurry to get me that way."

She turned her attention back to Oprah. James looked at the television. Now there was an African-American who knew how to rake in the bucks. Oprah's stardom had jumped the bounds of racism, even though she had awful taste in literature. Like Bill Cosby and Michael Jordan, she'd never be thought of as a nigger. All you had to do was get rich and famous, and you were accepted. Well, at minimum wage plus a quarter, he'd be accepted in seven centuries or so.

He bent down and kissed Aunt Mayzie's cheek. "Call if you need anything, you hear?"

"Old Buddy'd love that, wouldn't he? 'Don't pay you to talk, boy,' " she growled, trying to imitate the cook. Her laughter rattled the faded wallpaper.

James smiled despite himself. He was a chronic worrier, that was all. The sun was out and the birds were mating and springtime was almost here and Aunt Mayzie was far from defeated. And Georgetown had advanced another round in the tournament. Even with living in a white town, things weren't so bad.

"You take care on your way, Aunt Mayzie," he said at the door. "Love you. Bye, now."

James stepped into the sunshine and the breeze and the white eyes of Windshake.

"Where's Sylvester?"

"Like I would know." Peggy Mull pulled the phone away from her mouth so she could draw on her cigarette. She huffed out the smoke in a long, sighing trail. "Bryson's called and asked how he was feeling and to see if he was up to coming in after lunch. That's two days in a row he's missed."

"Reckon where he is?"

"Probably off in the woods somewhere, stroking that rifle of his. Anyways, I told them he wasn't even able to get out of bed. If his sorry ass loses that job, I'll be up shit creek with a toilet brush for a paddle."

"There's ways to get money. Don't you worry your pretty head none."

"And what's that supposed to mean?"

"Nothing," Jimmy Morris said at the other end of the line. "If Sylvester's off hunting, how about if I come over? You said yourself he usually stays till the sun drops."

"I don't know, Jimmy. I think he's starting to suspect something. It's hard to keep a secret in a damn trailer park."

Peggy knew that firsthand. Old Paul Crosley next door had noticed Jimmy's comings and goings, and Peggy had had to serve *him* a helping of home-baked panty pie to keep his wrinkled mouth shut. Not that Peggy minded much. She just hated to feel obligated.

"Peg, you know what you do to me. Just your voice is driving me nuts."

Peggy pushed away the pile of dirty dishes that covered the cracked Formica counter. *Thank the Lord peanut butter doesn't mold,* she thought. *Probably the oil in it. But I'll have to take a hammer and chisel to those egg yellows. Maybe tomorrow.*

"Tell you what, Jimmy. Why don't you get a fifth of that Millstream and swing by, and maybe we'll talk about it?"

"Talk, hell. I want to do more than talk."

Peggy giggled like a teenager. "Well, the kids *are* off at school."

"I'll bring back that old lawn mower and stick it out in the shed so's the neighbors will think I've been fixing it."

"You're a regular fix-it man, that's for sure. You gonna fix me up?"

"Let me check my tool, darling. Yep, raring to go."

Peggy stubbed out her cigarette and rummaged through her purse for another. Her fingers felt the ring of her

Earnhardt key chain, the one Jimmy had given her. Sylvester hadn't given her a damn thing except a hard time, and not the good kind, either. "Say, Jimmy . . ."

"Yeah, honey?"

"Why aren't *you* working today?"

There was a silence on the other end of the line, and Peggy listened to the faint electronic hum as Jimmy got his story straight. She glanced out the window and noticed that the trailer park was deader than usual. The curtains were drawn in Paul Crosley's Silverstream and the sawed-off Bronco was gone from the Wellborns' puddle-filled driveway. A patch of lilies poked up behind a rotted row of railroad ties at the park's entrance.

"Lemly Building Supply didn't drop off the blocks like they was supposed to. No need to mess around that muddy foundation all day for nothing. Can't lay what I ain't got."

"And you ain't got *me* yet."

"I'm working on it. See you in about twenty minutes?"

"I'll leave the door unlocked. And, Jimmy—"

"Yeah?"

Peggy found a half-full cigarette pack and crinkled the cellophane trying to spill out a fresh smoke. She looked at her hand, red and raw and aging, a hand that had been delicate once.

"Tell me you love me." *Even if you have to lie.*

"I love you, Peggy."

"Bye now," she said faintly, slowly pulling the phone away from her bleached hair and hanging it in its cradle. She lit the cigarette with her bloodshot hand.

Tamara picked Kevin's baseball glove off the floor and tucked it in the hall closet amid fishing poles, deflated soccer balls, windbreakers, and tangled piles of Christmas lights. One of these days they'd have to get around to spring cleaning. Because spring was here. The season of hope.

Yeah, right. Hope is a dirty word. I hope Robert will talk to me before our marriage slides the rest of the way into hell. I hope we can understand each other, because he's in a mid-life crisis and I'm in the same old sanity crisis. I hope hope hope hope.

She opened the living room window and the breeze pushed the scent of flowers through the screen. Dampness still clung to the air, but the sun was strong, and in its glow, the mountains were deep blue. Tamara's gaze traveled up the slopes, over the ripples of dark ridges to the gray stone face of Bear Claw. The familiar tingle trickled through her, and she tried to ignore it and concentrate on the coming day's lecture instead. But the sound cut through her thoughts.

Shu-shaaa.

She had no idea what the word meant, or if it even was a word. She tried it on her tongue.

"Shu-shaaa."

As she said it, something drew her attention back to Bear Claw. She thought she saw a flash of green light near the distant peak, as if someone had signaled with a piece of mirror. A secret signal directed at Tamara.

No. Probably just a reflection off a rock.

Because you do not hear voices. You do not dream the future. You do not see invisible lights. You are NOT crazy.

You are a teacher, a mother, a wife, a sensitive soul who needs to grow a thicker hide. Maybe that's not the right order of things, but brush your teeth and get down the mountain, and stop staring off into space waiting for spy messages to zap themselves into your brain.

If she wasn't crazy yet, she might soon drive herself there. *Shu-shaaa* was a cavity and her mind was a tongue, probing, exploring, curious, even though the rot would only continue spreading until the hole was bigger than the tooth. She slammed the window closed and went down the hall, away from the secret lights of Bear Claw.

Chapter Nine

Bill Lemly shucked off his White Mule gloves. He spread his fingers to stretch away the soreness. The truck they had just unloaded lurched away from the dock, coughing a black ball of smoke as it departed.

Bill looked around the loading yard. He was amazed that the Lord had allowed him all this. A tin-roofed warehouse you could fit a dozen buses in, a store the size of a football field, forty people on the payroll, and his name in letters as tall as he was.

"Here, Ray, let me get that end," Bill said to a worker who was struggling with a sixteen-foot board. They flipped it up onto a stack of pressure-treated lumber and it landed flush, sending a loud report across the loading yard. Bill put his gloves in his back pocket and rubbed his hands.

He was a hands-on guy. He liked to keep up with his business, know the names of the people who worked for him, and peek at the books once in a while, even if he didn't have such a good head for math. And he still loved the smell of fresh-cut pine and cedar. It always reminded him of his grandfather.

His grandfather had started taking Bill out on summer carpentry jobs when he was thirteen. Before Bill ever hammered his first nail, he carried lumber for two months. It was another three years before Bill was allowed to operate the skill saw. But that powdery golden sawdust had gotten into his blood, and he always knew he'd be in the building business in some way or another.

Bill had learned a lot from his grandfather: how to bevel an edge, how to shim out a door so that it didn't jam, how to miter the joints where the baseboard molding met. How to use his eyes. How to not be satisfied until a job was done right, even if he had to work unpaid overtime.

"Drive ever nail like it's the one that's got to hold up the whole house," his grandpa had said, his words muffled by the nails tucked in the corner of his mouth.

Bill could picture him now, with the straws of his white hair poking out from under his little round ball cap. When Grandpa's hands weren't occupied with a tool, he'd have his thumbs hooked under the straps of his coveralls, "studying," as he called it.

"Ever now and then you got to look a way off," he'd say, and they'd stop work for a minute and look without speaking at the blue-green mountains that rose around Windshake. When Grandpa was satisfied, he'd draw a deep breath and turn back to his work.

Carpentry had helped Bill gain strength, to build up his chest and shoulders and forearms until he was as hard as a ballpeen hammer. By the time he was in high school, he was one of the largest kids in Pickett County and a natural for the football team. Not that he cared that much. He had plenty of girls already and he liked having his afternoons free to work. But his father had said Bill was going to play and that was that.

So Bill had bulldozed through the defensive lines of the tiny mountain high schools and collected a dozen trophies and a state championship ring. He had given the ring to his father; it was the only time Bill had ever seen him cry. Bill had gotten a scholarship to North Carolina State, where he'd been moved from fullback to tight end, and a few pro scouts charted his progress.

Then he'd slipped in a scrimmage one day, his cleats grabbing a seam in the Astroturf, and his knee ligaments had shredded. He hobbled through his senior year and got his Physical Education degree, but the first-round contracts and the big bonus money had disappeared faster than a cat in a rainstorm. The irony was that anterior cruciate repair was a common procedure now, and he would have been barely slowed down if his injury had occurred a few years later than it did.

Bill wasn't bitter about the injury. In his mind, it was God's way of telling him that He had other plans for Bill. And that was fine with Bill. The Lord worked in mysterious ways.

But Bill's father didn't think God's ways were best. Bill, Sr., wouldn't even look him in the eye after that, as if his only son had purposefully betrayed him. Even when Bill moved back to Windshake and opened his first store, he never regained his father's respect. Bill had planted Bill, Sr., in the old Baptist cemetery without having had a chance to say good-bye.

Bill had put his considerable energy into expanding his business, and money had flowed his way as God watered the gardens of his life. And Bill repaid the Lord's blessing by working in the community and the church. If Windshake Baptist adopted a building project on Wednesday night, Lemly's Building Supply delivery trucks were on the spot at dawn on Thursday, loaded down with donated materials. And Bill would be there with his hammer and tool belt and tape measure and good cheer, leading by example instead of the arm-twisting he could easily have used.

At those times, when he was doing something good, he felt as if the spirit of his grandfather was right there with him, checking up on his work and smiling in pride. Bill believed God let His angels go down among the mortals to help guide them along, to keep them nudged onto the path of righteousness. And he believed that idle hands were the devil's playground.

So he would remain a hands-on guy, except when it came to Nettie Hartbarger. She was hands-off, at least for now. He looked down at his broad, blunt fingers.

"Hey, Mr. Lemly, any more trucks due in?"

Bill broke out of his thoughts and looked at the slim young man in the ragged Levis who was standing on the loading dock. Lorne Easterland. Most likely a distant cousin of his, as were the members of all of the old mountain families. "Naw. That's the last one today."

"Is your knee all right?"

Bill realized he had been unconsciously rubbing it. "Twinges a little when it rains, but it still works okay."

Lorne nodded toward the sun. "Don't look like you'll have to worry about that for a while."

"Yeah, we won't need to cover up the lumber until later." Bill slapped his palm on the pine. "Why don't you take yourself a break? Go in my office and help yourself to a Coke."

Lorne's face split with a crooked grin. Bill sat on the stack of two-by-sixes and watched him walk away. Sweat clung to the hairline at the top of Bill's spine. The mild breeze felt good as it blew across his skin.

Bill looked a way off at the smooth worn mountains, "studying," and thought about Nettie. That was a fine woman, and he was going to do right by her. He'd already failed once. He'd broken a sacred vow to God. But that wasn't entirely his fault. He could easily blame his ex-wife for that.

But when you're roasting over the flames of hell, when the devil's got you on the spit and giving you a slow spin, it doesn't matter where you lay the blame. So what if she had cleaned out his savings accounts and ran off to Nashville with that drugged-out country singer? So what if her crooning lover was starting to get some airplay? So what if she was eagerly sleeping his way to the top?

She'd have to answer for her sins on Judgment Day, same

as everybody else. Bill was planning to keep his own list of sins as short as possible. There had been a little fornication in his younger years, when the girls had been drawn by his muscles and his football stardom. Well, maybe more than a little. But the devil practically owned you when you were a teenager anyway, sitting by your ear and telling you to do all those nasty, horrible, pleasurable things.

But he'd been faithful to his wife, had trusted her and honored her. So "adultery" would never be scribbled into the Golden Book beside his name. And he'd prayed for forgiveness for those other things, and he believed his merciful God had wiped the slate clean, even if some eraser marks were still smudging up the record.

Now, with Nettie, he was going to be extra careful. He'd been in love that first time, no doubt about it, but sometimes he wondered if that had been a smoke screen thrown up by the devil. If the Lord worked in mysterious ways, then the devil probably worked in ways that were downright under-handed. Maybe the devil had been hoping to load Bill down with hatred and bitterness, to harden his heart and turn him from the Lord's good works.

But Nettie was a walking angel in Bill's mind. Just her smile lit up a whole room, and Bill didn't doubt that it could shine the way out of the darkest pit. She always did for oth-ers, and not in search of admiration either. Bill had first met her down at the Hunger Society. She was tucked away in a little kitchen, her hands raw from shucking corn and peeling potatoes, while the county commissioners were having their picture taken in front of the Thanksgiving buffet table.

"You're Bill Lemly, aren't you?" she'd said, barely glanc-ing up from her work counter.

"Yes, ma'am. Haven't I seen you in church?"

"Most Sundays. Once in a while, I take off to visit some friends of mine down at the Barkersville old folk's home."

She whittled at a potato, then glanced up again, and Bill had looked into her blue eyes. Of course he'd seen her at

church. How could you not notice her? As much as he bat-
tled the devil and tried to ignore those dark little whispers,
he was still a man. And he still had eyes.

Eyes had a way of latching onto Nettie. Even the potatoes
were ogling her.

"You one of those people who appreciates hard work, as
long as it's from a safe distance?" she asked.

Bill gulped, feeling as awkward as a barefooted eighth-
grader at a barn dance. He took off his Brooks Brothers
jacket and loosened his tie and scooted an upside-down five-
gallon bucket over to the counter. He got out his pocketknife, washed it, and started peeling the potatoes without
saying a word.

"People hungry today will be hungry tomorrow," Nettie
said in her soft, strong voice. Then she had started humming
"Amazing Grace," and Bill thought the gates of heaven had
just opened up and God was taking him home, lifting him on
those lovely, airy notes and carrying him to the Kingdom.

They had started dating in December. It was hard to find
a decent movie to go to. Even the Christmas movies seemed
to have more "X" than "Christ" in them. So they mostly went
to dinner or read each other Bible passages in Nettie's two-
room apartment above Oswig Realty.

Bill would sit at her little dining table and try hard to
focus on the good words of Psalms or the Gospel According
to Saint Luke, but his language skills were almost as bad as
his math skills. Except the way she read them the words were
music, God's poetry, inspiring and full of life. And Bill tried
hard not to think of her small neat bedroom just around the
corner, with its snow-white bedspread and the Jesus portrait
on the wall above the maple headboard.

Bill tried to heed the wisdom of Moses and Solomon. But
they were with the Lord and not in the same room with that
warm, small woman whose skin glowed with a purity that almost made her translucent. And Bill tried hard to listen to
her saying Christ's own words, the parts that were in red ink.

But the devil was putting *his* words in Bill's head, too, and they were buzzing like a bee. And the devil's words had a lot to do with that bedroom around the corner, and what kind of things he would like Bill to do there.

Nettie's hair smelled like those meadows at the foot of Fool's Knob, where he'd bought a hundred acres to keep a developer from snatching it up and bulldozing the wildflowers and whittling down the copses of silver birch and hickory. Not because he was one of those tree-hugging hippies, but because, when he saw the place, he felt it was God's country and Bill wanted to build a house there one day. And lately he'd been picturing Nettie in that house.

But that little vision would disappear like mist if he gave in to the devil. So he'd clenched his hands under the table and nodded at Nettie's recitals and blocked the devil out, even when the devil made him study the fineness of her long brown hair and the delicate curves of her ripe lips. Even when the devil made him tingle down *there*.

Like he was doing right now, as if he had a mildly electric feather at work, tickling Bill into arousal. Bill slammed his hand against a cube of cinder blocks and the bright rush of pain drove the devil back into his hole. Bill looked around the loading yard, hoping no one had seen him. The coast was clear.

"Praise to Thee, Lord," Bill said, looking up at the blue sky and the glorious sunlight filtering through the thin clouds. "And I pray that you watch over Nettie and give me strength and deliver us from evil and walk with me as I do Your holy work."

Bill stood up and lifted a sheet of plywood and carried it across the yard, letting it cover his waist where the evidence of the devil's work still strained against his jeans.

Nettie Hartbarger put her book aside. She was having trouble concentrating on Clive Barker's latest trip into the

shadows. Normally she loved Clive, even when he was
mocking Jesus and making dead children eat their own flesh.
Maybe especially then. But this morning her thoughts kept
returning to Bill.

His face was constantly in her mind, and had been ever
since she had started attending Windshake Baptist as a teenager.
A healthy tan, a strong but not Neanderthal brow, a twice-
broken nose that somehow gave an impression of nobility
rather than roughness, flat cheeks that crinkled when he
smiled. Sensitive brown eyes, with pupils constantly large,
like an excited schoolboy's. Clean-shaven, not that she minded
facial hair, but it meant he cared for his appearance and
probably wouldn't let himself go to seed in his old age.

And he had muscles. Broad shoulders. Tall. She'd heard
that he used to play football, and she wasn't surprised. He
looked like the kind of man who could pick up his enemies
by one hand and shake them into submission.

But he seemed so gentle. He was soft-spoken and de-
ferred respectfully to his elders. Any woman would fall all
over themselves to go out with him. A dream man, a prize
catch, a—*well, admit it, girl*—a stud puppy.

Which was her problem. She wasn't intimidated by his
money. He didn't flash it and she didn't make him. But she
was afraid he wasn't physically attracted to her.

She had hoped the other night might have been different.
She looked across the cramped living room that was also her
kitchen at the tiny table where they had sat, Bill making her
furniture seem undersized, as if her apartment were a dwarf's
hovel. But the night had ended with closed Bibles and clean
sheets.

She had dreamed of him and had woken up horny. Nettie
sighed and rubbed her thumb along the paperback cover of
the Clive Barker paperback. The memory of her dream with
Bill left her in a mixture of exhilaration and despair. Things
were going very slowly between them.

Nettie wasn't promiscuous, but neither was she celibate.

She had taken lovers before and hadn't felt the least bit guilty. Premarital sex was condemned by Preacher Blevins, but she thought it was natural and blessed. She couldn't imagine the Lord frowning down on any kind of love, or the acts that resulted from it.

Maybe Bill was gay. Maybe he was only dating her to keep up a front in the eyes of the church. But even a gay man would have at least *kissed* her by now. Several had in her life.

Even if he were gay, she would still be in love with him. She didn't believe homosexuals were automatically doomed to hell, either, the way Preacher Blevins said. Everyone was welcome to the salvation that the Lord offered, in her opinion. Not that she was going to express her opinion, because she didn't want to lose her job.

That was another problem. Being the church secretary was a good job, certainly a blessing. But a couple of things bothered her. She was afraid that Bill might have used his influence to have her hired, because she had started work three weeks after she first met him, or at least really talked to him, at that charity Thanksgiving dinner. She was qualified for the job, but so were the half-dozen others who had applied.

And lately, she had been noticing minor discrepancies in the church books, numbers that didn't add up and accounts that didn't square. She had re-checked her work but couldn't find any errors on her part. Nothing to really be alarmed about, but a little electric wire of worry jiggled in the back of her mind.

She had mentioned the discrepancies to Preacher Blevins, but he had dismissed her fears with a wave of his thin hand.

"The Lord takes care of what's His," he said. "Let's not take our eyes off the true prize, which is the Kingdom of Heaven."

Then he stroked her hair in a fatherly fashion, but Nettie had not been wholly reassured. She was planning on keeping a closer check on the church funds.

She glanced at the clock. Time to get ready for work.

She thought of Bill while changing clothes. As her cotton dress slid over her head and down her bare skin, she imagined it was Bill's gentle hands. She sighed. Good things took time. And when it came to Bill, she was willing to wait. She would have the patience of Job.

"So that whole mountainside belongs to one family?"

"Yes, sir. And they're in a selling mood. I talked to one of the sons already. His father got rid of a chunk of it a few years back."

"Cheap?" Emerland handed the binoculars back to his assistant.

The assistant strung them over his neck, the strap tangling with his tie. The wind ruffled the papers on his clipboard. "Ninety thou for twenty acres. Can you believe it?"

"The people are strange up here in the mountains. One minute they're giving it away, and the next they want an arm and a leg and your firstborn thrown in as a down payment."

Emerland gazed at the blue, stubbled face of Bear Claw, picturing three ski slopes, a glass lodge, and a condominium complex. The outlying areas that were too steep for serious development could be carved up into tiny lots and dotted with log cabins. The environmental regulations would be a bitch, with these new run-off laws, but Emerland knew how to go around or through red tape. He'd built Sugarfoot without much of a problem and he could do the same thing again. Maybe more than twice. There were mountains as far as the eye could see.

"Who did you say you talked to?" he asked his assistant.

"Johnny Mack Mull is the name."

"Johnny Mack, huh? What does he say?"

"Apparently the father doesn't want to sell out completely. Now that he's got some money he feels like he's set for life. And the two sons don't get their share until he's out of the picture."

"How far is the father from the edge of the picture?"

"He's sixty-seven but in pretty good health. Johnny Mack was asking me if there was some way they could have his father ruled incompetent. Says he's got mental problems."

"If the old man's out of the way, then we'd have to work with *two* owners. What about the other son?"

"Sylvester Mull. Delivery truck driver. Lives in a mobile home. Has two kids. Probably an easy sell there."

Emerland squinted into the sun, listening to the wind bending the pines in the valley below. He felt like a conqueror, like Napoleon or Balboa, looking out and knowing that all this could be his. He had the investors. "And Johnny Mack?"

The assistant cleared his throat. "All he talks about is wanting to move to Florida. But he'd probably want lawyers and residuals. He's not too bright, but he knows how to pick a wallet."

"Best to try the old man first. I'll make the contact."

"Yes, sir."

"There are ways to deal with these people. You've got to open a dialogue. Speak their language."

And Emerland knew the language.

It talked in more tongues than had the builders of the Tower of Babel.

Money.

Chapter Ten

Junior Mull looked out from under the bushes, watching the silver strand of his fishing line where it entered the dark water of Stony Creek. Damned trout were taking a day off, he decided. Scarcely a nibble all morning.

His jeans were wet from where he'd been sitting in the black mud of the creek bank. Still, it beat the hell out of having his ass parked in a hard chair at Pickett High. He could be there right now, staring at the ceiling tiles and picking his nose as Old Bitch Moody droned on about integers.

The raw fish smell of the creek and the thick swampy odor of decaying weeds filled his nostrils. The water was a little murky from yesterday's rain, but the fish were supposed to bite better after a rain. That theory had gone all to hell today. Didn't those scaly bastards read *Field and Stream*?

He dried his fingers on his army jacket before reaching into his chest pocket. *May as well fire up another joint. At least I can keep up my sense of humor.*

Junior gripped the rod with his left hand as he flicked the lighter and drew in a lungful of harsh dope. He exhaled and fanned with his hand to disperse the smoke. Not much traffic on the road this time of day, but no need to advertise his location. That pea-headed truancy officer had been after him since the fifth grade. Plus, now that he was on probation for shoplifting, it was a good idea to keep a low profile when breaking the law.

He took another drag and looked around his hidey-hole. A stand of laurels hid him from passing cars and an old tired cedar drooped protectively overhead. Empty liquor bottles and rusted cans were scattered around the perimeter of the clearing, and black chunks of wood huddled together inside a ring of creek stones. The charred smell of the dead camp-fire mingled with the mist that drifted off the creek as the sun rose higher.

His old man had shown him this place. Sylvester was no slouch at playing hooky, either, and that was one of the few qualities Junior had inherited. That, and what his dad called a "kinship with nature." Junior giggled and took another hit.

Kinship, hell. Kinship was fucked up, that's what it was. Like Gramps, stewing away on that big old farm, sitting on a goddamned fortune. But did he ever give Junior a red penny of it? Hell, no.

Junior used to hang out up on the farm, especially in the summer when his dad was away on his hunting trips and Mom was staining the sheets with that redneck Jimmy Morris. Junior liked the smell of the hay in the barn and the rich dust from the tobacco that had hung drying in the rafters. He even liked the smell of chicken shit.

There was lots to do on the farm, playing "fort" in the corncrib with his brother Little Mack or fishing out of season in the branch. Or going up in the briars and eating goose-berries until your belly was about to bust. Even hoeing the garden beat the hell out of hanging around the pool halls in Windshake.

But then Gramps had caught Junior getting into the white lightning. All he'd taken was half a cupful, and he'd been real careful to mark the level in the jar so he could fill it back with water. But the leathery old bastard had taken one swig, then sniffed at the jar like a dog sniffing between a girl's legs.

"Something ain't right," he said, his scrawny old skull bobbing. Junior watched as Gramps took another drink and swished it around in his creased jaws.

"Watered to hell," he said. "I'm going to have a talk with that damned Don Oscar Moody."

Gramps staggered across the living room to take his shotgun from the wall, where he kept it hanging on wooden pegs. Gramps shoved two shells in the double-barreled twelve-gauge, cussing a blue streak and weaving drunkenly on his thin legs. He leaned against the old chestnut bureau, making the mirror quiver. Gramps's shakiness was doubled in the reflection.

Junior gulped, afraid that Gramps would lose his temper and shoot somebody. Maybe even Junior. But surely the bastard would forgive his own kin, wouldn't he?

"It was me, Gramps," he'd said, cringing a little, holding his arms in front of his twelve-year-old face to absorb the shotgun pellets.

Gramps's jaw dropped loosely, and Junior looked at his black gums.

"Fuck a mother hen, boy," he said, his eyes swimming in their swelling sockets. "*You* did that?"

Junior nodded, still tensed and waiting to die. Gramps had stared off in space for a moment as if he'd been punched in the head with a plow handle. Then a wiggly smile had creased his face. "You're kin, all right. Mull, through and through."

He reached out and slapped Junior on the arm, laughing, then started rubbing Junior's shoulder with his strong bony hand. "Pretty damned sharp, you are."

And Junior relaxed, even started laughing himself, thinking *Damn, that was clever, wasn't it?*

But suddenly Gramps clamped his hand on Junior's cheeks,

stooped so close that Junior could see down his throat to his pickled tonsils, so close that Gramps's breath scorched his nostrils, so close that Junior could look into his yellowy eyes at the shadows that danced in the pupils.

"Don't you ever mess with my liquor again," Gramps said.

Well, fuck him and his liquor, Junior thought, sucking down another lungful of marijuana. Junior found out he could go over to Don Oscar's and buy his own moonshine. And Gramps could sit in his chair and rock until his bones came loose before *he'd* ever set foot on that scraggly-assed side of the mountain again. Crazy old bastard.

Junior chuckled to himself.

The dope was starting to work, making his eyelids twitch and the water glitter under the sunlight in a billion little speckled diamonds and the breeze was a whisk broom in the treetops and seven birds were singing different songs but the notes kind of fit together if you listened. And his stomach was clenched and the back of his neck tingled and he stared at the fishing line where it went into the water and at the round ripple that went out from there, and then another little ring inside that one, and then another, perfect circles that would keep spreading forever but never touch the one ahead of it.

And the water was even laughing with him, lapping up against the creek bank and tickling the muddy ribs of the earth. *Stony Creek was RIGHT,* Junior thought, snorting a little as smoke snot rolled down his lip. He took a final draw, scorching his fingers as he pinched the roach, but even the pain was funny, kind of dead and faraway, as if it were somebody else's and he was only borrowing it for a second.

He went back to watching the ripples where his line went into the water. *Might have to try some corn. They're not hitting night crawlers today. But I sure do like sticking those slimy, squirting bastards on the hook, though. And I'm as fucked up as a football bat and high as a Georgia pine.*

Suddenly the line grew taut, then slackened almost immediately. Junior's hand clenched around the rod.

Come on, you bastard. Hit it one more time.

Then he was standing and the pole was quivering and the water erupted in white-silver splashes. Four-pounder, it felt like. It had taken the hook and was trying to wind the line around an old black tree stump that jutted from the creek like an overturned molar.

Junior tugged and then cranked the reel, pulling in the slack he had gained. He cleared the fish from the stump, but it could dip around a rock just as easily, cutting the line on a sharp edge. Then the fish surfaced again, twitching like a convict in an electric chair, but the fight was over, the bastard was Junior's now, and all that was left was a little show of sport.

Junior reeled it in and flipped it onto the bank. It was the ugliest fish he had ever seen. If it even *was* a fish.

The thing was shaped like a bowling pin, with a blunt face and heavy tail. It had fins that were like fingers, three in a row down each side. Its single gill was a continuous gray slit across its forehead and gooey mucus dribbled out as the gill flapped in search of water. Its eyes were like wine grapes, green and round and bulging and without pupils. And its mouth—

The fucker's got TEETH. Not little bumps of cartilage like hog suckers and knotty heads have. This thing's got a mouthful of bone briars, and no way in hell am I gonna stick my hand in there and work the hook loose.

The fish-thing stopped wriggling as dirt and twigs collected in the gill. Junior put his boot on its belly so it wouldn't flop away while he figured out what to do with it.

Now, I may be fucked up. And after two joints of Tijuana Taxi, that's more than a maybe. But there's no way I'm as fucked up as this here fish-thing.

So, Junior, you can take this thing home and show the old man and see if he's ever seen anything like it, since he's caught and killed just about everything that bleeds in these Appalachian Mountains, except maybe humans. But that would mean having to explain why you were fishing instead of attending the tenth grade, which would lead to an ass-busting or at least a good bitching-out.

Or you can boot this deformed hunk of fishfuck the hell back into the creek and pretend you never saw it.

Junior pulled out his pocketknife and started to cut the line. The fish-thing writhed under his foot, spinning free and snapping at his leg.

"Goddamn it," Junior yelled, hopping back. The thing's eyes were glowing, green and bright as the neon on the pool hall's pinball machines. Junior whipped the pole, carrying the thing into the air and then back onto the earth. He whipped again and sent the thing's head cracking against a rock with the sound a dropped watermelon makes. He lashed again and again, sweating and panicky, until the thing was a green-red hunk of shredded meat. Then he put his boot on the raw corpse and jerked the pole with all his strength, and the line finally broke.

"Son of a bitch," he gasped, catching his breath. He kicked the thing into the water and watched as it turned once, slowly, then spiraled toward the creek bottom like a soggy log. He looked down at the twin rips in his denim cuffs.

He looked back at the thing and wished he hadn't. The tenderized fillet of dead meat had flipped its mutilated finger-fins and twitched its broken clubby tail, and headed upstream.

Junior's buzz left him, jumping from his skin like a ghost from a guillotine victim.

Terry McMillan wasn't on the Oprah show. Mayzie turned off the television.

James was gone. That was a fine young man, but he needed to get the chip off his shoulder. The whole blessed world wasn't out to get him.

She leaned over the chair arm, groaning a little with the effort. She slid open the coffee table drawer and pulled out her notepad.

Mayzie wasn't sure why she was so ashamed of what she did. She just kept picturing James laughing if he ever found out, and that would just break whatever little crumb of a heart she had left.

She sat back with her notepad in her hand and looked at the old photograph on the wall. That man was sure handsome and that baby was his spitting image. The photo didn't make her as sad as it used to. Lately, she pictured the three of them together again up in heaven, laughing and carrying on just like the good old days, only this time the days would last forever.

Mayzie looked down at the stump where her foot used to be. She'd heard that people with an amputation could still feel the missing limb, that it itched and you'd think you were wiggling your fingers or toes. But her limb was just gone, dead, invisible, like a lot of her heart.

She wondered if she'd get her foot back when she went to heaven. God wouldn't want her hobbling around up there, scuffing those golden streets with her crutches. But then they said that the angels got wings, but if they got wings then what did they need the streets for?

Another thing that bothered her was that she was afraid she'd be old when she got to heaven, and Theo would still be in his prime. And would she ever get the joy of watching her precious Oliver grow up, or did he remain an infant for the rest of eternity? And would Theo be like he was before, or *after,* the Lord called him home by means of that cotton press?

Best not to think of such things. The Lord has the plan, and it's best left to Him.

Mayzie wondered what she should write about today. She thought about the crocuses, but she'd done enough nature poetry, plus it was easier in the late spring when there were more smells and colors to choose from. Maybe she would write about her foot.

But now she was too worried about James. He didn't like Windshake one little bit, and he barely tried to hide his distaste. Mayzie didn't really need the help, but she did enjoy the company. James saw his visit here as too much of a duty. She only hoped that his hatred wouldn't harden him at so young an age. There was also this complicated mess of her family being raised to take care of their own.

She sighed and put her pencil in her mouth, then tapped it against her teeth.

"This old world's just full of little problems, Lord. But I trust that You know best and will take care of things as You see fit," she said aloud.

Mayzie put the pencil lead to the paper and started pressing words.

Something about the trees ain't right, Chester thought. I know I been in the white lightning just a mite early today, but that only makes a body see double or else see things that ain't there. And this IS there, whatever it is.

Chester stepped off the porch and Boomer reluctantly followed. Even the hound dog sensed something was wrong. Boomer lowered his head and growled at the underbrush that was thick along the fence line. Boomer never riled himself enough to waste a good growl on shadows.

Chester looked at the forest that bordered his weedy cornfield. The trees swelled with buds and new leaves. The dandelions were popping their yellow heads out of the pasture. Usually at this time of year, Chester could practically feel the trees stretching up to the sky, fighting for sunshine and begging for leaves.

But these trees above the house looked kind of sick. Not quite withered, but droopy, like they were sad about something.

Trees ought to be happy in spring. Their sap-blood was frozen up all winter, when all they could do was shiver in the north wind while their bones snapped off. But now the thaw had come and you'd think the wooden-hearted things would be jumping for joy.

And that green glow was back, only it was real faint, so that only a buzzard-eyed mountain man like himself would ever notice. The few airplanes that flew over wouldn't have seen anything out of the ordinary.

He heard a cracking sound, then a rumble of falling timber. Trees only fell like that when struck by lightning or else coated by an ice storm. They didn't snap like that in March, when the roots were busy soaking up the melted snows from the soil.

"Well, I don't expect it's that acid rain that DeWalt's always going on about," Chester said to Boomer after climbing back up on the porch and settling into his rocker. "I mean, even if the trees is—now what's that twenty-dollar Yankee word that DeWalt used?"

Boomer looked up expectantly.

"Oh, yeah. 'Distressed.' So even if the trees is 'distressed,' as they say, they ought not be falling over for no earthly reason."

Another tree dropped near the ridge line, a few hundred yards up the slope, the brittle sound echoing off the damp mountains. Chester saw the top of a white pine swaying where it had been hit by the falling tree. Something funny was going on. And he had half a mind to go out and investigate. But later was as good a time as now, maybe even better. That was the kind of philosophy that Chester credited with helping a body live to a ripe old age.

"I might have to give DeWalt a call," Chester said, twisting the lid off his moonshine jar. "See if he's got any book-learning on dropping-down-dead trees."

Boomer slowly wagged his tail. Chester looked out at the strange woods. He had a feeling that the trees were waiting, holding their breath in that moment of stillness that always comes before a storm.

"Yep. DeWalt will know what to do."

Boomer curled up at his master's feet to wait.

Chapter Eleven

Nice little piece of ass there.

Forgive me, Lord, for I have committed the sin of lust. I have committed adultery in my mind. But, Sweet Jesus Christ, did you SEE that stuff bounce around inside that cotton dress? No church secretary should dress like that and expect a God-fearing man not to weaken a little.

And her without a bra. Mercy, mercy.

Armfield Blevins pulled a handkerchief from the front pocket of his JC Penney jacket. He wiped at his forehead, the high glaring brow that his daughter said looked like Edgar Allan Poe's. Whoever the hell that was.

Probably one of them damned washed-up rock stars they couldn't seem to drive off the stage. Them ancient rock stars that would keep on rocking even if they had to do it from a rocking chair, and keep on rolling until their wheelchairs needed an overhaul. Getting up and spreading the devil's message just like Armfield spread the Word of God, only they delivered to packed stadiums and their message was blasted from a million stereo speakers. Armfield was lucky to draw two hundred for Sunday services, less during football season.

But the devil worked through everybody. The devil didn't
need two-hundred-watt amplifiers. He whispered right in
your ear. Look what he had done to Armfield. Steered his
eyeballs right onto Nettie Hartbarger's smoothly sloping ass.
Given him a hard-on from hell. He could feel it pressing like
a hot and vile snake against the inseam of his slacks.

*And, forgive me, Lord, but it feels good. And Nettie is just
a door away, at her desk in the vestry, doing the books,
doing Your work, back there all alone and warm-blooded
and curvy.*

But Armfield knew it was the devil working on him, soft-
ening him up, to coin a phrase. Just as the devil had laid out
the shining cities before Jesus, sweeping his cloven hoof out
like a real estate salesman, offering them to the Son of God
free and clear and with a righteous right of way if Jesus
would only forsake His Father. But Jesus had resisted, and so
would Armfield.

*But, damn it, we all fall short of the perfection and glory
of God. And what would Jesus have done if the old devil had
offered him a piece of Nettie's tail instead of some old Jew
cities built of mud and stone?*

Armfield gazed up at the mahogany crucifix hanging on
the wall behind the pulpit. Jesus looked down in return,
wooden and Indian colored and sad, peering from under His
crown of briars.

Armfield had scored the crucifix at a foreclosure sale,
from a Catholic church in a nearby rural county. The Catholics
had suffered declining membership and the diocese decided
to close the doors. Armfield saw the purchase as one more
victory, one more proof of the rightness of the Baptist way.
Some of his parishioners had grumbled when he'd placed the
icon on the wall, but Armfield had persuaded his flock that
the display was conservative, hearkening back to the old
days of Christianity. There was only one Old Time Religion,
and that was the Baptist faith.

Jesus didn't belong to some bunch who worshipped Mary and ate wafers. The Son of God belonged to those who were willing to have their heads washed clean of sin. Armfield looked up at the darkly stained wooden face.

"Forgive me, Jesus," the preacher whispered. Then, hearing a door creak open at the rear of the church, he added loudly, "And thank thee, Oh Lord, for thy continued blessing, that it may shine on this, Your church. Amen."

"Amen," added Bill Lemly, his deep voice filling the narrow church hall. Armfield turned and saw Lemly's wide-shouldered frame filling the doorway against the backdrop of the dark, wet world outside. Lemly walked up the aisle, his shoes leaving prints on the red carpet, that tongue of sanctity that carried the sinners forward, nearer to God and close enough to smell the five-dollar-a-pint aftershave that Preacher Blevins wore on Sundays.

"Good evening, Preacher," Lemly said. "Looks like the Lord's brought us some more rain."

"Yes, Brother Lemly. We may need to build ourselves an ark before this one's over with."

"Now, God promised He'd never do that to us again. The next time He destroys the world, it will be with something different. Something good."

What would it be next time? Armfield wondered. *Nuclear rain, man-made brimstone and fire from heaven? Cancer-causing chemicals in our sugar substitutes? Or another eight years of a Democrat-controlled Congress? The Lord worked in mysterious ways.*

"So right, Brother," Armfield said. "But the prophecies are coming together, just as the Bible promised."

"The Lord will be coming soon to take us home, and what a glorious day that will be."

That was one part of this deal that made Armfield uncomfortable. He wanted to go to heaven, wanted to waltz through the Pearly Gates and huddle at the feet of Jesus, plucking a harp and adding his thin voice to the choirs that would sing His praises, forever and ever without end. Armfield just didn't want to do it anytime soon.

One of his secret fears was that one day he'd be plugging along, minding his own business—maybe out checking the trim job on the graveyard hedges or working up the lead paragraph of a kick-ass sermon—and he'd feel a tap on his shoulder. He'd turn around and there would be the Lord Himself, tall and blond and blue-eyed and glowing.

Armfield didn't want to die. At least, not for a long time to come.

"Yes, Brother Lemly, a glorious day that will be," he said, licking his thin lips.

Armfield parted his Bible and tucked his purple nylon bookmark smack in the middle of the Gospel According to Saint Luke. *Good a place as any to quote from come Sunday.*

One of these days, he was going to get around to reading the Good Book, and from cover to cover, too, not with all this skipping around. He'd started it once when he was six-teen, sat down and zipped through Creation and Adam and Eve and Cain and Abel, the greatest story on earth unfolding before his eyes. Then he'd hit the "begats," and it had been like slamming face first into the wall of a Jewish synagogue: "Such-and-such begat thus-and-so, who in turn . . ."

Armfield wasn't the world's most educated man. He was a poor reader and the only original thoughts that popped into his head were when he was trying different poses on the fan-tasized flesh of Nettie Hartbarger. But he'd been the loudest in his class at Henneway. He had been the most outspoken critic of the liberals and the baby-killers and the Catholics and other lower forms of life. And he knew how to sell snake oil. But the "begats" had nearly bored him to tears.

He had prayed for strength and guidance so the Lord might sit on his shoulder and shine His Holy Reading Lamp so that Armfield could do the Lord's will. And finally he'd come to accept that the Lord's will was for Armfield to *never* finish the Bible. Armfield's dad couldn't even read, but he'd certainly gone to heaven, the way he'd tossed the family's cookie jar money into the collection plate every week. Money that Armfield could have used for orthodontia so his damned front teeth didn't stick out like a knot-sucking beaver's. Money that his mother could have spent on a mammogram, which might have detected the breast cancer that took her to the Lord while Armfield was at Henneway. Money that might have kept his malnourished sister from running away and becoming a hooker in Charlotte.

A flash of lightning blinked outside, once, then three times in succession, flickering the colored plate-glass windows as if they were movie frames. But the Jesus in the plate glass didn't change position, just knelt among those lambs like He was giving them the Sermon on the Mount translated into bleats and baas. Then the thunder rumbled, shaking the hand-hewed arches of the church.

"The Lord's pitching a fit tonight, Preacher," Lemly said, his laughter rumbling as deep as the thunder. "Must be somebody's doing some serious sinning."

Armfield nodded from the pulpit. Even though he was on the dais, with a solid oak rail between Lemly and himself, Lemly somehow towered over him, dark eyed and broad faced and muscular and tanned. Lemly had been a football star at State, then had moved back home after graduation and opened a building-supply business. Now he owned four stores among the surrounding counties and had another in the works.

This man could sell dogwood timbers to Jesus, Armfield thought in admiration.

But Brother Lemly was also a church deacon and generous benefactor and county commissioner and leading citizen. If Armfield wanted to get a grip on public opinion, to find out how a certain action or statement might play in Windshake, he asked Lemly. Hell, Lemly *was* public opinion, when you got right down to it.

The front door opened again, and the top of an umbrella poked its way into the church. It spun, sending a silver shower of water drops across the foyer, then lifted, and Armfield's lightbulb-shaped head lit up with a smile.

"Hey, darlin'," he said, forgetting his "preacher voice" for a moment.

"Hi, Dad. Hi, Mr. Lemly," Sarah said. She shook back her hair, her long red hair that was just like her mother's, only not scorched from too many hours under a dryer cone down at Rita Faye's Beauty Salon. Sarah smiled, white and perfect teeth showing between her lips. Armfield had made damned sure his kid had gotten her braces, if for no other reason than that she'd never have to look in the mirror and be pissed off at her miserly old man.

"Hello, Sarah," Lemly said. He turned back to Armfield. "Say, Preacher—"

Armfield had insisted that the congregation call him "Preacher" instead of "Reverend." It was much more folksy. Put the parishioners at ease. Got him invited to dinner come Friday. Loosened the purse strings come Sunday.

Kept their guard down. No association in their minds with the Reverend Bakker or the Reverend Swaggart. Or even Falwell, who hadn't been convicted but seemed to leave a bad taste in everyone's mouth just the same. He turned his attention back to Lemly.

"I was wondering if Nettie was here," Lemly said. "Said for me to pick her up at six o'clock sharp, and it's nigh on."

"She's in the vestry, Brother. Probably didn't hear us because of the rain on the roof."

"Mind if I go on back?"

"Help yourself, Brother. Just don't take Nettie away before she's got the Lord's bank account balanced."

Lemly's laughter thundered again, and he left the room, his wet shoe soles squeaking across the oak floor of the dais.

Damn. Armfield had been hoping Lemly might have some new angle to work, a tent revival or gospel singing to fill up the old coffers of Windshake Baptist. And maybe a few dollars could trickle their way into Armfield's pockets. But Lemly was here after Nettie.

Hmm. Might not be too seemly. Both of them single and dedicated to the church. Still, fairly young and prone to the call of lust, weak against the devil's whispers. And local tongues might wag.

He'd have to keep an eye on them. That wouldn't be much of a problem, especially in Nettie's case.

"Now, what are you doing here, young lady?" he said to his daughter.

"Mom sent me over to tell you supper's ready," she said.

Her face practically shone with innocence and youth, like the Virgin Mary's did in those Renaissance paintings. She had her mother's fair skin, with some delicate freckles on her smooth cheeks. Of course, he didn't really know what her mother's skin looked like these days, because she wore more makeup than a white-trash trailer queen.

Armfield looked down at the open Bible, then cupped it in his hands as if it were an infant. He held it lovingly to his chest. The weight of the book comforted him. Its gilt-edged pages gave him strength. And it made a damned fine prop when he went into one of his "whopped upside the head by the staff of Jesus" routines, when he twitched and gibbered across the dais on those Sundays when the congregation needed a little extra stimulation.

The routines were the reason why Windshake Baptist Church had recruited him. While a lot of the Southern Baptist churches were letting divorced ministers and liberals and even a few converted Episcopalians do their preaching, Windshake was going to hold the line. At last year's Baptist Convention, some formerly conservative pastors were arguing for what they called "continued accessibility in the face of modernity." Whatever that translated to in common English, it sounded like selling out to the devil to Armfield.

So a touch of fire and brimstone was welcomed in Windshake. Most of the congregation felt that if it was good enough for their grandparents, then, by God, it was good enough for *them*. Except some rivals had popped up along the outskirts of Armfield's territory. First Baptist over at Piney Ford was starting to pack them in. There was a Methodist church around the back side of Sugarfoot and a little Lutheran church in a converted vegetable stand out in the Stony Creek community. He'd even heard a Unitarian group was meeting in the basement of a used bookstore.

But Armfield wasn't worried. A little competition just made you work harder. It was also a sign that Windshake was prospering, as some big-money tourists had settled in the area over the last few years. Windshake Baptist's take had picked up about eight percent a year during Armfield's reign at the pulpit. Well, make that *three* percent, after Armfield skimmed off his "tribute."

"So, are you coming, Daddy?" Sarah said, her voice echoing off the polished wood and plate glass and into his hairy ears.

"Depends on what's for dinner. If it's another one of those vegetarian omelets, then I'll be heading down to the steak-house." Armfield snickered.

"Oh, Daddy," she said.

"Just picking, honey."

Armfield noticed that Sarah's accent was fading, her open vowels getting flattened like a flower in an old diary. She was a sophomore down at Westridge University, and she had been picking up all kinds of figures of speech and mannerisms from those Yankee intellectuals. Armfield wondered what else she might be picking up.

"May the Lord watch over her," he offered in silent prayer, then set his Bible gently on the pulpit, where it would be ready to provide inspiration on Sunday. He wondered if he should tell Nettie and Brother Bill that he was leaving. Naw, Nettie would lock up. Besides, he didn't want to walk in on the lovebirds.

Armfield was afraid he would suffer the sin of envy. He'd suffered enough sins for one day. It was going to take a good half-hour heart-to-heart chat with the Lord to wash those wrongs away. But the Lord would forgive. He always had.

Armfield walked down the aisle, under the high wooden ribs of the church. The only noise was the creaking of his knee joints and the muted roar of the rain pounding on the roof. He joined his daughter in the foyer, where she held the umbrella poised and open outside the door, ready for the thirty-yard trot to the parsonage.

Armfield was so focused on his looming penance that he didn't resent the falling rain. As he looked at it slicing across the streetlight in fat needles, he thought he saw a faint green shimmering. He shook his head and hunched under the umbrella.

"Race you," Sarah said, then she was gone, along with the umbrella.

Armfield laughed, then the sky split with a streak of thunder and lightning, the bolt touching ground near the church.

"Spare me, Jesus," he whispered, then dashed against the rain to the house.

Don Oscar was tangled in a forsythia hedge, its sharp green buds scratching into his skin. He felt ready to bloom, ready to explode into velvety yellow orgasms. He felt alive, more than he had ever felt while human. He was chlorophyll and carotene, watery tissue and carbon, a metastasis of animal and vegetable. He burned in joyous rapture as his energy was drained by the parent.

He was food of the gods.

The parent's slender white tongue-roots were stretching under the skin of Bear Claw, siphoning and converting the

Appalachian fauna all across the stony slopes. Now it had sent out its disciples, fish and fowl and man and beast, all marked by the touch of the cosmic reaper. And Don Oscar was one of the children, providing nourishment to the beloved space-seed so that its mission could continue.

He was dimly aware that his wife Genevieve was nearby, nosing in the dirt like an old sow snouting up succulent truffles. The wild lilies were sending green shoots into the sky along the banks of the creek, and Genevieve was among them, rolling in the rich swampy mud. Her torn calico dress was damp and black, sticking to her ample thighs as she wallowed without shame.

Don Oscar had never loved her as much, had never appreciated the glorious depths of her organic wealth as much as he had while converting her. Now they were bound in a far holier matrimony than they had ever achieved in their human relationship.

Now they served the parent, and it, in turn, served them, blessing them with the radiance of the sun, granting them the boon of moisture drawn through their epidermis, allowing them the pleasure of transpiration. Parting the clouds of their ignorance so that they might be aware, sloughing off their sinful skins so that they were made pure.

Don Oscar had lost his sense of time, but he thought maybe it was all science, only now there was a new science, with new natural laws. He regretted the wasted mortal effort of survival, the long struggle of the flesh. He was filled with self-loathing for the resources he had needlessly piddled away, for his avarice and selfishness. But then, his path had been worthwhile if it had ultimately led to this perfect day.

Was it only yesterday that he had been converted? Or did days matter anymore? Now there was only eternity, a blissful servitude that stretched forever ahead as the hot golden rays of the sun reached across the fingers of the galaxy.

He sprawled among the forsythia, leaning against the slender branches, leaking opal fluid from his wounds and scratches, absorbing carbon dioxide as he died and was re-born a million times over.

As he soaked and absorbed, as he swelled with verdant joy, he was overcome by a rapturous desire to share. He would pay a call on the neighbors.

Chapter Twelve

Tamara looked out over the auditorium at the sea of young faces and the tops of a few heads that had drooped over their desks. She despised these meat market classes. But what did she expect?

After all, this was Psychology 101. It was designed so that even an athlete could make a solid "C" while saving the sweat for scholarship payback. All you had to know was that Jung wasn't spelled with a "Y" and you had it made. Sure, there would be maybe five students out of the eighty who would put forth an effort, who would actually read the material and turn in four-page papers when she asked for a minimum of three.

Of those five, maybe two would go to graduate school and become psychologists.

But she knew that the line between an amateur and a professional psychologist was thin. That line was as wavery and elusive as the difference between sanity and madness. To teach or to be officially insane, all you had to do was be certified.

But that was part of the challenge, wasn't it? Being the one without becoming the other.

She flipped back her hair with one hand and gripped the

lectern as if it were a dance partner. She drew in enough air to send her voice across the room.

"How does the mind work? Why does it work one way and not another?" she said firmly without shouting. "Is it really only billions of nerve cells reacting chemically and electrically with each other? Are our thoughts and reactions only scientific processes over which we have no control?

"If so, what differentiates one person's emotions from another's? Social influence and outside stimuli? At what point does spirituality and ego step over into rational, measurable brain activity?"

She could tell she was losing them. She was even losing herself. Time for an icebreaker. "And what does it have to do with *us*, and why should we care?"

A few snickers rippled across the room. From somewhere in the back, a voice shouted, "Who says we care?"

The class erupted in laughter. That was good. At least they were momentarily awake. She fixed on the area from which the remark had come and saw a crew-cut teenager with one thick eyebrow across his forehead, smiling smugly.

"So, Mister—," Tamara said, meeting his small eyes.

"Watkins."

"—Mister Watkins, since you know all about yourself already, why don't you tell us? Why are you the way you are? Why are you self-confident enough to blurt out in class what half-a-dozen others were thinking but didn't say?"

The lone eyebrow made a vee in perplexity.

Tamara continued. "What makes you different from the young lady beside you, who keeps checking her wristwatch as if she's planted a time bomb somewhere?"

The lady blushed slightly.

"And why is Mister Watkins's mouth at a no-doubt temporary loss for words when his mind is spilling them out by the hundreds?"

Whew. That was a lot of questions to start off a lecture.

But she was supposed to be teaching *psychology*, wasn't she? The field had no answers, only more and crazier questions. And that was just the middle ground. When you branched out into clairvoyance and precognition and telepathic signals that said *shu-shaaa*—

Lone Eyebrow recovered his wits. "Because I'm the way I am, that's all."

"You are the way you are. But what makes you that way?"

"Good drugs," somebody yelled, and the class laughed again.

Tamara laughed with them. The morning's Gloomies were gone, maybe swept off on the magic carpet of dreams, maybe flushed down some subconscious toilet, or maybe just stuck in a mental desk drawer under the pages of her unwritten worries. Or maybe just hanging around Windshake waiting for her return.

She glanced at the front row and noticed a male student staring at her figure. If she couldn't keep their minds interested, at least she still managed to keep a few males awake. Robert didn't even seem to notice she was female anymore. Robert barely seemed to remember he had a wife.

She turned her attention back to the lecture and kept the discussion rolling. It was a good session, lots of class participation and fun besides. Not really anything she could test them on, but maybe it would get them thinking, and that was half the battle.

She was gathering her notes after class when a redheaded woman approached the lectern. Tamara flashed her a smile, and the woman smiled back, clutching her books to her chest.

"Dr. Leon, I just wanted to say how much I'm enjoying your class," she said

"Well, thank you," Tamara said, cramming her papers into her scuffed portfolio. She wondered if this was a brown-noser or the real deal, someone who took learning beyond the classroom.

"I'm thinking of going into psychology, and I wondered if you could recommend some outside reading."

Tamara looked into the woman's clear blue eyes. She saw no hidden motives in them. She considered herself a good judge of character. That was one of the few fringe benefits of her profession.

"More psych books?" Tamara said. "That way lies madness."

"Didn't you say madness is a matter of opinion?" the woman asked, uncowed.

Now I'm turning into a cynic, Tamara thought. This woman reminded her of herself a decade ago. Inquisitive and ambitious. Both handy qualities for a psychologist. She was pretty, though, which might be an academic liability.

Tamara said, "I tell you what, Ms.—"

"Blevins. Sarah Blevins."

"That name sounds familiar."

"Do you live in Windshake, by any chance? My daddy's the preacher up at the Baptist Church."

"And a preacher's daughter wants to be a psychologist?"

"I have to be something."

Tamara smiled. Psychology was just another belief system, and so was the Baptist faith. Neither was better nor worse, just different. And more truth was found in asking questions than in swallowing the company line, in either case.

"Tell you what," Tamara said. "I'll make a list of good books that you should be able to find in the university library. If you can't, maybe we can work it out so you can borrow some of mine."

Sarah's freckled cheeks dimpled as she showed her straight teeth. "Thank you, ma'am."

"Ms. Blevins, you can thank me by actually reading them and maybe someday writing better ones."

Sarah nodded seriously. "See you on Monday," she said

brightly, then went out the door, her coppery hair swinging from side to side.

Tamara stopped by the office she shared with two other associates. She wedged herself into her cubbyhole and worked on her research project. When she looked up, hours later, she noticed through the tiny window that the sun was sinking low in the sky. She hurried out to her car and drove home, dreading the Gloomies that might be drawing ever closer to the windows of her soul. And the secret lights of Bear Claw that might pierce the darkness of her troubled heart.

Of course they weren't real, but she was afraid she might see them again anyway.

Virginia Speerhorn looked across her cluttered desk at Chief Crosley. *What a fat stereotype, a Buford Pusser Keystone Kop lardass,* she thought. *Just look at him, sitting there munching on a doughnut while the buttons are already straining to pop off his shirt. He's ten pounds of manure in a five-pound bag.*

And that pathetic comb-over, it looks like a half-dozen greasy threads stretched across a red billiard ball. He may as well have a sign on his head that reads, "I'm just a heart attack waiting to happen, but I still think I'm a love machine." Doesn't he believe in bringing dignity to public office?

Still, he was an adequate law enforcement agent, and that was all she needed. Crime wasn't a problem in Windshake, and had never been a campaign issue. And a more ambitious person might have proved dangerous.

Virginia cleared her throat. Crosley's eyelids rolled sleepily open.

"What security measures are you taking for Blossomfest, Chief?"

Crosley parted his lips, allowing Virginia a glimpse of saliva-packed bread and raspberry filling. Then he swallowed, his knob of an Adam's apple pogoing dryly.

"Got five men—er, five *officers*—assigned for weekend duty, meaning two will be drawing overtime."

Virginia pursed her lips. "And you?"

Crosley became intensely interested in a flap of frayed rayon on the arm of his chair. "I'll be there, too."

"And not billing the city for overtime?"

Crosley looked up. Virginia noticed, with pleasure, that he cringed from the heat of what she thought of as her "withering glare."

"Now, Mayor, that was years ago. You still don't hold that against me, do you?"

"Chief, I'm not surprised when some of the sanitation workers fudge on their time sheets, putting down an extra half hour when they only worked a quarter. But I *do* expect my more visible officials to follow the letter of the law. Especially those who are commissioned to uphold it."

Crosley slouched even deeper into his seat. "I made good on that."

"I have a budget to maintain, Chief, and in my budget, every dollar has a place and must be answered for. You have a decent salary and your standard of living is above the city average. You get a measure of respect from your peers, and from me. I should think that would be satisfaction enough for anyone."

"Yes, ma'am," said Crosley, duly defeated.

Virginia leaned back in her splintery oak swivel chair, its old springs creaking like a vault door. She had rescued this chair from the dumpster behind city hall and exiled her predecessor's leather chair to storage. This uncomfortable, battered relic was perfect for the image she wanted to cultivate.

She looked out the window at the busy street. Nearly twice as much traffic now as when she had first taken up her post behind this desk twelve years ago. And this little town—

no, *city*, it was a city in her mind, no matter what the charter said—had bloomed under her careful tending. Tax revenue was up, the budget surplus was expanding, and her margin of victory in each successive election had grown accordingly.

She turned back to Crosley. "I want a good time for the whole family this weekend, just like the Chamber of Commerce ads have promised. That means no open consumption of alcohol, no littering, all vendors following the traffic and fire lane restrictions, and—my god, I better check something."

She stabbed her speakerphone. "Martha?"

"Ma'am?" came a tinny voice from the speaker.

"The live music for Blossomfest, do you know what the Chamber has scheduled?"

Virginia heard a shuffling of papers.

"Mayor, it looks like a solo acoustic guitarist at ten, then a student string quartet from Westridge after that. The headline act is that country singer, Sammy Ray Hawkins."

Virginia smiled in relief, her facial muscles twitching from the unaccustomed workout. "Thank you, Martha," she said, cutting the connection before Martha could say "You're welcome."

Virginia said to Crosley, "I was afraid the Chamber might have been dumb enough to line up one of those rock 'n' roll bands. *That* wouldn't square with the Windshake image, now, would it?"

Crosley grunted, a pastry crumb falling from his lips. "I'll keep things under control, Mayor."

Virginia nodded, only half listening. There would be at least a couple of thousand visitors this weekend, drawn up the mountain by the lure of Appalachian crafts, folk art, old-timey storytelling, and a chance to spend big-city money. They weren't voters, but the income greased the wheels of Windshake commerce and thus the wheels of local politics. What was good for Windshake was good for Virginia.

She planned on being highly visible. She mentally rummaged through her closet, selecting an outfit that would be regal without being ostentatious. She had forgotten Crosley.

"Is that all, Mayor?"

She waved him away and heard him groan in a duet with his chair as he stood, his rump wobbling like a sack of wet pastries as he left. Then she was back in her closet, trying on clothes.

Robert had finished his production for the day. He'd remixed the Petty Pleasures spot, reaching down into his intestines for a growly, fake bass. And he'd rattled off a promo for the upcoming City Slicker 300, along with a fresh liner that said "WRNC and Blossomfest, Windshake's Winning Combination." Since Patterson had scheduled him for unpaid overtime this coming weekend, Robert felt justified in taking off early.

"See you, Dennis," Robert called into the cramped News Office as he walked past. "Hope you get your Pulitzer today, or whatever it is radio guys get."

Dennis was packing his Marantz field recorder into a leather briefcase. "Big doings tonight, Bobby," Dennis said, closing the case with a prissy flourish. "The Blossomfest Committee is having its final meeting before the weekend. And I've got the exclusive."

It's only exclusive because no one else gives a damn, Robert thought. *But ease up, you cynical old bastard. Dennis is just like everyone else, trapped at WRNC until that magical ship comes in.* "Free doughnuts?"

Dennis flashed expensive teeth, that false anchorman's smile that Robert had seen him practicing in the mirror. There was a speck of roast beef between his bicuspid and incisor.

"You got it, Bobby boy. Say, I've got an interview with WDTV next week. Might be my ticket out of Windshake."

"What will we ever do without you?"

"Stumble on through the darkness, I suppose."

"Well, good luck, man, and I mean it." Robert stepped back, the cologne making his eyes water. Dennis nodded absently and checked his watch, then took his jacket off the coat rack and headed for the back door. Robert was about to follow him when Patterson's voice boomed down the cheap paneling of the hall.

"Mister Bobby."

A command, never a question. Robert froze with his hand on the door knob, a little Wonka melody running through his mind. *Oompah-loompah-oompadee-doo.* "Yes?" Robert said, smiling.

"Going somewhere?" Patterson's hair was slicked back and his cashmere sweater vest hugged him like wet rubber. He looked like he'd had a turn in a tanning salon.

Must have an appointment with that little gal Mrs. Patterson doesn't know about. He's buffed and polished and powdered, ready for a tumble in the Super 8.

"Thought I'd leave early. I've finished my spots and I want to spend the afternoon with my kids."

Patterson nodded, his beady eyes unfocused, as if trying to peer into the intricacies of the statement. "I just wanted to let you know that I've put Sammy Ray Hawkins in rotation for the rest of this week. He's on the hot current list."

"Isn't he country?"

"Yeah, but I'm stretching the format to get him in because he's headlining Blossomfest."

"Oh, yeah. I guess that's a pretty big thing around here, isn't it?"

"I keep forgetting this will be your first one. It's good for the community, and a good chance to get WRNC out among the public."

"I heard Sammy Ray Hawkins used to play around here."

Christ, we're practically bonding. Next thing you know, old Melv will be telling me about his days in college radio, back when Elvis was on his last legs.

"Yes, he was a scraggly folk type," the GM said. "Greasy hair and all that. Used to play the coffeehouses down at Westridge University. Then he got a few breaks and turned a little bit twangy and bought some fringed buckskin. Now he's the biggest thing since white bread, at least in these parts."

Robert nodded, wondering what else Patterson wanted. He couldn't just be shooting the breeze, could he? Making a little friendly conversation? Stepping off his high white horse to mingle with the masses?

Patterson continued. "And I'll tell you he wasn't cheap, either. I'm on the Blossomfest Committee for the Chamber, you know."

No, Robert didn't know. But Patterson was always rattling on about "Chamber" this and "Chamber" that, sending Dennis out to do stories on Chamber of Commerce businesses. Maybe that explained why WRNC's news was always soft-selling, sidestepping, and whitewashing the issues. And maybe that explained the Chamber of Commerce Community Development Awards that lined Patterson's office walls like family photographs.

"Dennis said you guys were meeting tonight."

"Finalizing plans. We want things to go off without a hitch. Mayor Speerhorn's going to be there."

"Well, hope it goes well. I'll see you tomorrow."

"Okay. Bye now."

Robert stepped out the door, laughing to himself. Patterson was so dumb that he had forgotten to prevent Robert from leaving early.

Robert had just pulled into his driveway as the bus dropped off the kids. Kevin long-jumped from the jaws of the door, high on life as only a child could be. Ginger followed, stumbling because her eyes were fixed on her picture book instead of the bus steps. Robert's heart soared.

Kevin never got into real trouble and he washed the dishes every night without complaint. He had grumbled the first time, but Tamara had explained that it was his chore from now on, that it was part of being a family, and there was no room for negotiation. Robert admired Tamara's firmly gentle child-rearing techniques. Maybe that psychology business paid off once in a while, even if it made messes in other areas.

Ginger was a miniature Tamara, with her shining eyes and blond hair. She was growing up too fast. Soon Robert would have to beat the boys off of her with a stick. Let her enjoy her Dr. Seuss while she could, because soon Clark in the Park in the Dark would be a rapist instead of a would-be pet.

We're doing okay, Robert thought. *Better thank God and count your blessings. Because, Robert, my man, you've got love, and I doubt if a whole hell of a lot of people ever have that.*

Except he'd been letting Tamara drift away. Or else she was putting up glass walls between them. Last night she had turned frigid again, as if the cold mountain rain had been pumping through her veins. She had been talking about her dad's death again, her extended guilt trip. She wasn't able to bury the past, which was another reason Robert was afraid to tell her about his little affair.

Their sex life hadn't been so great lately, and it wasn't all Tamara's fault, though Robert tried to convince himself it was. Every time Tamara aroused him, he thought of Betty and was filled with a horrifying excitement, as if the dirty secret added spice to his passion. But the guilt also roiled in his guts like a barbed-wire enema. If he didn't confess, he'd probably burn up from the inside, immolated by his own private hellfire.

Maybe he would talk to Tamara tonight, heart-to-heart, and hopefully, someday after the healing, tummy-to-tummy.

He opened the car door and hugged his kids.

Chapter Thirteen

The thing that had been Sylvester Mull shambled through the trees. It still had shards of Sylvester's memories and personality, but added to that, like a cancer that mimicked a healthy cell, was the consciousness of the space spore that had sparked this rebirth. Energy coursed through his flesh, pulsing in rhythm to the distant parent's metabolism. Sylvester wondered why he didn't care that he had left his beloved gun behind. Perhaps because now he wanted to merge with the wildlife instead of shoot it.

He dimly remembered his encounter with Ralph, only he recalled his conversion with pleasure, not pain. He wished he could have thanked Ralph, because Sylvester saw that his whole life had been spent wandering in the wilderness. Now he had purpose. Now he served.

But Ralph had stumbled away in the opposite direction, on a separate mission and beyond the intimacies of gratitude. He was following the call of his own inner voice.

Sylvester leaned against a wild cherry tree, his hands pressing into the coarse strips of split bark. He felt the tree's cells in their photosynthesis, converting light to energy, and that energy now flowing back through him and feeding the parent-creature. He felt the white roots plumbing the ground, tapping into the water table and drawing nitrates from the dark loam. The tips of the branches were his fingers, ready to explode into glorious bud. He was joined, no more tree or man, only dust and energy bound in bizarre and wondrous form.

Sylvester fell back, his head swirling with the tree's memories, memories of a bursting seed-germ, its agonizing fight through the soil, its climb into the light. He writhed in the damp dead leaves, absorbing the thick rot and bacteria, drunk on the teeming microscopic life, stoned on the richness of cellular activity. He rolled onto his hands and knees, his face erupting into a tortured beatific smile. The joy of realization drummed in his dead heart. His mind was singing green.

Sylvester rose under the crazy tilted sky, the great blue ceiling with its clouds like distant kin, all part of one big, loving biosystem. He walked on the earth that was only a garden, grown to feed the planet-eating parent. Sylvester shared the parent's hunger, *was* the hunger; the conversion had not snuffed his hunter's instinct. Their united drive was to consume and move onward, to reap nature's bounty, to excrete dark matter. He flowed like water, swept along on currents that carried all things toward one destination.

Home.

Paul Crosley looked out the window of his Silverstream. Jimmy Morris's pickup was in the Mull driveway. That could only mean one thing.

Hell, you could practically see the back end of the trailer bucking up and down like an old seesaw. Jimmy must be doing the boot-scootin' boogie like there's no tomorrow.

Not that Paul blamed him. That was some right good stuff, as he remembered it. And he planned on heading over after Jimmy left and refreshing his memory.

That was *if* he could get the old soldier to stand at attention. But the way it was starting to twitch in his lap, he thought that wouldn't be much of a problem.

Paul adjusted the patch over his right eye. The damned thing was itching like hell today. Maybe he should have gotten a glass eyeball like those VA doctors had recommended. But it was enough trouble just putting in his teeth every morning. He didn't want to mess around with a bucketful of other body parts.

He snickered, spraying liquor mist over his beige curtains. He had just pictured himself rolling out of bed and attaching a penis between his legs, like snapping a socket arm on a ratchet.

One of the Mull kids walked around the corner of their trailer. It was the oldest one, the one in the army jacket that Paul had seen smoking dope out in the toolshed this morning. Little bastard ought to be in school, doing his booklearning. No wonder society was going to hell the way it was.

Why, back in Paul's day, his daddy would have blistered his ass with a hickory switch if he'd have skipped school. And that wasn't the worst part. The worst part was having to go out and cut your own switch. And you'd better not bring back some slender little twig that was limper than a strip of licorice, either. You'd better get a good healthy sapling, or by God, Daddy would get his own, and then the skin and blood would really fly.

Now they couldn't even raise a hand against them at school. Damned liberals were coddling these snot-nosed delinquents like the brats were the victims. Paul had seen the cops bring the boy home once. Peggy had stood in the doorway in her crusty flower-patterned nightgown and nodded her tired bleached head and said *Yeah, Officer, I'll keep an eye on him from now on* and *I know he really ain't a bad boy at heart* and *I don't know why he'd ever do such a thing*. And the cops had just shrugged and nodded back and driven away.

And the brat had the balls to wear the uniform of the United States military, when that boy had 4-F written all over him. Ought to be a law against that.

Paul watched as the boy put his ear to the trailer door and turned, rage reddening his sharp young face. The boy kicked the gravel and spat in disgust. Then his eyes narrowed to slits, viper's eyes, as he looked around the trailer park. Paul ducked back into the shadows, knowing he'd be invisible because of the bright sunshine outside.

The boy quietly opened the door of Jimmy's pickup and rummaged around. Paul heard the faint clatter of tools and saw an oily rag fall to the gravel driveway. The boy lifted a bottle from under the seat, and Paul saw its brown liquid contents glinting in the light. The boy tucked the bottle into his army jacket with a secretive smirk and jogged toward the stand of scrub pine at the back end of the trailer park.

And he's a little thief to boot, Paul thought. *What that boy needs is a good ass-whooping. I've been whooped by hickory switches and thumped with the Bible and ground under the boot of the military and it ain't hurt me not one little bit.*

He strained his ears toward the Mull trailer. A window was open, and he could hear bedsprings groaning in rhythm. And Peggy was panting in that way that half the town knew. The wrinkled fingers of Paul's left hand cupped the jar of moonshine while his right hand went down to salute the old soldier.

Preacher Blevins looked up from his lunch. He wished he hadn't.

His wife, Amanda, was looking at him through the greasy black slits of her eye-liner. He choked down the throatful of bland tuna salad and reached for his coffee cup.

Was she trying to become the next Tammy Faye Bakker? The preacher believed one was enough. He didn't need a caricature trophy, a tin-voiced verse-spouter sitting on his shoulder.

"Do you like your sandwich, Armfield?" she asked in her whiny Georgia twang. She stretched his name into three syllables: *Ahmm-fee-yuld*.

"It's just fine, dear."

"I'm going down to Belk's today to buy me a new dress for Blossomfest. What color do you think I should choose?"

Armfield thought she'd look good in funeral black, with her dewy eyes sewn shut and the Alamo Rose troweled off her lips. Those big puffy lips that he'd once made her use in the way that had gotten the Sodomites burned. The image of him slipping on top of her while she was in her coffin popped into his head. Not that she could perform much worse dead than she did while living.

The devil was at him again. He took a gulp of coffee and said, "Get whatever kind of dress you want, dear."

"Maybe I'll get something that will work for Easter, too. Maybe something robin's-egg blue with a touch of pink lace and a yellow chiffon scarf."

Armfield nodded and chewed his sandwich. *Forgive me, Oh Lord, for wishing harm on this woman that I promised to honor,* he silently prayed. *The devil's working overtime today, so grant me strength.*

He took another bite of his sandwich. Damn that Sarah and her whole-wheat bread. Now she had taken to keeping tofu in the refrigerator. It looked like an albino cowpatty to him. He thought of his wife, then of Nettie, who was coming in to work at the church that afternoon. The image of the church secretary made his pulse beat faster. He drank the grainy dregs of his coffee and looked at Amanda, wondering if he might spend his sudden passion in her well-preserved lap.

No, never after she'd already put on her makeup. And never in daylight. And never on Sunday. And never when

Sarah might hear. And never when her favorite shows were on television. And never when—

"Armfield, how do you think I would look with a perm?" She touched her burnt red hair with a wispy hand.

Even more like a twenty-dollar whore, he thought. *But, Lord, the devil's in me DEEP today, please forgive me my weakness.*

"I think you look fine the way you are. But whatever makes you happy makes me happy." He tried on a smile that stretched his top lip over his twin beaver teeth. "And you know you're shining in the eyes of the Lord, and that's all that matters."

"Oh, Armfield." She tittered, and she may have blushed under her sheet of foundation, but Armfield couldn't be sure. Her clotted smile was enough to shrivel away the last of his erection.

He stood, pushing his empty plate toward the center of the table. "Got to go to the church, honey." He walked over and kissed the top of her head. The kiss tasted of chemicals and her hair didn't move.

"I think I'll buy me a hat, too," Amanda said. "Then I'm going to ride out to see Genevieve Moody about this year's blood drive. See if she wants to spend some of her husband's money. Maybe get her to go with me to the mall down in Barkersville."

"The Lord wants us to enjoy the fruits of our labors," Armfield said, heading out the door.

Just don't max out the fucking credit card. I can only steal so fast. Even the Lord's bank accounts aren't bottomless.

"Have a good day, dear," he called cheerfully, before crossing the yard to the church. "Say hello to the Moodys for me."

Jimmy Morris rolled over onto his back, sweat ringing his unwashed neck. The room smelled of chlorine and olives.

Peggy curled into the crook of his tattooed arm, nuzzling his coarse chest.

"Jimmy, you sure know how to treat a lady," she purred.

Jimmy grunted and reached for the bottle that he'd left on the bedside table. He fumbled among the condom wrappers and cigarette butts and old dental floss until his hand struck glass. He reached his arm over Peggy's damp stringy hair and twisted off the cap, then poured a slug of brown liquor into his mouth. He swished a couple of times to get the taste of Peggy off his tongue, then swallowed. Fire raged through his gullet and he smiled in satisfaction.

Peggy lifted her head, making a splotching sound as her cheek lifted from Jimmy's sticky skin. She took the bottle from him and sipped at it like a baby taking suckle.

She don't know what she's missing, Jimmy thought. *If she ever got ahold of the good stuff, she'd be spoiled rotten. But she's happy with this four-dollar-a-pint antiseptic that passes for whiskey, so I might as well save that Jim Beam in the truck for the gals who need to feel pampered.*

"That sure was fun, sugar," Jimmy said. He winced against the light pouring through the trailer window. It must be getting toward evening. He wondered how long he dared to stay. Sylvester could drive up any moment. Not likely, but a possibility.

But the danger was part of the thrill. And if he could get Peggy to go along with his idea, there would be a whole hell of a lot of thrill. He took another painful swig and put the bottle down. He cupped Peggy's worn chin in his hand. Dark grease filled the swirls of his fingerprints.

"You know you're good at that, darling. The best I know of," he said, in what he thought of as his Burt Reynolds voice.

"Jimmy, you're just saying that," Peggy said, not hiding the happiness in her voice.

"I mean it. You're worth a little risk."

"You mean to do *this,* or do you mean it's risky to love me?"

Jimmy frowned and looked for a different path, one that led away from fool emotions. "What I mean, sugar, is you're too good to waste on Sylvester. What kind of man stays out in the woods all the time when he's got something like this at home?"

He ran a hand over Peggy's freckled breast. Her nipple flexed and stiffened, like an earthworm caught with its head out of the ground.

"Now, Sylvester's a good man," she said. "He's never raised a hand against me—well, at least not much. And he provides for me and the kids."

"Just what the hell do you got, Peg? Look around."

She looked. Leak marks on the ceiling resembled coffee stains. A hole gaped in the thin paneling where a shotgun blast had ripped through the siding. Mice had gnawed at the foamwood baseboard. The closet doors hung awkwardly off their tracks like two drunks dangling from a railroad trestle. Peggy took a sharp breath, as if he had just slapped her across the face with her own autobiography.

"If Sylvester loved you, he wouldn't keep you like this," Jimmy said quietly. No need for added cruelty. Awareness had heaped enough pain on Peggy Mull.

Peggy put her head on his chest and was still. Then he felt a small warm wetness on his skin, and the mattress quivered with her sobs.

"Hey, honey, it's okay," Jimmy said, stroking her matted and tangled hair. He'd have to get her to take better care of herself. Maybe he'd buy her some fancy shampoo. To increase the value.

"J—Jimmy. I just get lonely sometimes," she said in her broken voice.

"We all do, sweetheart. Misery loves company, too."

"I try so hard. But Sylvester don't make much, and he

won't let me get a job. Says it would make him feel like less of a man."

Jimmy chortled and went for the other nipple. "How much of a man is he? Can't even give his wife a little loving when she needs it."

"But he's my *husband*. And I love him, in some kind of screwed-up way." Her sobs eased and she craned her neck to look at Jimmy's face. "But I love you, too."

Jimmy smiled and looked into her smoky blue eyes. They were her best feature. He'd have to figure out a way to make them stand out more. Packaging was what made the merchandise.

"And I love you, honey," he said, touching her lightly on the nose with his index finger. "And I want you to be comfortable."

She burrowed into his chest hair. "I'm comfortable right here."

"I mean with money."

He felt her tense a little.

"Good money," he said, breaking the silence.

"How?"

"I've got it figured out."

"What?"

"Five hundred dollars a week, free and clear."

He let that sink in. Twice what Sylvester probably made trucking feed all over Bumfuck. When he even worked, that was.

"What are you talking about, Jimmy?"

Her words crawled across the air like baby spiders down a thread of web, fragile and cautious.

"I'm talking about putting you to work, woman. Turning pleasure into business."

She thumped him on the chest, the fleshy sound echoing hollowly off the cluttered furniture. "I ain't no hooker, you asshole. I like to fuck. I like to do lots of things. But I got my pride, see?"

She sat up in bed, pulling the dingy sheet around her waist. The knobs of her spine flexed as she started crying again. Jimmy let her cry until the hurt and shock dulled. He took a drink of cheap whiskey while he waited.

Finally she turned, her eyelids puffy and red. He waited for her to speak. She shook her head from side to side. "I can't do it," she whispered, speaking more to herself than Jimmy.

"Think about it, sugar," he said. "You won't have to scrap for cigarette money. You won't have to beg for liquor."

Her fury returned, a storm blowing in from a half-forgotten wasteland. "If you think I've been fucking you for liquor, then you better think again."

Jimmy reached out and touched her flushed cheek. "Easy, honey, I didn't mean it that way. I just mean you can have the good things a lady like you deserves."

He let his hand trail down her neck to her breast and he gave a gentle squeeze. "Stuff this nice ought to be wearing silk, girl," he said. He let his hand slide lower. "'Cause it's silky smooth."

Not a bad little advertising pitch, Jimmy thought. *I'll have to remember that, come Friday nights at the Moose Lodge when the boys are peckered up and out for foxtail.*

Peggy relaxed a little under his caress. Her tears had stopped but the salt of their tracks still ran down her sharp cheekbones. As Jimmy stroked, he decided that this was seventy-five-dollar stuff if he'd ever seen it.

"I don't know, Jimmy," she said, then gasped from arousal.

"Shh. Don't say anything. Just think about it for a while."

"What about Sylvester?"

"You and me managed to work around him just fine. Don't you worry about that."

"And the kids?"

The kids. Might make evening business a little awkward, but Jimmy was an optimist. Besides, if this got rolling, he could branch out into dope peddling. And it would be convenient to have distributors in both the elementary and high schools.

"Just think of what you can buy for them," he said. "Won't have to run around in ratty-assed boots anymore. They can get Nikes like the rich kids. And they could have hamburger for dinner instead of macaroni and cheese."

"What if Sylvester starts noticing all the little extras?"

"Tell him you've been stretching the dollar. Hell, it's not like he notices things anyway."

Peggy trembled against his caress. A low moan escaped her lips.

Damn, she is a hot one, Jimmy thought. *She can probably turn a half-dozen tricks a day. Maybe even do a party scene once in a while. I'll have to work out a rate card for various positions.*

"Jimmy," she said, breath coming fast now.

Jimmy rolled away. He wanted to leave her aching. Might make the idea of an endless parade of prick seem more enticing. He started to get out of bed. She grabbed him by the most convenient handle.

"Jimmy, where are you going?"

"Got to run, honey."

He reached for his clothes as she wrapped her hands around his waist. Her lavender nail polish glittered in the sunlight. He stood and she fell back onto the bed, her legs wide. "Jimmy, don't leave me like this," she pleaded.

Perfect. If she could act this good with him, there was no reason why she couldn't pull it off on demand. He looked at her while he stepped into his pants.

"Think about what I said, Peggy." He tugged on one of his snakeskin boots, resting his other foot on the bed.

Peggy lay still and pouted, her lips curling. *Those lips are worth a hundred bucks a pop,* thought Jimmy. He picked up the whiskey and turned to leave the room.

"Jimmy?"

"What, darling?"

"What would that—you know, what you're talking about—do to *us?*"

"Not a thing, darling. You know I love you, no matter what."

"Wouldn't it make you jealous, knowing?"

"There ain't no room for jealousy. There's business, and then there's you and me. What we got is special."

Peggy scooted out of bed and wrapped a nightgown around her torso. She followed him to the door with quick, shuffling steps, kicking the dirty laundry away from her ankles.

Jimmy looked out the glass slats of the trailer window, making sure the coast was clear. Peggy was at his shoulder. He reached out and absently stroked her hair. "If you won't do it for yourself, do it for me," he said.

"How much did you say we could make?"

He looked out the window again. "I figure forty bucks a shot for the basics, fifty for special treatment. We split it fifty-fifty."

And Jimmy would keep the extra.

Peggy gnawed at a thumbnail, clattering her small sharp teeth. "I don't know," she said around her thumb.

"I'll round up the customers, and all you have to do is send them away happy. Everybody wins."

"But it's so—*dirty.*"

Jimmy faced her and took her firmly by her bony shoulders. "Look here, Peg. It might be a way out of *this*," he said, jerking his head toward the interior of the trailer. "Maybe we can get away someday, just you and me."

"But the kids—"

"It'll take a few years."

"I don't know." She looked down at the ragged welcome mat.

"Think about it," he said, his hand on the door.

She leaned forward quickly and pecked him on the cheek. He handed her the nearly empty whiskey bottle.

"Are you *sure* you'd still love me?" she asked.

"Of course, darling." Just like he loved his Ford F-100 pickup with the Leonard camper top and CB radio. Just like he loved the hunting knives that he traded at the Piney Ford flea market. Just like he loved his silver Dale Earnhardt belt buckle. Like he loved all his favorite possessions.

"And things will be just like before?"

"Sure. Maybe better." Except there was no way in hell he'd be parking his meat limousine in her flesh garage after she started working. Not with the kinds of things that people spread around these days. But she'd learn all about that later.

"I'll call you," he said, before putting his weight on the corrugated trailer step.

Peggy sat at the kitchen counter with the bottle in front of her. Jimmy's tailpipes thrushed as he backed out of the driveway and headed downtown. She idly scraped at a flake of dried gravy with her fingernail as she thought about Jimmy's offer. She took a sip of the whiskey, enjoying the numb tingling feel of her lips against the glass. Just for practice, she slid her mouth over the bottleneck. It went in easily.

Someone knocked at the door. She wondered who it could be at this time of day. The kids wouldn't be home for another hour or so, what with the long walk from the bus stop. She wrapped her nightgown around her waist and held it in place with her arm, then opened the door a crack.

It was Paul Crosley, wearing his terrapin grin.

Chapter Fourteen

Mayor Virginia Speerhorn looked down from her seat at the podium. She enjoyed her elevated view of the Chamber of Commerce members. She saw the pink tops of bald spots, the stray hairs that sprang free from severe barrettes, the seam lines of wigs and toupees. "Progress report, Mr. Patterson?"

"Yes, ma'am," said Melvin Patterson. He looked as if he'd love to put a tongue on the tip of her strapless dress shoe. WRNC provided good coverage for her during the election seasons, and Patterson was too dull-witted to know he was giving away free political advertising every time WRNC interviewed her.

"I've gone over security for the weekend with Chief Crosley," she said, her authoritative voice rattling off the oak rails and teak walls of the Town Council chambers. "That leaves entertainment, which I believe is your area, Mr. Patterson."

"Yes, Madam Mayor. The musical acts have signed contracts and the storytelling group will be there. Except they perform for free, of course. Then there are the usual attractions like the Volunteer Fire Department turkey shoot—"

"With air pistols, correct?"

"Yes, ma'am. The library will have a book fair and the Baptist Sewing Circle will be making quilts for auction. And most of the vendors will have displays and free activities to draw children to their booths."

"Very good, Mr. Patterson. All family-oriented, correct?"

"Yes, Mayor."

She insisted on formality at town meetings even though everyone knew each other. It kept things on a firm footing. This was civic business, after all. "And who's in charge of the vendors?"

"I am," came a watery voice from the table where the Blossomfest Committee sat. It was Margaret Staley. Her husband Horace had run a weak campaign against Virginia eight years ago.

Virginia had nearly ruined both of the Staleys. All it took was a simple background check to find out that the Staleys had not reported a toolshed, a speedboat, and a Ford Taurus on their county tax listing. Then there was the interesting fact that Margaret's sister had an illegitimate son by Margaret's husband's cousin. After the gossip had "leaked," the town had been whispering behind their hands for months.

Horace Staley had called Virginia, saying he wanted to respectfully withdraw from the race. Virginia didn't want to win an unopposed election. She felt that would make her seem politically vulnerable. So she had threatened Horace with the secret she had held back, that Horace had worked for the American Civil Liberties Union for a year after he had gotten his law degree.

Horace had stayed in the race and taken his beating, and had recovered enough to put his wife in the Chamber hierarchy. Virginia, feeling magnanimous, nodded at Margaret's trembling head.

Margaret stood, the legs of her chair digging into the parquet floor. Virginia winced. A few whispers fluttered in the back of the room among the two dozen spectators.

"We've got forty-one vendors enlisted, Mayor." She seemed to spit out the last word.

Some people just wouldn't let bygones be bygones, Virginia decided. *But Margaret is competent enough with fund management.*

"And they have their state and local business licenses, Mrs. Staley?"

"Yes. Their fees are paid up front, with a rain date clause in the agreement."

"No need for pessimism, Mrs. Staley. Please knock on wood."

Margaret clenched her jaw and twice tapped lightly on the table.

"Rain is a fact of life, my friends," Virginia said to the room at large. "But it's never rained at Blossomfest since I've been in office, and I don't plan on letting it start now."

This wasn't entirely true. There had been misty sprinkles at last year's Blossomfest, but Virginia had refused to postpone the event. The vending fees were already in the city coffers. So everyone had shuffled through a miserable weekend, too chilled to dig through their wallets and purses and buy useless items.

"Mayor, we have a variety of arts and crafts this year, pottery and woodcarving and weaving," Margaret said. "A solid mix of mountain folk art and consumerist-type merchandise. Something for everyone, as you like to say."

"Is that all, Mrs. Staley?"

Margaret dipped her weary, defeated head and sat down.

"Mr. Lemly?"

Bill Lemly stood up, seemingly blocking out the polished glow of the woodwork with his shadow. "We've got the street plans drawn up, Mayor Speerhorn. I personally supervised the building of the stage in accordance with all the local codes."

"And how much of a bite did that take?" Virginia was tallying up the estimated cost of promotion and weighing it against the expected profit. She fondled the gavel that she had used only once, in her first year in office, and it seemed as if that single rap still reverberated off the walls like a threat.

"None, ma'am. I donated the labor and materials."

She searched his face for smugness and found none. She hoped she never had to run against him. He might prove to be more clever than he looked. But she was sure she could find something on him, if it came to that. His ex-wife, for instance.

"Very good, Mr. Lemly. So we have everything in place. I'd like to personally thank the committee for all its hard work, and I'm confident that this year's Blossomfest will be the best ever."

She looked at Dennis Thorne to make sure he had gotten that last bit on tape. Patterson was looking at him, too. Dennis held his microphone in the air as wooden applause scrabbled across the council chambers.

"This meeting is adjourned," Virginia said, rising between the North Carolina and United States flags that flanked her like bodyguards. She watched as her subjects spilled from the room into the cool night air.

The kids were in bed. Tamara had tucked them in, although Kevin was starting to get a little squeamish about the good-night kisses. She had read Ginger *The Butter Battle Book*.

How true that was, she thought, as she turned off the light. *If people wouldn't worry about how other people buttered their bread, the world wouldn't be so out of whack. Dr. Seuss was way ahead of his time.*

"Mommy, what does 'out of whack' mean?" Ginger asked as Tamara was leaving.

"It means not sensible, not neat and orderly. Where did you hear that?" Tamara asked.

"I don't know. I just thought of it."

Coincidence. She probably heard it at school.

Tamara kissed Ginger on the nose. "And you're going to be all out of whack tomorrow if you don't get some sleep."

She went into the living room and collected an armful of papers, then sat on the couch beside Robert, who was watching basketball.

"Damn those cheaters," he said, his carotid artery swelling in rage.

"Calm down, honey. It's only a game."

"Only a game? *Only a game?*" He ran a hand through his dark hair, which was beginning to show the first signs of silver. "It's the *Tarheels* playing. Down by six with a minute left. And the Antichrist forces of St. John's are holding the ball."

Tamara almost made a remark about Robert living out a gladiatorial macho instinct by proxy, but she let it pass. There was enough friction between them lately that an innocent quip might flare into a free-for-all. Robert leaned back and took a drink of his chocolate milk. Tamara looked at him out of the corners of her eyes.

He's just like a little kid, she thought. *Still enthusiastic and energetic, excited by life. He's pretty good-looking, too. And not all of him is little.*

He pumped his fist as the Tarheels nailed a jumper.

Maybe if the Tarheels win, he'll be in a good mood. Maybe tonight. The Gloomies are away on vacation, even if they're keeping in touch via long distance.

She looked at her work and the words swam without meaning. She needed a rest. From psychology. From thinking. From *shu-shaaa*. She put her books aside and leaned her head on Robert's shoulder.

She watched as the Tarheels made what the announcer called a "trey," and her head fell to the sofa cushion as Robert leaned forward. She put a hand on his knee and rubbed his thigh as a skinny Carolina player hit a pair of free throws.

"Comeback City, baby!" the announcer shouted.

The crowd roared as if they were at a Nazi rally. Tamara pictured all that excitement taking place as a library opened its doors or a community theater dropped the final curtain on a staging of *Our Town*. The suspension of disbelief was too much of a stretch. The final horn sounded on the television set and Robert was airborne, pumping his arms just like Kevin did when excited.

"The Redmen are Deadmen," Robert said, imitating the announcer. "Aw, baby!"

Tamara watched him pace excitedly for a minute as the sportscasters droned nasally about tournament brackets and Sweet Sixteens and Final Fours and seeds. Sports had its own secret language, just as psychology and academia and religion did. Just another competitive belief system, only the score was much clearer in sports.

Everyone needs their buzzwords, she thought. *Even would-be clairvoyants need names for their Gloomies. Names like Shushaaa.*

Later, in bed, Robert touched her, his palms still moist from the tension of watching the game. "How did your day go, honey?"

She smiled against the dark pillow. "Fine. No Gloomies."

"I'm glad."

"So, are you excited about Blossomfest?"

"I'm agonna buy me a Rebel flag ashtray, and maybe one of 'em little wooden outhouses, you know the kind, what's got the hillbilly with the corncob pecker."

She laughed, surprised that she was surprised by it. Laughter sounded strangely out of place, the way their bedroom had been lately.

Robert spooned against the warm flannel of her night-gown. The night was a little damp and chilly, but she mostly wore the gown so that Robert could take it off. She hoped.

"Listen, honey. I know I've been a little distant lately," he said. "Been worried about work and stuff, wondering if we did the right thing moving here."

"Robert, we've been over that enough. You like the station. I know it's not as demanding as a big-market FM, but it's just as important to the audience. And the kids really love it here."

"But what about you? I just feel so selfish, pulling you away from Carolina just when things were starting to happen for you."

"Things can happen at Westridge, too."

"Are you sure you're happy?"

She turned to him, close enough to feel his breath in her hair. Twin sparkles were all she could see of his eyes.

"Honey, I'm doing fine," she said. "I *told* you that. And you know I'm honest with you, and I trust that you're always honest with me."

There was a long heavy pause. Tamara was afraid that Robert still didn't believe her.

"Honey," he said. "There's something I've been meaning to tell you—"

Suddenly the Gloomies washed over her in a gray-red tide, pounding the cliffs of her mind.

SHU-SHAAA.

She sat bolt upright and listened to the dark world outside.

Crickets. A chuckling chipmunk. A dog barking down the street. There—a snapping twig.

"Something's outside, Robert."

"Honey, it's the middle of the night. Things don't *move* at this time of night in Windshake. It's against the laws of nature up here."

"Robert, you know me."

Robert sighed heavily and rolled out of bed. He leaned his face against the window and looked out into the woods that lined the backyard. Tamara liked not having streetlights glaring all night, but there were times when they came in handy. Like when the Gloomies stormed and she needed reassurance.

Robert turned and Tamara saw the black outline of his arms raise against the dim moonlit backdrop.

"Nothing there, honey," he said, the mattress squeaking as he slid under the covers.

"The Gloomies are back."

"I know," Robert muttered. "Do the bastards ever leave?"

Tamara was stung. Tears welled in her eyes. Then her pain turned to anger. The son of a bitch would *not* make her cry.

"You could be a little more sympathetic," she said. Her voice was cold. Her body was cold. Her heart was cold, like a shriveled dead star collapsing under the tired weight of its own gravity.

"I've been sympathetic," Robert said. "For years. Your father's dead and you can't bring him back."

"But it was my fault."

"No. You just had a dream. You happened to have a dream that he was hurtling through the dark in a metal tube and then it exploded into fire." Robert's voice was flat, as if reciting an overly familiar line.

"But nobody believed me."

"It was just a dream."

"But see what happened?"

"Your father died in a car crash the next morning."

The tears tried to come back. She fought them and lost. "I tried to make him stay home," she said, her throat aching. "But he just tweaked one of my pigtails and laughed and said that he'd be fine. Only he wasn't fine. He was dead, ripped to pieces by metal and glass."

"And by bad luck. Fate. Coincidence. God's will, or whatever. It could have happened on any day, or never at all."

"But the dream."

"Premonition. You know it's fairly common. You're the psychologist, after all."

Tamara thought he said "psychologist" with the trace of a sneer.

"But what about the other times? When Kevin broke his leg?"

"We can't stop living every time you have a bad dream."

Tamara pressed her face into the pillow, drying her tears. She was afraid that the tethers were broken, that whatever connected her to Robert had snapped its moorings, that she and he were tumbling apart like lost astronauts, drifting into a nebulous gray territory. She was alone, at the mercy of the Gloomies.

The inside of her brain tingled, an itch that was beyond scratching. She wasn't sure whether she had slipped into sleep and suffered a bad dream or if *shu-shaaa* was talking to her again. All she knew was that the noise was loud, a scream, as if the source of the signal had been turned up to ten and a half.

Except the voice doesn't exist. You can't see the future and you can barely see yesterday. Now quit this stuff before you go crazy.

She wrapped the pillow around her head, thinking of the kids, psychological theories, her failing marriage, anything but the vibrations that shook the walls of her skull.

Sylvester staggered against a garbage can, spilling refuse on the sidewalk. He couldn't flow as quickly without sunlight, but he was determined. He left the paved street for the quieter glory of the forest.

The oaks throbbed, their mighty limbs rich with sap. He merged with the ash and poplar, the hickory and laurel, and reveled in the generous sharing of the thorns and nettles as they tore at his flesh. In the jungle of his mind, among his tangled synapses where the seratonin oozed, he was aware of the parent channeling nature's energy through him. He was a vessel.

Something in the house stirred. His fingers found the earth, his dead heart hummed a night song. The air hung thick around his head. He swatted away the confusion, but the vibration tickled and pricked him.

Tah-mah-raa.

Sound.

Meant.

Nothing.

He passed the dark, hushed house with its sleeping bioenergy units. He would return for them, or other children would follow and do the work. All would be harvested for the greater good of the parent. First he had an ache, a longing, an inner instinct that compelled him forward, just as a sapling's leaves were driven to reach for the brilliance of the sun.

A dim shape stirred within him, an image, a memory. The memory became a symbol in the swampy nitrate soup of his brain. The human remnant of Sylvester recognized the symbol.

He tried the symbol on his fibrous tongue:

Peg-gheeee.

Chapter Fifteen

At first, Chester had thought it was old Don Oscar, walking out of the woods like he sometimes did when he got a wild hair up his ass, coming out of the evening shadows like a cow at feeding time. Chester's old failing eyes followed Don Oscar as the figure rolled over the fence into the sow's lot.

He wondered why the hell Don Oscar wanted to mess around in that black swampy gom. Then the sow had started squealing like somebody had clipped its ears. Chester pulled his bony hind end out of the rocker and peered into the hog pen. He saw Don Oscar wrestling with the sow.

Then the sow went quiet and Don Oscar climbed over the fence and went after the chickens. But the chickens high-stepped across the matted grass as if the flames of hell were licking at their tail feathers. Don Oscar moved after them as if he was up to his knees in cow shit, wading instead of walking. And Boomer, who knew Don Oscar's sour-mash scent, brayed to beat the band, sounding so deeply that Chester's papery eardrums rattled.

Chester stepped forward, knocking over the jar of moonshine that rested between his boots. He hoped Don Oscar had brought some more along, as payback for coming over and scaring the death out of a fellow. Chester stopped at the edge of the porch, leaning on the locust railing as he called out. "Don Oscar, what are you stirring up the livestock for?"

Don Oscar turned at the sound of the voice, awkwardly but fluidly, and Chester got his first good look at his old friend. His friend was in there somewhere, because the wide bald head was still shining and the round cheeks were swollen with a shit-eating grin. But the eyes were all wrong.

The eyes were too deep and bright and green and empty.

Boomer bounded off the porch, limping a little, and closed on Don Oscar. Boomer's hackles were up and his tail was low to the ground as he crouched to attack. Chester knew that Boomer was getting the same uneasy signal that Chester was getting, only the hound's instinct was truer. And the signal was that Don Oscar had *turned,* changed from a goofy bootlegger into something contrary.

"Chesh-sher, it's *shu-shaaa*," the turned bootlegger said, but the words were all slobbery, as if Don Oscar's mouth was a mush of rotten persimmons.

Whatever the change was, it didn't look so wonderful to Chester. "What in hell happened to *you?*"

"Shu-shaaa," Don Oscar said, spreading his soggy arms wide.

Don Oscar was always going on about science, especially when it came to brewing shine. But it looked to Chester like science had fucked up good this time.

Boomer growled again and leaped at Don Oscar's trousers. The hound's teeth locked and he worried at the corduroy fabric, twisting his dense furrowed head back and forth. Don Oscar lowered his arms and knelt, embracing the old hound. Boomer jerked his head back, a patch of cloth and dripping, pulpy meat clenched between his jaws. The stuff that dribbled like blood from Don Oscar's wound was the color of antifreeze.

Don Oscar lifted Boomer's face to his and throated the

dog's snout. Don Oscar's eyes brightened, as if he was stealing Boomer's breath to recharge his own batteries. Then Don Oscar let the dog loll heavily to the ground. The hound lay still in the dirt, bits of straw and leaves stuck to his fur.

Chester was about to go for his gun. The thirty-caliber was hanging on two wooden pegs in the living room, and a loaded shotgun leaned in the corner. But Don Oscar moved closer to the door, and even as slowly as the monstrous form was moving, Chester didn't want to risk touching those starchy, rubbery arms or getting anywhere near the bad wind of Don Oscar's rotten breath.

Chester ducked under the railing and ran helter-skelter to the fallen feed shed, then doubled back to the barn, his heart aching like a fist clenched around a razor blade. He opened the door to the corncrib, wishing he'd taken the trouble to oil the hinges sometime during the last twenty years. But he never figured a squeak would be a matter of life or death.

He wrestled his way underneath some dangling scraps of rotten harness. Bars of light spilled between gaps in the plank siding. The dust of dead corn husks spiraled in the sharp sunbeams, and Chester was afraid he was going to sneeze.

He held his breath, wiggled his nose, and strained his ears. He heard leather rustling against chestnut, bridle straps still swinging from his passage. Rats scurried in the bowels of the corncrib, their dinner disturbed. The tin roof rattled and popped as the metal contracted against the cooler evening air. Chester heard none of the watery sounds like the ones Don Oscar had made as he walked.

Chester climbed the rickety stairs to the hayloft and closed the trapdoor. The door had no latch, so Chester nudged an old gray hay bale over it. He fell into a pile of loose hay, his bones aching from the effort. Then he tried to gather his breath, though his lungs felt as ragged as his long-john shirt.

That was when Boomer barked.

Good boy, Chester thought. *Now you can show that deformed bastard who's boss in this neck of the woods.*

Boomer barked again, only this time it was more of a marshy, slushy yelp. The bark bore too much resemblance to the way Don Oscar had talked. Chester crawled across the floor, his bony knees catching on nail heads and splinters. He looked through the siding at the farmyard below.

Boomer still looked like Boomer, only his eyes were green now. The damp dot of a nose lifted into the air and quivered, and Chester hoped Boomer's sense of smell had gone to hell along with his vision, or else the hound might seek out his loving master. Don Oscar must have gone around the house, because Chester could hear chickens squawking in the backyard. Then Boomer dropped his tail and headed into the dusky forest, the way he did when he was going out to roust night owls and raccoons.

Chester waited as the sun slid down like dying hope. He felt naked and vulnerable and his throat was clogged with straw chaff. He would have traded his soul for his rifle and a quart of corn liquor. He was debating making a run for the farmhouse when Boomer padded back across the yard and climbed onto the porch, his ears drooping toward the ground. The dog's toenails clicked on the pine planks as he disappeared through the open farmhouse door. Another hour passed before Chester saw the headlights.

DeWalt stepped out of his Nissan Pathfinder. His headlights had flashed across the gray murk of the porch as he drove up, and he expected Chester to be waiting there, rocking back and forth with Boomer at his feet. The evening was a little cool from the rain, and he knew Chester cherished the fresh air almost as much as he did his moonshine.

No lights were on in the house. The natural kind of moonshine was flooding the tiny valley where the farmhouse rested. DeWalt looked up at the rising moon that was nearly full, with just a dull sliver shaved off of one side. A couple of stars pricked the darkening sky.

He drew in a breath through his nose, inhaling air heavy with the scent of spruce and balsam and pennyroyal and springwater. A few hens clucked quietly, the only sound in the valley besides the breeze that whistled through the gap in the barn doors.

In the moonlight, DeWalt could see the rest of the Mull farm, where it veered up the slope of Bear Claw. The farm was surrounded by Antler Ridge and Wellborn Mountain as well, with the lesser mountains huddling in shadows at their feet. DeWalt took in the view that stretched for miles in every direction. He saw the dark bulge of Fool's Knob, black against the dusk.

Then he cussed under his breath. The monolithic outline of the condominiums that rose from Sugarfoot blighted the vista. The distant building's bright orange lights twinkled in the atmospheric distortion. Floodlights lined the weaving course of the ski slope like white stitches in the belly of a beast.

Why didn't you join that Ridge Law committee that was trying to block the construction?

It's not my battle, Mr. Chairman. Nor is it any business of the Royal Order of the Bleeding Hearts.

And just what is your battle, Loyal Lodge Brother?

Removing the itch from my balls, sir.

Scratch on, Oh Brother.

Part of what bugged DeWalt was the thought that it might have been some of his own money that had built the monstrosity. He didn't keep up with where his brokers made their investments, and he knew they handled North Carolina real estate. He couldn't deny that he'd raped a little land in California during his salad days. Even knocked over a few redwoods.

Is that what this is about, Brother? "Guilt" with a capitalistic "G"?

Maybe a little, Mr. Chairman.

I believe I speak for the entire lodge when I say this, Oh Brother: My heart just BLEEDS for you. Now, back to your balls.

DeWalt stepped onto the warped planks of the porch steps. The eyes of the nail heads glared darkly at him. The boards creaked under his weight like old bones.

"Chester?" he called, his voice like a scythe in the hush. No answer. Why had the drunken old fool called and invited him over, anyway? He'd said something about trees falling down, and a green light up on the ridge, then hung up right in the middle of a sentence as if he'd left something burning on the stove.

Maybe Chester hung up because he knew that a bleeding heart always came when summoned. It wasn't like DeWalt had a full calendar or anything. Or maybe Chester just needed a city-slicker California-Yankee liberal to make fun of.

DeWalt crossed the porch, the toe of one of his boots slipping into a gap between the boards. In the fuzzy light of the moon, he saw that the front door was open, its brass knob glinting from a stray moonbeam. The living room was black, as dark as the storm clouds in DeWalt's troubled head.

He jumped at a snapping sound behind him, then realized it was coming from the woods. A tree fell in the darkness near the ridge line. DeWalt wondered if that was what Chester had been talking about on the phone. Maybe Chester hadn't hung up on him, maybe the line had been broken by a falling tree. But why didn't the old coot answer him now?

He wondered if Chester had suffered a heart attack. The old man had to be nearly seventy, and he wasn't exactly a follower of any New Age health regimens. More likely, he had passed out with the lights off and was snoring on the couch with one wrinkled hand tucked into the crotch of his overalls, dreaming of the days when his equipment still functioned.

Then why is the door open, Oh Brother?

Let's go in and see, Mr. Chairman.

After you.

DeWalt pushed the sagging screen door open and stepped into the darkness.

Emerland, the developer, gazed through the dark glass at the silhouettes of the mountains. A few lights twinkled, orange and green and blue and yellow, across the sparsely populated slopes. The denser brightness of Windshake pocked a small glen between the bases of Antler Ridge and Bear Claw. It was the clean glow of civilization, a jewel in a dull crown, the kind of gift that Emerland wanted to give the region.

Wilderness was too tame and ordinary, nature was too natural. God or the elements had carved that granite outcropping over there on Antler Ridge, the outcropping that resembled stag horns. But God or physics had spent billions of years on that little piece of accidental art. Give Emerland two years, a fleet of bulldozers, and a truckload of dynamite, and he could build not only the horns, but the rest of the stag as well.

Emerland pressed his nose against the cool window. The view was exquisite, worth every cent of the half million these top-floor condominiums sold for. Emerland had saved this suite for himself, making it his field office and second home, what he liked to call his "war room."

His eyes roamed the upper slopes of Bear Claw. He didn't see any lights. He hoped he'd be able to pinpoint the location of the Mull farm, to get a bearing on his next opponent. Maybe there, where that cut in the ridge was, in the black wedge of valley surrounded by trees.

The trees would all be coming down soon. Emerland savored his pending victory. He rubbed his palms together and noticed they were moist.

The phone rang and he picked it up. "What?"

It was his assistant. "Mr. Emerland, I went to the Register of Deeds office today like you wanted, and you'll never guess what I discovered."

Emerland never guessed at anything. He waited.

"Sir, Chester Mull owns the entire peak of Bear Claw and most of the south slope. He's the sole surviving heir of the original Mulls who settled here. But the bad news is, there are at least two dozen relatives who can lay claim to the land if he dies."

"That means I can't let him die. What else?"

"He sold twenty acres to Herbert DeWalt about three years ago. That's *the* Herbert DeWalt."

"Damn. I knew money talked. DeWalt must be up to something, trying to make a comeback in real estate."

"Sir, I've uncovered no other attempts by DeWalt to purchase more land in the area."

"That bastard's slicker than an oil rig. Probably put together some dummy corporations to do the purchasing."

"Believe it or not, DeWalt actually lives here. Built a cabin and everything."

"You sure it's not just a summer home?"

"Year-round."

"Damn. I wondered what had happened to him." Emerland looked at his Rolex. Nearly midnight. He had a big day tomorrow.

"Apparently he's laying low, in some kind of retirement," came the tinny voice from the earpiece.

"Who else holds land over there?"

"A few Moodys, Painters, Oswigs, McFalls. Mostly old mountain families. Apparently nobody's laid the hard sell on them yet. One of the Oswigs is a realtor."

"They're just the minnows. First, I've got to land the big fish."

"Did Mull talk to you when you phoned?"

"He just said 'who?' a couple of times. Bastard's never heard of me. At least that means he hasn't been bombarded with anti-development propaganda. Then he said he wasn't interested and hung up. *Hung up* on me."

Emerland clenched his hand around the phone at the memory, feeling the veins swell in his neck.

Then his assistant spoke again. "What's the next move?"

"I'm driving out there tomorrow. I'm going to talk turkey, and Mull's going to go 'gobble.'"

The assistant laughed from the other end of the phone.

"And DeWalt's going to shit a brick when I gouge a ski slope across his backyard," Emerland said. "Then he's going to shit a brick shithouse when he finds out he was one of the silent investors that made it all possible."

The assistant laughed again. Emerland looked out the window at the mountains. *His* mountains. It wasn't about money. Hell, everybody had money. It was about making a mark. "I'd better get to bed. The early bird and all that happy shit."

"Good night, sir."

Emerland hung up without responding.

Chapter Sixteen

DeWalt stepped into the dark living room of the Mull farmhouse, blinking as his pupils expanded. The room smelled of animal hair and gunpowder, wood smoke and corn husks. DeWalt slid the soles of his boots across the uneven plank floor, probing for obstructions. He knew from previous visits that an old horsehair settee lurked somewhere underfoot, and in the middle of the room stood a walnut highboy that would fetch ten grand in a New York antique shop.

"Chester," he called. Dust stirred from the air draft of his voice.

A door creaked upstairs. He ran his hand along the walls. Chester had nailed linoleum sheets over the siding in an attempt to cover the cracks in the walls. The house had been built before insulation had become common. DeWalt was surprised that a fire wasn't burning in the potbellied stove.

DeWalt walked to the end of the room, using the wall to guide him to the stairs. His fingertips glided over the smooth surface of a mirror, then over the splintery, rough-cut window frame. The window had been boarded over, so the light of the moon didn't penetrate. He passed the window and bumped his head on an outcrop of wooden coat pegs.

Then his boot thumped into the hollow riser of the stairs.

He'd never been up to the second floor. A piece of fabric hung in front of him and he brushed it aside like a cobweb. Running his hand along the wall, he found a light switch. He flipped it once, then again. Nothing.

It was even darker in the narrow stairwell. He strained his eyes at the murk above him. Something shuffled in the shadows.

"Chester?" He wished he had brought a flashlight.

Some pioneer you are, Oh Lodge Brother.

I'm concerned, Mr. Chairman.

To what do you attribute your accelerated pulse and the faint quiver of your limbs?

The unknown.

Brother, all is unknown. Except for your overly familiar testicular organs.

Sir, I object. No need to get personal.

The first tenet of the Royal Order of the Bleeding Hearts charter is "Know thyself." Perhaps that scares you more than anything else.

Mr. Chairman, pardon me, but I've had enough of your Flower Power sloganeering and half-baked solipsism.

Brother, do I detect mutiny in the ranks?

Walk with me, Mr. Chairman. I dare you.

DeWalt headed up the stairs, staggering on the narrow runners, his arms pressing against the walls for balance. The air was cooler up here, and he felt a draft as he stepped into the room. A shard of light cut between the curtains like a silver sword blade. The room, apparently Chester's bedroom, took up the entire floor. The moon glinted off the green brass of a bed railing.

He moved to the bed, checking among the ragged quilts for Chester's parchment-covered bones. He uncovered nothing but the vinegary odor of stale sweat and piss dribbles. He was about to go downstairs when he heard a shuffling under the bed.

That wasn't a dust bunny, Oh Lodge Brother.

Shall we investigate, Mr. Chairman?

It's your mutiny.

DeWalt stooped, one of his knees popping. He put one hand on the metal bed frame, a stray mattress spring digging into the back of his wrist. He tilted his head so his eyes could collect enough light to see. He heard another shuffle and saw a thin dark rope quivering on the floor.

The rope moved toward him, and he saw the shadowy body attached to it. Boomer. Chester's droopy-eared best friend and resident methane factory. The dog turned to him, and DeWalt saw a moist glistening dot that must have been the dog's nose.

DeWalt wondered why the mangy beast hadn't barked upon his arrival. The dog knew his smell, and surely Boomer had heard the Pathfinder driving up. This was a hound dog, for Christ's sake.

Chester usually took Boomer everywhere he went. Even in the truck, Chester would be behind the wheel and Boomer riding gassy shotgun, the worn pads of his paws splayed on the dashboard. But Chester's truck was out in the yard, so Boomer's master wasn't out for a solo spin.

"Here, boy," said DeWalt in a soothing voice.

Boomer wiggled on his belly, working the joints of his legs. DeWalt could hear the bones knocking on the pine floor as the hound scooted toward him.

"That's a good Boomer," he said. He was about to reach out and stroke the dog when it lifted its heavy wrinkled head out of the shadows.

DeWalt jumped back as if electrified.

The thing on the dog's shoulders couldn't rightly be called a head. It was more like an inverted boot, with a long, dry, leathery tongue dangling toward the dusty floor. An eye shone on each side of the face like a radioactive green pea. The moistness DeWalt had seen was a blowhole that gaped in the slope of the skullbone like a Venus's-flytrap, opening and closing with a faint, marshy sigh.

The eyes lit up like twinkling Christmas lights, a limey neon decoration for a nightmare. Ears—*no, cactus bulbs,* DeWalt's horrified mind screamed—pinned themselves back as the head tilted toward him.

DeWalt processed all this insane information in a heartbeat, but it was a long heartbeat, because his aortic chamber had frozen in fear. When his lungs resumed hammering oxygen into his bloodstream, he backed toward the stairs.

The thing that had been Boomer crawled to the center of the room, its flytrap orifice gurgling. The creature had no fur, only bristles that flexed as the body stubbed toward DeWalt. Worst of all was the snakeroot of a tail thumping the floor, as if the mutated Boomer still wanted human affection.

DeWalt half fell, half ran down the stairs, hurtling forward with his arms crossed in front of him. He stumbled through the living room, imagining that the clutter around his ankles was creeping myrtle vines and the table edge at his knee was a birch branch. A dry crash filled the farmhouse as the highboy toppled, and then DeWalt was at the screen door, flailing through the mesh. He scooted into the Pathfinder and was turning the key when he saw a dark form coming around the barn.

The figure moved with a shambling gait, the way Chester did when the old fool was on a three-day drunk. DeWalt opened his door and got out, leaving the engine running.

"Chester, what in God's name happened to Boomer?" DeWalt said, surprised that his vocal cords found room to vibrate in his tight throat. The figure shuffled closer, and DeWalt could smell him now. Chester had never been a chronic bather, but even *he* knew enough to at least stand in a rainstorm once in a while and let the worst odors wash away.

DeWalt was about to call out again when he saw the eyes. Neon eyes that he shouldn't have been able to see from twenty feet away. The figure lifted its arms. "*Shu-shaaa,*" it said.

DeWalt spun, slipped in a pile of Boomer's excrement, then got up and dashed to his vehicle.

The Pathfinder cut twin dark curves in the grass as DeWalt sped away before the figure by the barn could shuffle out of the shadows and fully into the moonlight. DeWalt didn't *want* to see it. His imagination was painting mad enough nightmares without any more help from reality, and the Lodge Brothers in his head were, for the first time in years, speechless.

"Working late tonight?"

Nettie jumped. Preacher Blevins had crept up behind her without her hearing. She thought he had left hours ago.

Her heartbeat pulsed against her eardrums. The preacher always moved with meek, reverent steps, as if noise brought chaos to the House of God. Still, he could have at least knocked on the vestry door.

"Oh, I didn't startle you, did I?" he said, the filament of his smile beaming from the lower portion of his pale light-bulb head.

She put a hand to her chest in exaggerated fear. "I thought it was the devil himself."

"The devil will never touch one as pure as you," the preacher said, resting a hand on her shoulder. He bent over her, his necktie curling out and brushing her hair as he looked at the papers covering her desk. "I was watching television over in the rectory when I looked out the window and saw the lights on. What's so important that it's got you working this late?"

"Just these figures I was telling you about. I can't make sense of them."

"Oh, the money. You shouldn't worry your pretty head about a few missing dollars. I'm sure the Lord's put them right where He wants them."

Nettie could smell tuna and onions on his breath. She

said, not turning because his face was so close she would have had to bend her neck away, "Well, since you're here, maybe you can have a look. See here, in the column marked 'Miscellaneous Charities'—"

She ran a finger down a row of numbers. "I've been through the entries covering the past two years, but almost every entry is incorrect; for example, last June twelfth we have a donation of $1,000 recorded to Windshake Nursing Home's ministry fund. But I was a volunteer there, and I remember the gift being $500. I know because I ordered hymnals and paid to have the piano tuned."

Preacher Blevins nodded gravely, his smooth light-bulb features furrowing.

"And here," Nettie said. "September twenty-third. A $350 withdrawal to pay the Baptist Convention. I checked with their office, and membership dues are only $200."

He peered over her shoulder, and Nettie was struck with the notion that he was sniffing her hair. Then he straightened up and crossed his arms. "I'm sure there were administrative fees and that sort of thing. And a lot of that money is earmarked for little things, like helping out widows and buying refreshments for church socials. It's hard to keep track of every little dollar. And it all comes out in the wash, anyway. The bottom line is that we're a growing enterprise. It's the Lord's will for us to flourish and share the church's blessings."

Nettie's head itched, as if the preacher's breath had deposited nits and fleas in her hair. She turned and looked up at him.

The preacher spread his hands in supplication. "I used to do the books before we hired you. I'm not too good with numbers. The Lord didn't bless me that way. I'm sure I made some errors along the way. But as it's written in St. Matthews, 'When thou dost give alms, let not thy left hand know what thy right hand doeth, that thy alms may be in secret, and thy Father who seeth in secret will repay thee.'"

"But so much is unaccounted for."

"Worry not, my child. I'm sure you'll get everything straightened out." He lowered his eyes. "Well, I believe I'd better go say my prayers and get some sleep. Might have a big congregation this weekend, what with Blossomfest and all, plus Easter's coming up."

He yawned and tilted his head back, his pungent exhalation rising beneath his beaver teeth.

"Preacher, can I ask you something?"

"Certainly, honey."

"When I got hired as church secretary, whose decision was that? I mean, was it the Board of Deacons's?" She prayed that Bill hadn't been involved.

"Well, they made recommendations, but the decision was entirely mine."

Nettie sagged in relief.

The preacher must have noticed. "Why do you ask?"

"Just curious, is all."

The preacher stepped toward her, hovering, and put his hand on her shoulder and gave it another squeeze. "I think I made a good decision, don't you?" he asked, and again he lowered his eyes.

Nettie felt them roving over her skin as if they were tongues. *No,* she told herself, *that's just your imagination.*

She had been working too long, that's all, stooped over the church accounts until her guts were tied in knots. All this needless worry had put her on edge.

"Good night, Nettie," Preacher Blevins said, giving her a final pat on the head. "Lock up when you leave."

Nettie nodded at his flashing light-bulb smile and began clearing her desk. "See you tomorrow, Preacher."

"May God keep you and watch over your sleep, my precious child."

"Thank you. Same to you."

She listened for his footsteps as he left, but he was as silent as a mouse, as if he were walking on air. After a couple of minutes tucking papers in drawers, she switched off the light and headed into the worship hall.

A dark church is kind of spooky. She stepped under the hushed arches and walked down the aisle.

Goddamn.
Forgive me, Father.
Goddamn.
Forgive me, Father.
Goddamn.
Forgive me, Father.

Armfield leaned against the cold marble monument, his pants unbuckled.

I could have had her tonight, he thought. *I saw it in her eyes, Lord. I saw how she wanted to reach out for the forbidden fruit. She must be the devil, a Sodomite. Because You've said all along that Satan would wear the gowns of angels.*

But You never warned me what would be UNDER the gown. Talk to me, Lord. Give me a sign. You've forgiven me my avarice. You've overlooked my sins because of the greater good that I serve. I have delivered many souls unto you. I have trumpeted Your glory before the people. But now you repay me with a last temptation.

Armfield looked around the graveyard, at the white stones that jutted from the ground like frozen ghosts. The remains of those who had gone before, who were now home in the Kingdom. Who might be looking down from on high, watching him humiliate himself.

The church door opened and Nettie stepped out. Nettie, the small, curvaceous Delilah who had driven him to this wicked frenzy. The bow-lipped little whore whose cotton dress swirled as she walked. Who should be taking his seed, instead of him spilling it on the ground like the hapless Onan.

He watched as she passed under the streetlight and got

into her car. He ducked behind the monument as her head-lights swept over the graveyard. His fingers returned to that sinful spot. He fixed Nettie's image in his mind, but the image of the crucified Christ kept superimposing itself.

"Thy will be done," he gasped, gripping the monument's cross as the devil took his hand.

Chapter Seventeen

James Wallace shouldn't have had that third beer down at the Hayloft Tavern. In fact, he shouldn't have gone there at all. The blue jeans, cowboy hats, and flannel shirts should have tipped him off, plus the name of the place wasn't exactly a drawing card for the yuppie generation. And he could have picked up a clue from the band that was playing at one end of the huge old barn. "Big Willie and the Half-Watts." *Yee-haw*.

But driving by, he'd seen that big-screen TV through the window, and March Madness was in full swing. He liked to watch the tournament even if the teams playing were Fleaspeck Valley State and Bumfield Tech.

The people had been nice enough at first. The bartender, who resembled Festus from the old "Gunsmoke" show, had taken his money without drawing back his hand from the contact. Not a single overt response to James's skin. Probably a few remarks slithered from the corner booths, but midway through the second beer, the edges of his awareness had tunneled considerably, and about the only white eye that bothered him was Dick Vitale's glass one.

Then the girl had talked to him. She was two stools away, but that was close enough to make James uncomfortable. He could almost hear the rustle of the nooses tightening behind him.

"You like basketball?" the redhead said, turning and smiling at him.

"Yeah. I'm a Georgetown fan. Got my degree there."

His tongue felt a little thick. Still, it was pleasant just to talk to someone. Aunt Mayzie was good company, but she sometimes got tired of having him around. Besides, this was different. A lot different.

"Georgetown, huh? That's a tough school. I go to Westridge myself."

"I've heard that's a good school. Pretty long drive, isn't it?"

"I live up here, so it's cheaper than moving down to Barkersville or staying in a dorm."

"What do you study?" James took another sip from his heavy mug of beer.

"I'm a psych major."

James nodded. *Psychology, huh? She might have all kinds of games going on. Maybe this was some kind of black-white social experiment.*

"I'm in library sciences myself," he said, licking the beer foam from his upper lip. "Used to work at the Smithsonian."

"Wow. That's a really cool place. I went there on a class trip a few years back. If you don't mind me asking," she said, rolling her blue eyes to indicate the town outside, "What brought you to Windshake? I mean, it's not exactly a happening place."

"My aunt lives here. I'm keeping her company until her health improves." *Or until she dies, whichever comes first.*

"Isn't that sweet?" the redhead said, smiling again. "I've seen you around town. I mean, it's not like you don't stand out or anything."

James dipped his head and waited. *We don't like darkies 'round these parts. Spooks belong in the graveyard. Coons are fer huntin'.*

"I thought you'd be an interesting person to talk to," she said.

What kind of a lily-white liberal was she? Takin' pity on the po' old suppressed African-American. That's NIGGER to you, ma'am. James stared into his beer at the salamander eyes of foam.

"Well, am I right?" she said.

"I'm just a regular guy." James shrugged, then let his shrug continue into a hunch, as if he could duck his head into his shirt like a turtle.

The redhead moved to the stool next to his. James felt the white eyes crawl out of the rough-cut woodwork. *Fuck them,* James decided. *It wasn't against the law for him to talk, even to a local white girl.*

"My name's Sarah. What's yours?"

"James."

"Look, I'm not on the make or anything. I like to dance. And I get tired of the same old guys around here. All they want to talk about is bow hunting and tractor pulls and big tires."

At last James smiled, a slightly beery grin that was warm and relaxed. And he had to admit it felt damn good. He hadn't smiled in a coon's age, to coin a local phrase. "At least you're up-front. Can I buy you a beer?"

"I'm underage, plus my Daddy's the preacher at Windshake Baptist. He doesn't even approve of me dancing. But thanks, anyway."

Holy hell. He was messing around with a *preacher's* daughter. He could practically hear the gasoline splashing onto the wooden crosses. Still, she was pretty cute. Her company was worth a little risk.

They talked and watched the game and James learned that Sarah wanted to move to Oregon after graduation. And though she had been raised a Baptist, she had started hanging around with a Ba'hai group on campus and thought they had some good ideas. World unity and all that. Brotherhood of man. Sisterhood of woman. Peoplehood of people. Sounded pretty hip to James.

But then she asked him to dance.

James looked at the stage at the far end of the converted barn. Hay bales propped up the amplifiers and Big Willie was twanging on a jaw harp. A fat boy who looked like that old Shoney's restaurant statue was thumping a stand-up bass, and the other Half-Watts were sawing on fiddles and plucking banjoes. A group of middle-aged cowboys and cowgirls were galloping around in a square dance, hoeing on down like there was no tomorrow.

He could dance with a white girl. Sure, and he could even do that "change-yer-partner" bit and get belly to belly with a buckskinned belle. But he was positive the next dance would be a dozen white men doing the Tennessee Two-Step across his hide.

"No, thank you," he said. "Contrary to stereotype, not all blacks are good dancers."

The corners of her mouth sagged in disappointment. She talked a few minutes more and then mumbled that she had classes tomorrow and better be getting home. He watched her leave, and the tension died in the bar as if the power had been cut.

James had been so nervous talking to Sarah that he couldn't resist that extra beer. So there was no way in hell he was going to slide behind the seat of his Accord and drive through the tight streets of Windshake, where white cops blossomed like popcorn whenever James was at the wheel. Nothing to do but hoof it the eight or ten blocks home.

He didn't like walking the streets of Windshake at night. His fuzzy brain conjured voices from stale old radio dramas.

Who knew what evil lurked in the brick alleys and shadows of Windshake? Probably redneck evil. Yokel vampires with buck fangs and Oshkoshbegosh overalls.

He walked with his head down, not that there were many white eyes to avoid at this hour. He passed Luther's Hardware, glancing into the window at the wheelbarrows and bird-houses, and noticed that there was a special on snow shovels. Then he turned the corner onto the darkened back street. It looked kind of spooky at night, with the ragged awnings hanging over like big hands and the fence-top shadows resembling black teeth. Broken glass glittered under the street-light like tiny hungry eyes in a dark forest. A loose piece of guttering flapped in the night breeze.

He wished he had talked to Sarah longer. She was really nice, and gorgeous to boot. He wasn't sure how he felt about interracial dating, though it might be time to find out. But maybe she was just being kind. She hadn't given him a phone number or anything to indicate any real interest. The summery aroma of her perfume wisped across his nostrils in memory, but the back street odors of rotten asphalt and spilled kerosene drove it away.

James climbed onto the abandoned railroad track and headed home. He stretched his legs to keep rhythm to the spacing of the creosote timbers that passed under his feet. Then he tried to walk on the rail, but his coordination was too impaired. He was passing the rusty, corrugated water tower when he heard a sound in the dark gridwork underneath it.

Stray mutt? James took a step, his sneaker sending a chunk of gravel skipping down the tracks. The noise came again, louder. A rasping, wheezing sound.

He wouldn't look. He told himself to keep the old head down, submissive-like.

Somebody stepped out of the shadows. At first, James thought it might be one of the rednecks from the Hayloft Tavern, come to share a little two-fisted Southern hospitality with him.

But whoever it was staggered like a bum on a sterno binge. Only, Windshake didn't have any homeless that he'd ever seen.

James aimed his foot for the next cross tie, but came up

short because his eyes had shifted toward the person in the shadows. He stumbled and nearly fell down the gravel bank. One of his feet had lodged under a track coupling.

Fucker's got one of those glo-tubes, like they sell in the dime stores at Halloween, James thought. *No, TWO of them.*

The person wobbled out of the shadows.

A good Southern boy, all right. Regulation-wear Levi's and ball cap. And he's coming this way.

Only his goddamned legs aren't moving.

The man oozed into the streetlight, and James saw that the glo-tubes were eyes stuck inside the lump on the man's shoulder's. Only now he could see that it definitely wasn't a *man.*

Glistening ropes clung to the thing like poison sumac, slick and fuzzy. The thing moved like a slug, the lower part of it leaving a trail of mucus. The tall weeds wilted under its passage.

The wheezing sound was coming from the thing's shoulder-lump. A gummy flap opened, and James looked with fascinated horror into the fluorescent green throat. Tonsils dripping with foul nectar wiggled in the back of the dark opening. Gray thorns rimmed the edge of the flap and it clamped shut with a sigh of longing.

No. James, you are not making this up. Four beers doesn't make you hallucinate. A HUNDRED beers couldn't summon this out of your imagination.

James was frozen, his synapses hot-wiring his reflexes, beaming an urgent message through the hellish insanity that his visual perception had cursed him with. The message was: *haul ass and don't spare the gas.*

Except his foot was caught in the godforsaken railroad trestle, hooked in a hollow place in the timber where a coupling joined two rails. He almost snapped his ankle trying to lurch away.

The thing slugged closer, its arms jutting ahead like gnarled tree branches, pungent foliage pluming from their tips. While James worked to free his foot, he got a close look at the thing's head. Closer than he wanted, close enough to guarantee him a lifetime's supply of nightmares. If he even had a lifetime left.

He could see the gill-like ridges in the thing's throat as the thorny flap opened again. Inside was a pulpy mass that looked like a cow's well-chewed cud. Then the flap worked again, and swampy steam rose from the mouth. Worst of all was the Red Man cap perched atop the bristled lump, because it made the horror all too human.

The thing was oozing noise, spraying sibilants into the night air like the blowholes on those whales James had seen on The Discovery Channel. Only this thing was trying to form syllables.

James knelt, tugging at his foot, feeling the skin scrape from his ankle as he twisted. Gravel dug into his flesh, but he barely noticed the pain.

"Shu-shaaa . . ."

The fucker is not talking to me, James told himself. *Please, Lord, don't let it be talking to me.*

And it now was close enough that James could smell its tainted raspberry breath, an acrid minty fog, as if the husband-murdering Blanche Taylor Moore had made a batch of herbal tea. Suddenly his foot came free from his shoe and he rolled over, then was hobbling down the tracks, one white sock flopping in the darkness. He dared a look back to make sure the vegetative nightmare wasn't gaining on him. The thing wasn't fast, but it sure as hell looked *determined.*

The thing in the Red Man cap misted a final plaintive call after him, like a child left all alone on a playground.

"Shu-shaaa . . ."

You saw it, too, Mr. Chairman.

That was definitely the result of your Haight-Ashbury vacation in '67, Oh Lodge Brother. And '68. And '69. The ghost of lysergic acid past coming back to haunt you.

What the hell did *you* see, Herbert Webster Fucking DeWalt the Third? Lucy in the kennel with cauliflower?

Flashbacks, Oh Brother. First the green rain, now the incredible vegetable dog. I didn't see anything THAT vivid when I flashed the first time. Bum trip, man.

But it was Boomer, wasn't it? He even oozed an oily fart, just like the real article.

"All is but a dream within a dream," Oh Brother.

Mr. Chairman, enough of your cosmic horse manure. It's not a dream when you can feel pain.

DeWalt held the match to his thumb before moving the flame to his pipe. He smelled the acrid stench of his burnt flesh. So he wasn't dreaming. His hand shook as he lit the pipe. He drew in a gasp of smoke, comforted by the stirring in his lungs.

He had nearly sprung the shocks on the Pathfinder bouncing over the old logging roads on his way home. If he had been more sure of his sanity, he would have punched in some numbers on his cellular phone and bleated incoherent alarms to the outside world. But he decided he'd better be certain of the inside world first.

And now the Chairman of the Royal Order of the Bleeding Hearts was giving him a hard time, as if time wasn't hard enough as it was.

DeWalt had bolted the cabin door and now huddled in his chair with the lights off. He strained his ears against the night, hearing only the rush of the stream and the fingers of windswept branches clawing across the cedar shake shingles. Suddenly, he wished he'd cleared the trees from the perimeter of the yard.

Because he had the feeling that the trees wanted *in.*

Ah, hands on the testicles, Oh Brother?

This is no ordinary case of the male itch, Mr. Chairman. This is the fucking heartbreak of psoriasis.

Brother, are you going to cower in ignorance, or seek the truth?

Shove the truth up your rump, Mr. Chairman. Because the truth means that animals are mutating into flora and fauna. The truth means that Chester has screwed-up eyes, and I'm not talking Bette Davis eyes or even Marty Feldman eyes. I'm talking neon-green twin-laser light shows. And, remember, my eyes don't lie.

The truth is bitter medicine, but one must swallow so the healing may begin.

The only thing I want to swallow is a dose of Quaaludes. Nothing like a basket of stumble biscuits to make the nightmares go away.

You can't escape that easily, Oh Brother. The truth has a way of finding you, no matter where you hide.

As long as the light of truth isn't neon. Now, pardon me, Mr. Chairman. I have an appointment with my itching balls.

"Police Department."

"Listen, I want to report . . ." What the hell *did* James want to report?

"Yes, sir?"

"Uh—downtown, I saw . . . I was nearly attacked."

"In Windshake?"

"Yeah. On the back street, behind the hardware store."

"ID the perp?"

"What's that?"

"Identification. Did you see the perpetrator's face?"

Oh, yes. Unfortunately, I got up close and personal. "Yes, Officer, only . . . I'm not sure what it was."

"Sir, have you been drinking? You're starting to slur a little."

"I'm fine. Listen, could you just take a look?" *Because I need to know that I'm not losing my mind.*

"We have an officer on patrol. I'll give him a call."

"Thank you." *And you, too, sweet Lord.*

"Do you want to come down to the station and file charges?"

Wasn't there something in the U.S. Constitution about the criminal getting to face his accuser? "No, I'm okay. I just thought you might want to check it out."

"You were *nearly* attacked, you say? It's not against the law for someone to be out at night, I'm afraid."

Oh, Officer, this thing was definitely breaking some laws. Maybe not the laws of humankind, but certainly the laws of nature. "Well, just check it out, okay?"

"I need your name for my report."

James hung up. The sweat from his frantic run had dried but the fear still clung like salt. Fortunately, Aunt Mayzie had already been asleep when he got home. At least he didn't have to offer her any explanations of things he didn't understand himself.

James checked the locks on the doors and windows and went to bed. He left his light on, trying not to think of all the raw vegetables he had eaten in his life. He fell into a restless sleep praying for Aunt Mayzie, hoping that heaven's gate didn't have a sign posted that said "No coloreds allowed." Because if the world was ending, she'd have a hard time hobbling through the stampede to get a place before the throne.

The alien felt the mist of its spores scatter in the night. A tingle of air pressure altered its surface chemistry, took shape, and imprinted sound vibration on the creature's skin. The symbol throbbed against its heart-brain, causing a disturbance in the pacific state of healing.

May-zee.

The creature analyzed the symbol and compared it to the "shu-shaaa." No connection. No pattern. No hint of higher intelligence.

The creature fed and rested.

Chapter Eighteen

"What do you make of it?"

"I ain't touching it."

"Looks like some kind of jelly to me," Chief Crosley said. "When did you find it?"

"This morning. Dispatch got a call last night, some drunk said he was nearly attacked back here." Arnie McFall ran his sleeve across the sweating bone of his forehead. The sun glinted off the car windows into his eyes. "Sent Matheson out, but Matheson didn't see nothing. I figured I'd poke around this morning, in case we had a bum hanging out back here. A bum could live in style, what with Sonny's dumpsters and all."

Crosley looked down on the milky pool of slime that even now was congealing and crusting under the warm sun. Ordinarily, he would have figured it for a chemical spill or some kind of underground leak, nothing that would hurt anybody. But it was the clothes splayed out in the middle of the foamy gom that was the mystery.

He didn't like mysteries. Mysteries were for those cop shows on TV, the kind that you watched while you put up your feet and killed a cold one or two. He didn't need any mysteries in Windshake, because he didn't have any snoopy writers or doctors or priests who could solve them like they did on TV.

"Maybe somebody just put these clothes here for a joke," Crosley said. "When I was a kid, when we went to the beach, I'd sneak off at night and make weird tracks coming up out of the surf, twisting my hands and feet and crawling on my belly. So whoever saw it in the morning would think a monster had crawled out."

"Might be shenanigans, Chief. But it looks kind of natural."

The Chief had to admit that the clothes covered the ground in the shape of an actual person. The angles of the knees and elbows were curved instead of bent like a stick figure's. Dingy white socks jutted from the cuffs of the jeans, their bottoms worn completely through. A Red Man baseball cap had rolled a few feet away, where it leaned against a rusty transaxle.

Somebody had gone to a lot of trouble for a prank. And who'd want to waste a good pair of Levi's like that?

"Looks like whoever it was came down the tracks there into these old junk cars."

"You're calling it a 'who,' Arnie. I don't like the sound of that."

"Sorry, Chief."

"I don't see no shoes nowhere."

"I've looked all over the back street. Nothing out of the ordinary. Besides *this,* I mean." Arnie pointed to the imprint.

Crosley rubbed his belly the way he always did when he was uneasy. He looked around the car lot, at the water tower and the weedy train tracks. The backs of the buildings were streaked with tarry runoff and fire escapes clung to the bricks like giant broken spiders. Traffic echoed off the storefronts from the jams of people pouring in for Blossomfest.

"You want me to scrape up a sample to send to the SBI boys down in Raleigh?" Arnie asked.

"No, let's just keep this to ourselves until we know more. Run a missing persons check and that sort of thing."

"The way this is drying out, it looks like it'll flake off in the breeze. Won't be much left soon."

Good, thought Crosley. He said, "Who called in that report last night?"

"Didn't give his name. Like I said, Dispatch thought it was a drunk."

"The Virgin Queen is going to love this," Crosley said, referring to Mayor Speerhorn by her departmental nickname. "Especially right here at Blossomfest and all. She's going to shit a silver teapot."

Crosley resumed rubbing his ample stomach.

Chester didn't see Don Oscar out in the farmyard.

It ain't Don Oscar, Chester told himself. *Let's just call it "Mushbrains" from now on.*

Because the last time Chester saw Mushbrains, about an hour ago, it was looking kind of milky and droopy, like a mushroom did after the steamy sun had worked it over. Sort of wilted from rot and turning to gooey liquid.

Yeah, like that, except this fungus thing used to be your drinking buddy.

Chester tongued his chaw and flexed his arthritic joints, grateful that the Lord had seen fit to throw down a sunny day. If it had been raining, Chester probably would have laid in the hay till the storm passed, his muscles cramped up like a pine knot. He tiptoed down the stairs, grimacing at every squeak of the dry chestnut.

He pulled the twine strap that lifted the corncrib latch from the inside. If Mushbrains was outside the door, Chester knew he was done for. He kicked open the door and bounced out onto the packed matted dirt of the barn floor, arms up like a karate fighter. Nothing stirred but a scrawny rooster that hobbled out of a stall, its red comb quivering as it swiveled its head.

Chester clung to the wall as he edged toward the barn opening. He didn't know what was safer, the cool dark shadows or the sterile exposure of daylight. He was debating a run for the farmhouse when the decision was made for him. Swampy breathing came from the far side of the barn.

He bolted across the yard, his limbs flailing like a crippled hay rake. Forty feet of fiery lung pain later, he was on the porch, kicking aside the broken screen door. He staggered into the living room, blind from sunshine, and bumped into the splintery carnage that DeWalt had strewn. He felt along the wall for his thirty-caliber, then decided on the shotgun.

He wanted whatever corpse old Mushbrains left behind to be unrecognizable.

He thumbed back the triggers, comforted by the feel of the cold steel. Mushbrains was easy meat now, if "meat" was the right word.

"Old Mushy ain't moving too swift lately," he said, his spirit soaring now that he was armed. He peered through the door, waiting for Mushbrains to slog within range. Toenails clicked on the floor behind him. He turned and saw Boomer.

Good old Boomer.

Good old Boomer, his fur now bristles, his spine bowed from the weight of whatever roiled in his bloated belly. His old stringy eyes had flowered into purple hyacinths, and the nose resembled a moldy peach. The drooping leathery tongue was veined like a maple leaf. Stinkweed thorns crowned the forehead and his grapevine tail wagged in stupid joy.

Chester jerked one trigger and his hound dog shredded like a December jack-o'-lantern. Chester wiped at his eyes, eyes that were too dry and tired to make tears. He opened a bureau drawer and filled his overall pockets with twenty-gauge shells. It was time to deal with the mushbrained monster that had pissed on his corn flakes and crammed grit in his craw.

Chester walked into the sunlight, feeling like Chuck Conners in "The Rifleman." Mushbrains sloughed toward him, leaving behind glistening clumps of itself as it closed. Chester looked into the glowing, scallop-edged eyes to make certain there was nothing of Don Oscar left inside.

The thing tried to lift its arms, limbs that were like a wet scarecrow's. The moist flap in the middle of Mushbrains's face lifted. Milky bubbles spewed into the air.

"*Shu-shaaa*," it was saying, but a fistful of number ten shot peppered into its pulpy flesh. The soggy stump of the creature remained upright, and Chester reloaded and gave it another double helping of hot pellets. Still it stood, a fungus leeched onto the earth and quivering like a windblown cornstalk.

Chester flipped out the spent shells, the acrid tang of gunpowder suffocating the scents of spring. He was sighting down the barrel again when he heard a revving engine. Somebody was coming around the bend toward the farmhouse.

DeWalt's Pathfinder came roaring out of the pines and down the red dirt road. At the same time, a loping hunk of something that might once have been a buck leaped out of the woods and cut in the path of the sport utility vehicle. The sport utility vehicle swerved, then its front left wheel dipped into a rut. The bumper glanced the deer-thing and caused an explosion of foul green fluid. The Pathfinder bounced once before going over on its side.

The fallen beast shook itself, shedding the antlers that sprouted like dead shrubs from its head. The back end of its body had disintegrated from the impact of the vehicle, but the deer-thing rose unsteadily on its front legs. Then it skittered into the woods on the other side of the road, pieces of its spongy flesh and organs dribbling out behind. Chester glanced at Mushbrains and saw that it wasn't going anywhere, so he jogged painfully up the road to the Pathfinder, his gun at his hip.

The left tires on the SUV were still spinning, trying to grab traction in the air. DeWalt crawled out of the cracked sunroof. He was halfway free when Chester reached him. DeWalt's head had a gash in it, and Chester was relieved to see that the man's California Yankee blood was red.

Chester checked the woods to make sure the deer-thing was gone. He heard some boughs snapping, but it was just another tree falling.

Funny how dropping-down-dead trees somehow seem just plain ordinary now, he thought. *I guess there's different shades of normal.*

He leveled the shotgun at DeWalt, who was still on his hands and knees, shaken by the crash.

"Let's see your eyes," Chester said.

"Let me see yours."

They looked at each other, Chester's brown rheumy eyes gazing into DeWalt's blue-ringed pupils.

"Okay, then," Chester said, leaning the shotgun against the bent hood of the SUV and stooping to help his friend. DeWalt stood with a groan.

"Anything broken?" Chester worked his chaw rapidly.

"I don't think so. Couple of dings, that's all." DeWalt touched his head and examined the blood on his fingers.

Chester nodded toward the Pathfinder. "Told you that was an uppity piece of shit. Shoulda got a Ford." Chester shot a brown stream of saliva onto the cracked windshield.

"I'm glad to see you, Chester. After last night—"

"Yeah, I know. I wondered if you had turned, too. That's why I didn't try to warn you."

"What the hell's going on?"

"I ain't rightly sure, but why don't we go up on the porch and talk about it. Can you walk okay?"

DeWalt nodded and took a step, pain creasing his face.

"Have a seat in the rocker. I'll be up in a minute. And watch out for the chickens."

"Chickens?"

"They move slow, but the little peckerheads might have caught whatever it is. Me, I got some unfinished business."

Chester walked toward the barn to finish off Mushbrains. Then he would have to put whatever was rolling around in the hog pen out of its misery. After that, he planned on rounding up his guns and twisting the cap off a smooth jar of moonshine. Times like these, a man needed to be fortified.

They were running through a jungle. Only the jungle was actual size and they were tiny, like in a *Honey, I Shrunk The Kids* movie. Rick Moranis was Robert. Huge pollen motes rolled after them like tumbleweeds, and hairy clover stems were bending down to swat at their bodies as they ran.

Ginger tripped over a pine needle and she bent to help her up and looked right into the jaws of a fallen dandelion that was a bright yellow lion. The lion opened its mouth but they ran away. Now Robert and Kevin were lost somewhere in the green-wire black-shadow twig alleys.

She heard them call, but when she tried to run with Ginger in her arms, she sank into moss. Its fingers clutched at her bones as she saw Robert and Kevin run inside a long pale hallway. The hallway unfolded like a parachute, so she followed with Ginger and then they were inside the throat of the lily.

The throat shook and vibrated, and a great roar rose from deep in the thing's belly: *SHU-SHAAAAA*.

Then the throat of the lily was closing and the kids were wallowing in amber nectar. She tried to scream but the honey-dew filled her mouth and she was suffocating—

—then she woke up on Robert's side of the bed, a pillow over her face.

Tamara glanced at the red eye of the clock. Nearly nine. The high sun pierced the shutters.

Friday was her day to sleep late, since she had no classes. Robert had gotten the kids off to school. Her tongue was dry and starchy, as if the Russian army had camped in her mouth. She tried to raise herself and head for the bathroom, but she was heavy with sleep, confused by the dream. And the Gloomies were tap dancing across the stage of her psyche.

Maybe Robert is right, she thought. *We can't stop living because of dreams. Waking dreams or otherwise. And at least this one can't come true.*

Unlike the death of her father, which had been vividly pre-created in a dream, this particular subconscious brain flick wasn't filmed in an earthly setting. Well, at least not a natural-sized one.

But the time she had dreamed of Kevin soaring over a canyon like a bird, with his wings failing in mid-flight, he had broken his hip the next day while jumping a gully. So maybe it was all symbolism. But as a psychologist, she knew the danger of reading too much into random brain activities. Sometimes a cigar was just a cigar.

Robert had been wonderful while Kevin was healing. Kevin's cast came up to his waist to keep his pelvis immobile. There was a bar slung between his legs, and Robert had to carry him like that, with one hand on the bar and the other under Kevin's back. Robert insisted that the family keep up their routine, and since Tamara had her hands full with Ginger, Robert hauled Kevin everywhere they went, to the zoo, the circus, basketball games, or Tamara's academic functions.

Robert's forearm was rubbed raw from the plaster, but he never uttered one word of complaint. He bore whatever pain was necessary to keep the family together. He was always ready to make time for the kids. In fact, she sometimes suspected that might be the reason he'd never made the kind of selfish sacrifices it took to become a radio star.

What had changed? Why is he so cruel about my Gloomies? What has happened to us?

She had always been able to sense things, feel things. Not like those characters on paranormal shows, the ones who could read minds and bend spoons and scramble computer systems just by wishing. Hers was more of a sympathetic understanding of living things, with an occasional prescient dream thrown in. And she had been getting chaotic vibrations from Robert for months now, ever since Christmastime. She hated to bring it up, because it only caused more disharmony between them. And the last few days, she had sensed that something larger was out of balance, something outside their lives, as if the earth had tilted slightly and gravity was failing.

"Yeah, and the Dalai Lama will be reincarnated as Chicken Little," she said to the ceiling. "*Shu-shaaa,* my foot. If I'm so damned smart, why can't I figure out my own husband?"

She kicked away the covers and stood, peeling off her nightgown. She walked to the window and raised the shade, letting the sun warm her. The woods that bordered the back of their lot were airy and calm and full of songbirds. The new buds seemed to have swollen and exploded almost overnight.

The forest could be a symbol for unknown danger, or it could just be a bunch of trees, she thought. *Depends on your belief system, or the complete lack thereof.*

Either way, she was going to do her thirty sit-ups, take a shower, and go down to Barkersville to do some shopping. Maybe she would buy Ginger a yellow Easter dress. Then maybe she'd go for a drive, just for the hell of it. Stay out late just to bug Robert. Let *him* worry, for a change. She flipped on the radio and heard Robert talking over the fade of a Celine Dion song.

"This is Bobby Lee with you, stick around, Dennis Thorne's going to have a Blossomfest preview and the rest of WRNC's High Country News, coming your way right after these messages."

Why did she love that insensitive bastard so much?

She looked out the window at the top of Bear Claw, preparing herself for the expected flash of light. The ridge was golden in the sun, the striations of its slopes like waves in an ocean of soil and stone. No strange beacons signaled her, no meaningless syllables pierced her skull. The clouds brushed the mountains as if scrubbing away the nonsense of telepathy and an overactive imagination.

Maybe Robert was right. Gloomies didn't exist.

Eggs . . . shish.

The alien collected the symbol, added it to the others that had drifted into the cave. It had received more input from its roots and tendrils, but the symbols made no discernible patterns. After the symbols passed through its filters and reached its center, they were digested along with the bright energy of the forests. The alien fed on the information, but could not focus on all the new signals that flooded its raw senses.

The creature pulsed against the granite, heated by the solar rays that leaked from the mouth of the cave. It was growing stronger from the sustenance. Soon it would be able to move, to crawl from the darkness and expand its search for food. In the meantime, it would rest and analyze.

James dropped a plate, sending thick ceramic shards across the concrete floor. Buddy appeared in the serving window, his face purpling like a plum above his stained apron. "That's the second one you dropped today, boy. What's going on?"

"It's a little steamy back here, that's all." James felt the invisible white eyes burning from the counter and booths right through the wall. "Makes things slippery."

"Well, you watch it now, or those plates are coming out of your paycheck."

"Yes, sir."

James swept the dishroom floor, the slushing sound of the wet broom straws reminding him of last night's encounter. But then, everything was reminding him of last night's encounter: the boiled brussels sprouts, the day's vegetable side that everybody ignored; the pallid green of the creamed broccoli crusting around the edges of bowls; the parsley garnishes pasted to the plates by Buddy's award-winning gravy; even the zucchini he had sliced, making him think of green fibrous fingers with every stroke of the knife.

"We're in a quandary, Mr. Tin Man," he said quietly. "What you might call a smorgasbord of problems."

The Hobart didn't answer, only opened its dewy steel jaws in hunger for more dirty dishes.

"On the one hand, you've got a creature running loose in Windshake, something that might be dangerous to other people. But on the other, you've got me as the only witness, and what am I but a crazy drunken nigger, probably freaked on angel dust and spouting voodoo Zulu nonsense?

"And on another hand—and let's hope you never get three hands, because then you'll be as creeped-up as that hothouse nightmare I saw last night—I've got Aunt Mayzie to worry over and protect, so I can't hop in the Honda and rediscover the Underground Railroad. Because she's not going to budge, even if the devil himself and his skinhead hordes come to stake their rightful claim to this sorry town."

The Hobart stared, uncomprehending. James lifted his eyes to the food-specked ceiling of the dishroom.

"Lord, I hope you're listening, because I have a feeling we're going to need some help. I take back all that stuff about asking you to give Mayzie her angel's wings early because you needed a black face to spice up Your choir. And I take back that 'White makes right' guilt trip that I used to lay on you. And I'm sorry for—hell, Lord, this could take the rest of eternity, and I don't have that long. Just get Your white ass in gear. If you really want to save us the way the preachers claim, now's your chance."

James didn't feel any more secure because of the prayer. He checked the lock on the back door and kept a close watch on the brussels sprouts that swam in the garbage can like leafy eyeballs.

Chapter Nineteen

Nettie lifted the shades and looked out on the sun-soaked morning. The dogwood trees that lined the sidewalk, slaked by recent warmth and water, had gained their buds. Yellow lilies rose from the mulch island that surrounded the Oswig Realty sign. Only a few clouds marred the pink-fading-to-baby-blue sky. The smell of mocha drifted from the dough-nut shop down the street. The whole world reeked of Easter.

Nettie thanked the Lord for the glory. He had made a per-fect day for the picnic. Maybe this meant that the Lord was giving His blessing to the couple.

She had hardly believed it when Bill called last night to ask if she had any plans for today. Bill wasn't the sponta-neous type. So when he asked if she wanted to go out for a picnic lunch, she had agreed so fast that Bill had to ask again, because she had replied while he was still in the mid-dle of inviting her.

She wanted to look as good as the weather. She pulled a cream-colored cotton skirt with a floral pattern from a hanger in the closet, then held it up to her body and studied herself in the full-length mirror. The gold and violet floral patterns accented her dark brown eyes and hair, highlighting the ocher flecks in her irises.

"Oh, you Delilah, you." She wrinkled her nose at her reflection. Then she stuck her tongue out at the thought of being a seducer.

But that was the idea, wasn't it? To get Bill away from telephones and Bibles and delivery trucks so that he couldn't help but notice her.

And Bill said he had a secret place he wanted to show her. She shivered with pleasure at the way he had said *secret.*

Nettie called Preacher Blevins and told him she wouldn't be in until late afternoon. She worked flexible hours, but she liked to keep in touch in case something pressing arose. The preacher asked where she would be, and she told him. An uncomfortable silence followed.

Ah, well, she thought. *The preacher's probably worried about the missing money.*

"Be careful of him, little Nettie," the preacher said before hanging up. "He's been known to follow wicked ways."

She wondered if those wicked ways were the same as the ones she had in mind. She began dressing, wondering if she would be reversing the process for Bill before the day was done.

Peggy fingered the torn flap of the envelope. She sighed a blue lungful of tobacco smoke. The electric company was going to cut the power on Monday. January's bill was seven weeks past due. And this morning, the kids had to eat oatmeal for breakfast, from two little brown packets she had found in the cupboard behind a rusty can of beets and a hard-crusted sack of cornmeal. It had been plain flavor oatmeal, at that.

Her puffy eyes welled with tears. She tried to be a good mother, Lord knows she tried, but she wasn't getting much help on the home front from Sylvester. Bastard hadn't even made it home last night and apparently hadn't bothered to show up for work for the third day in a row.

She stubbed out her smoke and laid the butt aside for later. Might be hard times ahead.

Hard times is here, girl, she told herself. *The question is, what are you going to do about it?*

She lifted the phone, her nicotine-stained fingers trembling as she punched the buttons. Jimmy answered. Jimmy didn't seem to be big on going to work these days, either.

"Hello?" he said, his parched throat cracking.

"Jimmy? It's Peggy."

"Peggy, darlin'. You're up with the birds this morning."

"You up yet?"

"Uh—sure, honey. Just a sec."

She heard the unmistakable sound of a hand covering the mouthpiece and Jimmy's muffled voice beyond that.

"Is somebody with you, Jimmy?"

"Huh? No, you know I'm a one-woman guy these days. And you're the woman got me that way."

Peggy might have blushed slightly, maybe even gotten a small tingle, if she didn't know all about Eula Mae Pritcher, Peggy's crosstown rival. Eula Mae lived on the other side of the tracks, and one day Peggy wanted to have a catfight with her over which side of the tracks was the *wrong* side. But maybe when it came to loving Jimmy, both sides of the track were wrong.

"Cut the shit, Jimmy. I called to talk about your . . . proposal."

"Really?" His voice squeaked like an adolescent experiencing his first hand-job. Then his voice lowered again. "I mean, I'm glad you're coming around. I think it can be good for both us."

She wasn't sure what she thought of having Jimmy as a business partner. But her back was to the wall, with pricks at every side.

And what was the difference, anyway? She was already doing the synchronized snake dance with Jimmy, Paul Crosley, that Speerhorn boy who was Junior's friend at high school, and occasionally her own husband, Sylvester. And all she had to show for it so far were sticky thighs and a heartache.

"Jimmy, Sylvester didn't come home last night. I don't know what he's up to this time. And I'm starting to get to where I don't care."

"No telling where he's off to. But that might make this little enterprise go a little smoother, right here at the first. So I can get some customers over there."

"Here?"

"Sure, darlin'. It's convenient for everybody. And we already know how to work around Sylvester's schedule."

Peggy wasn't sure she liked the idea of a parade of drunks in her trailer, dirtying up her dishes and spraying jism and liquor vomit all over her bedroom, using up her toilet paper and leaving mud all over the doormats. But she knew that Jimmy sure as hell didn't want anybody whoring out of his own mobile home. He wouldn't even let Peggy set foot in the place.

"When do we start?" she asked.

She heard a bristling sound, probably Jimmy rubbing the hangover off his stubbled cheeks. "Soon as I round up some johns."

"Who the hell is John?"

"Just the lingo, baby. I told you, I've been studying on this some."

She stabbed the thumb-length cigarette butt between her lips and fired it up. "Well, I've got some bills coming up, is why I'm asking."

"It's Friday, honey. I can line up some action, no problem. If we can set something up for this afternoon, hell, I can go down to the Moose Lodge and probably load up a cattle truck. Plus, if Sylvester *does* turn up, he'll be at the Moose Lodge, too, just like every Friday night. So I can keep an eye on him."

"Whatever you think is best. I'm just tired, Jimmy. Real tired."

"Honey, that ain't the way to be, if this is going to work."

"Don't worry, I know how to pretend. Fooled *you,* didn't I?"

The worst part was that she had loved him, and all the things he did to her. But love was another thing that didn't matter a rat's ass in the new real world. "Love" was up there with "pride," words you knitted onto those heartwarming little samplers you hung on the kitchen wall. Just threads and knots, when you got right down to it.

Jimmy broke the silence. "No need to get mean, Peggy."

"Just bring them on. However many you can find. And one more thing—"

"What, dah—?" He'd been about to say *darling.* "What?"

She sucked in another tarry hit, then exhaled slowly. She felt like a worn-out whore already. "Nothing on credit."

She slammed down the phone. *Fuck them. Fuck them all.*

It couldn't be any worse than acting on a stage. In sixth grade, she'd played the part of Sleeping Beauty in the class play. Her Momma was so proud, she'd gone out and spent money the family could barely afford for costume materials. Peggy remembered the feel of the dress her Momma had made, virginal white cotton with lace edging, billowy sleeves, and a veil. She'd worn it for the first time at the dress rehearsal the night before the play.

She felt like a real fairy queen, her small nylon slippers seeming to barely touch the stage as she crossed. The lace swished lightly with each movement and the veil wisped out behind. She had tingled, made of feathers and warm snow, puffy clouds and helium. For that one night, she believed in magic.

She noticed how the boys watched her during rehearsal. Even the girls glanced at her as if she were a stranger, with a mixture of awe and envy and scorn. The drama teacher, Mr. Anderson, said that she looked absolutely perfect.

"Good enough to eat," he said to her privately, in the wings behind the curtains. And when everyone was gone and it was time for Mr. Anderson to drive her home, he locked the school and darkened the gym and turned on the spotlight. Then he led her to the sheet-draped plywood altar where Sleeping Beauty would drift in pretend dreams the next day and await her prince's kiss. Mr. Anderson leaned her back among the plastic roses and lifted her dress and put himself inside her, said that was how princesses found true love.

There was pain and a little blood, but even that couldn't wash away the magic feeling. She had never felt so loved, so treasured and worthy. Even though the play was a disaster and Mr. Anderson never looked her in the eye again, she had carried the memory of that airy feeling ever since. And she'd spent her entire life trying to regain the magic, to step into a bright starring role, to slip again into those soft folds of make-believe.

Well, you can add "make-believe" to that sorry little list, alongside "love" and "pride," Peggy thought. *If my prince ever does come, he is damn sure going to have to pay for the privilege.*

Junior passed the joint to Reggie Speerhorn. Reggie took a hit and rolled his eyes.

"Good smoke," he grunted as he exhaled, leaning against the dumpster. They were skipping study hall, hiding in an alcove behind the gym. The air-circulation pump kicked on, making the wall vibrate, and Junior jumped in stoned surprise.

Wade, the third member of the stoogish group, broke up in laughter. He said, "That reminds me of the way you jumped when that lightning struck the other day, while you were taking a whiz. About pissed all over your boots."

Reggie took another toke and said to Junior, "Yeah, man. You been tight lately. What's got you so spooked?"

Junior huffed a little. He about told them to fuck themselves and the horses they rode in on, but they were two of his best customers. The guys had the scratch, and that's all that mattered.

Wade was an import, from Chicago. His parents were loaded, something about his old man retiring from IBM, whatever that was. He said his parents moved him down here to get him away from the niggers and spics and gangs and drugs. Well, the plan was three-quarters of a success.

Wade didn't care what he paid, either. He was used to big-city inflation, and Junior could charge him ten bucks a gram for sensemilla bud. Good virgin smoke from the fields of Meh-hee-co, grown by dot-headed beaners specifically for U.S. consumption. Wade kept asking Junior to score some smack and crack, but Junior didn't need that scene.

Wade had it going on with the chicks, though, Junior had to admit. Blue-black curly hair, the kind the girls seemed to like, what Junior called "Superman hair." He was tall with a cocksure walk, and that northern accent made him sound exotic to the Bojangle's Chicken-and-Biscuit crowd. Butt-loads of money didn't hurt, either.

Junior had been smoking dope with Reggie Speerhorn since the fourth grade, when Reggie had found a roach outside the teacher's lounge at Fairway Elementary. Junior often wondered what the mayor would think if she discovered her only son had been brain-basted almost half of his waking life. Might put a dent in that "Just Say No" horseshit she'd picked up from the Reagan era, the words she always ended her speeches with at the school assemblies.

Wade and Reggie were good customers, and probably the closest thing Junior had to friends. Even though they were a little older, they were sort of like kin. Brothers in the family of dope. Still, there was no way in hell he could tell them about the fucked-up fish he had caught yesterday. He took the joint from Wade.

"Yo, man, blow me a shotgun," Reggie said.

"Naw. That's too faggy." Junior didn't want his lips anywhere near Reggie's. He took a draw and leaned against the bricks, listening to a PE class on the football field, the temporary jocks grunting like hogs rooting for acorns.

Reggie thumped him on the chest, and Junior looked at the freckly green-eyed stoner.

"I ain't no fag, man." Reggie tried to sound as tough as his leather jacket.

Wade grabbed Reggie by the shoulder. "Chill. You're fucking up my buzz."

Reggie squirmed his shoulder free. "Nobody calls me a fag."

Junior knocked off an eraserhead of ash and handed the joint to Reggie. Reggie pinched it between his thumb and forefinger, still sulking.

"Did I say 'faggy'? I meant 'froggy.' *Ree-deep,*" Junior said. He and Wade broke into moist laughter. *Froggy* was a nickname for Reggie that went whispered around the halls behind his back. And he did resemble a frog, with his squat, spade-shaped head and bulging eyes.

"I'm getting me some good pussy," Reggie said, spitting out a pot seed that he'd accidentally sucked into his mouth. Apparently, he wasn't aware of his nickname, because he didn't clench his bony fists in rage. But he had to make a play for manhood now.

"Anybody we know?"

"You don't, Wade, but Junior knows, don't you?" Reggie flashed a bloodshot wink at Junior.

Junior had no idea what he was talking about and really didn't care. The lunch bell was about to sound, and who wanted to be standing around with their thumbs up their asses, smoking dope at school, when they could be downtown or out in the woods, smoking dope with their thumbs up their asses?

"Are ya'll interested?" Junior said. "Got thirty grams of Panama Red and ten grams of Tijuana Taxi. I can probably score a half kilo of what we're smoking, but it'll be Monday, at least."

Junior was glad drug dealers had started using the metric system for weighing dope. Always made it sound like you were getting more for your money. Plus you could cut a bit out and customers couldn't tell the difference. Still, using the metric system was about as close as Junior ever wanted to get to being a French Commie.

"I'm in for the Red," Wade said.

Junior did some math, but the numbers wiggled and sagged in his smoky head. "For you, man, one-fifty."

"Deal." Wade dug into his tight Levi's to get his wallet.

"I'm going to make a liquor run up to Don Oscar's. Ya'll want to come?" Junior said, slipping Wade's cash into the pocket of his army jacket.

Reggie spat a chunk of phlegm that clung to the side of the dumpster for a moment before it slid to the ground like a coddled egg. "That stuff kills your brain cells, man. Mom's sending me to Duke next year, and I hope there's enough left upstairs to get to medical school."

Wade reached up and tapped him on the skull. "Anybody home, Doctor Dope? What do you think you're smoking, cloves or something?"

"I can maintain on this stuff. Liquor messes with me. Plus, getting caught for drunk driving would play hell with my home life. Not to mention skipping school. That would fuck up my citizenship grade, and I want to graduate in June."

"You need to quit worrying about the future, man," Junior said. "There ain't no damn future."

"I'm up for a liquor run. I'm failing anyway." Wade nodded toward the main body of the school. "My ass is going to be in the pine all summer as it is."

"Cry me a river, man," Reggie said. "Say, you clowns going to Blossomfest tomorrow?"

"Kind of artsy-fartsy craft bullshit, isn't it?"

"Yeah. But Sammy Ray Hawkins is playing. And there'll be all kinds of pussy in town."

"Reg, admit it. Your mom's making you go."

Reggie's froggy eyes looked at the litter on the ground. "Well, she *is* the fucking mayor."

"Me and Junior always go fishing on Saturdays," Wade said.

Like hell, Junior thought. *This old southern white boy ain't never casting another hunk of bait. Because of what might take it. Because of what you might catch.*

Or what might catch YOU.

"You know," Junior said, "Blossomfuck might be good for a laugh, especially if you got the right attitude." He patted the pocket where he kept his dope.

"Hey, where's my Red?" Wade said.

"You want to go to Don Oscar's?"

"Does a bear shit in the woods?"

Junior punched him lightly on the biceps. "You drive, I'll roll."

"Since you ain't old enough to have a license, I guess I'm elected." Wade brushed back his Superman curl.

The two teenagers stepped out of the shadows of the alcove and headed for the parking lot. Neither cared if they were seen. Suspension just meant a few days of dope-filled vacation.

"See you guys tomorrow," Reggie said, sniffing and tugging at the collar of his leather jacket, feeling as high as a god.

Armfield Blevins gripped the pulpit and looked out over his imaginary flock. The Lord had brought Armfield this station, and now it was his own.

"The time is at hand," he said in his brimstone voice.

"The wicked are among us, poisoning our spirits with their drink, tempting us with the burning vessels of their flesh, reaching into our hearts with hands that turn to claws. They come disguised as angels, as loved ones, as friends. They come dressed in smiles and shapely clothes and flashing jewelry. They come with golden skin and fine hair and beckoning eyes. Because Satan is clever. Satan is mighty. Satan is determined."

He slammed a fist on the pulpit and the sound reverberated off the stained glass and dark wood of the church. With Easter approaching soon, the house would be packed. A wide-eyed hush of faithful, the men in stiff ties, the women in lavender and yellow chiffon, their perfumes floating like incense in the church's sacred air. Children sniffling and dreaming of chocolate eggs, pinned to their seats by the steely stares of their mothers. All wanting Armfield to lift their spirits and beat off the dusty sin, to then return them to the world pure and new and whole.

He would use this coming Sunday to whip them into a holy froth, to drive their sins to the surface so that they might see their own mortal wickedness. He would force them to look inward at their own black hearts so that all could see for themselves how much they needed Armfield. He would burden them with guilt and darken their brows with trouble. He would make them ache for their preacher, the only one who could shape their flawed souls and make them perfect once again.

But only practice made perfect. He dropped his voice from thunder to a whisper, making sure the words carried to every corner of the empty church.

"And Satan walks among us now. He sees the things the Lord has put on this world and claims them as his rightful keep. Satan builds his throne upon our backs, sets up his kingdom in our tall buildings and our space ships and our science laboratories. He walks in the fields of life as if he is the reaper, as if the fruit of this earth has grown ripe for his dark harvest."

Now Armfield scanned the room, silently accusing every imaginary face. He let his voice crack slightly as he continued.

"And we invite him in. We open the gates of our hearts and say, 'Come in, Satan, come into our homes and hearts and gardens, for you blind us with your glory. You offer us pleasure and wealth and earthly goods, and for that we embrace you. For you are more human than that other one, that faraway God who has no face and who asks us to make sacrifices of time and love, who promises treasure that we cannot see or hold or spend or fornicate with.' "

Now he could let his eyes mist a little, so that those in the front rows could see.

"That faraway God, who seems small and useless in the shadow of almighty Satan. That faraway God who seems not to hear when we ask for pay raises and better golf scores and a multitude of attractive lovers. That faraway God who asks us to give our precious money to His church, who asks us to walk upright and do unto others and ignore the lusts in our heart. That faraway God who seems to take more than He gives."

Now Armfield nodded gravely and lowered his eyes, as if all hope were lost, as if the Lord were extinguishing the sun, as if the storm clouds of the Apocalypse were gathering outside.

"Satan offers much. Yes, his gifts come in pretty packages. He brings joy to our flesh. He speaks our language."

Now the long, heavy silence, so that his words could settle into the flock and the woodwork and the red carpet.

"And God offers only one gift."

Armfield turned and looked toward the crucifix at the heart of the church, that solemn icon that was bought with embezzled church funds. Someone would cough now, someone whose throat was thick with harbored tears. Another would shuffle his shoes in discomfort. An infant would bleat in borrowed shame.

And Armfield would again face the crowd. His head would lift toward the arches of the church, as if seeing through the pine planks and shingles to a brighter ceiling. Now the tears could come, just two tiny trickles at first. He would repeat the hook: "God offers only one gift."

Armfield was fully in the moment now, as if the crowd was actually before him, arching and leaning forward to hear every divine word. Armfield lifted his arms slowly, as if Satan had weighted his flesh.

"The gift of salvation."

Now the tears could flow, now the tears could glisten on his cheeks, now he had the whole world in his hands.

He spoke, voice rich with emotional tremolo, his shoulders shaking with agonized bliss.

"Because He sent His only begotten Son to die on the cross. So that the blood of the Son might wash away the grime of our sins. That one would die so that all might live eternal. That one light might shine so that all darkness is banished. That one heart could hold all our pains and troubles and sins, so that we might be spared."

He rose to a crescendo, and using tears and rhythm and tone and all the weapons of his craft, Armfield could lift them into the light.

"That one named Jesus-ah, who took the nails in His flesh-ah, who endured His crown of thorns-ah, who looked down from His high windy cross-ah, and forgave us for what we had done. Because He knew we were weak-ah and human-ah and full of Satan-ah. Jesus gave His earthly life so that we would not have to die, so that we could dwell forever in the House of the Lord-ah.

"And all God asks is that we let Him in-ah. That we open our hearts so that His love can heal-ah. That we desire the everlasting life He has promised-ah. That we join Him in the Kingdom-ah."

An abrupt halt, so the silence could ring. Then a final husky whisper, squeezing out the last passionate drops of his testimony.

"He asks so little, and His gift is so great."

Now he could droop his head and nod solemnly at the

ushers. Now the plates could pass as the organist played "O Sacred Head Now Wounded."

Armfield looked out over the empty gleaming pews and sighed. The Lord had blessed him. The Lord smiled on his work. The Lord had ordained him general of a shining army. While rehearsing, Armfield always felt as if the Lord had invaded him anew. Had bathed him and made him clean. Had briefly taken Armfield's flesh and bones and skin as His own.

He closed his Bible. He could work on a resurrection bit next week. Right now, he was full of glory but empty of food and drink. He would have an afternoon snack and then go into town to see how the church's quilt display booth was coming along. Hundreds, maybe even thousands, of Satan-infected people would be in town for Blossomfest, all with full pockets and empty hearts.

He allowed his summoned tears to dry.

Chapter Twenty

"As I see it," Chester said, wiping a dribble of moonshine and tobacco juice off his chin as he leaned against the porch rail, "we got some kind of freak-o'-nature thing going on. Like those two-headed calves a body hears about, or when you cut open a tomato and the seeds inside are already sprouting. Carnival sideshow stuff."

DeWalt's head had stopped bleeding but it throbbed dully with pain. He almost asked Chester for a swig of corn liquor, but then Chester's brown-stained backwash slogged into the jar as the old mountaineer pulled it from his lips again. DeWalt drew his pipe from his pocket and inhaled its gummy comfort instead.

"But *why?*" DeWalt said around the stem.

"*Why* is a fuck-all, pardner," Chester said. "Why Windshake? Why the hell not? *What?* is a more likely question. And *how?* The facts is that my longtime pal and the best damned shine cook to ever set foot in the Blue Ridge Mountains turned into a rotted stack of mush. And my good coon hound ended up more dandelion weed than dog. My hog was pretty much a hunk of soybean squeezings by the time I got to it. Now, I got my eye on those pea-brained chickens."

"Shouldn't we notify the authorities, Chester? I mean,

this might be widespread by now. There might be others. If this is some kind of infectious disease—"

"Now, what kind of a disease turns a man into a mush-brained mess like that? Ain't heard no old mountain tales such as that. And I'll bet bear for cornmeal that it ain't wrote down in none of your books, neither."

DeWalt gripped the arms of the rocker. Chester had teased him about his folklore studies for the entire three years they'd known each other. Chester was the voice of experience, the man who had hunted in the Appalachian snow and foraged under the silent trees. Chester carried the mountains in the cracks of his boots and skin, in the linings of his lungs, in his sluggish blue blood. But now the rules of the Living Game had abruptly changed and the rug of natural law had been pulled from underfoot.

And DeWalt was fed up with Chester's digs.

"Look here, you hairy-eared bastard. Just because you're full up to your bloodshot eyeballs with mountain wisdom doesn't make you an expert on whatever's happening *now,* in a world where trees fall for no reason and animals get turned inside out. So let's just admit we don't know a goddamned thing, and maybe work together to get to the—uh, well, to the goddamned *root* of the problem."

Chester drew back as if he had been slapped. His eyes narrowed and he looked at DeWalt as if seeing him for the first time. Then he nodded in admiration and broke into a hacking spasm of laughter.

"I was wondering if you had any sand in your gizzard, DeWalt. I guess maybe you're real settler stock after all. Wouldn't have sold you that land if I thought you was a *hopeless* Yankee sonuvabitch."

DeWalt looked across the farm at the surrounding woods. "Well, you can ridicule me later. Right now, I think it's best that we contact the authorities. We don't know what we're up against."

DeWalt's instinct was to turn to the comfort of civilized

thought, research, and investigation. To let others worry about the problem. To sit and scratch his balls while the cavalry rode over the hill.

"You expect anybody else will know what the fuck's going on?" Chester said. "Like you said, things have changed. Something ain't right in these woods. Ever since them damned lights—"

"*Hey*." DeWalt punctuated his shout by slapping his palms on the worn rocker. "I'll bet all this has something to do with that green radiance that permeated the water."

"Oh, that glowing shit, like?" Chester rubbed his rough chin. "Come to recollect, the trees got funny right after the lights started up. Thought I was having one of those heebie-jeebie fits, the kind you get when they run you through detox and you start seeing things. So I sort of paid it no never-mind, the way a body does when they see something that don't fit the big picture."

"Except nothing fits the picture anymore. Where did you see it, exactly?" DeWalt stood with bone-bruised effort and walked to the edge of the porch. His eyes followed Chester's quivering index finger.

"Over that rise. Right at the ass end of my lot and right above—Sweet Mary, Jesus, and Joseph the goddamned Carpenter. Right above Don Oscar's acreage. Probably not far from his cookhouse, come to think of it."

"It might be some kind of chemical spill, or, who knows, maybe a secret nuclear waste dump. It wouldn't be the first time the government's put its citizens in danger without their knowledge."

"Now you just hold it right there with that Commie-liberal talk. The good old U.S. of A. wouldn't ever do such as that. Not unless they were exterminating suicide-bombing trash. Or them that don't pay their taxes."

"I'm just trying to consider all the alternatives."

"Well, I would have heard trucks and such. Old logging roads run all back through there, but the way sound carries before the trees flesh out, you can about hear a squirrel fart. So I ain't buying that idea. Think it's about time to go have myself a look-see."

"You *saw* that deer or whatever it was that I hit. No telling what might be out there. You can't just go off half-cocked."

Chester's shotgun had been leaning against the rail beside him, but now he picked it up and nestled the butt against his hip, the barrel pointed to the sky. He thumbed back both triggers.

"Ain't no *half* about it. And there's another thing. Cops messing around out there might come across Don Oscar's still. And I think it would be disrepecting the man's memory to have him go down on the books as a lawbreaker."

Chester worked the jar again, his knobby throat pumping the corn liquor to his stomach. He wiped his mouth on his gray long-john sleeve, then added, "We got a mountain tradition. Called 'taking care of our own.' "

Then he swung his bones off the porch. He walked twenty feet before turning. "You comin'? Or are you a yellow-bellied, chicken-livered California Yankee?"

DeWalt debated action.

Permission to risk life and limb, Mr. Chairman?

Oh Brother, you have nothing to lose but your pathetic, directionless life.

And yours as well, Mr. Chairman.

Remember what I was saying about the unknown? Better to curse a thousand candles than to light the darkness.

Better to sit here and scratch my nuts and call it somebody else's problem, right?

That's the spirit of the Lodge, Oh Brother. The Royal Order of the Bleeding Hearts doesn't want solutions. We want sympathy, compassion, useless lip service. Passive resistance. Working to promote change within the system. A kinder, gentler self-destruction.

Well, with all due respect, I'd like to resign my membership.

Sorry. It's a lifetime commitment.

Go to hell, Mr. Chairman.

I'm already there, Brother. And so are you.

DeWalt braced himself for the agony of rising. "Hold on, Chester. I'm coming, if I can get my legs to work."

He rattled down the stairs, feeling as old as Methuselah. He was huffing by the time he caught up. "What do we do when we get there?"

Chester smiled, the late afternoon light making shadows in the valleys of his face. "Daddy always told me to make hay while the sun shines, pardner," he said, leading the way across the fields. "Didn't say nothing about what to do in the dark."

"Look at this fucking rot, man." Junior stomped the planks of Don Oscar's porch and moldy dust rose in the air around them. The porch was covered with a blue powdery fungus that was about an inch deep. The mold reminded Junior of the blue mold that tainted the tobacco that his grandfather used to grow, back before the old coot had gotten so lazy.

"Where's Don Oscar?" Wade asked, a little uneasy at messing around a bootlegger's house with no one home.

"Probably up the trail doing business. See those cars in the driveway? That Mazda ain't Don Oscar's, it must be some customer."

"No, that's the preacher's wife's car."

"The preacher's wife? How in the hell do you know what she drives?"

Wade looked down. " 'Cause I go to the Baptist Church."

Junior let out a chortle. "You're fucking with me."

"Naw, man."

Junior looked at Wade with his head tilted. Maybe the guy was serious. He was from up north, after all. "Hey, how do you reckon getting wasted works in with religion?"

"What's that got to do with believing in Jesus?"

Junior thought it over for a second, until his head started hurting. "Uh, nothing, I guess."

Wade crinkled his nose against the ripe, rank odor. "Shoo. That damned wife of Don Oscar's needs to do some cleaning."

"What is this shit?" Junior said, drawing a trail on the moldy porch with the tip of his boot.

"Who knows? Let's get our moonshine and get the hell out of Dodge."

Junior led the way up the dark muddy stitch of ground that followed the creek. There was more mold along its banks, veins of faded avocado green and powder blue and dried mustard. Puffballs dotted the dead leaves under the trees like leather eggs. The glen smelled like a forgotten laundry basement.

Wade stopped and looked along the creek. "Hey, Junior, is it my imagination, or is all this grass dying?"

"Who the fuck are you, Ranger Rick or something? Let's get up to the springhouse."

But Wade was right. All the plants seemed to be wilted, as if tapped out by a late frost. The trees sagged toward the ground, already tired from holding up new leaves. Some had fallen, their trunks snapped in half, branches stunted. But Windshake hadn't had an ice storm in weeks. The plants were supposed to be thriving this time of year.

Junior and Wade stepped from under the oak and hickory and balsam limbs into the springhouse clearing. The mold in the clearing seemed to have dried out from exposure to the sun. Junior lifted the heavy padlock on the springhouse door to make sure it was locked.

"Hey, Don Oscar?" he yelled, his eyes searching the edge of the clearing. "You out here?"

"Maybe he's on vacation, man."

Junior giggled at the image of Don Oscar in Bermuda

shorts, sitting on the deck of an ocean liner with his shirt off, his Indian-red neck and arms meeting the pale gooseflesh of his bare chest in the perfect outline of a T-shirt. "Naw, man. Bootleggers don't go on vacation. You saw the cars in the driveway."

"Do you want to wait a while, or what?" Wade looked around uncertainly.

"Why not? Good a place as any to smoke a little number." They sat on a fallen log and replenished their buzz, blowing smoke pillars into the clear sky. Junior saw that the stovepipes were bare mouthed, meaning Don Oscar had let his cooking fire die out. That wasn't like the old bootlegger at all. He liked to brag that he kept the still cooking around the clock.

And thin powdery roots had crawled up the walls of the springhouse, veining out across the warped planks. Don Oscar usually took a lot of pride in his operation.

"Hey, look at that," Wade said, pointing into the shadowed pocket of a soggy stump.

"Just some mushrooms. Sons of bitches grow all over the mountains this time of year."

"But those are the psychedelic kind. Used to pick them out of the cow pastures down in Florida, when we went for vacation. Hippies down there showed me which ones were the right kind. Pop a few, and a half-hour later, you're as fucked as a Homecoming cheerleader."

"I got news for you, Ranger Rick. In case you ain't noticed, this ain't fucking Florida."

"I heard they grew in the North Carolina mountains, too."

"Since when did you turn into a goddamned nature boy? As I remember it, you're making an 'F' in Science, the same as me."

"If it's got something to do with getting fucked up, then I'm an expert. Like peyote and acid and stuff. You ever tripped, man?"

Junior's stoned smile was plastered across his face. His

cheeks tingled. He shook his head from side to side. That Panama Red was some ass-kicking shit. No wonder those spics just wanted to lay in the shade all day.

And what the hell was Wade doing, going over and picking some fucking mushrooms when they had a pocketful of pot, and maybe some moonshine in the near future as well?

Wade sat back down and broke the moist splintery stem of one of the mushrooms. "See, if the stem turns blue where it's broken, that means it's a magic mushroom, or 'shroom,' as the hippies call it."

"You're full of shit, Wade."

"Hell, no, I'm not. We had hippies up north, too. Some of my best connections were hippies. Once you get past that peace and love horseshit, they're just like regular folks. And they know a hell of a lot about getting wasted."

"Give me a joint and a jar, and I'm set. I don't know about that other stuff. Plus, what if it's one of the poison kind, death angels or whatnot?"

"Look here. The stem's turning. It's safe as mother's milk."

Junior looked dubiously at the stem, at the blue-green ring that was starting to emerge where Wade had broken the flesh of the fungus. Junior was starting to get thirsty. *Where the hell was Don Oscar?*

"You ain't seriously going to eat that shit, are you?" Junior asked. But from the look in Wade's eyes, he didn't have to bother asking. Wade popped a couple of small caps in his mouth as if they were M&M's. Wade chewed and grimaced, then swallowed with effort.

He smiled at Junior, and it was a preacher smile, the kind people wore during weddings and holidays, or funerals where they didn't know the dead person too well. Wade held out his palm, and a couple of tan moist mushrooms lay across his lifelines.

"Magical Mystery Tour," Wade said, grimacing as if he had eaten a handful of earthworms.

"I don't know. I want to see if you drop over dead first."

"See you in the clouds, fuckface." Wade leaned back against the crisp, leaf-covered bank, oblivious to the moldering roots that threaded across the soil. "I'll say hello to God for you."

Junior was curious now. He hated missing out on a chance to escape from this fuck-up of a reality. What was the worst thing that could happen?

It was almost as if Wade read his mind, because Wade said, "What's the worst thing that can happen?"

"I'll die."

"Well, there's grass in heaven and there's booze in hell, so what have you got to lose?"

"Not a damn thing, I reckon."

He picked up the mushrooms that Wade had left on the log. They were light and innocent-looking. They couldn't be any worse for you than pot. His dad said that nature was there for a reason, and nature always did you right.

Junior put them in his mouth and bit down, then his taste buds were flooded with bitterness. *Wow man Wade is talking but his words are mushy and far away and they're not matching up with the way his lips are moving and the wind is painting my skin and I can feel every hair on my body and that tree has so many tiny flecks of bark, every one is alive, and the leaves are waving hello and the tree is slithering like a snake and the sky is an ocean if you look at it upside down and I can swim in it and Wade is smiling and I thought he said it took a half hour to kick in only how long has it been, hours or seconds, there's no difference because it all feels like now and I'm falling into the orange pool of the sun except these vines are holding me down and what the fuck these vines are holding me down and Wade's eyes are glowing, he didn't tell me it would be so fucking weird, no wonder those hippies are so goofy, this can't be real but what is real, and I want to lift my arms only the vines are holding me down but my arms are the vines and the vines are fingers reaching into the ground and I am the dirt and the trees and far-fucking-out I've come from the stars to swallow this land and I must eat the trees that I am and I am* shu-shaaa *and I must feed myself so I can go home and Wade's eyes are glowing green and he's part of me now and we are all children of the parent and boy am I fucked up and I bite the trees and I squeeze the life in my jaws and I come from space to eat the trees and I'm hungry and that is the wind in my throat and not my heart because my heart is not beating and this is really fucked up because I come from space to eat the life and eat myself who is the earth so I can go home and*

I am Shu-shaaa *Mull but what the fuck is* shu-shaaa *that is me that is the tree that is the sky that fills the fucking sky and*

I can't feel the end where my skin used to be and I can never turn back until all is shu-shaaa *and I come from space to eat the trees and I must go with the flow toward nothing and everything and always all at once and boy am I fucked up*

Chapter Twenty-One

"This is a gorgeous place, Bill," Nettie said. Bill watched her eyes as he helped spread the blanket across the warm clover.

They were on a rise of meadow that overlooked a laurel-covered river valley. The gray face of Bear Claw sloped upward from the meadow, the mountain harsh with rocky shadows. The softer outlines of Fool's Knob and Antler Ridge met the sky on the southern horizon. The surrounding trees wore their new buds like a regal finery of jewelry and lace. A scattering of sparrows erupted from the forest and soared over the grass, their wings tilted at odd angles.

Bill smoothed the blanket with his hand and sat beside Nettie. He smelled dandelions and wild onions, fried chicken and raspberry tarts. He had planned on stopping at the Sav-a-Ton and buying one of those ready-to-go deli picnics, but Nettie had insisted on providing the food. And she looked tasty herself, in that lavender blouse and light-colored skirt, a yellow scarf tying her hair back in a dark ponytail, little wispy curls brushing her cheeks.

Now get that stuff out of your mind, he told himself. *Is the devil going to follow you even out here, into the heart of God's country?*

Nettie opened the basket and passed him a napkin. "Bill, what made you ask me out on the spur of the moment?"

Bill avoided her eyes and looked off at the mountains, just as his grandfather had. "I just wanted to show you this place," he said, waving his work-roughened hand out toward the woods.

"I love it here. I feel so . . . free," she said. "Close to the Lord. Pure." She said the last with a small blush.

Bill saw the blush and gulped nervously. He nodded and said, "I've loved this place since I was a little boy. Used to go up there by that ridge and pick huckleberries."

He didn't add that he used to bring his high school dates out here to give the Corvette's shock absorbers a workout under the ogling moon. But that had been a different, devil-ridden Bill, before the Light had found him. Those sins had been washed away by the blood of the Lamb. He helped Nettie unpack the food.

"I'll bet you were cute as a boy."

Now it was Bill's turn to blush. Even his ears tingled. He dropped the bowl of mashed potatoes, tipping over the plastic container of sweet tea. He hated that he was always so clumsy around Nettie.

"Even as a boy, I knew I wanted to live out here one day. Finally I was able to make enough money to buy it."

"This place is *yours?*" Her eyes widened.

Bill hoped he didn't sound like he was bragging. "Well, actually, it's the Lord's, but I get to keep it until He comes back for it. The lot goes over to the base of the mountain and across that ridge there, the one with the stand of oaks, on down into that old-growth thicket by the river."

Nettie picked a buttercup and tucked it behind her ear. "Wow, Bill, you certainly have an eye for beauty."

Bill studied her face, wondering if she were fishing for compliments the way some women did. He decided she wasn't insecure about her looks. She couldn't be, not with all the gifts she had been blessed with.

"Well, I've been wanting to settle here one day. Only . . ." He gulped again, feeling his big stupid vocal cords locking up on him. He'd never been very good at expressing himself, and now, when the bright sun and the swaying daisies and the velvet green fields demanded poetry, he could only stack words as if they were cinder blocks. " . . . only, the time's never been right."

"It's a nice dream, Bill. I hope it comes true. You deserve every good thing in the world."

Nettie was talking about dreams, and his heart clenched like a fist. He had shared dreams with his first wife, and she had vomited them back in his face every chance she got. She had ridiculed him, laughed at his idiotic plans that she said were a waste of money, snickered at his sexual performance, and taunted him with a string of lovers, from the entire land-scaping crew to Sammy Ray Hawkins, making sure to time her trysts so that Bill had a fifty-fifty chance of walking in on her adulterous acrobatics.

Bill had tried hard to forgive her, even asked the Lord to forgive her, too. And he draped her in silk, adorned her with diamonds, wrapped her in gold chains, hoping he could buy her approval and affection. But he only built the wealth of her scorn. And the devil had gained final victory by forcing him to break a vow to God and divorce her.

He wasn't about to risk that pain again. Nettie must have sensed something, because she put her hand on his big fore-arm. "Is that the secret you told me about? You owning this?" she said quietly.

"Well, yes," he said, after he jump-started his tongue. "But it's not just that. There was something else I wanted to tell you.

"Confession is good for the soul."

"We've been going out for a while now. And I've enjoyed every minute we've spent together. But I'm afraid I better tell you something before you waste much more time on me."

Bill watched her wilt. Her eyelids dropped, her dark, delicate eyelashes flickered like the butterflies that were cutting patterns over the grass. She bowed like one of those long-ago English queens, readying herself for execution. She nodded gently, as if praying that the ax-blow be swift and sure.

"I've been married before," he said, in a rush, wanting it over with. "And I got a divorce. I've sinned in the eyes of the Lord, Nettie."

She blinked twice. "Is that your deep, dark secret?"

Bill braced himself for her counterattack, the cruel feminine laughter that would slice like a saber. It didn't come.

"Bill, everybody makes mistakes," she said. "And God's heart is bigger than the sky. There's plenty of room up there for forgiveness. That's one of the best things about His love."

Bill looked up at the high ceiling of the sky with its thin stucco of clouds.

He wiped the sweat from his palms onto the blanket. "I was afraid you'd think less of me, like I was a hypocrite or something, the way I promote the church and stuff. While I'm eaten up on the inside with black sin."

And now Nettie *was* laughing, but it was a laugh of relief instead of ridicule. "Bill, I've got deep, dark secrets that would put that one to shame. And someday, I might tell you about them. Now, let's eat before the ants figure out we're here."

The tension that Bill had sensed from the moment they arrived seemed to lift into the March breeze, as if God had waved a soothing hand overhead.

"Too late to fool the ants," Bill said, blowing one off the back of his hand. It landed in the spilled mashed potatoes. Nettie laughed again, an airy music that was as natural to the meadow as the song of sparrows. Bill grinned at her and lifted the plate of fried chicken. His grin froze as Nettie pulled a bottle of wine from the basket. He looked into her deep, shining, curious, tempting eyes.

"I hope you don't disapprove." She twisted a corkscrew in with a firm hand. Her face clenched with effort as she popped the cork. "One of *my* dark secrets."

Bill's smile tried to shrink like drying plywood, but he kept it nailed into place. She was pouring the blood of Christ into two clear plastic tumblers.

No, he thought, *this is white wine. The blood of nothing but dead grapes. Do you mind, Jesus? Of course, You used to drink it. But what if it makes me weak, prone to the devil's whispers? Or is this a test of faith?*

But then he was taking the cup from Nettie and bumping it to her raised cup in a toast, and he was swimming in her beautiful eyes and the wine was on his lips and in his throat and then warming a small spot in his belly. He sipped again, nervously, and the warmth spread.

They ate chicken, her a breast, him two legs and a thigh. They had scratch biscuits that were as good as Bill's grandmother used to make, back before she bought her first microwave. Bill's plate was emptied of the mashed potatoes that Nettie had covered with a thin gravy that was good even cold. The buttersweet taste of the raspberry tarts clung to his lips, and he wondered if his smile was as red as Nettie's.

They lay face to face, leaning on their elbows, and talked under the warm fingers of the sun, sharing their third cup of wine. Bill pointed to a sycamore branch and a flutter of bright red.

"Male cardinal," he said. "Watch for a second."

A small brown bird flitted from the growth of a spruce and the cardinal gave chase.

"Going after a piece of tail feather," Nettie said.

Bill was stunned. The Nettie he had known and dated and studied scriptures with must be back in Windshake, and this Jezebel had been sent by the devil to draw Bill back into the hellish fold. She giggled behind her hand and her eyes were alight with amusement.

And his lips were mildly numb and now the warmth had

spread all over his body and he was laughing, too. Then he was laughing so hard that he fell toward her and then their eyes met and their lips met and they shared laughing breath and raspberry saliva and Chardonnay tongue and then the devil was on Bill's shoulder, whispering in his ear. But the Lord was on the other shoulder, drowning out the Prince of Lies with an orchestra of blinding sunburst heartbeats—

—and Nettie couldn't believe this was finally happening. Her heart had almost stopped when Bill said he had something to tell her "before she wasted much more time."

He was going to tell her that, while she was a nice girl, he didn't think they should see each other anymore. He would be too kind to say the truth, which was that she was homely and independent and not the picturesque queen he envisioned at his side. He would just say that even though her company was pleasant, their relationship wasn't going anywhere because the tinder just wasn't taking the spark. And they should remain friends and continue the Lord's work together at the church and not have any ill feelings toward one another because the Bible said to turn the other cheek.

But he didn't say those things, only some ridiculous thing about being divorced, but marriage wasn't as sacred as love, so why should he worry about it? But Bill was sweet to consider her feelings, even if his solemnity almost made her laugh. Some people took the covenant of marriage more seriously than others, and she respected Bill's tenets. Her own relief had gushed through her body so forcefully that she was afraid it was going to burst through her skin.

And Bill had not frowned on the wine. Well, perhaps briefly, but he had taken a cup, and then more, and she could feel his awkwardness fall away into laughter and now into this kiss, which was making her head expand, this kiss, which was drowning her in a pool of light, this kiss, which was a moist dew, this kiss, which was a free fall, this kiss, which was tangling their limbs in liquid knots, this kiss, which was one long heartbeat, this kiss that was a pillow cloud that was her body that was fighting out of the blouse and cotton dress and winding inside Bill's shirt and trousers and skin and now the kiss spread over their entire flesh as the hot white honey wax arms of heaven embraced them and swept them aloft on a cream silk fire breeze and dropped them into a milk sky sun ocean and then they were racing together toward a frozen forever only now they were exploding like golden flowers and she was melting and flowing and arriving and disappearing only to find herself back in Bill's arms where her journey had always led.

Junior stumbled through the laurels along the riverbank, ignoring the sharp branches that gouged his skin, not caring that the flesh peeled from his bones like shucks from an ear of yellow corn. Because it wasn't his skin, it was the parent's, and *shu-shaaa* had no awareness of pain or decay. There was no death, only change. Only a joining into the life that must become *shu-shaaa* so the journey could continue.

Junior heard the life in the trees and under the thickets and behind the shrubs and in the meadow, and he stepped into the sunlight and saw the life that was like his own used to be.

A memory of being human, of a time before *shu-shaaa* Mull, swam in the swampy mist inside his head. He was about to cross the green earth skin to reach the writhing human lives so that he could touch their hearts with the hand of the parent. Because they sang with light and stole the sun that fed the life and their animal cries filled *shu-shaaa*'s air.

But another force pulled him away, tugged at him like vines and creepers and kudzu, and compelled him to cross the river and ascend the mountain that rose from the earth to return him to a bed of memories. A place from his human past, a place of roots. An old human who deserved to share the glory, a human whose name was Mull, only its own name had once been Mull, but that didn't matter since they would soon all be one.

Fording the river, something fell from his pocket and rode downstream on the current, glistening in the sunlight. Another memory waded into his altered consciousness, a recollection of pleasure and smoke followed by a sharp prick of sorrow at things long gone. But the human thoughts were fleeting and quickly suffocated by the verdant rhapsody that was *shu-shaaa*.

He flowed toward the Mull farm, biting trees along the way.

Tamara pulled her car onto the shoulder of the road, trembling. She was lucky that no cars had been approaching, because she had veered into the other lane and back again, tires squealing in complaint. The creature that had dashed in front of the Toyota had the fuzzy, arched tail of a squirrel, but its eyes were bright wet specks and its head was as slick as that of an otter.

The animal's sudden appearance hadn't startled her. It was the way those radiant eyes had peered through the windshield and flashed with the same secret light that Tamara had seen on the mountaintop. The oozing gash of mouth had opened, and the word *shu-shaaa* filled her brain and numbed her fingers, and if she hadn't half believed that such a creature could speak, she might have lost it completely and run the Toyota into the ditch.

She sat with the engine idling, her forehead against the steering wheel. When her breathing steadied, she looked in the rearview mirror. No creature there, though a thin trail of liquid marked its crossing of the road. Tamara got out of the car and went to the trail. Two black curves of thin rubber showed where the car's tires had skidded.

"I'm not listening to you," she said. She looked in the

weeds on the far side of the road. A stretch of barbed wire bounded a hay field. Though the growth was low, the creature could easily get lost in the grass. Maybe it had been infected with rabies.

She'd heard of the "thousand-yard stare" that rabid animals had, the way they'd look at you as if you were a hated thing. At the same time, they were gazing at a point miles away. But Tamara had never heard of a disease that made a creature leak mucus the way a car with a busted pan leaked oil. And she'd definitely never heard of a disease that caused an animal to bombard you with a telepathic message.

She knelt and studied the glistening trail, which had already dried on the sun-warmed asphalt. She was about to touch the flaking material, then decided against it. If the animal had been infected, then its saliva or droppings or oozings were best left alone. As she watched, the flakes grew smaller and more transparent, then lifted on the breeze in a cluster of pale motes.

A truck approached and the driver slowed. He rolled down his window and stuck his head out, his face red from an early seasonal sunburn. The back of the truck was piled with worn furniture, a boxy television, rugs, and stuffed garbage bags.

"You broke down, lady?"

"No, I'm fine. I just thought I saw something."

The man looked at her with narrowed, sick-looking eyes. "Was it something that was there or something that *wasn't* there?"

"What do you mean?"

He gazed at the sky. "Been seeing birds, myself. Except they can't keep up with their own shadows. And green rain. Seen some green rain that wasn't there."

Tamara eased closer to the Toyota, wondering if she should make a run for it.

"It's up on Bear Claw," he said. He turned on his windshield wipers, though the sky was nearly clear.

"I have to go," Tamara said.

"What's your name?"

Tamara regained her composure. Maybe the man was mildly schizophrenic and his medicine wasn't working today. She, of all people, should know that brain chemistry could go out of balance through no fault of the brain's host. Suffering a mental illness was no cause to treat the man like an ax murderer.

"Tamara," she said, peering into the cab just in case the man happened to be carrying an ax.

"Tamara," he echoed. "That's what I figured."

"Why is that?" Seven miles from nowhere in every direction and she had no way to protect herself. She eased two steps away from the truck.

"Didn't you hear it?"

"Hear what?"

"You ought to listen better."

She looked around. No vehicles were approaching. She was about to ask if the man had seen any other strange animals when he waved toward the forest that climbed the slope of the mountain.

"The *trees*," he said. "They're saying things that ain't right."

"Excuse me?"

"They're liars."

He rolled up his window and headed down the road, the truck's exhaust lingering in her nostrils. Tamara looked up the face of Bear Claw, wondering what sort of "it" the man had imagined there.

The alien aspirated, drawing air through the plants it had converted, and absorbing the energy of the animals that had become part of its own flesh. As it expanded and its roots probed deeper, more symbols collected in the heart-brain center. The symbols brought pain, but pain was necessary, because pain was survival. If the creature was going to become part of this planet, the planet must join in return, a symbiosis that was thicker than blood and sap.

The symbol pierced its fungal walls and lodged in its center, where the other symbols were stirred in the confused soup of sleep.

Tah-mah-raa.

Chapter Twenty-Two

Jimmy had rounded up Peggy's first official customer.

Howard Pennifield entered the trailer behind Jimmy, his shoulders sloped like a gorilla's. He blinked stupidly and looked around at the clutter, trying not to stare at Peggy sitting splay legged on the couch with a drink in her hand. She eyed him, trying to size him up. She knew him from Little League, because his kid was on Little Mack's baseball team. She wondered if Howard could wield a bat better than his slow-witted kid could.

Peggy had spent almost an hour deciding how to dress. She wasn't sure if she should go for the sophisticated look, with fake fur and that kind of stuff, or just act naturally. She didn't think men wanted to pay for "natural," they could get "natural" from their wives, bruised-looking eyes and hair in curlers and wrinkles backfilled with foundation. She didn't have a whole lot of accessories. Maybe she would make Jimmy invest in some of those see-through garments and thin-strapped lingerie they sold in that Frederick's of Hollywood catalog that kept showing up in the mail.

In the end, she had chosen her Kmart negligee that was a shimmering pink with ruffles along the bustline. She had skipped the panties. May as well give them an eyeful. It wasn't like she was going to be standing on a street corner or anything. She gave the two men the provocative look she had been practicing in the mirror. She noted with amusement that Jimmy licked his lips like a weasel.

"We parked behind the woods, Peg, and walked in around the back way," Jimmy said. "May as well keep a low profile, at least here at first."

Howard nodded as if his head were a sack of feed.

"Then what are you doing here, Jimmy?" Peggy said. "You going to hold it for him?"

A shadow crossed Jimmy's face, then he said, "This here's Howard. Don't know if you know him or not."

"We've met. Hello, Howard." She gave him a painted smile. He nodded again. She hoped the bulge in his wallet was as big as the bulge at the front of his pants.

"Well, let's get this show on the road," she said, dragging at her cigarette and taking a painful pull of cheap whiskey. Jimmy, looking a little uncomfortable, leaned down to whisper to her.

"I was wondering if, you know, you and me first? Just for old time's sake. Plus"—he leaned right to her ear—"he wants to watch."

"What's half of fifty? That'll be twenty-five bucks, Jimmy."

"Damn you, girl, it's supposed to be like before. Us being in love and shit."

She let the negligee ride up a little more, until the soft down of her love nest showed. Jimmy licked his lips again.

"Twenty-five bucks," she said. "Take it or leave it."

Peggy enjoyed this new feeling of power. Maybe this little enterprise had more advantages than just bringing in some cash. She stood and walked to the bedroom, curling her feet a little so that her rear wiggled under the hem of the negligee.

Howard spoke for the first time. "You said seventy-five, and she said fifty. What's the deal, Jimmy?"

"Hush up, you peckerhead. You ask for extras, you got to pay for extras."

The men followed her into the room where she lay in the sagging curve of the bare mattress. Jimmy dropped a pile of green bills on the bedside table and began shucking off his boots and shirt. Howard nodded at her. She winked and stared at the ceiling, imagining a prince swooping from the clouds on a winged white horse.

Reggie Speerhorn parked his Camaro behind the GasNGo. He walked through the kudzu-draped jack pines where he and Jimmy had smoked bushels of dope together, then hopped over the oily little stream that bordered the trailer park. He had found that afternoons were a perfect time to get a piece off Junior's mom, before the bus dropped off Junior's dipshit brother. And Junior was probably drooling and puking right now, his guts ripped by moonshine. Reggie hoped Peggy's boot-brained redneck lover hadn't beaten him to the punch again.

He walked past the silent huddled trailers that were crowded together like sardine cans on a grocery shelf. He didn't understand how people could live like this. Car engines and baby-doll parts were strewn through the bare red yards. Clotheslines sagged from the weight of ragged blankets and underwear with big holes in the crotch. Even the scavenger birds avoided this place, as if instinctively knowing that not a crust of bread would escape these sorry tables.

The Ford pickup wasn't parked in front of the Mull trailer. Neither was Junior's dad's truck. Reggie crept around a rusty oil barrel toward the trailer, feeling a shiver of excitement ripple up his spine. He tried to picture Peggy at the window, her hand on her pale cheek, waiting for him to drop by, a maiden longing for her prince.

As he passed the end of the trailer, he heard voices coming from inside. He stooped and ducked under the trailer through a ragged gap in the white aluminum underpinning. He put his ear to the floor. Peggy was saying something, and the mattress was squeaking. Reggie could hear the bed's bare iron legs lifting and settling, lifting and settling, on the groaning floor.

He looked at the tar-papered toolshed twenty feet away. He could get up on top of it and see through the window. That old apple tree would hide him, that tree with the split trunk and gnarled nest of elbows. A few snowballs of white blossoms protruded from its upper branches as if the tree hadn't yet realized it was dying.

He glanced around the trailer park. Somewhere a kid was squalling like she had a razor blade under her fingernail, and a dog barked weakly from the end of its chain. Traffic flared past on the distant highway, but the rest of the park was hushed, as if smothered by poverty.

Reggie slipped behind the shed and scrabbled up its boarded side, pushing his feet against the knots in the apple tree. He wriggled onto the roof, hoping the shed wouldn't collapse. The tips of the tree branches skittered on the tin sheeting around him like wet chalk on a blackboard. He held his breath and looked through the trailer window, still slightly buzzed from his lunchtime smoke break.

A man was standing in the room, someone Reggie didn't know. He was nodding his big head and scratching at his gun blue stubble. His shirt was off, and his plump red shoulders hunched into a pale, hairy chest. Then Reggie craned his neck and saw the rest of the room. Peggy was in bed with a man who had a Rebel flag tattooed on one side of his back.

How many other guys do I have to compete with, he thought, *before I get a turn with my pretty Peggy-O?*

Then he saw her face. Her cheeks were wet with tears, her nice yellow hair spilling on the pillow, her eyes fixed on the ceiling. She was smiling, but it was a frozen smile, the kind you got when you were in church and the preacher told you somebody had died for your sins. Sort of like "Isn't that nice?" but you wouldn't mind being somewhere else.

Peggy never wore that expression when Reggie was making love to her. She would giggle and nip at his earlobe, her breath fresh on his neck like a morning wind. And she always caressed his back and wrapped around him like one of those eight-armed Buddha babes. But right now her arms were spread out at her sides, palms turned up and fingers slightly curled, as if surrendering to something.

Whatever that redneck was doing to her, she wasn't fighting it. But she also wasn't enjoying it. Maybe she really did love Reggie, the way she said. And he hoped that she was saving her special stuff for him. Reggie couldn't complain about other guys fucking her. After all, she was married. But he knew she would stay true to him in her heart.

And now her redneck lover was getting up and pulling away from her. The other man got into bed with her. He was still nodding, but Peggy didn't even blink, just winced a little as he entered her. Her head rocked back and forth as he went to work, but her eyes never left the ceiling.

Reggie felt a hot firmness in his pants where the fabric pressed against the sun-baked tin. Maybe he could wait until they left, then he could have Princess Peggy to himself, to tell her that he was in love with her and would she mind letting him show how much? But he was afraid Little Mack would come home any minute, and then word might get back to Junior. Damn the world, always getting in the way like that. Love ought not be so fucking complicated.

He slid backward off the roof and hooked his sneakers on a fat branch. Then he looped down to the ground and peered around the corner of the shed, ready to sneak back through the woods. But somebody was coming.

A wrinkled, leather-faced old man with an eye patch stepped out of the silver trailer next door. He staggered slightly, as if his knee bones were realigning themselves with every step. The man walked to Peggy's door and knocked lightly, then put his bat-winged ear to the door. He was grinning like a mud turtle as he pulled the latch and went into the trailer.

This must be one of those gangbangs the football players talked about, Reggie thought. *That old bastard looks eighty, if he is a day. If he can get it up, then sweet Peggy is a miracle worker. But I don't want to stay around to see if that particular wonder comes to pass.*

Reggie shuddered at the image of the one-eyed old-timer's stained khakis dropping down around those varicose legs and knobby knees. He was sick now, disgusted at himself for sharing his soul with something that opened up for anything that moved. He was about to jog off, blind with tears, when a hand fell on his shoulder. He turned and found himself in the arms of a new kind of lover, one that made him forget all about Peggy Mull's lies.

Sylvester had traveled many miles. But distance no longer mattered to him. Or to the parent.

Distance was only time, and *shu-shaaa* had forever. Forever to return to the bright hot center of everything where the universe began. Forever to cross space and rejoin its kind in a white collection of energy. Forever to gather its seeds together, the seeds that had been scattered by that cataclysmic explosion at the dawn of chaos. Forever to retrace the explosion that had spread the stars and matter and atoms and galaxies across the black mist of nothingness.

Sylvester dripped with the glory of the parent, stewed in cleansing juices of perfection, and wallowed in the brilliant healing rays of the sun. Its warmth washed his flesh and the sweet breath of the far trees sang in his ears as his budding fingers found memory of the door latch. His mind screamed words, but words had no place upon those flowery lips. He dimly recognized the trailer park and the white metal box that had once had meaning, that drew him forward on some buried instinct.

He was still much too human, human enough to know the parent was beyond names. Human enough to remember Sylvester Mull and the existence of pain. Human enough to know that hunger came in many forms. And the parent's hunger drove Sylvester to harvest.

He grabbed the boy by the shoulder, watched the human eyes widen as Sylvester bestowed the parent's flawless blessings. They communed, mouth to mouth, and Sylvester tasted speerhorn stooge stoner prince, all crazy images, as their juices swapped genetic mutations. Then he let the boy fall, left him to answer his own calling, and continued toward the white metal box that had once been home.

He wished he could say words. He wished that the parent would lift its green veil so that he might speak his human heart. But wishes were fruitless. His tongue had gone to seed.

No matter. This was his door and doors were made for going through.

The parent was hungry.

"Shu-shaaa."

Chapter Twenty-Three

Emerland negotiated the narrow, twisting road, cursing the stupid hick loggers who hadn't bothered to remove all the stumps. The branches that hung low on both sides of the road swatted at the candy-apple red paint on the flanks of his Mercedes. He winced at the grating of wooden fingernails.

Calm down, he ordered himself. *This time next year, or two years from now, this will be a two-lane blacktop. Hell, maybe even by autumn. These winding dirt roads can be yanked straight and these mountains can be shaped the way they were intended.*

He drove out from under the trees into the late afternoon sunshine. Blinded by the sudden light, he didn't see the capsized SUV in front of him until he was almost upon it. He jerked the steering wheel to the right, hoping his tires didn't fall into the same deep rut that the Pathfinder had hit. He bounced onto a flat patch of land and steered around the wreck.

"What in the hell is going on here?" he shouted to the empty passenger compartment of the Mercedes. His only answer was the purring German diesel engine.

Once safely past the Pathfinder, he slowed and looked in the rearview mirror. A thin layer of dust covered the overturned vehicle and the front grill and bumper were spattered with green goo. A small rivulet of brackish gold oil ran down the rut. He couldn't tell if the wreck had occurred hours or minutes ago.

The scene didn't make sense to Emerland, and that made him uneasy. Someone who could afford to drive a new SUV could pay for a tow truck. And what was somebody with a new car doing in this neck of the woods? Or was it Mull's, bought with DeWalt's money? And where was the driver?

He saw the Mull farmhouse a hundred yards down the slope. An old pickup truck was parked by the porch, its grill and round headlights making a grinning mask. The farmhouse itself was supported by locust poles and bordered with field stones, constructed back before the days of building codes. Emerland noticed that Mull had electricity and a telephone line, but no cable television or satellite dish. No doubt the old bastard had been dragged kicking and screaming into the twenty-first century, but probably had developed a taste for technological and material comfort by now. From such seeds, Emerland grew gardens.

He drove up to the farmhouse and got out, smelling the damp woodsy humus and barnyard rot, and the rich odor of manure and stale hay. The air was heavy with the pollen of poplar and wild cherry blossoms. It seemed that the leaves had come out in the last few hours. The fields were actually rolling hills, just like the cliché, and Emerland tried the words on his tongue as a possible name for the new resort.

"Hello. Mister Mull!" He was peeved that Mull hadn't come outside to greet him. At least the old bastard could have stood on the porch barefoot with a flintlock across his arm, the way Emerland had imagined.

But whoever had spilled that Pathfinder might have gotten such a cold and menacing reception, which may be why the driver lost control.

He had acquaintances who were developers, and they always talked about how obstinate these old mountain families were. Rumors went around that some of these backwoods rednecks shot at every three-piece suit that turned a cuff on their land. That they believed anybody who showed up without a hound at their heels was either a revenuer or an evangelist, both of which meant you'd better be on your toes. That anybody who had all their teeth couldn't be trusted. But that was ridiculous. The movie *Deliverance* was not a documentary. At any rate, Emerland wasn't scared off that easily.

Emerland enjoyed the hunt. The faint-hearted could go elsewhere, to backfill the Everglades or build shopping malls over abandoned toxic dumps in Jersey, making easy money. But their dreams were flat. Even if they built an eighty-story office building in Atlanta, they'd never reach as high into the sky as Emerland did with his mountain monuments. No one would be able to look down on him.

He shouted Mull's name again, growing impatient. He'd at least expected barking dogs. In the city, he would have clamped down on the car horn until he got results. But right now, he wanted to be the slick seducer, not the head-butting goat.

He looked around at the land that would be his. The decrepit outbuildings looked like they'd be no challenge to a stiff wind, let alone Emerland Enterprises's bulldozers. But maybe he'd let the barn stand, renovate it into an old-timey saloon, with rusty cross saws and staged photographs of moonshiners on the walls. The bar could charge six bucks a shot for drinks named "Mountain Squeeze" and "Blue Ridge Brandy" and "Olde Firewater." And maybe he'd leave the outhouse standing so the tourists could have their pictures taken in front of it.

He yelled once more, then stepped onto the porch. Yellow-green chicken shit and old black stains covered the planks. The windows were boarded over and shuttered with pine slats. An old rocking chair, held together by twine and spit, showed an imprint of two bony buttocks in its frayed seat cushion.

Yes, this old bastard would hop at the chance to move into a high-class condominium.

The screen door was broken, splinters and wire mesh sagging from brown hinges. The front door was open. Emerland peered into the dark interior. The place was a mess, with furniture tilted over and shattered mason jars covering the floor like spilled silver. Mull must have pitched a hell of a drunk.

"Mister Mull, are you home?" he shouted through the doorway. His words were swallowed by the cold-warped walls.

Damned old coot, thought Emerland. *True, I didn't make an appointment, but that must be his truck there. I doubt if that SUV came to take him away. And from the seedy look of this place, I'm positive Mull's not out somewhere tending his farm.*

Emerland put his hands on his hips. He might as well walk around and get a feel for the place. Maybe he'd step into the woods and peek over the ridge at the view. Look at Sugarfoot and admire his own handiwork. But first, he wanted to check out the Pathfinder.

He was breathing hard by the time he reached the top of the slope. He owned a fitness club over at Sugarfoot but didn't spend much time there. When he did stop in, he was so preoccupied watching the spandex leotards cutting into the crotches of the women that he didn't get much exercise. Unless he happened to smooth talk one of those tight-bunned aerobics addicts up to his suite for a little private workout.

Emerland pressed a hand to the SUV's hood. The engine had cooled, which meant the vehicle had been there for a while. He knelt and stuck his head inside the shattered sunroof. Papers and cards had spilled from the glove box to the driver's-side door. He shuffled through them until he found the white registration sheet. He pulled it out into the sunlight, looked at it, and let out a grunt.

"I'll be damned. Herbert DeWalt. Now what the hell is *he* doing over here?"

He put this piece into the puzzle. Could DeWalt have

been tipped off about Emerland's plans? Emerland didn't trust any of his assistants. He'd bought or stolen most of them from rivals, and he knew that the practice worked both ways. A well-placed bribe, forty pieces of silver here and there, had been known to tempt even the most faithful of inner circle members.

But DeWalt had had three years to make a move on this property and apparently hadn't reached Mull's price yet. If DeWalt was after the land, he must have lost his old edge, the skill and instinct that had chopped millions from the bank accounts of others. True, the rich bastard had wheedled a few acres off of Mull, but that was a drop in the hat. Emerland believed in buying entire mountains.

He stood up and looked at the bristled pine ridge tops. Mull might be showing DeWalt around right now, pointing out boundaries and right-of-ways. And it would be just like DeWalt, from what Emerland had heard, to pretend not to give a damn that he'd just wrecked his expensive toy. Probably wrecked on purpose just to show off, like a cartoon character lighting cigars with a hundred dollar bill. Emerland clenched his fists in rage. If DeWalt wanted to go to war, Emerland was ready to bring out the big guns.

Because he had made up his mind that this was *his* land. He walked toward the woods.

James walked beside Aunt Mayzie, prepared to catch her if she stumbled. He wondered why she couldn't watch from the porch like any normal person would. She could have seen plenty from there, the city workers decorating the stage and some of the vendors setting up their displays. But no, she just had to stick her nose into things, get right in the middle of those white people and bump their shiny shoes with the rubber tips of her crutches, smiling and saying *'scuse me*.

All around them, people shouted and chatted happily, ex-

cited about tomorrow's Blossomfest. Decorations hung from
the light poles, giant yellow tulips that could be turned upside down and spray-painted silver for use as the town's
Christmas bells. Traffic had been detoured from Main Street
and the asphalt was covered with hay-packed replica wagons
and folded plywood booths. A banner proclaimed "Welcome
to Blossomfest" in red letters on white vinyl, with Mayor
Speerhorn's blown-up signature at the bottom. The banner
fluttered stiffly beneath a power line, catching the spring
wind.

James felt like a period typed onto a blank page, the way
the white folks clustered around them. But with Aunt Mayzie,
that made two periods, or maybe a colon. And he was so
busy helping Mayzie weave through the crowd that he couldn't
keep an eye out for the mushroom creature in the Red Man
cap.

*Oh, but I thought you decided that was a dream, bro'.
Just a drunken nighttime sideshow. A wrong turn by that
gray ball of meat you keep under your flattop.*

But James hadn't convinced himself it was only his imagination. Because he wasn't really the imaginative sort. In
grade school, when the English teacher had told the class to
get out a sheet of paper and play "What if?" James had
stared at the tip of his pencil until his eyes crossed. He was
always more concerned with "What had been." And at the
end of class, he'd turned in a page with one sentence
scrawled across the top: *What if I can't think of anything?*

But if the subject was history or science, something with
a past, James filled the front and back of a page in fifteen
minutes. He was too analytical and left brained to create
phantasms, fictions, or things that go bump. Not to mention
thinking up a fruit salad scarecrow with green eyes and an
alfalfa wig. So that would be that.

Still, he found himself looking into the white eyes,
searching for green light.

Aunt Mayzie was having a grand time, talking to people

she knew or asking vendors about the merchandise. They wandered past the soap makers and the tobacconists and barbecue cooks. One old man wearing fireman's suspenders and a dark "NYPD" ball cap was weaving a basket from brown reeds. A blotchy-faced woman at the next booth, who was almost as wide as an elevator, stapled canary yellow bunting to the edge of a table.

"What are you going to be showing, ma'am?" Aunt Mayzie asked, leaning forward on her crutches, her shortened leg angled behind her.

"We're delivery florists, but we also do flower arrangements. Weddings, funerals, that kind of thing. You want our business card?" the blotchy woman said without looking up.

James looked around. The words "floral arrangements" had flooded his mind with too many unwanted images. He looked into the tops of the trees that lined the main street, expecting some sort of overgrown spider to drop down.

"I'm not in any danger of either a wedding *or* a funeral," Aunt Mayzie said to the woman. "Where's your store?"

"Down in Shady Valley. We get a lot of business from the university. You know, academic functions and such. And boys saying thanks to the girls, if you know what I mean."

"I thought they did that with a six-pack and a vial of penicillin these days," Aunt Mayzie said. The women shared a laugh while James rocked uncomfortably on his heels. As if penicillin were enough to knock out the infections that went around these days.

"Oh, to be young again. But I was serious about the business card. I've got to get rid of five hundred this weekend," the florist said.

"That shouldn't be no problem. I've lived here since way before the first Blossomfest, and more come into town for it every year. I expect there'll be a couple of thousand this year."

The blotchy woman opened a gym satchel and handed Aunt Mayzie a card.

"Petal Pushers," Aunt Mayzie said. "Ain't that a cute name, James?"

James nodded, anxious to move on. The sun was starting to flatten out above the western ridges, growing fat and orange the way it did before it dropped over the side of the earth. And then the darkness would come. And even the sodium street lamps and the heavy police patrols wouldn't make James feel safe. He cleared his throat.

"We'd better go on and see the rest of the sights before dark, Aunt Mayzie. Plus, we have all day tomorrow, and I'm sure this lady wants to get back to her work."

"All right, James. You young folks are always in such a rush. Good luck to you tomorrow, ma'am," Aunt Mayzie said.

The woman nodded absently, already turning her attention back to her bunting, the heady aroma of flowers rising on the evening breeze.

They walked to the Haynes House, a nineteenth-century home that had been restored as a community center. The music stage had been built on its grassy lawn beneath a big, dying oak that had been throwing down leaves since before the Cherokee hunted the hills. A couple of husky guys in flannel shirts were setting up the sound system, black Marshall stacks that had cones as big as manhole covers. Teenage kids hung from the porch rails of the Haynes House or clustered around the stage, sipping Pepsis and dreaming rock-star fantasies.

Aunt Mayzie pegged up to the Haynes House porch. Hay bales had been scattered around to make seats for a story-telling area, and one end of the porch had been blocked off with hay to muffle the music that would be blaring from the stage the next day. James helped Mayzie up the stairs and she leaned against the Colonial columns that supported the roof.

"Why don't you have a seat, Aunt Mayzie?" James said. She was breathing a little too hard to suit him.

"I'm okay, honey," she said. "Just let me look around a little more and catch my breath, then I'll go on home. I know you want to watch the basketball tonight."

James had forgotten that Georgetown was playing in the tournament. He took it as one more sign that his brain was out of alignment. He had it together now, though. And as long as the hay bales didn't rise up and start walking, he'd be okay.

They went home just as one shimmering edge of the sun hit the far mountains. The clouds tapered out in pink and red swatches, the ridges as bright as hell's foundry. The evening air was fresh with new life, the blossoms arriving just in time for their namesake festival. He looked past the hills that crowded the town, off toward the distance where the granite face of Bear Claw loomed like a great majestic beast. James thought perhaps moments like this were why Mayzie endured the harsh winters, the isolation, the white world.

The white eyes.

Eyezzzz.

The alien assimilated the symbol, gathered it into its collection. *Shu-shaaa tah-mah-raaa eyezzzz.*

The symbols were nonsense, free of any pattern. This planet had no intelligent life. The creature could feed without fear of destroying higher life forms. It was growing faster now, healed from the impact with the soil, its roots and spores spreading. The heart-brain throbbed in unison with its tendrils.

A symbol triggered itself again, repeating, like the pulse of a quasar.

Tah-mah-raaa tah-mah-raaa tah-mah-raaa.

The creature opened itself, let the vibrations of its new home settle into its center. The symbol's source of origin had grown more intense, nearly meaningful. The creature took that as a sign of healing.

Soon it would have enough strength to contact the others, those also making their journeys across distant space. The closest could join it here and help convert this planet. It was rich in microorganisms, wealthy with cellular activity. The creature was fulfilling its biological imperative.

Growing.

Thriving.

Harvesting.

It shivered in the verdant pleasure of survival and propagation.

Tamara slowed the Toyota and gazed toward the top of Bear Claw. She should be getting back home, she knew. But something about the mountain compelled her to search its slopes. It was an itch, a tingling of some deep-seated knowledge.

She braked slowly, finally able to open her eyes. The world was exactly the same as it had appeared before, only more vivid somehow. The grass along the sloping hills was a swaying green sea, the trees reached for the sky like happy worshipers, and the clouds had stitched themselves into the fabric of the sunset. The air tasted rich and her head swam in its intoxicating glory.

Something pinched her arm and she looked down to see a mosquito perched there, its proboscis needling into her skin. Its wings were slim and irradiant, almost glowing, and its body was jeweled with amber sap. The eyes were bright and she was struck by its intelligence; it appeared to study her in a speculative manner.

As if I'm on the wrong end of the magnifying glass, she thought. *Well, you're on the wrong end of a free meal.*

Tamara raised a hand from the steering wheel to swat at it. She was suddenly struck blind by darkness, gasping in pain and surprise as her skull reverberated with that phrase she had come to dread:

Shu-shaaa.

And behind it, so fast that it seemed to blur into the same blend of symbols, came *Tah-mah-raa.*

Her own name.

She clutched her head, the mosquito forgotten. She'd heard that migraine sufferers could become physically incapacitated from the agony of their attacks and wondered if that was what was happening to her. Her stomach knotted in nausea at the intensity of the invasion. The piercing needles withdrew a bit and the pain lessened enough for her to open her eyes.

Brain tumor. Oh God, what if I have a brain tumor, and that's what's been causing my delusions? Or what if I'm schizophrenic?

She tilted the rearview mirror and a stranger gazed back, one with wild eyes and tangled hair, a twisted face that would make a convincing textbook picture for a schizophrenic. The pain had moved from the center of her cranium to the back of her eyeballs. She rubbed her forehead and the sharpness receded to a distant, dull throbbing.

When she felt a little better, she rolled down the window and let the cool breeze dry the sweat beneath her eyes. She scratched at her arm, then remembered the mosquito. Its bite had left a grayish green ring, a tiny red dot of dried blood in the center.

Tah-mah-raaa tah-mah-raaa tah-mah-raaa.

She looked around, confused. Maybe this was how brain tumors progressed, the obscene mutated cells manipulating the healthy cells, multiplying and altering, squeezing out the host cells in their drive to spread. Maybe the thing inside her head was even programmed to know that it was killing its host, but could no more turn away from its silent mission than a hungry mosquito could ignore warm flesh and blood.

No. She was fit and healthy, in the prime of life. Such a thing could never happen to her. She would rather believe—

Shu-shaaa

—that she was nuts, losing it, having a nervous break-down.

But, in her heart of hearts, she couldn't buy that, either. Hearing imaginary voices was one thing. She was quite sure this voice was real.

And she knew now from where it was speaking.

The mountain called to her again. She put the Toyota in gear and headed for the gravel road that her instincts told her climbed the spine of Bear Claw.

Chapter Twenty-Four

Jimmy wanted the last time with Peggy to be special, but it was hard to get intimate with that moron Howard watching. The bills rustled in his shirt pocket and that made him feel a little better. The bed squeaked as Howard and Peggy went at it. Jimmy put on his boots, anxious to leave the room. He was no saint, but there were some things that turned even *his* stomach.

He opened the hollow door and an old one-eyed bastard in a faded military uniform stood there, his ear cupped to the door. One-Eye was grinning like a possum in a dumpster. Jimmy pushed him backward and closed the door, shutting off the sound of Peggy's sex factory.

"Who the hell are *you*, fuckface?" Jimmy said.

The old man licked his lips. "Just a concerned neighbor, is all. Thought there might be trouble over here."

"Ain't no trouble and ain't nobody else's business."

"Old Sylvester might think otherwise, don't you reckon?" The old fart squinted past Jimmy with his good eye as if trying to see through the door. "Seeing as how you fellows is over here taking turns with his wife."

Jimmy grabbed One-Eye by the throat. The knot of the man's Adam's apple pumped feverishly under Jimmy's palm.

"And how's he going to find out?" Jimmy pulled the pale face next to his own. He could smell the old soldier's rotten gums, the stench blowing from his mouth like a graveyard wind.

"Hold on, hold on. I ain't no squealer," the man wheezed. "Just want my piece of the pie, is all."

Jimmy relaxed his grip on the man's throat. His fingers had made red prints in the flesh.

"Costs fifty bucks, old man. More for extras." He looked dubiously at One-Eye's wrinkled and pallid face. "And there ain't no guarantees, in case you don't, uh . . . come through."

"Fifty bucks," One-Eye yelped. "She been giving it to me for free."

Howard must have heard them arguing, because the bed stopped squeaking. Or else he had finally clocked out.

"Who's that, Jimmy?" Howard shouted from inside the room.

"Oh God, not *Sylvester,*" Peggy said.

"No, it ain't Sylvester," Jimmy hollered back over his shoulder through the door. "Just another customer, Peg. Get on with it, now."

My first try at ass-peddling ain't going as smooth as I'd hoped, Jimmy thought. *And if Peggy's turned to this old geezer for companionship, then I must not have been keeping her satisfied. My feelings would be hurt, if I had any.*

But he might be able to turn the situation around yet. Maybe One-Eye still had enough of his government pension check left to at least sniff Jimmy's product. It was a classic case of supply and demand, and demand seemed to be high at the moment. And the supply wasn't going anywhere.

He opened his mouth to tell the old fart the new facts of life, but his mouth kept dropping, his jaw nearly hinging down to his chest. Because of what he saw coming up the hall behind One-Eye.

Sylvester had come home, or at least, *part* of Sylvester. Sylvester approached the back bedroom with stinging green eyes and ripe skin and arms stretched outward like a junkie sleepwalker. His mouth dripped with amber sap and opened to show the wiggling little fibers inside. His outstretched fingers hooked like crabapple sticks. He looked hungry and horny and happy and pissed off and long buried all at the same time.

One-Eye turned at the marshy sound of Sylvester's footsteps, right into the dewy zombie's—*zombie,* Jimmy's mind screamed, taking its first small swan dive into madness—widespread arms. One-Eye didn't even have time to register the horror and cry for mercy before Sylvester was upon him, embracing the frail, bone-covered parchment of the man's skin and lowering his mouth to One-Eye's thin, cracked lips.

Jimmy backed against the bedroom door, the only action he could inspire his lost muscles to produce. The Sylvester-zombie—*zombie,* the word flashed across the impossible gaps in his brain—slopped its mushy mouth across One-Eye's face, sucking and blowing. The old soldier's eye widened and swiveled in its socket, looking for a Grim Reaper or an escort to hell or maybe just a last earthly image to take to the grave—a light bulb or a paneling nail or a velvet Elvis painting—something sane and common to comfort him in the eternity of death.

Except when the Sylvester-zombie released One-Eye, the wrinkly bastard slumped to the floor, dead and *smiling.* Dead and happy about it. Dead and still flicking his rheumy blank eye at the world. Dead and back again, as if to prove, especially for Jimmy's benefit, that the good times kept right on rolling.

Jimmy's mind collapsed like a wet house of shoe boxes, crawled into itself and curled into a fetal position as the Sylvester-zombie—*zombie*, his last thought, *will I be a zombie, too?*—gave him the soul kiss, the magic, the glory and the power, and the slippery tendril of its tongue as they shared a deep cosmic breath of stardust and stumpwater.

*   *   *

Peggy looked over at the nightstand, at the money stacked between the overflowing ashtray and the dusty alarm clock. That was plenty enough payoff. She could worry about her own needs later, after she took care of the kids. They could have a square meal tonight for a change.

Howard rolled off the mattress and the bed almost sprang up like a trampoline from the load reduction. She watched him wrestle his legs into his underwear, then bend over to get his pants. "How did you like it, handsome?"

She could get the hang of this line of work. Lying was just another part of the job. Hell, this wasn't much of a stretch from her usual day.

Howard nodded and grunted.

"You sure are good at that, big man. You let me know when you want a second helping," she said. This was no worse than playing Sleeping Beauty.

But there was no magic, no redemption. All she had was emptiness.

And fifty bucks. Don't forget the fifty bucks.

She reached for a cigarette and lit it as she looked at the clock. Little Mack would be home in about fifteen minutes and Junior might be home in an hour, if he bothered to make it home before dinner. Junior was becoming as unpredictable as the man he'd been named after.

"My kids will be home soon, Howard. Maybe you'd better just hit the road. But you come on back sometime, when you have the money. I got lots of other places for you to try out," she said, running her tongue over her lips. She winked at him and he almost blushed. He was getting excited again.

"But not right *now*. You're broke." She laughed and pulled the sheet over her body. She was flattered to be so arousing to someone, but it might take the rest of the evening to get him off again. She didn't feel tired, but she wanted to straighten up the trailer before Little Mack got home.

She would wash the dishes and pretend that everything

was normal. Maybe even mop the kitchen. A regular house-wife.

Howard nodded dumbly. "You're purty," he said, putting on his pants. He draped his shirt over his shoulder and headed for the door.

"Glad you think so, big man. Tell Jimmy to get his scrawny hind end back here on your way out, will you?" She stubbed out her smoke and the ashtray spilled over. Brown tarry butts rolled off the night stand to the vinyl flooring.

She locked her hands behind her head and stared at the ceiling, at the little swirls she had studied while the men sampled the goods. She had seen faces up there, and wondered if she would see them now. She heard the door open and Howard grunted again. She looked at the doorway, expecting to see Jimmy's scraggly grin.

Instead, she saw her husband of twelve years standing there like a sick stranger. Howard screamed in a girlish voice, fell, and crawled on his hands and knees down the hallway, the sleeve of his shirt caught on his foot and trailing behind him. Sylvester stepped past him toward Peggy, but something was wrong. His eyes were like radioactive marbles. Sylvester had *turned,* like a sweet potato that had fallen behind the stove and gone rotten.

Her mind was a Popsicle, cold and sweet and hard, as she watched her husband slog to the bed and stand over her with his ragged jack-o'-lantern smile and his moist, impossible flesh, as he slid onto the bed with a noise that sounded like sixty pounds of earthworms. Sylvester pulled the blanket away and she crossed her arms over her breasts, feeling suddenly shy in the face of this insane homecoming. He touched her bare thigh and his finger was slick with pulpy rot. The jack-o'-lantern gaped and she thought he was trying to speak, to perhaps whisper her name or tell her that she looked good enough to eat.

Then she saw that Sylvester had no tongue, only wiggly things that flickered out in the direction of her face. She smelled her late husband as his swamp-gas fog overwhelmed her and then she was in the grasp and surrendered without a fight because it was her husband, after all, and this was his rightful place between her legs and she embraced his neck and pulled his impossible swollen head to her lips because she was staring deeply into his eyes and seeing the Magic Land and she was Frenching him with a fierce desperation because she wanted to feel the Magic and *shu-shaaa* throbbed in time to her last heartbeat as the cosmos puked magic into her throat and she at last became Sleeping Beauty again, this time forever.

She had never felt so loved.

Little Mack was scared.

He heard the noises in the trailer and didn't want to go inside, even though the door was open. The truck with the big tires wasn't here, so maybe that mean, skinny man wasn't with his Mommy. But *somebody* was in there. And it sounded like a whole *lot* of somebodies.

He ducked down by the steps and looked into the living room. He couldn't see because his eyes were full of sun. But he heard people moaning like the ghosts did in those scary movies that Junior made him watch when Mommy was out late at night. Or else when she and Daddy went to bed early and Junior turned the television up real loud.

He wished, wished, wished Daddy was home, but Daddy didn't come home much these days. Little Mack thought it might have something to do with the skinny man. Little Mack didn't like the skinny man, even though the man fluffed Mack's hair and gave him a nickel once. Mack didn't like him because he smelled like those green pellets that the janitor put on the floor when some kid threw up at school.

He didn't see the skinny man and he didn't see Mommy, but he heard people moving around in the back of the trailer. He almost yelled for Mommy but all of a sudden he was afraid, because he saw the one-eyed old man from next door who looked like he was two-hundred years old, except right now he looked like he was *four* hundred, because his skin was the color of art paste and something that looked like rubber cement poured out of his nose and mouth. And the eye that didn't have a patch moved funny, like it couldn't see anything but still wanted to *look*.

The old man tried to stand, but his legs didn't work right. He rolled over on the floor and he must have seen Little Mack, because he smiled real funny. Smiling like he had a secret. A bad secret.

Little Mack turned and ran, hoping that his Mommy wasn't in there with that bad man, that she wasn't part of the secret. He ran into the woods where he always hid, ducking under the blackberry briars and clamping his hands over his ears because he didn't want to hear the scary things that were in his head. He was afraid that the dark might get here before the scary things left.

He hoped Daddy would come home soon and make everything all right again.

Tamara turned up the old dirt road and started to climb the winding grade. The Toyota's engine whined in protest as she downshifted. The steep slopes of Bear Claw rose before her, taunting her, solid and ancient. The car juddered as it fought over the ruts and granite humps.

This was the mountain in her dream. And she trusted her dream. If she didn't trust her dream, something bad might happen. Or something bad might happen no matter what she did.

The Gloomies are up there somewhere, she thought as she looked up at the forested slopes. *They're not in my head this time. They're real. They're here.*

She considered turning back, running away from the thing that had haunted her for the past few days, the feelings that had gripped her heart, the unease that lingered in the base of her skull like a hibernating snake. But she knew these Gloomies were different. They wouldn't let her hide. They had secret spy lights.

They wouldn't be satisfied until they had her. And she wouldn't be satisfied until she had faced the enemy.

Because, in the dream, it had taken her family.

The Gloomies had already taken her father.

No way in hell would she lose anyone else.

Chapter Twenty-Five

Chester leaned against a locust tree and waited for DeWalt to catch up. DeWalt was slowing him down plenty, even more than the age and arthritis and fear that had leadened his legs. Twenty years ago, Chester would have covered twice as much territory in the last hour. But, twenty years ago, he hadn't been looking for neon-eyed freaks or strange green lights.

He glanced up at the treetops as he fumbled for a refresher hunk of Beechnut. The trees looked like October witches, with long arms and sharp elbows and dark skirts. He could hear himself wheezing through his nose. He was glad he had never taken up smoking. Maybe that was what was causing his Yankee sidekick's ass dragging.

Chester looked down the slope at DeWalt, whose face was plum colored and whose jawbone was hanging like an over-chased fox's. DeWalt's eyes were fixed on the ground as he stepped over stumps and fallen logs, shuffling over the brown carpet of leaves as if his high-dollar boots were filled with mud.

A lonely crow swooped over, landing in the top of an old sycamore tree. The bird cawed a couple of times, and the sound was swallowed by the sickly blooming treetops. Chester worked his fresh tobacco into the old, enjoying the sting of nicotine against his gums. The moonshine jar in his pocket was half empty. He thought about taking a swig but decided against it.

Hell, must be getting religion or something. Next thing you know, I'll be blaming the devil for what happened to old Don Oscar. Maybe the easy answer is the best. Then at least it would all be God's fault and the rest of us could go on home.

He swiveled his head, looking around the ridge. They were getting close to Don Oscar's property. If there were green lights, they should be able to see them from this rise. The sun was just now falling into the fingers of the trees and would soon crawl behind the mountains and die for the day. Chester was reconsidering his newfound abstinence when he first saw the opening.

"Well, I'll be dee-double-dipped in dog shit," he muttered. Then, loud enough for DeWalt to hear, he called through the trees.

"What's that . . . Chester? Did you . . . say something?" DeWalt yelled, between gasps.

"Get your flatlander ass up here and pinch me. Just so's I can be sure I'm not dreaming."

"Coming . . . you flannel-wearing . . . bastard," DeWalt said, breaking into a tortured trot. "Don't . . . let your long johns . . . ride up your rump."

Chester's thumb trembled on the twin hammers of the twenty-gauge. Not that buckshot would do a whole hell of a lot against *that*.

Then DeWalt was at his side, saying "Good God" in a hoarse, weak voice.

"It ain't nothing to do with God," Chester said. "More like the garden gate to hell, if you ask me."

Below them, in an outcrop of mossy granite boulders, the light radiated green, fuzzy, and dismal. Chester thought it looked like the bonus light on that pinball machine down at the GasNGo over on Caney Fork. You had to knock a ball into the caved-out belly button of a painted Vegas showgirl to get the bonus. But this light looked like the jackpot for a game that had no score.

There must have been a springhead in the rocks, because a sluggish trickle of fluid roped down the gully. But it was no clean, pure mountain stream. It sparkled like rancid grapes, as if only part of the light were reflected, and the rest was swallowed and absorbed into the oozing green tongue that wound its way through the trees toward Stony Creek. The mud of the gully banks was veined with stringy white roots, as if a thousand giant spiders had spun sick webs.

The trees that bordered the outcrop were stunted and gnarled, darkened as if lightning-struck. Chester had the fleeting notion that they had grown heads and had bent low to eat their own trunks. No animals stirred in the heavy, still air of the ridge slope. It was almost as if the source of the green light had swallowed the atoms of the atmosphere.

Swallowed was the word that came to mind, because the thing definitely gave Chester the impression of a mouth. It was a grotto, a jagged opening under the rocks. Soil was spilled around the edge of the opening as if around a wood-chuck's hole. Chester could clearly see inside the grotto because the fluorescence was coming from somewhere within the earthen throat. Along the walls of the cave, which angled downward toward the base of the mountain, yellowish tendrils and umbels dangled like tiny slick stalactites, as long as arms. They writhed and curled like eyeless maggots searching for dead food.

The mouth of the grotto was large enough to hold a dozen people. Paste-colored stones huddled inside like teeth that were impatient for something to grind. In the throat, ribbed bands of unnatural color shimmered in chartreuse, electric lemon, and cadmium yellow, greasy glow-in-the-dark colors. Deeper inside, leathery pedicels quivered like thirsty tap-roots.

"Is that your government conspiracy?" Chester said, after they'd both seen more than enough. They had reflexively crouched behind the locust, as if the cave-thing had eyes and would spot them.

"What in heaven's name is it?" DeWalt said, still struggling to catch his breath.

Chester almost said, "Oh, just one of those Earth Mouths you hear about, like the ones in those old folk stories. No big deal. Hills are covered with them."

Because he was afraid that he was becoming used to the idea of mushbrained people and a world where the unreal was commonplace.

Instead, he took a serious bite into his chaw and said, "You're the man with the book-learning, why don't you tell me?"

"You can only be taught what is already known. And I don't think this falls into the category of 'natural phenomena.' "

"What the hell do we do now? We've hunted down the bastard—and pardon me for giving it credence by calling it an *it*—but it ain't the kind of thing you shoot between the eyes and field dress and carry back home to the dinner table."

Chester was relieved to see that DeWalt's color had faded from beet red back to pink. Maybe the Yankee wouldn't up and die on him just yet.

"That creek might explain the green rain I saw," DeWalt said. "It's like that cave is spewing the stuff out. Those roots are spreading out, whatever it is. And the mouth—"

Chester looked over his shoulder and met DeWalt's eyes. *There, DeWalt had said it first.*

"Yeah, the mouth," DeWalt repeated. "The mouth goes into the mountain, but it feeds here. Can't you *feel* it?"

Chester nodded. He supposed he'd always had what DeWalt called a "kinship with nature," but he didn't want to be kin to whatever this thing was. He had enough fucked-up kin already, with his worthless sons Sylvester and Johnny Mack. Not to mention that liquor-pinching grandson of his, Junior. Now this mouth had squatted on his land, just crawled into the belly of Bear Claw and made itself at home with no respect for property lines.

But wasn't there something in the Good Book about forgiving those who trespass against you?

Chester wasn't ready to fall back on religion, especially when it meant inviting something like this into your life. And he'd never had much use for God, ever since the Baptists had told him that drinking moonshine damned you to eternal hellfire. But he found that he was fast needing something to believe in, because his sanity was dangling like a rusty bucket over a dark, bottomless well.

"I can sure feel *something,* DeWalt. Like when you're standing under one of those transfer stations with all the electric cables crisscrossed over your head. Something invisible but strong enough to make the hair stand up on the back of your neck and make your innards tingle. And if you listen close," Chester said, realizing for the first time that they had been whispering, as if the knotholes of the tainted trees were ears, "you can hear a little murmur inside the mouth. Almost like an ass-backward birdsong with a hard wind thrown in for good measure."

"Yes, I hear it. Sort of like music. The orchestra of the oubliette."

"Talk plain, you cufflink-wearing Yankee. I'm getting left far enough behind as it is."

"Something that sounds *wrong.* And looks wrong. But there it is. We can see it with our own eyes."

"But what are we going to do about it?" Chester's knees ached from stooping. "I don't think a shovel would do much good, even if we'd have brought one."

"Time to plan our next step, I suppose."

"I want all my steps to be *backward,* away from this damn dirt mouth that looks like it's ready to suck something in."

They had scarcely noticed that darkness was settling around them like black ink. The fluorescence from the mouth was so bright that it lit up the pocket of woods like a used car lot. The sound of distant crickets warned Chester that night was pitching its tent. "I see enough. *Too* much. Let's get the hell out of here."

"I'm game," said DeWalt.

"Don't say that, especially when that mouth looks like it's ready to do some hunting of its own."

He led DeWalt back toward the farmhouse, hoping his directional memory and woodsman's instinct held true. They reached the ridge overlooking the farm just as the sky turned from pink to violet. Chester was leading the way down one of his old hunting trails when he heard a twig snap. He spun, lowering his shotgun to waist level and pointing it toward the sound.

"Uh, pardon me, folks," the man said, stepping from behind a laurel thicket. "I got myself lost here."

"Stop where you are and open your eyes," Chester said.

"They *are* open."

No green lights. Chester exhaled and let the gun dip. His trigger finger relaxed, but only slightly.

"What in bluefuck blazes are you doing out in my woods this time of an evening? Trying to break your fool neck?" Chester hoped the man didn't realize how close he'd come to getting himself a new blowhole. He could feel DeWalt at his back, peering over his shoulder.

"Just out looking, sir," the man said.

"Trespassing ain't looked on too kindly around here. Ever damn thing and its brother's took up residence on my property." Chester didn't like the smell of the stranger's cologne. Smelled like sissy stuff. But at least his eyes weren't glowing green and he wasn't dribbling mush from his face.

"I apologize, sir," said the smooth-talking man. "You wouldn't happen to be Chester Mull, by any chance?"

"Depends on who's asking."

"Emerland. Kyle Emerland." The stranger stepped out of the shadows and extended his right hand. DeWalt muttered under his breath.

"That's fine and dandy, Mr. Emerland," Chester said, ignoring the offered hand. "Can't say as I'm glad to make your acquaintance. You still ain't said why you're out here, and you don't look like a midnight poacher in that fancy suit of yours."

"I'll be blunt then, sir. You seem like a man who appreciates honesty. I'm here to make a business proposition."

"I'm not in no business. What have I got that you want?"

"About four hundred acres of mountaintop, for one thing," DeWalt interrupted. "You're pointing a gun at the man responsible for the development of the Sugarfoot resort. I'll turn my head if you want to shoot him without any witnesses."

"Herbert DeWalt, is that you?" the stranger said cheerfully. A little too cheerfully, in Chester's opinion.

Slick, like. Maybe he's in on this Earth Mouth deal somehow. Maybe it's some sort of high-dollar pollution. Or a secret government test of some kind.

"Yes, it's me, Emerland," DeWalt said. "I'm sure you've done your homework, so let's not play games. You're just wasting your time. Chester's not interested in selling."

"Come now, let's be reasonable. Let Mister Mull decide for himself."

"Hold on, hold on," said Chester, irritated. His mind had been forced to make too many leaps already today. He was just coming to grips with a strange unworldly visitation, and now a stranger wanted to talk real estate. "Anybody mind clueing *me* in, seeing as how I seem to be the bone that the dogs are tugging at?"

"At least hear me out, Mister Mull," Emerland said. "Let's sit down and put it all on the table. I think you'll find my offer's extremely generous."

"Do *what?*"

"He wants to buy you out, Chester," DeWalt said. "He wants Bear Claw so he can fill it in with concrete and steel, shiny glass and ski lifts, and the finest tourists that New Jersey and Florida have to offer."

"Come on, DeWalt," Emerland said. "You know I'm a fair man. And I'm not a cheapskate."

"He's got a bulldozer in place of a heart," DeWalt said to Chester.

Chester squinted at the stranger's face. "A little earth moving might not be a bad idea, if this here Emerland's got a big enough shovel for the job."

An early moon had risen, a crisp wide ball that looked like it would drip milk if squeezed. Chester was uncomfortable standing out here at night, with a forest full of mushbrains and Earth Mouths and Lord only knew what else.

"Why don't we take this little powwow down to the house?" Chester said. "I don't trust these woods this time of night. Never know what you might run into."

DeWalt was looking at Emerland as if watching a rattlesnake that might decide to strike. Chester headed down the trail, glad he'd shut the flatlanders up enough so he could listen to the trees.

Because the trees were whispering, and the language was soft and slushy and strange. He picked up speed as he headed downhill, leaving the two men to make their own way back. But they must have experienced the same uneasiness, because they stayed at Chester's boot heels until the trio reached the forest's edge.

Chester breathed a sigh of relief when they stepped out from the canopy of the woods into a meadow. He looked at his farm spread out below, at the dark buildings and the barbed-wire stitching that marked off the fields. Under the stars, it was a beautiful, peaceful place. Except for its unwanted visitors.

The evening dew soaked into Chester's boots, making his

feet heavy. He dug into the pocket of his overalls for his moonshine. DeWalt stepped beside him, breathing hard.

"Let me warn you about him, Chester," he said, low enough so that the trailing Emerland couldn't hear.

"Shoot, pardner." Chester screwed the lid off the jar. He hoped DeWalt didn't launch into his tree-hugger bit. He glanced back at the mountain. He could just make out the green glow in a pocket between two ripples of black land.

"You know that song 'This Land is Your Land'?"

"Sure. Learned it in third grade. My last year of schooling."

"Well, there's a new version. It goes"—DeWalt drew in a breath and sang in an off-key bass—"This land was your land, this land was my land, now it belongs to . . . that bastard Emerland . . ."

Chester chuckled. "You couldn't carry a tune in a galvanized washtub. But I get your drift."

"What's that, gentlemen?" Emerland called.

Chester stopped and lifted the moonshine jar to his lips. "Oh, just talking about you behind your back, is all."

"Don't believe everything DeWalt says. He's only protecting his own interests. We'll top his offer by twenty percent."

"Don't matter none," Chester said. "I ain't selling. And I got other problems at the moment."

"Mister Mull, we're talking a high six figures here," Emerland said. "Maybe bumping seven. And our development will be ergonomically designed to fit the environment and protect the viewshed. The impact on the natural beauty will be minimal. My architects—"

"You can shelve the twenty-dollar words, Emerland," Chester said. "Won't make no difference."

"Chester, his idea of 'low impact' is a truckload of dynamite," DeWalt said.

Chester had lifted the jar for another sip but stopped with the jar inches from his lips. "What's that?"

"Emerland likes things that go boom."

Chester took the delayed swallow, wiped his mouth with his sleeve, and said, "Dyn-ee-fucking-mite."

"Are you thinking what I'm thinking?" DeWalt said.

"Yeah, but probably in plainer words."

"Blow the fucker back to hell?"

"Can't get no plainer than that."

Emerland's eyes shifted back and forth.

Probably wondering how he ended up with such a pair of fruitcakes on a cool Appalachian mountain under a grinning moon, Chester thought.

"Hey," Chester said to him. "You got some dynamite over there at the construction site, don't you?"

"Huh?" Emerland's clean-shaven jaw dropped.

"Ka-blooey stuff. TNT. Instant avalanche."

"You're insane." Emerland raised his palms in protest. "That stuff is seriously regulated. It has to be double locked and every damned piece has to be accounted for—"

"Locked, huh? And I reckon you got the keys, Mister Big Britches?" Chester let his few teeth catch the moon in what he hoped was a crazed grimace. He pointed the shotgun at Emerland to complete the lunatic image. He was pleased to see Emerland gulp frantically.

"You can't do this. Why, this is . . . it's against the *law.*"

Chester cackled. He'd discovered that pretending to be insane wasn't much of a character stretch. "There's a new law in town, stranger. And it ain't wrote by the likes of us. Now, get on to the house."

He let the barrel of the gun flash under the moonlight for emphasis. DeWalt held his arm out like a doorman, indicating that Emerland should go first.

"Lead on, MacDuff," DeWalt said.

"Who the hell?" Chester asked.

"I'll tell you about it someday, after this is all over."

Chester wondered if it would ever be over as they walked under the seemingly endless night sky.

Chapter Twenty-Six

Driving yourself crazy.

What else could you call it when your car almost seemed to steer itself, when the road beneath the wheels was predetermined, when God's skyhook towed you toward an unknown destination?

No. Tamara wasn't heading toward craziness. She was either already there or miles from it, saner now than she had ever been. The green light on the ridge above her grew stronger as she approached, and though the curving dirt road often took the glow out of her sight, the electric throb in her head was constant, more intense with each heartbeat.

She'd slammed some breezy, take-it-easy Jackson Browne into the tape deck, as if mindless melancholy were the proper soundtrack for this unwanted mission. As she ascended, and the road grew more rough and rutted, the forest had taken on a dark look, the canopy hiding quick shadows. The houses had grown sparser along the way, here and there tucked in little glens, gray outbuildings warped with age amid pastures worn low by diseased-looking cattle.

Tamara downshifted and cut around a particularly steep curve, and for a moment the world fell away at the shoulder of the road, and she could see Windshake below, brick and wood blocks with some sunset lights already on, the uneven highway leading away from town like a black river. Jackson sang something about not being confronted with his failures, as if the mirror didn't do that to every human being on earth. Then she was between the trees again, and the creeping insistent voice tickled the top of her spine.

Shu-shaaa tah-mah-raaa.

The Gloomies were around, floating, seeping, flowing. If she couldn't come to them, they would come to her, or perhaps they would collide with each other. She hadn't dreamed this part. Or maybe this was a waking dream, one where her own life was the centerpiece, not her father's or her children's. This was the forest of night, the oaks surreal and the pines undulating their branches, the tint of the leaves slightly off-kilter, as if viewed through a smudged kaleidoscope.

She took another curve, skidding on the moist stones where a ditch leaked springwater across the sodden road. The tires spun and caught, but as she straightened the wheel to head deeper up the cut of the mountain, the bank on the far side gave way and a gnarled giant oak fell toward the Toyota. She swerved, but the thick branches batted the side of the car in falling, cracking the windshield. The weight of the tree nudged the Toyota into the ditch, bottoming out the car and leaving the left front wheel hanging suspended. She shifted into four-wheel drive, but the mud, the tangled grip of the tree branches, and the grounded oil pan kept the Toyota from doing anything more than quivering in place.

After a minute of revving the engine, Tamara tried to open her door. It was pinned by a splintered branch as thick as her arm, its new leaves pressed against the glass in greasy smears. Up close, the leaves looked as if they had turgid blue veins, like the varicose veins of an old person.

She crawled across the seat to the passenger door, opened it, and wriggled out. She stood and looked at the oak, with its gray bark and dark knotholes that seemed to be watchful eyes. The exposed roots, thrust up from the soil, undulated like white worms.

No. The tree isn't alive, not in THAT sense of the word.

She looked past the fallen oak to the forest beyond, which was pocked here and there with granite outcroppings. Other trees lay fallen or bent, almost in a line up the slope. The destruction led in the direction of the glow, and she could see a faint shimmering between the stick figures of the trees.

Tamara sensed a change in the atmosphere, as if a storm were approaching, but the clouds of sunset were thin and red. The thing, the source, the *shu-shaaa,* had brought her here, and now she was alone. Now the tide had turned, giving the advantage to whatever strange force haunted the ridge top. The air was electric with it, and the March wind carried its taint.

She should have gone home. Robert would be sitting at the kitchen table with milk and cookies for himself and the kids, frowning as he watched the hands spin on their wooden owl clock. Then his face would become a rictus of anger as the Six O'clock News came and went on the television. Then he'd put on a mask of studied calm while at the same time trying to reassure the kids by telling them their mother was probably out picking up pizzas. Even though it wasn't like her to just take off without leaving a message.

She looked around at the forest shadows that grew long like sharp arms. Small animals chittered in the tangled boughs and tree limbs creaked in brittle agony. Red buds and bright green sprigs fought toward the sinking sun in painful birth. Trees screamed into the sky as if burning alive. Even the loamy soil cried from the harsh clutch of roots.

No, she thought. *I am NOT sensing the forest. Having a few dreams is one thing. Listening to my Gloomies is another. But I'm not a nature child, hearing the songs of Mother Earth. Sounds like something Jackson Browne would write in a sappy moment.*

I am not feeling the dead leaves sigh as they decompose. The laurels are not waving at the sky, drawing air into their waxy leaves. The firs are not transpiring their juice as if crying joyful tears. The woodears and fungi are not pulsing as if the dirt and water and air have aroused them. Centipedes and grubs and termites are not rooting around in lush bacterial cemeteries, whistling like industrious dwarves.

The creeks are not hammering like lead pipes on bricks, instead of gurgling like fed babies or tinkling like tiny sleigh bells. The rocks cannot throb like rotted teeth. The saplings do not scream as if pierced by their own splinters. I am not going insane here. The mountain is not talking to me.

The MOUNTAIN—

is not—

talking—

to ME.

Tamara clasped her hands over her ears as if to block out the unwelcome call of the wild. But the sound was already inside, circling the globe of her brain, spinning its fibrous web in her psyche. She leaned against the Toyota, bright sparks streaking behind her closed eyes. The Gloomies had joined in harmony with the forest's raging chorus.

She fell to her knees on the weedy roadside. Among the clatter of bonelike wood and harping briar and babbling brook and frenzied fern, she didn't hear the footsteps kicking leaves as they neared. But she didn't need to hear, because she *felt*.

She looked up to see a teenager standing over her. He had dark hair and a Bulls jacket and a wide jaw, a typical teenager who happened to walk out of nowhere—normal, everyday, out-of-the-ordinary—his flesh swollen and moist. Menace flashed in his eyes, which glittered deep and green and empty. Tenderness flashed in his blissful smile, showing petrified teeth. And now he groped her with mental hands.

Because he was one of the Gloomies, part of whatever had been niggling at her mind like a loose jumper wire. And she was inside his mind now, only his mind was pulp and mush, a fruity tree made paper. A name, yes, "*shu-shaaa*" was his name, and it was also "Wade." But that made no sense. Then again, nothing did at the moment. No sense, only a sensing.

And she was pounded with the impression that she'd better fall beyond his reach, because he wanted to make an offer. An offering. Of her.

Then his hand was on her shoulder, pulling at the fabric of her blouse, loosening her bra strap and exposing her shoulder to the fading sunlight. He pulled her close, his breath like a dead mist rising over the wooden corpses of a windfall. And in his touch, she felt the parent behind him and inside him. She felt its hunger, its instinct, its will to possess.

She saw the vision it carried in its hot seed of a heart: the great *shu-shaaa* reunited, the bright pinwheel of galaxies folding back upon itself, the nebulous clouds of space being summoned home, matter consumed and excreted as dark matter, the universe swallowing its own tail. Then, after the hands of time reversed, after the sand had been stuffed back into the top of the hourglass, after history was once again unwritten and unmade, only a calm black nothingness would remain. The horrible eternal peace of a collapsed cosmos, with not a glimmer of light or life. She saw the future.

The vision came through a single touch. But now the touch was gone and the contact no longer burned, because she dropped on her back and kicked at the teenager. His flesh yielded like an overripe peach. The initial stunning power of the psychic invasion had eased. The impressions of galactic anticlimax still stormed Tamara's mind, but she compartmentalized them, put them aside for later study. First she needed to survive.

The teen fell away, but approached again like a drugged snail. The boy throbbed, pulsed with dewy joy, steaming like a hothouse orchid. Tamara instinctively knew he wanted to rape her. Not just a rape of orifice and flesh, but a violation of her deeper self. Her organic being, her fluid and cells and neurons and synapses, her blood and spit and sweat. Her soul.

She rolled to her feet and grabbed for the car door. Her fingernails screeched across the sheet metal until she found the door handle, then she was diving inside, banging her knee on the gear shift as she struggled into the bucket seat. She slammed the door just as the boy reached into the Toyota.

Tamara heard a sound like green beans snapping as the car's weight shifted. No surprise flashed across those fluorescent eyes as his severed fingers dropped into her lap. She slapped them into the floorboard, and milky fluid leaked from the wounds. Even disconnected from their host, the fingers worked, wriggling in some blind and silent search.

Then the boy's face was low on the windshield, soggy lips pressed against the glass in a cold kiss. The eyes gleamed longingly as oozing palms searched the glass, seeking entry. Tamara slammed down the door lock.

Did the shu-shaaa thing, the source of her Gloomies, have knowledge of locks?

She sensed that *shu-shaaa* was growing strong, eating the mountain, spreading like kudzu, soaking up sun and water and bacteria. It was ravenous, like the boy at her window who ached to convert her, to consume her energy and reduce her to a rotting husk. Just as its parent would leave the entire world as a husk after it had taken its fill.

She didn't succumb to any internal debates over such impossibilities. She simply *knew*. She might deny the evidence of her eyes but she couldn't deny the sensing. The sensing never lied. No more voices. No more doubt.

All that was left was survival in a world gone mad.

Tamara crawled into the back seat and put her hand on the door lever. The boy sloughed his way down the side of the car, his marred hand leaving a wet trail on the glass. He moved slowly, but Tamara wasn't sure that flight was wise.

She could outrun this one, but she sensed that others of his kind were out there. Lots of others.

Still, she couldn't stay here all night. It might be hours before anyone passed this stretch of nowhere road. Or it might be tomorrow. Mountain folks had a tendency to turn in early. And how could she expect help when the entire mountain seemed allied against her?

She decided to risk it. If she followed the road, she would soon come to a house. And with the moon coming out, she didn't really need light to avoid the others who had become infected—*converted*—like the boy had. She could easily pick up their chaotic vibes, because her sensitivity seemed to have grown with the nearness of the *shu-shaaa,* as if the Gloomies were as psychically tuned in to her as she was to them. Whatever had shaped the mind or consciousness or soul that called itself *shu-shaaa,* it was growing stronger and more at ease in this environment.

In its natural environment.

And its understanding of Tamara mirrored her own understanding of it.

"Mah-raaa . . ." the boy said. "Tah-mah-raaa . . ."

Oh, God. It's speaking. It knows my NAME.

Tamara flipped the latch and then kicked the door open with both feet, shoving the boy backward. As he staggered, she hopped to the roadbed. She ran toward the east in the direction she had driven up. She took one glance back at the boy, who stumped slowly after her, his feetless legs—*no, STEMS, not legs*—scissoring with a wretched slosh.

She heard its pathetic call with both her ears and her mind.

"Shu-shaaa . . . mah-raaa . . . eyezzzz."

But underneath that voice, which was piped directly from whatever force drove the Gloomies, inside the blissful mist of that cosmic possessor, Tamara sensed the human part, the boy who wished he were somewhere getting high or flirting

with cheerleaders or singing in the church choir. The part
that was aware enough to know what it once was and could
no longer be. The part that screamed inside, even while the
parent hummed its pacific lullabies.

Then she fled down the road. She wasn't a jogger, but she
exercised daily and found the work was paying off. Of
course, she never thought her life might depend on it. Even
one who sometimes saw the future wasn't always prepared
for the worst.

Her mind turned cartwheels as she covered her first quarter mile with darkness falling like a dark shroud from above.
She was out of immediate range of whatever had clogged
her senses, the raging mountain that had croaked its appetite
upon the world. She tried to understand what could have
brought something like that into the world. But maybe it had
always been there, somewhere across a billion skies, across
the not-quite-endless universe.

And it was not only growing, it was *learning*. It had
adapted to the strange environment and was evolving in
order to survive, assimilating itself into the biosystem. Or,
perhaps, it was assimilating that system into itself in a mutual transference, a symbiosis where both predator and prey
were the same.

Because it knew her name . . .

She was so lost in her thoughts that the car was almost
upon her around the bend before she saw it. Its headlights
washed over her as she jumped to the side of the road. Her
ankle twisted as she fell in the ditch. The car slid to a halt,
tires rasping on the gravel as they grabbed for traction. A
door opened, lighting up the passenger compartment.

"You okay?" called a voice. She counted the heads of
three men. Risky, even here in the low-crime region of the
mountains. Still, she didn't have much choice, if she wanted
to get home before the sun rose. Before the Gloomies
swarmed.

"Uh, sure," she said, limping cautiously to the open door. "Had a breakdown up the road."

"Yeah, saw the car," an old man in the front seat said. He talked with the rural drawl that marked him as a native. "And the . . . uh . . . *boy* . . ."

Under the interior light, she made out the faces of the men inside the Mercedes. The man in the back seat, who looked to be in his fifties, was well-dressed and had friendly blue eyes. The driver wore an expensive suit, his styled blond hair trimmed evenly three inches above his collar. He seemed a little nervous. She watched in the rearview mirror as his eyes kept flicking to the leather-faced old man beside him.

"Hop in, young lady," said the man in back. "You don't want to be out there on a night like this." He slid over behind the driver. "I'm Herbert DeWalt. Your chauffeur is Kyle Emerland and that there's Chester Mull."

"Tamara," she said. "Tamara Leon. Thanks for the lift."

Tamara got into the seat he'd vacated and looked at the two men up front as the Mercedes pulled away. They had driven out into an open stretch of valley, with hay fields on both sides. The rising moon bathed the valley, making the distant ridges look creamy and vague. She almost relaxed. Then she saw that the old man in the front passenger seat had a shotgun.

"Don't be alarmed, ma'am," DeWalt said. "Nobody's going to hurt you. We're on a little business trip here."

Chester turned and grinned at her, showing his few teeth as if they were precious jewels. A dark knot of tobacco was lodged in one jaw. He smelled as if he had crawled out of a whiskey barrel.

"Ain't a fit night for man nor beast. Nor woman, for that matter," he said, glancing appreciatively at her face. "We don't mind the company nary a bit. You got green eyes, but they're the *right* kind of green."

"Hush, Chester," DeWalt said. "We don't need to frighten her any more than she already is."

The driver glanced at the shotgun. Chester tilted the gun toward him. "Nothing to be scared of, Emerland, as long as you don't drive over any big potholes and make my trigger finger slip," he said to the driver.

"Emerland," Tamara said. "You're the developer."

Emerland beamed a little at the recognition, even though his eyes twitched with anxiety.

"Nothing personal, but I heard you were a real jerk," she said. DeWalt and Chester laughed. Emerland seemed to shrink in his seat a little.

"Goddamn, look out!" Chester yelled. Emerland yanked the wheel, dodging the figure that seemed to have risen from the roadbed out of nowhere. Tamara heard a thump against the rear quarter panel.

"Did I just hit somebody?" Emerland's eyes were wide in the rearview mirror.

"It was a frigging mushbrain," Chester said, gurgling from a mouthful of brown saliva. He relieved his burden onto the Mercedes's burgundy carpet. "Saw its green eyes flashing. Sonuvawhores must be all over the place by now. Keep driving before it decides to stand up again."

Chester pointed the shotgun again for additional encouragement. Emerland floored the Mercedes and kicked up a rash of gravel. Emerland's cell phone rang, and Chester lifted it from the seat, cracked open his door, and chucked the phone out of the car. "Don't want you blabbing to your buddies before we're done," Chester said to Emerland.

"We were right, Chester," DeWalt said. "I don't know if it's a disease, but it seems to be spreading. That's what—the fourth one of them?"

Tamara startled them by saying, "There are dozens by now."

DeWalt and Chester turned to her and Emerland dared a glance in the mirror.

"It's up on the mountain, whatever it is," she said. "The thing that caused all this."

"Hey, that's what *we* was thinking . . ." Chester trailed away.

"I know about them," she said, not sure how to begin. "They've been in my head . . . I see things."

She knew she sounded insane, but the *world* was insane, as if God had tipped the universe upside down and shaken the laws of existence. And right now, she needed allies. Some madnesses were best shared. Robert was miles away, safe with the kids. At least, she hoped they were safe. She'd have to trust Robert to take care of the family.

"You *see* things." Emerland shook his head. "Christ. I've been kidnapped by a freak show."

"Shut up and drive," Chester said. "And don't open your yap till we get to your dynamite shed. You seen them things as plain as we did." He turned to the back seat, giving Tamara his wet, crooked smile. "Go ahead, now. We're listening."

She told them about her knack for seeing the future—the quick version, no frills and no embarrassment. It was the first time she'd ever told anyone besides Robert. It gave her confidence somehow, to tell a bunch of strangers who weren't in a position to be skeptical. But it also made the clairvoyant gift seem more real than ever before, as if she could no longer deny it, even to herself. They didn't laugh once.

As the Mercedes slid through the greasy night onto the main highway, she described the *shu-shaaa,* what she had sensed from the forest and the boy. She told them about its "cosmic mission," realizing as she explained it just how far-fetched it sounded. They didn't interrupt, only nodded and grunted. When she finished, DeWalt told her about the Earth Mouth they had found.

"That's it," she said. "The strange music I heard that wasn't really music. It's the source. Its voice."

"You mean it *talks?*" Chester said.

"It called me by my name. Through the boy."

Chester had lowered his shotgun so that the occasional passing motorist wouldn't see it in the flash of headlights. He said, "Ordinarily, I'd call it a bunch of hippie claptrap and think somebody's been smoking some funny weed. But I seen it with my own eyes, and ain't no dope ever filled this old head. But *something's* as fucked up as a football bat, and it ain't just me. They're like zombie creeps in some picture show."

"Well, it's got its 'mission,' as you say, Tamara," DeWalt said. "And we have ours."

He told her about their plan to dynamite the cave. "We know it's probably a job for the military or the FBI or whoever has jurisdiction over alien invasions—"

"But it would take days, maybe weeks, before you convinced somebody you weren't crazy," Tamara said, the resident expert in being called crazy. "And it's getting stronger by the minute. I can feel it. It's learning about the world, growing, getting smarter."

Chester peered at her with one bleary eye, crow's feet crinkling as he squinted. "One more thing's bothering me. Hell, *lots* of things is. But what's this '*shu-shaaa*' business?"

"Maybe it absorbed the sound from some life form in the woods. Something it converted. But the boy tried to talk to me. So it must be learning language. Human language."

"I expect it already knows tree talk, then. And the talk of pigs and chickens and whatever rot Don Oscar's head was filled with. Maybe that explains why old Boomer was trying to bark, but kept on making them swampy sounds."

"And the people who have turned, they still have some of their own thoughts, but the thoughts are trapped and mixed in with the parent, the *shu-shaaa.*"

"I'm no Einstein," DeWalt said, "but what you're saying doesn't really follow what we know about physics."

"Well, Einstein didn't know about this thing, either," Tamara said. "Rules are made to be broken."

DeWalt thought for a moment and nodded, then looked out the window.

Chester turned to her again. "You say there's more of these dirt-bag zombiemakers up in the sky somewhere?"

Tamara nodded. "All heading for their version of heaven, nirvana, whatever you want to call it. This may sound corny, but each is like a spirit energy going home, and one day, maybe ten thousand, maybe ten *million* years from now, they'll join together and . . ."

Emerland shook his head again. Chester looked out the window at the stars. DeWalt said, "And *what,* Tamara? You're preaching to the converted here. You're the closest thing to an expert we might ever have."

"They'll become a god."

"Shit fire," Chester said.

They rode on in silence as the pavement sloped up toward Sugarfoot.

Chapter Twenty-Seven

"Why didn't you tell me about this sooner?" Virginia Speerhorn pressed a polished thumbnail into her palm until the pain helped her control her anger.

"Didn't think it was any big deal. Just a report of attempted assault. And you've got plenty to worry about as it is, what with Blossomfest and all."

"I might be worrying about finding a new police chief, Mister Crosley," Virginia said into the phone. She couldn't use her withering glare, but she could drip the sarcasm. "You know I want to be informed about such matters."

"Sorry, Mayor. I hate to bother you at home—"

"You're just afraid you'll piss me off. Don't want to rile the Virgin Queen, is that it?"

There was silence on the other end of the line. Virginia knew Crosley was rubbing his fat belly with his free hand.

Blossomfest was barely nine hours away, and she wanted to appear fresh and vigorous in front of tomorrow's crowds. Even though she enjoyed the iron grip she kept on Windshake, she hadn't completely ruled out a run for state office. Crosley had called shortly before midnight, interrupting her wardrobe reverie.

"And now you have some missing persons reports?" she said, prompting his attention away from his gut.

"Uh, yes ma'am. Kyle Emerland, for one. You know, that bigshot developer?"

"Of course I do." She made it a habit to know all the bigshots.

"His assistant called in about seven o'clock. Said Emerland missed a board meeting and a dinner date with some out-of-town investors. The assistant said Emerland never misses a board meeting. No answer on his cellular phone, either."

"When was he last seen?" Virginia was glad that the local paper was a bi-weekly and wouldn't have an edition out until after the weekend. And Dennis Thorne at the radio station would hold any story if he was afraid somebody might give him a bad job reference. No negative publicity until *after* Blossomfest.

"The assistant says he was planning to visit a fellow named Chester Mull this afternoon to discuss a business proposal. Mull lives out on the top of Bear Claw."

"That's outside the town limits. Have you contacted Mr. Mull?"

"No answer on the phone there, either. I sent a black-and-white up there to check it out, even though it was county. Officer found an overturned vehicle, but it wasn't Emerland's. Belonged to a man named DeWalt. No sign of any people on the premises, though. Just the truck. I ran the plates, and it checked out as Mull's."

"Something sounds fishy. I presume you're still searching."

"Yeah, but we've only got three men—I mean, *officers*—on duty. Two are keeping watch downtown over all the set-ups. Everybody else has the night off because of having to patrol Blossomfest tomorrow."

"Call in a couple. I'll authorize the overtime. Who else is missing?"

Virginia hoped this didn't turn into an epidemic. Most missing persons showed up the next day with a sheepish grin and a hangover, or sometimes were traced to motels that rented rooms by the hour.

"A Mrs. Tamara Leon," Crosley said. "Teaches down at Westridge. Her husband says he hasn't heard from her all day. He tried the university and all their friends, but nobody's seen her. Whereabouts unknown. Plus there's a high school kid. But he's a regular. Likes to take little trips, if you know what I mean. Drugs."

Virginia allowed herself a sigh of relief. At least those two were nobodies. She wondered if there was a connection between them and Emerland. It seemed unlikely.

"Concentrate on Emerland, and keep an eye out for the other two. But they're strictly back burner for now."

"Yes, Mayor," Crosley said. "Oh, and there's one more thing."

She listened as Crosley explained the case of the mysterious Melting Man, the one that had "disappeared," leaving behind only some dirty clothes and a Red Man cap. By the time he had finished, Virginia decided that she was definitely going to have to find a new police chief.

"I'm not in the mood for games, Chief. Call me if you get something."

"But I *saw* it . . . uh . . . good night, ma'am."

She hung up the phone and thought for a moment. Three people missing in one night, when Windshake usually might expect one every six months. Something was going on that was beyond her control. She hated that feeling. She wondered if it would dampen Blossomfest, then decided it wouldn't. She wouldn't let it.

She went to check on Reggie, to make sure he had made his eleven o'clock curfew. Surely he understood how important this weekend was to her. She almost wished his father hadn't died, but he'd been deadweight anyway, holding her career back. The only thing he'd ever done right was giving her Reggie.

She could see from the dark crack under Reggie's door that his lights were off. She knocked lightly. He was old enough to have his privacy respected. He didn't answer. He must have already been asleep.

"Sleep well, my angel," she whispered, then headed for her own bed.

Nettie hummed "Amazing Grace" at her desk in the church vestry. She felt as if she were glowing, like the Madonna in those Renaissance paintings. She hadn't felt so wonderfully alive since she had gotten saved at age fourteen. Now she had been saved again, this time from loneliness and unrequited attraction.

Maybe it's even . . . yeah, you can say it: LOVE.

The day with Bill had been wonderful, her wildest fantasies come true. He had touched her, held her, taken her. His smell clung to her skin, a strong and masculine odor of sawdust and clean sweat. She tingled under her dress as she thought back on their tumble in the clover.

She was having a hard time concentrating on the computer layout she was doing for Sunday's church program. She'd push her mouse to drop in a clip art Jesus and then her mind would take off and Jesus would end up over in the birthday announcements. And when she typed "Windshake Baptist Welcomes Blossomfest Visitors," the event came out as "Bosomfest" and then "Blosomfset." She would be here all night if she wasn't careful, and she didn't plan on being here all night. Because Bill was coming to her place later, before he started his volunteer shift providing security for the Blossomfest arrangements.

She was high, brushing God's clouds with her mind. She thanked the Lord a thousand times for bringing Bill into her

life and heart. She was afraid that Bill would feel guilty after-
ward, that he would think she was some kind of wicked woman
out to sap his strength and turn him from God. But when
their eyes had finally opened after that searing hot explosion,
they had looked at each other for a full minute without
speaking. Then Bill said "I love you" in his deep, honest
voice, and she could tell he meant it.

She replayed the words like a reel-to-reel tape, over and
over. And she was still hearing them when Preacher Blevins's
feet crept across the floor. She spun in her swivel chair to
face him. She wasn't going to let him sneak up and put his
hand on her shoulder again.

He looked down on her, his lightbulb head brightened by
his beatific smile. "Burning the midnight oil for the Lord,
Nettie?"

"Finishing up the program, is all," she answered, watching
as his dark vulture eyes did their cursory crawl over her body.

He grinned his beaver grin that now seemed sinister instead of friendly. "Fine, my child. Fine. Ought to have a big
crowd this week. And next week, with Easter coming up. It's
an important time for the Lord."

Nettie wondered if the preacher knew that Easter had
originally been a pagan fertility holiday. Thinking of fertility
made her glad she was still taking birth control pills, even
though she hadn't had a sex partner in over a year. In the heat
of the moment, neither she nor Bill had mentioned condoms.
Nor, heaven forbid, disease. She found herself blushing,
thinking of rubbers in church.

"Your cheeks are pink, my child," the preacher said, stepping close so that he was standing above her. "What thought
is in your head that brings the devil's shade?"

"Oh, just a minor sin, Preacher. Hardly worth feeling bad
about, but when you're in the House of the Lord—"

The preacher raised a beneficent hand. "I know, child. We
humans are weak. We fall short of the perfection and glory
of God."

He touched her knee with a hot, moist hand. His breath smelled of copper and blood, a hunter's breath.

Bill's love gave Nettie courage. She decided it was time to confront him. "Preacher—"

He leaned closer. "Tell me your sin, my pretty one."

She arched back in her chair, trying to shrink away from his leering face.

"My sin is silence," she said, her teeth clenched. "I didn't speak against something I saw was wrong."

"But the Bible says 'Judge not, lest you be judged also,' " he said, lowering his voice. The rafters settled in the vast quiet of the empty church, as if the night was pressing heavily upon it.

She hesitated, wondering how to put her doubts into words. "It's about the money, Preacher."

"Money?" His eyes shifted like well-oiled ball bearings.

"The missing money. Only one person had access to it before I started working here. Only one person could have taken it."

"I told you, child—"

"I'm not your child, either. I'm a child of God, and you're a far sight from God."

"What are you talking about?" His face creased with confusion, breaking its practiced calm.

"It has to be *you* taking the money, Preacher. There are just too many discrepancies to laugh them off as honest mistakes. I've discovered ten thousand dollars that have fallen through the cracks just in the last year."

"Oh, my child, my child, the devil has put lies in your sweet little head, cast visions in your bright eyes," Armfield Blevins said in his smooth preacher voice.

She heard the slight sibilance of snakiness in his delivery. *God, had she been blinded by this deceiver all along? Had they all?*

"I've been hoping that I was wrong," she said. "But I can't fool myself any longer. It's eating me up inside."

She drew back as he smiled at her. Blevins's hand clutched her knee as he loomed over her, his form somehow made larger by the way he seemed to soak the shadows from the corners of the vestry.

"Thou shalt not bear false witness," he said without emotion.

"And thou shalt not suffer false prophets," she answered. The church would be torn apart, but Nettie knew that God would heal the congregation and make them stronger through the trials and tribulations. And she would make certain that Mister Blevins had his trial. In the court of humankind, that is. God would pass the final judgment elsewhere.

"There's plenty for both of us, Nettie. It's part of His plan. Part of my plan."

The preacher's right hand rubbed her knee and his other one began lifting the hem of her skirt. "For both of us," he repeated, voice husky. His breathing was harsh and shallow and fast.

"No." She shrank away.

"Hush, my child," The preacher's raw breath was on her cheek. "Armfield forgives you. You know not what you do."

"Preacher, what in the hell do you think you're doing?" She was cold inside, dead as stone.

"Why, saving you from Lucifer's fire, Nettie," he whispered. "You have gone astray, and I must bring you back into the fold. I'll show you the path of righteousness. But you must bow to my will. You must open up and let me inside."

Now his hand was under her skirt, on her bare thigh. She twisted away and tried to stand. His face purpled with rage and he tightened a fist around her hair, pinning her to the chair. His eyes leered with cruel promises.

"Harlot." He jammed his free hand under her skirt. "I smell the devil on you. I've seen the devil in your eyes. I've seen you flaunt your temptations before me. You're an abomination in the eyes of God."

Nettie strained to push him away, but his lean body was

leveraged against her, his knees pinning her legs and trapping her arms between their bodies. He had the strength of a demon. He yanked her head over the back of the chair, forcing her lower and exposing her neck to his frantic lips and slathering tongue. She could only stare at the ceiling, her arms trapped against his chest as he lifted her skirt to her waist.

His face was above her, wrenched and distorted and beet red. Through her shock and horror, Nettie realized that if Satan walked the earth, this was the mask he would wear. A mask of cruelty and mockery, eyes aflame with rancid lust, his breath a foul, soul-stealing wind. As she struggled, she closed her eyes and prayed to God to deliver her from evil.

A low voice filled her ears. "Uhmmmm . . ."

The preacher froze. At first Nettie thought he had moaned, calling out in a fit of possessed passion. Then the voice came again, from the interior of the church.

"Uhmmmmm . . . feeel . . ."

The preacher's taut-skinned head swiveled, eyes wide with fresh fear. His clawing hand slightly loosened in the tangles of her hair. She held her breath, waiting for a chance to break free, her heart hammering like a dove's.

The voice came again, louder, from the opening where the dais lead into the vestry. "Uhmm-feel . . ."

Nettie couldn't see who it was because her head was still trapped against the chair. But she could see the preacher's face turning ash gray as if he had seen a ghost. He released her.

The preacher backed away from Nettie and spun to face the door. His hands were out by his sides like a gunfighter in a showdown. His slacks dropped around his ankles from the loosening of his belt. Nettie lifted her head and doubted herself for a second time that night.

Because she didn't believe what her eyes were screaming at her.

Amanda Blevins moved across the room toward her faithless husband. But Amanda was only a small piece of what-ever the thing was, as if random bits of her features had been pressed into a dismal green clay. It had Amanda's henna red hair, but the styling had wilted, leaving damp straws. Her sharp nose protruded from the face—*God, can that be a FACE?* Nettie thought—like a curving thorn.

Amanda's clothes were torn and hung from her body in rags, and her flesh was in damp tatters as well. Her skin looked like old meat that had aged in a basement and grown moldy. As she moved, finger-sized chunks of her slid to the ground, leaving a slick trail on the floor as she approached the preacher. One sagging, flaccid breast swung free from her ripped blouse and dangled like an overripe fruit. Nettie's stomach knotted in revulsion and she tried to vomit, but her stomach wouldn't obey.

Nettie didn't know what was worse, the thing's mouth or its eyes. The eyes were glowing, deep green and translucent, as if rotten fires burned inside the watery skull. But the *mouth*—the mouth opened, gurgling and vapid, and sharp tendrils curled out like a nest of serpent's tongues from a pulpy den.

Then it spoke: "Uhmmm . . . feel . . . Uhmfeel . . . kish . . ."

The mouth sprayed viscous lime-colored drops, and Nettie could smell Amanda now. It was the stench of corpses, of graveyard rot and bad mulch, of stagnant puddles and tainted melons. Nettie tried to rise, but her limbs were thick, limp noodles and all she could do was watch in help-less fascination.

"Kish . . . shu-shaaa . . . Uhmmfeel," Amanda said.

The preacher backed away, his devil mask now turned white. Sweat glistened on his high forehead. His jaw locked open in horror as Amanda closed in on him. He staggered, his pants around his ankles tripping him, and he fell against the wall.

Then the thing that had once been Amanda was upon him, sliding down onto the preacher with a mushy, wet sound.

Her liquid flesh flowed over him and the inhuman mouth bent to his face. Nettie heard his muffled cries as he joined his wife in unholy union.

Then Nettie's muscles stirred to life and she pulled herself from her chair. She bolted across the floor, her shoes slipping on the slimy trail that Amanda had left. As she reached the vestry door, the preacher's voice clearly pierced the air in a final litany.

"It burns . . . it burns," he whimpered.

Amanda had tilted her soggy head to the ceiling, swamp suds dribbling from her vacuous mouth.

"*Shu-shaaahhhh*," the monster sprayed to the heavens before dropping its face once again to the preacher's.

Nettie ran into the unlit sanctuary, banging her knee against the pipe organ. She prayed to the Lord to shine on her from the darkness, this darkness that ruled the Earth, that rose in thick fogs around the edges of her mind and threatened to swallow her into the belly of madness.

Because hell had unleashed its demons, the Apocalypse had arrived, and she wondered if she had the faith to stand. For the first time since she had been saved, she wondered if faith alone would be enough.

Chapter Twenty-Eight

Robert turned off the television. He couldn't concentrate on the basketball game. He'd put the kids to bed and tucked them in with lies, hoping he'd done a good job of hiding his worry. He walked into the kitchen and stared at the telephone, silently begging it to ring, debating another call to the cops. He looked at the owl clock they'd received as a wedding present, its hands as dusty as their marriage.

It was nearly midnight. He balled his fists and wrestled the urge to punch the refrigerator. He longed to feel the pain flare up his arm and to pull his bloody knuckles from the dented metal, to hammer the idiotic appliance for standing there slick and mute while his wife was missing. He wished he could break himself in half as punishment for driving her away, because he knew it was his fault.

Suppose she'd had enough and couldn't face another of his temper tantrums? Robert couldn't really blame her. All because his guilt was chewing his intestines from the ass-end up. All because he should have been there for her, should have talked and confessed and opened his heart and asked for the forgiveness he knew she would have granted.

What if the unthinkable happened? That dream of hers,

the one she'd tried to tell him about. He'd only half listened while she related it. Something about the mountain eating them all. Maybe it was some kind of prescient view of an accident, maybe she'd driven off the road or fallen in a river or been suffocated or murdered or . . .

Don't even think about it, he thought. *But her goddamned Gloomies—*

Forget her Gloomies. That clairvoyant crap, seeing the future. Well, if Tamara could see the future, why had she married such a worthless piece of rat baggage?

But she'd been right about her father. And when Kevin broke his hip. If she is dead, and you never got a chance to say you were sorry, then how are you ever going to live with yourself?

He was reconsidering battering the stupid refrigerator because he couldn't reach inside and rip his even stupider heart out, couldn't hold it to the light over the sink as it dripped its cheating blood, couldn't watch it take its last undeserved beats. He couldn't, because of the kids.

"Daddy?"

Robert turned, his fists balled. Ginger rubbed a sleepy eye, clutching a stuffed frog to her chest. Her cheeks were wet with tears.

"What are you doing out of bed, honey?" He relaxed his hands and knelt to her. She looked so much like Tamara.

"Had a bad dream." She stood there sniffling in her flannel circus pajamas as he hugged her.

"It's okay now. Let me tuck you back in, and you can tell me all about it if you want."

"I want Mommy."

"Mommy's still not home, sweetheart. But she will be, soon."

"Not if the Dirt Mouth eats her."

"Dirt Mouth?" Robert almost grinned, but his daughter's serious green eyes stopped him.

"The Dirt Mouth in the mountains." She said it matter-of-factly, as if it were something she had seen in a nature program on television.

"Honey, there's no such thing—"

"Mommy said you have to trust your dreams. Because dreams are nature, and nature never lies. And the Dirt Mouth was in my dreams. And Mommy was on the mountain with it."

"Dreams are just little tricks the brain plays on us while we're asleep. Games to help pass the night."

"Where's Mommy, then?"

"Just . . . out somewhere, honey."

"Out with the Dirt Mouth. And it's going to eat the whole mountain, Daddy. It wants to eat everybody and all the trees and things."

Robert stroked Ginger's hair and held her to his chest. "It's just a bad dream, honey. Let's get you back to bed, and in the morning you'll see that Mommy will be home and the sun will come up and there won't be any mean old dirt mouths around."

He lifted her and carried her back to bed.

God, she's growing so fast, he thought. *Blonde and gorgeous and bright eyed. She's going to be sensitive, just like her mother. She has a wonderful imagination, too.*

Just like her mother.

He tucked her under the blankets and kissed her forehead. He couldn't help it. He had to know. Just in case. "Where was Mommy, honey? In your dream, I mean?"

"On the mountain, with the bad people. The barefooted mountain. Where the Dirt Mouth is, and the green light."

She yawned, then her tiny eyelashes flickered as her eyelids relaxed.

"Sleep tight, sugar. Daddy will make everything better."

"'Kay, Daddy."

He turned off the light. Her voice came from the darkness.

"Daddy, what's a *shu-shaaa*?"

"Shu-shaaa? I don't know, honey."

"It's scary."

"Don't you worry," he said to the dark bed. "Nothing bad can happen to you. Not while I'm around."

He found that lying was easy, once you got used to it. He started to sing "Baa Baa Black Sheep," and was on the third round of masters and dames when Ginger fell asleep.

He went out on the porch to smoke a cigarette and wait.

Nettie prayed.

She asked the Lord why He had allowed her to trip over that little round headstone that was really only a rock, the marker for an ancient, anonymous grave. She should have seen it gleaming like a white-capped tooth under the grinning curd of the moon. But she had run in a panic, out of the side door of the church into the dark graveyard. And she had been blind with fear.

What purpose could the Lord have in breaking her ankle? And she was scared to call for help, because help might come in the hideous form of the preacher's wife. Or the preacher himself, standing there in the glow of the vestry lights with his pants around his ankles and his eyes as deep as devil pits. Maybe if she could reach the parsonage, maybe if Sarah were home, maybe if she could crawl . . .

It was only forty yards. But the pain was a ring of dull fire above her foot and she had to pull herself along by digging her hands into the turf and dragging herself forward a few feet at a time. As she slid, the earth sent its small stones digging into her hip and the grass tugged at her skirt. She was only a dozen yards from the church when she heard the sounds.

At first she thought it was a burst water pipe, or a wet wind cutting through the rags of the treetops. Then she saw them, shadows shuffling out of the forest at the edge of the cemetery. She was about to call out, thinking they could help her.

But who would be walking around the cemetery on the dead edge of midnight?

Then she saw their eyes. Three pairs of fluorescent orbs, dancing in the dark like fat fireflies. It was more of *them*.

More of whatever Amanda Blevins had become.

Nettie bit her tongue so she wouldn't scream and a seam of bright pain flashed across her mouth. She grabbed her crippled leg with both hands and rolled over, trying to swallow her whimpers of agony. She huddled behind a huge marble slab, pressing against its cold smoothness. The inscription on the headstone, "William Franklin Lemly, 1902–1984," was carved in dark relief against the moon-bathed alabaster. Bill's grandfather.

"Help me, Bill," she whispered, her cheek against the slab. The three figures stepped—*STEPPED wasn't the right word,* she thought, *they're flowing*—into the moonlight, and Nettie saw the green pallor of their flesh. Their heads made her think of wax fruit dipped in motor oil. They flowed over the grass-covered bones of the dead as if they were dead themselves, with that same moist slogging that Amanda had made while entering the church, a dribble of mucus and gelatin. She recognized two of them, Hank and Ellen Painter, parishioners of Windshake Baptist who lived out on Stony Fork. The third was too rotten to be identifiable. It was sexless beneath its ripped and rotten clothing.

The three approached the light of the church door like wise men come to see a miracle image. Nettie peered around the stone as they passed, certain that they would hear her heart hammering. But their radiant eyes stayed fixed on their beloved church. Nettie watched them stumble up the stairs, mashing together as they all tried to go inside at the same time. They fell into the church and moaned in wet voices, singing praises to or raising curses against whatever god they now followed.

Nettie clawed her way across the grass, thinking of it as hair, the scalp of an earth that sweated dew and breathed the wind. A bright orange spear of pain flamed up her leg. She crawled behind a tall monument topped by an angel that held a harp and gazed toward heaven. Nettie rested her back against it, careful to keep the monument between herself and the church, and looked toward heaven herself.

Lord, what wonders you have wrought, she prayed. *If this is the End Times, please give me the strength to endure Your plagues. If this is the first trumpet note, then may all seven of Your angels blow in their turn. Thy will be done. Please forgive me, Father, but I'm going to try to live. Because I kind of liked the way my life was going before hell gave up its demons. So forgive me for being human, but I'm not quite ready to give You my ghost. Amen.*

Through a shrub twenty yards away, she looked wistfully at her car sparkling in the asphalt parking lot under the security light. But the car was a straight drive, and she couldn't operate the clutch because of her shattered ankle. Her best hope was to reach the parsonage and phone for help.

Assuming that either Sarah was home or the door was unlocked. Assuming that Sarah wasn't one of *them*. Assuming Nettie covered the open stretch of graveyard without being seen by the creatures. Assuming she didn't pass out from pain before she reached the front porch.

She clenched her jaw and wriggled on her belly like a serpent sent out of the garden.

Emerland unlocked the gate. The chain-link fence was topped with razor wire, designed to put second thoughts into the minds of would-be thieves. He considered fleeing for the darkness that hung on all sides of the compound. But the Mull geezer still had the shotgun, and Emerland could feel its blunt power throbbing anxiously somewhere behind him. Plus, to be honest with himself, all that talk of green-eyed plant people and mountain-eating Earth Mouths had put him on edge.

Though Emerland had seen the strange people along the road, he still thought Mull and DeWalt were nuts. This was the twenty-first century, for God's sake. Science had pretty much squashed any prospect of monsters or ghosts or vampires rising out of the ground. And aliens had become plastic clichés because of their overuse by hack fiction writers and low-budget movie producers. But good old human lunacy was a reliable constant, a proven horror that spanned history. And Emerland was positive that he could rely on Old Man Mull to do the unpredictable.

He turned back to the trio, flinching against the beams of the Mercedes's headlights. Chester, DeWalt, and the flaky psychic babe were black shadows against the yellow brightness.

"There you go," he said. "I just hope the security guards don't swing by."

But there were no security guards. The company that had brokered his construction company's insurance had insisted on around-the-clock protection because of the dynamite. Emerland had agreed in writing, but had never seen the point in wasting money on security. Who gave a damn if somebody stole something or if the whole place blew to hell if you had insurance that would cover the damage?

"Now unlock the dynamite shed," grunted the skinniest shadow, the one with the shotgun.

Emerland didn't bother arguing. He led the way past the metal hulks of bulldozers and cement mixers and stacks of fat-grooved truck tires to a small shed at the back of the compound. DeWalt carried the flashlight that Chester had found in Emerland's glove compartment, but the moon was so bright in the clear sky that they didn't need it. Emerland fumbled with the lock in the plywood door, cursing himself for being such a control freak that he needed a key to everything that had *Emerland Enterprises* stamped on it.

Then the lock popped and the door swung open with a rusty groan of hinges. DeWalt stepped inside with the flashlight. Emerland felt the gun barrel in his back and followed DeWalt.

"Do you know how to use this stuff?" Chester asked DeWalt.

"Sort of. I read the *Anarchist Cookbook* back in my younger days. You need a blasting cap, fuse wire, an electrical detonator switch. And some of those."

He pointed to the stack of small, paper-covered rods that were in an open crate on a shelf. "How many does it take?" DeWalt asked Emerland.

"How the hell do I know? I'm a developer, not a demolition man," Emerland said.

"Shut your rat hole, Emerland," said Chester. "Grab two dozen. Pass some to Tamara, here."

Emerland watched as Chester filled his overall pockets with the heavy sticks.

"Hey, DeWalt, you overeducated Yankee, why don't you read what it says under the red letters there?" Chester said, pointing to the warning written on the wooden crate. "Then, whatever it says *not* to do, just do the exact opposite. That ought to make some sort of snap, crackle, and pop or another."

"Chester, you're an idiot savant," DeWalt said.

"I don't take kindly to the 'idiot' part, but I'll take that other fancy word as some sort of praise."

"If I remember right—and you'll have to forgive me, because my brain was a little souped up back in those days— you attach the wire to this detonator and then to the blasting cap. This button sends an electric charge through the wire that heats up the stuff in the cap, then—"

"Fucking fireworks," Chester said. "Sets off the rest of the dynamite."

"Well, technically, this is TNT, not dynamite."

"What-the-hell-ever. As long as it makes a bang."

Emerland stepped back from the door, seeing that the two men were so intent on collecting the TNT that they didn't notice him. He glanced at the creamy-skinned blonde. Damn, she was good-looking. If only circumstances were different, he wouldn't mind having her in his hot tub on Sugarfoot, popping the cork on some Dom Perignon. He wondered if insanity was contagious.

"Um, guys," she said. "The thing's getting hungrier. I've got a feeling that we better move before the sun comes up."

Emerland's arousal shriveled. He tried to slink behind a broken motor grader.

"Not so fast, scumbucket," Chester said without turning. Emerland's feet locked. He passed the time by looking up the red mud slope of the clear-cut mountain to the shining tower of Sugarfoot Condominiums. It was beautiful against the starry sky, a man-made testament to the power of dreams. He wished he were there now, behind one of the tiny lights among the plush carpet and clean satin sheets and filthy-rich tourists. Away from grubby madmen and this sweet-cheeked Nostradamus.

They were walking back to the car, the woman and DeWalt clutching armfuls of dynamite, when something stumbled against the fence. Emerland heard the thin jingle of wire, then turned and saw the fruit of nightmares. It had once been a woman, he could tell that much, because its stringy hair fell like soggy bean sprouts over dripping breasts. The eyes glowed with deep, irradiant longing as its pale fingers hooked the metal links. "Shu-shaaa . . . kish . . . treeeez . . ."

Had the sounds come from that thing's raw wet mouth that gaped too widely to be human? Emerland was studying the vaguely familiar cheekbones and the wide skull that shone like pallid cheese in the moonlight. He suddenly recognized her—*no, IT, not HER*—as one of the aerobics instructors at Sugarfoot. One that he had shared several rather private workouts with.

No.

This wasn't happening.

Emerland was still looking at the face, looking for the woman who had once worn that skin before . . . *before the Earth Mouth-zombiemaker-worldeater came.*

Then the face disappeared as the thunder of Chester's shotgun shredded the thing's upper torso into a rain of pulp.

"They're out there. I see them coming," Tamara said in the sudden dead calm that followed the explosion.

Tamara led the way as they ran to the Mercedes. Emerland was frozen to the spot, unable to rip his gaze from the quivering stump of the creature that now sagged to the ground, leaving a viscous trail of fluid on the fence that shimmered in the moonlight. Then he regained the use of his legs and dashed to the car, passing the others and sliding behind the driver's seat of the Mercedes.

"Now do you believe?" DeWalt asked from the backseat.

Emerland nodded.

"Let's get the hell out of here," Chester said.

Chester didn't even have to threaten him with the shotgun this time.

Chapter Twenty-Nine

Bill hung up the cellular phone. He had dialed Nettie's number for the fourth time. No answer at the church, either. She wasn't in her apartment when he drove there to meet her at eleven o'clock. She had stood him up.

After *today*. After all they'd been through and shared. After Bill had bent his principles. After the sin that didn't feel at all like a sin.

After he'd said that word *love,* the clumsiest word that ever passed his lips.

He gripped the steering wheel and looked through the truck's windshield. The Blossomfest booths were silent, draped with vinyl and canvas and waiting for tomorrow's crowds. The brick faces of downtown were asleep, the streets black and empty. A police car threaded up the street between the stalls, its headlights washing over the plywood signs and stacked boxes and rigged backdrops. Bill studied the peeling white of the Haynes House, which would soon be filled with laughing children, polyester-clad tourists, frowzy-headed college students, and the locals in their overalls and starched pink dresses.

Bill looked at the stage where Sammy Ray Hawkins would be playing tomorrow for the adoring crowds. Bill's ex-wife would sit smugly at the foot of the stage and search the crowd for Bill's face. Her mouth would be thick with cherry lipstick, her hair cut in a style she had seen in some recent magazine. She would be wearing a poppy red blouse with a plunging vee front, the better to show off her braless chest. Her hair would dance across her laughing face, blown by the breeze that always seemed to follow her.

And Bill knew he would lust after her, if only for a moment. But maybe if he prepared himself now, if he prayed for strength, the desire would dissolve along with his hatred. And the scars on his heart where the Lord had healed him would not reopen and bleed fresh pain. It was strange to be thinking of her now when he had Nettie filling him, crowding his skin and mind and memory, filling his inner ear with her soft musical voice, but roots ran deep and vows lingered even when broken.

He only hoped Nettie wasn't regretting the afternoon. He didn't think so, but why hadn't she been at her apartment waiting to meet him as planned?

Bill's stomach knotted. He was sure that, somewhere down in those orange flickering pits, the devil was laughing at him. What a great joke the devil had played. Gotten Bill to turn away from God and answer the human call of his weak heart. Convinced Bill to commit sin with a virtuous woman, an act that condemned *her* to damnation as well. He could practically hear the Prince of Lies licking his dry lips in anticipation of torturing Nettie for an eternity.

But, dammit—excuse me, Lord—it hadn't felt wrong or dirty. It had felt real and right and joyful, there on the blanket in the meadow under the eye of God. It felt like love, something that had its own kind of glory, something that no Red-tailed Son-of-a-So-and-So Fallen Angel could taint and twist into something foul. And God damn—excuse me, Lord—any demon or human that tries to come between me and my newfound soul mate.

But the shadow of a doubt crossed his mind. Satan was

tricky. Satan could make Nettie pretend that she loved him when she really didn't. Satan could induce her to unbutton her blouse and offer her flesh to him as some kind of ritual sacrifice. Satan could use Nettie to siphon his spirit away.

Why couldn't Satan content himself with Bill's ex-wife instead of seeking to convert the pure? But perhaps that was so much sweeter, a seduction of the innocent, as much a lure to the Damned One as cake frosting was to a child.

And now Nettie could be hiding under her white bed-spread in her tiny room, crying in shame at being used. Nettie's stomach could be in knots, she might be praying for forgiveness. Nettie might be nothing more than a helpless pawn of that brimstone-breathing bastard who hoped to rule the world. Or at least hoped to spread a little misery along the golden road that led to eternal salvation.

But if the devil had hurt Nettie, there would be hell to pay. Because Bill would crawl under the earth and grab the goat-faced freak by the throat and wring his sorry neck. Because *nobody* was going to hurt Nettie as long as he had a breath and a prayer.

Excuse me, Lord. I get a little worked up when it comes to Nettie, in case you haven't noticed. But if it's Your will, I'd like You to bring us together. For our good and Your greater glory.

He looked down main street. The town looked dead as four o'clock. He hated to break his word, but he couldn't sit on his rear end, not knowing how Nettie was feeling about this afternoon. The police could watch over things here. He couldn't wait any longer.

Bill decided to try the church in case Nettie had worked late for some reason. It was a busy time, he knew, with Easter coming. But even the dedicated had to sleep some-time. And Nettie would have called him if she'd had to miss their date. Wouldn't she?

Or had she decided that someone who had already been in a failed marriage was damaged goods? Or that Bill was a serpent-tongued hypocrite out to serve his own desires instead of the Lord's?

He started his truck. Who could hope to understand the ways of God or Woman?

Crosley eased his cruiser through the trailer park, its tires crunching on the gravel drive. Someone had called in to report a prowler, and Crosley had taken the dispatch himself. Probably just another fly-blown drunk staggering home late, but at least it gave him something to do besides look for people who might not want to be found. For all he knew, Emerland was dipping his wick in that Leon woman right now, and the Mull fellow was sleeping off a drunk in a whorehouse somewhere. He'd rather deal with something simple and solvable, like a wino to shake down and maybe lock up, or a teenager caught puffing on a joint.

No Incredible Melting Man to deal with, no big mysteries. He didn't blame the mayor for not believing the story. Hell, he didn't half believe it himself, and he'd *been* there.

He rubbed his belly and thought about pulling another Black Label from under the seat. But he was close to the legal limit already. And he had the feeling that the Virgin Queen was just waiting for a good excuse to bounce his fat ass out of the Police Chief chair. Drunken driving on duty wasn't exactly kosher for a man who upheld the public trust.

But just look at my public, he thought. *Scraggly-assed white trash who would dry up and blow away—just like the Incredible Melting Man—if it weren't for their welfare checks. Only a third of the handout actually went to buy food. The rest went to moonshine and speed and pot and whatever else would give them a few hours of amnesia.*

One of his own uncles lived out here, and that made him sick to his stomach. The catch of it was, what really burned his ass, was that the white trash couldn't stop breeding like maggots. No matter how many rubbers they gave out at the

Pickett Health Clinic, no matter how many birth control lectures they gave to those doughy rednecks, they still manufactured an endless stream of yard monkeys. All with the same vacant eyes and slack mouth and growling belly and an inborn craving to get higher than a Chinese kite.

Ain't there some song about the circle being unbroken, in the sweet by-the-by, Lord? If the Lord had any sense, He'd turn these idiots to salt pillars and be done with it. Save Himself a little wear and tear and worry. But at least the Lord hadn't rained a plague of niggers on Windshake. Well, maybe a few, but they had the good sense to keep to themselves.

He'd visited his brother in Virginia Beach, and he'd felt like a grain of rice in a pot of black beans, there were so many little pickaninnies running around. So he figured he'd forgive God for salting Windshake with white trash if He wanted to, as long as He held the pepper.

Crosley cruised past the silent, dark trailers, wondering about the tin-boxed lives of the people inside.

Probably dreaming about their next handout. Hope none of them come down to fuck up Blossomfest. Maybe they'll hang out here all weekend, swapping out wives and spark plugs.

He didn't see any prowlers. Nothing worth stealing back here anyway. He decided to pop around the corner to the GasNGo and get himself a Snickers bar and a *Penthouse*. Then he'd park somewhere and finish off the Black Label before the sun came up.

He had almost completed the trailer park loop when he saw movement in the bushes that bordered the lot. A dirt trail led into the woods, and lights from the gas station blinked through the trees. The rednecks probably walked through there to buy their two-dollar wine and disposable diapers. He put the cruiser in "park" and heaved himself out from behind the wheel.

Crosley walked up the trail, his hand on the revolver that swung from his hip. No need for caution. Subtlety was lost on these bastards. He stomped around in the bushes as if trying to flush a covey of quail. "Come on out. I know you're in there."

A rustle of sprung grass and bent twigs answered him. He unsnapped his pistol strap and lifted his revolver.

"D—don't shoot me, Mister Policeman," came a small, sniffling voice.

One of the yard monkeys. What's he doing out this time of night?

"I won't hurt you, son," Crosley said in his calm cop voice. "Just come on out into the light where I can see you."

A boy, maybe eight or nine years old, stepped from beneath the low branches. Moonlit tears streaked his dirty face. Crosley knelt to the boy, hoping he wouldn't catch lice. "What's your name, son?"

"Mackey Mull, sir. They call me Little Mack." The boy sucked what sounded like a half pound of snot back up one nostril.

"Little Mack, huh? Well, what in the world are you doing out here in the middle of the night, Little Mack?"

The boy looked down at his feet. "You sure you ain't going to shoot me?"

Crosley realized he was still holding the pistol. He smiled and slid it back into its holster. He almost patted the boy on the head but decided against it.

"I wouldn't hurt you for a thousand dollars." *Unless it was tax-free.*

"I been hiding," the boy said. "Since way yesterday."

"Now, little man, what are you hiding *from?*" Crosley hoped it wasn't a child-abuse case. Domestic problems were a hell of a lot of paperwork, and the legal system never changed a goddamned thing. For all he knew, this brat deserved a slap across the lips once in a while. Most of them did.

"The bad men. With the shiny green eyes." The boy sobbed, small shoulders shaking. "I think they got my mommy."

"Your mommy? What bad men?"

"The bad men. Like in the scary movies."

"Look, son. Don't you worry. Mister Policeman will fix everything right up, now."

"My brother Junior says policemen are pigs. Are you a pig?"

Yep. No person alive could resist the temptation to back-hand this particular mucus midget.

"No, son, we're just plain folks working hard to make the town safer for everybody. You live here in the trailer park?"

"Yeah. Over there." He waved his hand.

"Okay. Just lead me to your trailer, and I'll make things all better."

"What about the bad men?"

Crosley chuckled.

"I'll take care of the bad men," he said, but noticed that he was rubbing his stomach. Something the brat had said about green eyes made him think of the Incredible Melting Man.

The chief followed the yard monkey back down the trail. They were almost into the open gap of worn yards and gravel when he heard limbs snapping. He turned just in time to see his uncle, his military clothes torn and stained. The old bastard usually took pride in his appearance, especially when he was wearing the uniform.

"Uncle Paul," Crosley said. "What you doing out this time of night?"

Uncle Paul took a staggering step forward and lifted his arms. His one eye was shining like a lime lighthouse. Crosley looked into the eye and saw empty carnival nightmares as the wrinkled and slick face pressed toward his own.

"See, it's one of *them,*" the brat shrieked beside him.

Crosley ordered his hand to lift the revolver, but his muscles went AWOL. Uncle Paul's rancid stench swarmed his senses and snaked into his nostrils. Then their faces pressed together and Crosley tasted bitter sap. The spores hit his tongue, flooded him, broke and burned him. His mind was already turning, already joining, already halfway there.

"See?" Crosley heard the brat squeal, just before he slid into the blissful fog. "See? I *told* you there were bad men. Stupid pig."

Then Crosley was overwhelmed by his uncle's moist slobbering, by the rotten rind of a mouth that kissed him hello and good-bye. As the brat's footsteps receded into darkness, Crosley entered a different kind of darkness, one that never ended, one he never wanted to end.

Nettie crawled across the patio of the parsonage, her belly cold against the flat tiles. Her arms ached, her ankle was swollen, her knees were rubbed raw, and her head throbbed with bright metal pain. But she was alive.

She might be the last person on earth, but she was alive. She heard the noises from the church as those creatures blew their bubbly praises to the rafters, sang their unintelligible hymns and blasphemed all that was good and holy with the very fact of their existence. If it weren't for those hellish visions described in the Bible, Nettie would have thought herself insane. A visionary shouldn't suffer doubt, and this was a sure vision of hell.

She had *seen* the preacher's wife sliding across the vestry. She had *seen* the snake-eyed preacher complete his conversion. She had *seen* the overripe parishioners crossing sacred ground on their trembling stumps of legs like lepers to a healing. She had witnessed and believed.

Nettie raised herself to a sitting position, pulled open the storm door, and tried the knob. Locked. Nettie hoped Sarah was home. It was her only chance. She gripped the doorknob with both hands and hauled herself to her knees. Then she rapped on the glass window.

No one answered.

A light was on in one wing of the house. Maybe it was Sarah's bedroom. Nettie didn't think she could crawl another inch. She banged again, louder. Her ankle throbbed like a crumbling tooth.

She was about to knock again when she saw the long shadows of the ones who stood in the distant church door. Those who had turned. Against nature. Against God. Against the light and toward her.

They shuffled down the church stairs under the quiet stars. The preacher led the way as the creatures crossed the graveyard, his thin twigs of arms upraised in rejoicing. Amanda followed, once again a chastened wife, only now she had the power of a demon. The Painters followed, meek and marshy and jubilant. The unidentifiable dripping stalk that had once been a person brought up the rear, one arm missing.

Nettie pounded louder and began yelling. The preacher was close enough so that she could see his lightbulb head, now lit with a neon green filament. He smiled at her as if she were a lamb that had hopped between the fence poles of the slaughterhouse holding pen. The musk of the others drifted across the dewy night, a stench of sun-split melons and swamp rot.

She was about to offer a final prayer for mercy, that she might die before she went to living hell, when a light blinked on in a far window of the parsonage. At the same instant, truck headlights swept up the road and across the parking lot, flashing over the marble teeth of the cemetery.

Chapter Thirty

"Hold on just a second," Chester said.

Tamara and DeWalt gathered around him like oversized scarecrows, their faces pale in the moonlight. Emerland stood by the Mercedes, arms folded. They were back at the Mull farm, about to head up into the dark woods. Chester hoped the other three were as scared as he was, because fear provided the kind of shock absorber that still worked even when corn liquor didn't.

Chester gave DeWalt the shotgun and nodded toward Emerland. "I don't reckon he'll be going anywhere, but just in case. Be back in a minute. I just thought of something."

"Chester? I think we'd better hurry." Tamara's hands were on her bulging pockets, where dynamite sticks poked out of the cloth like fat brown licorice.

"This might be worth waiting for, darling. We're gonna need all the help we can get."

He walked across the barnyard to the collapsing shed. He kicked open the door, hoping the wildlife was put to bed. Stale dust and powdery chicken shit filled his nostrils. A shaft of moonlight pierced the blackness where a few boards had fallen off the side of the shed. Stacks of feed, fertilizer, and other bags where piled by the door, cobwebs catching silver light among the moldering paper.

Concrete statues and birdbaths leaned against one wall like sentries sleeping at their posts. Plastic buckets holding dry dirt and the skeletons of shrubs formed a dead forest behind the feed sacks.

Enough junk here to open a lawn and garden store, Chester thought. *I'm glad I never got around to making Johnny Mack get rid of this mess. Like anybody around here—besides Hattie, God rest her soul—ever gave a damn about keeping the place up. And she would have had a fit if she knew her youngest boy had been packing away stolen goods. I ain't all that proud of having a sorry thieving no-account for a son, but right now I guess I can forgive him.*

Every time Sylvester drove his Bryson Feed Supply truck up to the farm, back before he'd moved out for good, Johnny Mack had swiped some of whatever happened to be in the truck bed. Johnny Mack didn't give a damn whether the products had any earthly purpose or not. He stole for the same reason a rooster crowed, just to celebrate the fact that the sun had come up again.

The rats had torn at the sacks of sorghum grain and the chickens had worked through the open holes until the meal had gotten so stale even the vermin wouldn't forage in it. But the other bags were mostly intact, covered with thick dust. Chester knelt to a pallet covered by smaller bags, his arthritic joints laughing pain at him and calling him a foolish old sonuvabitch. He'd have time to ache later. Or else he wouldn't give a damn one way or the other.

Chester glanced back through the door at the others. They seemed glad for the delay. Nobody looked overly anxious to go into the woods where the Earth Mouth gaped and the mushbrains crept around like mildewed snails, even though the three people paced impatiently. DeWalt held the shotgun down beside his waist like a city slicker, but Emerland didn't seem interested in making a run for it. He'd been quiet ever since that mushbrain had pressed itself against the fence back at the construction compound.

Chester wiped the grime away from one of the labels. "Screw a blue goose," he muttered. "Shoulda thought of this right off."

He lifted the sack, sending dust rising in the moonbeams like floating worms. He wasn't sure he could carry the twenty-pound sack through two miles of dense woods, but he had a feeling he had no choice. If they were trying to exterminate something that had come from God-only-knows-where, they'd better throw everything at it they could get their hands on.

Chester tossed the sack on his shoulder, then staggered for a moment until he got the load balanced. He wouldn't be able to take a drink with both hands occupied, but the corn liquor hadn't done him much good anyway. He'd gotten more sober as the night wore on, no matter how many sips he'd taken. He'd mostly been drinking out of habit anyway, taking comfort in the familiar way it burned his throat.

"What's that?" DeWalt asked when Chester stepped out of the shed.

"Sevin. Fungicide. What you put on the tomato plants to kill off mold and such."

DeWalt's mouth fell open and Tamara smiled. Chester liked her smile. If he were thirty years younger . . . hell, she'd be thirty years younger, too.

"I know the *shu-shaaa* thing looks like some kind of plant-creature," DeWalt said. "But how do we know if its chemistry resembles that of Earth vegetation?"

"I think it adopts some of the host's chemistry as part of its mimicking," Tamara said. "Like the old saying, 'You are what you eat.' Maybe in the thing's natural state, it's invincible. But I think it's vulnerable right now, at least compared to what it's going to be. If it gets smarter by absorbing from the environment, maybe it absorbs some weaknesses, too."

"Just the way it adopted the language of humans after it, uh, converted them?" DeWalt said.

"Yeah. And *shu-shaaa* also speaks the language of plants and rocks and dirt and water. Remember that strange music you heard?"

"Mushy shit," Chester said. "Like what old Don Oscar was saying. The thing fucks big time with their brains, that's for sure."

"Besides, what do we have to lose?" DeWalt said.

"They's some more stuff in here," Chester said. "If y'all are up to toting it."

DeWalt and Tamara walked up to the shed. Emerland followed with his head down. The developer had removed his tie and didn't seem worried that his fancy shoes would never serve in high society again. But the rules of society had changed, even a rock head like Emerland could see that, and the Earth Mouth didn't give a rat's ass how much money a man had. It would gobble him up and use his shoulder bone as a toothpick.

Emerland looks like a man who's had the truth slapped upside his head, Chester thought. *Like a man finding out the kids he'd brought up had been made by somebody else. Or that cancer is eating away his guts and there's not a damn thing to be done but pass blood and pray. Or that God didn't give two shits about the human race, or else He wouldn't let such bad things happen to it. A truth that ought not to be, but was.*

Tamara went into the shed, then DeWalt followed. "Hey, here's a five-gallon can of Roundup," Tamara called to Chester.

"That would kick like a damned donkey, all right, but that'll get mighty heavy mighty fast," Chester said, his words gurgling around his chaw. He spat and gummed rapidly, excited despite feeling every single one of his sixty-seven years. Or was it sixty-eight now? Or a *hundred*-and-sixty-eight?

"I can handle it, Chester," she said. "I know what's at stake more than anybody."

Chester figured this wasn't a good time to haggle about equal rights and that other uppity horseshit he'd heard about.

That was big-city worry, as far as he was concerned. In Windshake, women knew their place, for the most part. Didn't stir up trouble. Still, she was probably in better shape than he and DeWalt put together.

If she really *could* read the alien zombiemaker's mind— and Chester found himself believing all kinds of things that he used to laugh at when he saw them on the magazine covers in the grocery checkout line—then he might be wise to trust her judgment.

"Have a go at it, then," he said. "That's some Acrobat M-Z in the brown sack, DeWalt. Experimental stuff that's supposed to kill blue mold on tobacco. Got to have a permit to buy it." He laughed, choked on tobacco juice, spat, and continued. "But not to steal it, I reckon."

"It's concentrated poison," DeWalt said. "It says on the directions that one tablespoon of this stuff makes a gallon of fungicide. Making this bag about a thousand gallons worth."

"Maybe we can volunteer Emerland to bring it along, seeing as how your hands are full with that dynamite rig and the shotgun. What say, Emerland?"

Emerland stared vacantly ahead, then nodded as if he were a dummy on the knee of a stoned ventriloquist. He shambled into the shed, doing a pretty fair imitation of one of the mushbrains.

"Every little bit helps," said DeWalt. "Or hurts, if you want to look at it that way."

Emerland showed surprising energy in lifting the forty-pound sack onto his shoulder. Chester figured he probably worked out in one of those fitness clubs, with wires and weights hanging from metal bars and sweat seeped into the carpet. Probably hadn't done an honest day's work in his entire life, but that wasn't necessarily a bad thing, in Chester's opinion. Emerland's jaw clenched and his eyes shone with either grim determination or madness.

They gathered outside the shed, all looking silently toward the faint green glow on the far ridge. An owl hooted in the barn, lonely and brooding in the high wooden rafters. A wind tried to stir the brown leaves from the corners of the fence but gave up, too tired after a long winter's work. A dog barked, followed by another's, and the sound echoing off the cold mountains reminded Chester of old Boomer.

Tamara broke the peace of the waiting night. "Chester, can I use the telephone real quick?"

Chester looked up at the deep sky, at the gorgeous bright lights jabbed in the roof of forever, like holes put there so the world could breathe. He found himself wondering how many more of these Earth Mouth bastards were up there, riding the black wind on their way to wherever such as those were meant to be. He hated trying to look at the Big Picture, or worrying over the fuck-all Why. That was for preachers and college boys. Some things were just too big for a broken-down dirt farmer to understand.

"Power's out. Phone might be out, too. Tree musta fell on the lines," Chester said.

"I have to try," Tamara said. "My husband's probably worried sick by now."

"Better let me come with you. Might break your neck in that mess."

He laid the sack of Sevin across the Roundup can and led Tamara across the yard, wondering if all the chickens had turned by now, whether they were sitting with their stupid heads under their wings, their green eyes shut against the world. Probably dreaming of laying tiny rotten plums in their nests, come morning.

Chester wondered what might hatch out of those tainted eggs.

Or if he'd still be here when the sun pissed its yellow light down on the world again.

Little Mack crawled deeper under the trailer, his face pressed in the dry dirt. He was scared.

He could hear voices, only they weren't making words. Just wet sounds. And he sort of recognized his mom's voice. He wondered if she was one of *them* now.

Because he'd seen them fall out of the trailer, slide out of the door while he'd still been hiding in the bushes, just as the sun went down and he'd first started really getting lonely.

Jimmy, the mean one he'd seen lying naked on top of his mom that time, had walked like a drunk man across the yard and went into the Wellborns' trailer, and Mack had heard screaming and yelling inside, then the Wellborns were walking like drunks, too, Sue and Grady and their little girl Anita, as they scattered and stumbled into the woods.

Anita had lifted her dress one time and showed him her panties when he'd given her a nickel, and she said for a dime that she'd take her panties off. But Little Mack never had a whole dime, that was a lot of money. Now he didn't think he wanted to see under her dress even for free. Because her skin was slimy looking and her eyes glowed like Jimmy's. And Jimmy was so slimy looking when he came out of the Wellborns' trailer that he looked like he was dripping.

Mack held his breath as a familiar pair of boots appeared on the trailer step. Mack knew those boots inside and out. They had thick brown heels and smelled like old baseball gloves, and Mack had once hidden yucky oatmeal in them. Those were Daddy's boots.

Daddy was home and would make everything all right, just like that stupid pig cop had promised, only the stupid pig had let Old One-Eye kiss him on the lips, so he must be what Junior called a "queer." Daddy would beat up that ugly Jimmy and then they would all be happy and maybe Mom would slice up some wieners to put in the macaroni and cheese the way she sometimes did on special occasions. And maybe even Junior would come home, but this was Friday night, and Junior never came home on Friday nights.

At least Daddy was here, and maybe he'd even killed something and would be in a good mood. Sometimes he'd tack an old squirrel skin or raccoon fur to a board and give it to Mack, and Mack would rub it and sniff it and dream about playing out in the woods. Except now the woods scared him because it was full of the slimy people.

He crawled on his hands and knees to the front of the trailer and was about to call out when he saw that Daddy was drunk, too, only Daddy didn't drink, even though Papaw Mull did and Junior did and Mom did and One-Eye did and Jimmy did and everybody. But not Daddy. So why couldn't Daddy walk straight?

Then Mack saw that Daddy's jeans were damp, as if he'd peed in his pants. Except the wetness was slimy, like motor oil or syrup. Which meant . . .

Which meant that Mack better not make a sound.

Which meant if he was going to cry, he'd better let the tears slide soft down into the dust. He couldn't break into a bawling fit. Junior said Mack was just an old bawl-baby, anyway. And maybe he was, but he was scared, scared enough to wet his pants, and it was dark and Daddy was slimy.

His mom came out of the trailer.

She stood in the yard and tried to call. "Muh . . . aaaaaaaahck."

She was naked in the moonlight and covered with milky snot. He bit his tongue and didn't answer.

The alien pulsed, its glutinous sap coursing through its root system. Its spores were still spreading, but with the lack of solar radiation, its cellular activity had slowed. It took advantage of the rest to analyze the other symbols it had collected.

May-zee. Mush. Muh-aaack. Kish.

Jeesh-ush. Ahhm-feeel.

Chesh-urrr.

And those it had gathered before: *shu-shaaa, maz-zuh, nig-urrr, peg-heee, eyezzz, chreez.*

And the one its heart-brain kept returning to, the one which glowed deep in the furnace of its metabolism: *tah-mah-raaa*.

The symbol must have meaning. The alien had dissected many different kinds of patterns in its trip across the cosmos. Solving this one was only a matter of time. And it had forever.

Chapter Thirty-One

Tamara followed Chester into what she thought must be his kitchen. She saw only the outlines of things, lesser shadows in the blackness. An old wood cookstove lurked heavily in the corner. The bones of broken furniture protruded from heaps on the floor. She smelled the damp soot of the chimney, the sweet odor of liquor and decaying fabric, and the thick whang of rancid bacon grease. The cool March air seemed cloying in here, pressing against her like a second skin.

"This way, darling," Chester said to her. She bumped into his back as he stopped suddenly.

I can see into the future, but I can't see in the dark.

The random syllables skittered across her mind, as elusive as wet rats: *shu-shaaa, maz-zah, muh-aack.* The green glow radiating from the ridge was the visual equivalent of those sick psychic signals she was receiving, its dim pulse growing stronger in the forest beyond the door. As they'd driven past her Toyota on the way to Chester's farm, the signals had been more intense, direct, *personal.*

"There's a tone," Chester said, and she felt his leathery hand and cold plastic pressing against her arm. She took the phone and squinted at the old-fashioned rotary dial. She counted the holes with her fingers and rang her home number.

Robert answered before the first ring had died away. "Tam?" he said, breathless.

"Yes, sweetheart. It's me."

He sighed in either relief or anger. "Where the hell—I mean, I'm sorry, I've been worried sick—where are you, honey? Are you okay?"

She nodded, fighting the tears and laughter that wanted to mix themselves together. "Yeah, I'm fine. God, I miss you."

"I miss you, too. What's going on?"

"It's a long story. You know the Gloomies?"

"Um—"

"They're here. *It's* here."

"What?"

"And it's bigger than I thought. Are the kids safe?"

"Sure. They're sleeping. Now what the hell—"

"Keep them inside, no matter what. I've got to go, honey. I just wanted to let you know I was okay. I'll be home soon."

I hope, she added silently. *God, to be back in my warm bed right now, my flannel nightgown on and Robert snoring, with no Gloomies dancing and no visions painting themselves inside my head. No shu-shaaa and peg-heee and all this other random madness. Just plain old ordinary problems.*

"Don't go," Robert said.

"I have to. Take care of the kids."

"Tam, Ginger has it, too," he burst out before she could hang up.

"What?"

"Seeing things. You know. She said something about the people with green eyes. Honey, does that have anything to do with your Gloomies?"

"Yes. Oh, God, Robert. Don't let anything happen to them."

"Tell me where you are."

"No. It's better this way. I love you," she said, and this time she couldn't stop the tears.

Chester took the phone from her. "Your wife's in good hands, mister. Don't you worry none."

Then Tamara heard Chester draw a sharp breath. The phone dropped to the floor. Wet, oozing hands clutched her shoulders. The Earth Mouth must have overwhelmed her senses, because she hadn't registered the creature sloughing up behind her. Now, at the contact, her mind sparked and she was connected, for a fleeting moment, with the thing that had once been called Junior Mull.

His scrambled synapses shot her a broken jumble of symbols, *fishfuck moonshine taxismoke shu-shaaa cheshur cheshur cheshur chesssh—*

She twisted to escape, but he—*it*—was only pushing her aside, as if she were standing in the way of its dead heart's desire. Its green eyes were locked onto Chester, glowing like radioactive gemstones in the coal mine of the room.

"So, come to claim the family keep, huh?" Chester said, with more than just a touch of craziness in his voice.

The thing stepped past Tamara, leaving a slick trail on her shoulders where its limpid fingers had clutched. It closed on Chester, panting in a moist expiration that passed for its breath. Tamara realized the creature's instinct had brought it here as if reeled in by some ancestral fishing line. Her clairvoyance had been slow in picking up what Chester had instantly understood. Because Chester recognized the dripping, waxen hulk of swampmeat that reached its limbs toward him.

"Junior, just get the fuck on back. You ain't *right* no more. Don't you see that, boy?" Chester shuffled slowly backward across the wooden floor.

"Shu-shaaa . . . shay . . . home . . . ," it said, gurgling as if its wide, wet mouth was full of snuff. "Shay . . . kish . . . chesher . . ."

The green eyes cut a path like flashlights, and Tamara saw the rictus of Chester's face in their glow. She felt along the kitchen counter as the Junior-creature closed on Chester. The old man had his hands up in front of him as if to offer peace, but the creature's peace was more insistent, more urgent, more compelling.

Tamara's fingers brushed across some dishes and felt the rim of the sink. A jar tumbled, throwing a silver glint before shattering on the floor. Then her fingers closed on greasy metal and she lifted, finding comfort in the weight that filled her fist. She stepped forward quickly and swung with all her strength. The iron skillet smacked flush against the thing's skull with a sound like someone stomping grapes.

Milky luminescent fluid burst from the pulp-skin and oozed down the stem of the creature's neck. The thing turned to Tamara, flashing a toothless smile made bright by the iridescent scarlet-red pistils dangling in its deep throat. A throat that was the lily of her dream, the throat that was a smaller replica of the Earth Mouth, as if the creature and the *shu-shaaa* Gloomies shared a common hunger.

Pupil and master.

Acolyte and high priest.

The seeker and the enlightened.

The pollen mote and the God seed.

The yield and the harvest.

She swiped sideways with the skillet and it axed into the soft neck. The creature's head canted to one side like a cornstalk hit by a hailstorm. She chopped again, her hand slick with the thing's leakage, and the head rolled off, hitting the floor like a blob of wet dough. The decapitated body swayed for a moment, then regained its balance and took a juddering step forward.

Something gripped her elbow and she almost swung the clot-soaked skillet again. But she saw Chester's too-wide shining eyes and stopped herself. Through his touch, she

could sense his fear and revulsion, she could feel his hatred
of the thing that had brought such horrors. His anger smelled
like stale sweat and shorted-out copper wires.

Chester tugged at her, leading her out of the house, his
thin fingers pressing her flesh like iron bands.

"Who was it, Chester?" she said, once they were on the
porch, panting in the safety of moonlight.

"Guh—grandson." Chester gasped. "Just like fucking
chickens, these things is—they come home to roost."

Tamara tossed the skillet off the porch and rubbed the
creature's oily juice onto her skirt. DeWalt must have heard
the struggle, because he ran toward the porch steps, his
hands clenched around the shotgun.

"What happened?" he asked.

"Family reunion," Chester said, looking over the hills.
"Now let's go blow this alien sonavawhore back to Kingdom
Come."

They walked to the shed and gathered their makeshift
ordnance. Emerland was slumped like a puppet waiting for
its strings to be jerked. He lifted the sack of Sevin without
being told and followed Chester between the dark outbuildings. DeWalt walked behind them, loaded down with herbi-
cide, the shotgun, and the detonator. The wide white moon
shone down, throwing their long shadows over the field.

Back at the farmhouse, the headless Junior-thing stumbled out of the house onto the porch steps. Tamara watched
as it fell to the ground and scrabbled awkwardly among the
weeds, as if searching for its head and heart and hope and all
things lost. She lifted the can of Roundup and headed for the
forest.

Nothing made sense.

Those people walking across the graveyard, Preacher
Blevins in the lead—and was that Amanda behind him?—
shuffling like a pack of drunks in the moonlight, heading for

the parsonage. And Nettie's car, empty in the church parking lot. Where was Nettie?

Bill jumped out of his truck and hurdled the short hedge that marked off the cemetery. The preacher turned toward him slowly, as if the air were molasses.

"Howdy, Preacher," Bill called, a bit uneasily. It was well after midnight. Was this some kind of strange revival service?

But the preacher was Baptist. The preacher knew as well as anyone that Satan walked the night, especially when the full moon floated across the sky. Bill looked toward the church at the lamplight streaming from the open vestry door. The light cast an oblong yellow rectangle on the trimmed grave grass.

"Bill."

It was Nettie, weak and wounded. Her voice hadn't come from the church. Instead it had floated over the headstones from the parsonage.

"Nettie?"

He ran across the neat cemetery, dodging the white monuments, praying to the Lord to keep Nettie safe, not caring that he was treading over the graves beneath him. Out of the corner of his eye, he noticed something odd about the preacher and the others. They were *shimmering*.

Then the smell hit him, barbed into his nose like a winch hook. Skunk cabbage and stinkweed, moldy sawdust and rancid cedar. A moist and fungal stench.

"Help me, Bill," Nettie called again.

He dodged through the tombstones the way he'd skirted defensive linemen while scoring those high school touchdowns. But he had a feeling that this was the biggest game of his life, that more was at stake than championship rings and scholarships.

The parsonage's dark bricks were stolid against the trees, its windows with their neat white trim like sanctifying eyes. Nettie was on the porch, holding her left ankle and pulling on the doorknob. Even from twenty yards away, he could see the moonlit tears trailing down her cheeks, her eyes wide and frightened. He rushed across the dewy ground and knelt beside her.

"What's wrong, honey?" he whispered, afraid and feeling helpless, as if Nettie were a bird with a broken wing. He didn't know where to touch her.

"Ankle's broken, I think," she said between clenched teeth. She put her arms around his neck and hugged him, then put her mouth to his ear. "I'm so glad you're here."

He held her a little away from him so he could see her face. Then he saw her ankle, twisted at an awkward angle above her white shoe. "What's going on?"

"The preacher. Gone bad. His eyes . . . look at his eyes."

Bill turned his head. They were coming closer, wet and dripping, arms outstretched like trembling blasphemies. Their eyes shone inhumanly deep and unholy green. The preacher smiled and his mouth was alive, like a thing separate from his flesh, wiggling with bright worms.

Satan.

Satan was here, now, just the way the Bible promised. The Lord had called for the end without so much as a trumpet blast in warning.

"Sweet Jesus, save us," Bill said.

"I don't think Jesus can beat these things," Nettie said. "At least, not by Himself."

Bill shook his head, lost. "Green eyes. That part wasn't in the Book of Revelations."

Sounds drifted across the narrow strip of yard, flyblown hymns rising from those walking gates of hell.

"Bill, they're coming." She whimpered a little from pain. "They want me. Us. All of us."

Bill was thinking about bits of verse, words that had been thundered into him throughout his thirty years. "Yea, though I walk through the valley of the shadow of death—"

"Bill, the Lord helps those that help themselves. And each other."

"—I shall fear no evil."

Bill put his arms under Nettie, lifted her body that was still fresh and warm and naked in his memory. Her breath whispered across his neck. He looked around, wondering which way to run, but already they were upon him, wet arms and bright eyes and dead wet faces and ripped skin and finger-nails sharp as thorns.

The preacher pressed his mouth near, the thick rinds of his gums snapping hungrily. Amanda Blevins, or the demon that now owned her fermenting flesh, reached for Bill with viscid hands. Others of their kind had come out from the trees or behind the marble headstones or perhaps up from the very ground itself.

Bill grew confused, as if someone had pumped him full of six kinds of drugs, or Satan had thrown open the door to a crazy house. Because words and images flashed across his mind, things green and quick and not of this Earth. He felt Nettie being pulled from his arms as he squirmed under the hothouse assault. Tongues writhed near his cheek like snakes.

"Nettie!" he screamed, swinging his fists like sledge-hammers against the blanched pulpy meat of the hellspawn.

Floodlights suddenly erupted, giving detail to the horror, revealing the devil's hordes. Their mouths opened in apoca-lyptic glee. They had seen the light. And the light exposed their ungodly hunger.

Mayzie slid awake, up from the currents of sleep into her darkened bedroom. She had been dreaming of Theo.

They had been in the backyard, digging in the little flower bed. She was planting gladiola bulbs, except the bulbs had already sprouted, grown, and bloomed while she held them in her hands. She put them in the dirt, and Theo pressed the soil around them with his strong brown hands. Oliver was in his white woven crib, gurgling happily among the blankets, throwing tiny punches at the clouds.

Dogs were raising a ruckus at the end of the street. Their noise had awakened her. Mayzie threw the blankets off, feeling the humid hand of the night.

"Blasted dogs barking like there was no tomorrow," she said to herself. She'd have to pay a call on the owners in the morning.

The corners of the dream dissolved away as she looked out her window. A shadow moved across the moon spill. Mayzie fumbled for her eyeglasses on the dresser. She sat up, not believing her eyes. Not wanting to believe.

A liquid wax statue walked across the yard, its eyes two neon green orbs floating in a wide pale face. And the face, the gone-to-grave moldering face, belonged to Old Man Thompson, the postal carrier.

He's making the rounds early today, Mayzie thought. *What's that they say about neither rain nor hail nor gloom of night?*

She was still in that maelstrom of sleep, not quite ready to come to grips with reality. Especially a reality that had been stood on its ear, that could build and house such an impossible creature as the twitching old man. Thompson smiled as if he had seen Mayzie through the window, and his smile kept stretching wider and wider, until she could see the stipuled tonsils quivering in his throat. Then he stepped toward the glass, and Mayzie could no longer palm off the sight as a dream, because it was spraying wet sibilants into the air.

"*Shu-shaaahhhh.*" The last syllable drawled out across the air, matching the baying of the distant hounds.

Then Old Man Thompson was at the window, his leaking face leering, his thin fingers scratching along the sill. He held up his wrinkled hands, splinters beneath his fingernails. He waved his hands in the air, dripping his juice on the marigold border.

Mayzie felt a pressure in her chest as her pulse accelerated, changed gears, and raced past its speed limit. Bands of hot bronze pain girded her heart, and her breath lodged in her throat like a peach pit. She wheezed and fell back among the pillows, but her eyes couldn't leave that ghastly face. Old Man Thompson watched as she died, his beatific expression sagging as if in disappointment at being deprived of her company.

Then Mayzie closed her eyes, clamped her eyelids tight as those invisible razored fingers squeezed her aortic chamber. And she saw them, Theo standing in the golden mist wearing his favorite wool shirt, Oliver nestled small as a teddy bear in the muscular arms. Theo smiled and beckoned and Oliver kicked his legs in delight. They were young, just as they had been in her recent dream, and she wondered if she were young again as well.

She looked down at her hands, at the wrinkles and years washed away, at the lifelines that were now meaningless. Her heart no longer ached, it only swelled with an abiding joy, and peace descended upon her like a silk gown.

She stepped toward them, gently, one foot in front of the other.

Chapter Thirty-Two

DeWalt stumbled, then regained his footing. His legs were sodden tree stumps, dense granite pillars, tonnage. He absently reached into his front pocket for the habit of his pipe. He was putting it to his lips when he was struck by the vision of tobacco plants under a gleaming sun, rows upon rows waving their fat juicy leaves in shimmering reverence, full fields of rich decadence and sharp dewy blossoms, green armies with their nicotine arsenals. He tossed the pipe into the undergrowth.

DeWalt looked around at the long shadows of branches and the looming treetops. Even under the full moon, the night woods were secret and treacherous.

No wonder, Oh Lodge Brother. Whose side do you think they're on, anyway?

You're too xenophobic, Mr. Chairman. Maybe that's why you won't let anyone else join the Royal Order of the Bleeding Hearts.

Two hands, two balls. A balanced arrangement.

And what if I defect to that other club?

Which club would that be, Oh Brother?

Greenpeace's evil twin. The Royal Order of Shu-shaaa. The Earth Mouth. The God seed.

You haven't got the nerve. You wouldn't be here now if you weren't even more afraid of showing your true color. Yellow.

I object, Mr. Chairman.

Why do you think you were driven to make piles of money? Why you dodged Vietnam but didn't give a damn about the peace movement? Why your marriage didn't work because you could never give enough of yourself? Why you had it all but never enough? Why you always had to start over?

No fair. You're hitting below the belt.

It's your FEAR, Brother. Oh, not of death. A fear of being ridiculed. Of being found out. A fear of having lived. A fear of being caught giving a damn.

Fuck you and the horse you rode in on.

This meeting of the Royal Order of the Bleeding Hearts now draws to a close.

DeWalt looked at the shadowy forms of Chester and Emerland twenty feet ahead. He hoped Chester knew where they were going, because DeWalt was as lost as a preacher at a strip joint. Woodsmanship and sense of direction couldn't be ordered out of an L.L. Bean catalog. And other things also had no price.

His shoulder ached from the sack of fungicide he carried. The dust of its pungent poison wafted from beneath the tucked paper flaps. He had given the shotgun back to Chester, glad to be free of its power. But the dynamite bulged in his pockets, as heavy as the weight of responsibility. The detonator switch and blasting cap were in his vest pockets.

He hoped he would be able to rig the cap. Chester would never let him hear the end of it if he failed. Plus, the world might end. If he remembered correctly, the detonator sent an electrical charge to the cap, and the heat caused a chain reaction in the cap that set off the rest of the TNT.

But how do you expect to remember that, Oh Lodge Brother? Do you trust your memories after your long fling with free love and sex and every sort of mythical mother lode mindmuck known to the human race? Do you trust the ravings of those kitchen-sink radicals you used to swap bedbugs with?

Those were decent people, Chairman.

Quoting chapter and verse from the Anarchist Cookbook*?*

Well . . . times were different then.

Yes. You hadn't developed your itch yet. Whatever happened to promoting change within the system?

Viva la revolucion, comrade. Times were different then, but times are different *now*, too.

You're out of order, Brother.

Yeah, and for everything, there is a season. You know, what the hippies sang, back when we thought the world was worth changing, let alone saving. We couldn't even change our own damned minds.

He heard Tamara behind him. The can she was carrying sloshed as she changed hands again. The handle had to be biting into her palm, and her arms were probably numb by now. But she was faring better than the rest of them, urging them up the trail.

The moon had started its descent in the sky. Dawn was only a few hours away. Hadn't Tamara said something about the zombiemaker Earth Mouth thing getting stronger under the sun?

Yes, I did, Tamara thought.

Wait a second.

What did DeWalt say?

He didn't say anything. You heard him. In your head. Turn, turn, turn.

Nonsense. Clairvoyance is one thing. Telepathy is quite another.

And maybe you're getting delirious from fatigue and hunger and lack of sleep. And maybe, maybe, maybe you can chase arguments around your head like a dog chasing its tail until your brain collapses into a useless heap.

But LISTEN.

And she shut the flap of her own clamoring inner voice, closed up shop and concentrated. She heard DeWalt thinking something about lodge brothers and how the moon looked like a bad rind of cheese and how that reminded him of when he and his friends used to camp in the backyard up in Oregon and how he wished he were a child again so he could live his life all over—

Then she was out of him, her mind swimming with those extra thoughts.

She stopped walking and set the can of Roundup on the damp leaves.

"You okay, Tamara?" DeWalt asked from under the shadows ahead.

"Fine," she replied, thinking she would never be fine again. "Just resting for a sec. Be right along."

"Chester and Emerland are taking a breather, too. Chester says we're nearly there."

That made Tamara curious. Could she?

She opened her mind and sent her new telepathic ears tenderly into the night, swiveled her psychic antenna.

And she touched Chester's mind briefly, shared his thought that he was sure going to miss old Don Oscar's moonshine, but he was going to enjoy it while it lasted. She absorbed his bright fear, felt the raw spot where the overall strap's buckle dug into his shoulder, tasted the sting of corn liquor, and smelled sweat-stained long johns. Then she pulled back.

She was either reading minds or else she'd finally shattered into a thousand schizophrenic splinters. It had to be *shu-shaaa,* the pulsing alien that had brought her Gloomies back from their hibernation. The creature had amplified her sensitivity, maybe from an overload of its own hot cosmic power spilling over, maybe from some undiscovered wavelength that operated beyond the scope of human understanding, maybe a final boon granted by an omnipotent conqueror to the ants it was about to crush. Who could know such things?

A stray thread of thought spiraled up from her crowded subconsciousness, in Chester's thin brain-voice, a sound byte that had probably slipped in randomly during the telepathic exchange.

"Curiosity killed the cat and never did no good for the mouse, neither."

Maybe it was best not to understand. All Tamara knew was that her head was full, brimming with not only her own fears and worries, not only the *shu-shaaa* blaring its presence in a bright invisible beacon, not only the Gloomies making a comeback that would rival that of John Travolta's, but now she had other brains to wonder and worry and ache over.

She picked up the five-gallon can and carried it into a small clearing where the others were talking and resting. She instinctively shut off her third ear and listened to their words instead of their brain waves. She didn't know if she could handle all of their thoughts at once.

She didn't want to try.

"Oh, my God. *Daddy!*"

Nettie heard Sarah screaming from the open door, at the same moment that the porch lights exploded into brightness, at the same moment she felt the slick arms and leafy hands tearing her away from Bill.

The Painters loomed near Nettie, throwing their shadows over her face. Sandy Henning, the church organist, had joined them, and her nimble fingers flexed like turgid vine roots. Nettie looked past them at Bill and saw him fighting off the thing that Preacher Blevins had become. Bill's big fist disappeared into Amanda's leering maw. The preacher's mouth was inches from Bill's, but Bill thrust a forearm up and blocked the assault.

The preacher turned toward his own screaming daughter and his impossible smile got larger and more putrid, foul swamp sludge dribbling from his melon pink gums. Then Nettie's attention was ripped in half by an orange flare of pain shooting through her leg. One of the creatures had clamped its viscous jaws on her ankle, sucking at her sweat and salt and skin cells.

Then Ann Painter's face covered her own and she tasted the hellfire heart of carbon and the tangy artichoke air and the deep secret undergrowth of cellulose and the acid of aspen and ash as the tannic vaults and crypts of life's mysteries unlocked themselves and she was and she was and she was pulled free again and found herself in Bill's arms and he pushed her into the parsonage and pulled the flash-frozen Sarah by her pajama sleeve out of the reach of her own scabrous father.

Bill kicked the door closed and the arm of one of the demons caught against the jamb with a thick, glutinous sound. Bill dropped Nettie onto the carpet and she watched with distant eyes as he slammed his shoulder against the door and the arm split like a rotted weed stalk. It bounced off the welcome mat and rolled to a rest beside Nettie. She looked at its dark purple veins still pumping dews, the forefinger still undulating, beckoning, urging her to follow.

She was pollen. She floated on its breeze. Toward forever.

Armfield was lost in his ecstasy, drunk on the holiest of waters. All his life had been a fruitless search, small rituals and sacraments and blessings bestowed. All his life he had walked in darkness, tossing prayers to an invisible and unfelt God. All his life his soul had been a battleground for the stern Jesus and the understanding and encouraging Satan. And now the human soul had slipped away, danced free of dust and stigmata and beast-numbers and psalms.

Now, beyond life, he had found his true life's work. The true salvation and mercy and light. The one true master that demanded and deserved an eternal servitude. The kingdom and power and glory of *shu-shaaa,* forever and ever, amen.

But still there was an ache, an empty human ache that he knew was part of that old and pitiful fleshly life. An unfulfilled knot in his Jack-in-the-Pulpit chest, a hunger in his brimming mouth and hands, a nutrient throbbing in his gelatin organs. The family must be united, the circle must be unbroken.

"Sha-raaa," he sprayed to the deep night.

His wife was at his side, her mascara sliding from her face along with the congealing strips of her skin. She raised the stump of her left arm to the heavens, spilling her milky effluence onto the red tiles of the porch.

All in praise to *shu-shaaa.* Armfield had never felt so connected, so close to his congregation as he now did. They shared the same vision and mind and crusade. They were truly one in the eyes of their newfound god.

And, like any god, this one demanded converts.

They launched their soggy meat against the door.

"Nettie, are you okay?"

Bill gingerly sat her up and leaned her against the sofa. She didn't look hurt, except for her ankle, and she was smiling, a small, pink, dreamy smile.

Her eyes were pressed into tiny crescents and her eyelashes twitched like monarchs on sprigs of white clover. He had seen that monster blowing its rancid wind into her throat. Bill swallowed and prayed harder than he had in his entire life.

Oh, please, Lord, let her be all right. Because I need her more than anything on Your earth. And I don't know what plague You've loosed upon the world, but please spare Nettie from it. You can take me, I know I'm not the best catch there is, but I promise to serve to the best of my ability, I know I sing off-key but practice might make perfect if I have forever to work into the choir. And I know Thy will be done, on earth as it is in heaven, but Nettie's as pure as the driven snow. And I know she'll make a heck of an angel, but please just let me have her for one lifetime, and I swear we'll serve you for a thousand times a thousand.

I know You are merciful, I've felt Your goodness in my heart ever since I asked You in, ever since You gave me the hope and strength and wisdom. But please tell me that You're listening. Please give me a sign.

There was a crash of glass at the front of the house and the door groaned on its hinges, the thick wood panels warped from the stress of weight.

Bill looked up from Nettie's blank face to the frightened mask of Sarah. She trembled in her pajamas, her arms wrapped around her chest, her eyes bulging with the memory of impossible sights.

"Sarah."

She stared deeper, farther.

"Sarah!"

He stood and grabbed her by the shoulders, shaking her until her eyes met his. "Come on, you've got to help me. We've got to get Nettie to a doctor."

"D—doctor?" Her lower lip quivered. She shook her head, denying her senses.

"Something's happened. Something's wrong with the people."

"M—mom and Dad?"

"I'm sorry, Sarah. I wish I knew what was going on. But I don't. I only know that they've changed somehow."

Sarah bit her thumbnail, the rims of her eyes red from fear and shock. The door splintered and she glanced over at it.

"We don't have much time," Bill said. "You call the police, I don't know what to tell them, just get them out here. Then we're going to have to make a run for it. If we can reach my truck, we'll be okay. We can't stay here much longer."

Sarah nodded, suddenly grim and determined, as if awakening in a hospital bed and realizing she'd have to fight for her life. She padded barefoot across the carpet as the pounding on the door grew louder.

Bill laid his hand on her arm. "We can pray for their souls. That's all we can do. The rest is up to the Lord."

She looked at him coldly. "What kind of Lord would do something like this?"

He had no answer. Sarah went down the hall and took the telephone off the wall.

Bill looked out the window. More black shapes emerged from the forest, as if the trees themselves had come to life. He knelt to Nettie and lifted her again. She seemed lighter somehow, as if a vital part of her was missing. She was still smiling.

"We're about in its territory," Chester said, scratching idly in the dirt with a stick. "See how the woods is getting weirder? Them roots running through yonder like sick snakes?"

He didn't like the way the trees looked, dark skeletons with sharp dead arms. Small animals, either alive or else dead and green eyed, chittered among the crisp foliage. The spring leaves shimmered in the moonlight, starchy and shiny and curling like needy claws. And if he held his head just *so,* he could hear the faint, raw wind that blew from the Earth Mouth.

"How much farther, Chester?" DeWalt asked, breathing

heavily. The California Yankee was about tuckered out. They all were, except Tamara.

"Another hunnert yards and we'll be over this ridge, then we'll be able to see the mouth."

Chester looked at Tamara. She was leaning against a tree, looking up at the moon. He was about to warn her against trusting the trees, but he figured she knew better than he did. After all, she was the one with the juiced-up brain that seemed to know what the Earth Mouth—what did she call it? *Shu-shaaa?*—was thinking.

If you could call it "thinking." Hell, aliens weren't meant for God's green earth. This world was made for humans to walk across and piss on and plant in and pave over and generally use its thick dirty skin however damn well they pleased. But this Earth Mouth-zombiemaker thing, if it came from the stars, was liable to pay no mind to what God intended. Hell, hadn't He throwed enough planets and stars and chunks of rock into the sky to go around for everybody and everything, no matter how fucked up it was?

Why couldn't the shu-shaaa-shitbag take the MOON, for Christsakes? Nobody would miss it much, except maybe poets and poachers and other such trash. Well, maybe old hound dogs, too.

"What if this doesn't work?" DeWalt said.

"Then we'd best get used to the idea of wearing ivy undershorts." Chester worked his plump chaw to the back of his gums, then turned to Emerland. "You ain't said a word since we left the farm. Your tongue ain't turned to a turnip, is it?"

Emerland looked up from where he was sitting on the sack of fungicide. "When my lawyers—"

"When your panty-waist lawyers do *what?* Sue the alien?" DeWalt laughed. "I'd like to see what you were awarded for emotional damages. And, of course, the Earth Mouth gets to be judged by a jury of its peers. So we'll need at least a dozen more of them. And how would you like to have a heart-to-heart chat with *its* lawyers?"

Even Tamara laughed, brought back from whatever far corner of space she had been floating in. They all sat quietly for a moment as the crickets and night birds played their odd instruments, their tunes off-kilter in a music that seemed to slip into the spaces between sound and silence.

"Used to hunt these woods with my boys," Chester said. "Back in better days. We'd bag a half-dozen squirrels ever single trip."

"I'm sorry about your grandson," Tamara said. She came out from under the tree, the moonlight shining on her golden hair.

"Don't be. If there ever was a case of somebody getting their just desserts, that was it. That boy was sorrier than a cut cat." He spat for emphasis.

"Tamara, how many more of the creatures are out there, do you think?" DeWalt asked.

"Feels like a hundred, at least. I only sense them through *it*. They're feeding organic energy back to the *shu-shaaa*. And the more it eats—"

"—the hungrier it gets," DeWalt finished.

"We'd best give it an early breakfast, then." Chester stood up, the nerves in his knee joints flaring blue fire through his legs. The TNT in his coat pockets banged against his ribs. His side throbbed. He hoped his liver wasn't going out on him now, not after all those years of good service.

He headed up the sloping trail. The others fell in behind him.

Chapter Thirty-Three

James awoke suddenly, as if a broken knife had twisted into his guts. He found himself fully dressed. He had gone to bed not expecting to sleep. His ears had been dream sentinels as he slept, guarding the nervous bivouac of his brain. And they had sounded the alarm. He blinked into the darkness, listening.

Every tiny twig whisper, every breath of wind, every falling dead blossom was a monster, a ghostly creeping thing.

His heart twittered like a disturbed nest of rats that were now crawling up the walls of his insides.

Something wet slapped against the windowpane. He turned his head toward the spilled moonlight.

Oh, Lord, a FACE, a thick, rotten white plum.

Like the thing in the red cap.

The glass was stained with slick streaks. Pale vapor swirled from the distorted nostrils like smoke through an orchard. Then the face was gone.

James rolled out of the small bed and crept to the door. He turned the knob and the door swung open on silent, warped hinges. He stepped into the hall, the weight of his feet sending creaks into the still night. Somewhere in the living room, an old clock ticked.

James put his ear to Aunt Mayzie's door. She must have been lost in starry dreams, probably of her Theo and her little Oliver. She wasn't the sort to suffer nightmares.

But nightmares might walk through walls.

The liquid sound was now outside the house, at the side yard. James peeked through a window and saw it, swaying in the flower beds like a drunken scarecrow. The thing reached a trembling limb to caress a slim silver birch and pulled the fresh leaves to its mouth. It nibbled with toothless gums as a thread of viscous fluid trailed to the ground.

A gray cat flitted out from under the neighbor's gardening shed, pausing and arching its back as it heard the noises. Then the cat's muscles uncoiled and it silently merged with the shadows.

The mushroom creature's head swiveled like a periscope, wringing shimmering dew from the neck stump. It sloughed forward in the direction the cat had fled. The grass was wilted and bleached in the creature's wake.

James groped the air in front of him until his hand found the coffee table, then the telephone.

That's right, he told himself. *Call for the Man. Axt him to protect yo sorry black ass.*

But a nigger ain't got no business meddling. He ought to just hang in the woodwork and keep his big lips shut.

It's a whitey world. It's their trees and rivers and air and dirt. Their fucking problem, not no jazzbo's, no suh.

I's gwine see no fucking evil.

He turned quickly and saw a flash of movement, and his heart leaped into his throat. Then he saw that he was looking at the mirror that hung on the back of the open bathroom door. And the movement was only his own white eyes. He sat on the couch and waited for a morning that seemed years away.

*   *   *

Robert looked up into the deformed milk bone skull of the Man in the Moon, wondering if the moon was looking down on his wife somewhere. He drew a final puff off his third straight cigarette, then ground it into the ashtray. He always smoked out on the porch, in consideration of the kids. But now the ritual gave him no comfort. It was just a meaningless gesture, a murdering of time, a footless pacing.

He held his watch face to the moonlight. Four o'clock.

Robert thought about calling the police again to see if they'd turned up anything. But Tamara had told him that she was fine. And Tamara, unlike Robert, never lied. So all he could do was wait and worry.

And wonder about Ginger.

And the bad people with green eyes. And dirt mouths. And why he felt so helpless. He couldn't even worry worth a damn. All he could do was chain-smoke and count the stars.

Yep, he was one sorry son of a bitch.

He'd laughed at Tamara's Gloomies all along, tossed them off as a side effect of her psychology studies. As if *he* knew his ass from a hole in the ground when it came to the workings of the brain. He didn't even know his own mind, much less anything not directly related to feeding and mating and occasionally drawing a paycheck. Taking, that's all he ever did.

If he knew his own mind, maybe he could figure out why he was afraid to tell Tamara that he'd cheated on her. And that maybe he'd done it because he had reached midlife, had stood at the top of that hill and looked back and saw only his own worthless tracks. And now it was all over but the downhill slalom into the grave. And because she had power, sensitivity, imagination, she was a constant reminder of his own failings.

Robert had never fulfilled his great dreams, his expectations of fame and success and happiness and wealth. He hadn't made a single mark on the world. Even his footprints had disappeared under the shifting sands of time. And after he was gone, no one would notice his ever having *been,* much less mourn his passing.

In his ambition, his quest for radio stardom, his search for identity, he had urinated on the few flowers that had bloomed in the desert of his life. And the brightest, the sweetest, the great joy of his heart that had brought Kevin and Ginger into the world, was now beyond his help.

A siren flared in the distance and faded slowly across the dark hills. Sirens always made him think of his loved ones, especially when they might be the cause of the emergency.

He lit another cigarette and listened to the wind and other things sighing in the low branches of the forest. A winged creature flew low, brushed against the eaves of the house, and flitted back into the darkness beyond the yard.

Something pricked the back of his hand and he held it up to the square of the kitchen window light. A spider twitched on wiry legs, its plump body seeming to soak up light and cast it back like the glow-in-the-dark stars on Ginger's ceiling. He shook his hand and the spider fell to the porch. He crushed the arachnid with his shoe and studied the spot where he'd been bitten. The wound was raw and jagged, a small chunk of flesh peeled back as if the spider had fangs.

Tamara should have known it wouldn't be so easy. Did they expect the *shu-shaaa* would just let them walk up to its temporary home and fill it with dynamite and chemical poisons and then just blow a little kiss good-bye as they blasted it to smithereens?

Tamara sensed its awareness of them just as the green light fully came into view, just as they were heading down the soft-sloping ridge, just as she was stealing DeWalt's absurd thought. He was humming "When Iris Eyes are Smiling" to himself.

She sensed the white roots thickening under their feet,

turning into snakes and cables and lanyards. She heard the
trees bending low, cracking their knuckles and knee bones,
and felt the conspiracy of laurels and fern. The forest came
alive, armed with lances and clubs.

"Look out!" she yelled, ducking under a swiftly descend-
ing oak branch. DeWalt grunted as a dense limb dropped on
him from the night sky. Chester ran toward the source of the
glow, his bony shoulders stooped against the leaves that
slapped at him. Emerland ran, too, holding up his sack of
fungicide to protect his face, pale roots licking at his feet.
The two men reached the dead area around the Earth Mouth,
where the trees stood like bleached skeletons.

Tamara's mind went out to DeWalt and she felt the bright
spark of his pain and the black, swirling cloud of his panic.
Then her mind was swallowed by *shu-shaaa* and its frozen,
grinning fog. She fought it off and helped DeWalt stand.

"It's stronger," he said, his face pale and wide in the
moonlight.

She nodded. "We'd better hurry," she whispered, not knowing why she was whispering. Because *shu-shaaa* already knew.
Everything and more. It had probed their minds and souls,
plumbed the depths of their hearts, stolen the secret symbols
of their hopes and dreams.

And though it didn't understand, it knew enough to be
afraid.

It sent a thick root out of the ground and up her leg. The
root probed like a maggot under her skirt before wrapping
around her bare thigh. She slammed the can of Roundup
against it, bruising herself with the effort. The root twisted,
trying to pull her to the soil within reach of its brethren.
Struggling to stay upright, she twisted the can's cap and
pulled the plastic safety rings free, then splashed the concentrated poison on the base of the root. It writhed and shrank
back and then flopped to earth.

The shotgun exploded, both barrels, the thunderclap rumbling through the thickets and echoing off the ridge. Chester

stood near *shu-shaaa,* looking like a paper doll cut from black construction paper, gunsmoke silhouetted against the glow. Emerland hunched behind him like a rabbit. Tree limbs swatted stiffly at DeWalt, hickory and birch and wild cherry animated into action.

Her own psychic powers pulsed, charged with energy. She fought through *shu-shaaa*'s fog, pushed her psyche like a butter knife through cheese, bluntly reached her mind into Emerland's, feeling his fear and revulsion and hopelessness and his deep desire to lie in the soil and cover his ears and clamp shut his eyes.

"Stand up," she ordered him silently. Emerland looked around as if trying to figure out where her voice was coming from. He stood, trembling, the Sevin in his arms. Briars grabbed at his pants.

"Follow Chester," she thought at him. He nodded, and in the foul radiance, she could see the tears sliding down his cheeks. He was thinking of the voices of devils and angels and madnesses, each of them the same in his mind.

DeWalt pushed at the leaves that pattered against him like moths.

"I think I can make it," DeWalt said, rubbing his shoulder. Tamara hooked her arm in his, glancing warily at the carpet of leaves, wondering what might lie beneath it. Her skin itched where the root had rasped against it.

"I wasn't going to leave you," she said.

"What a noble woman."

"You've got the detonator, after all."

"It's nice to be needed for a change." He tried to laugh but coughed instead, and they stumbled toward the light, kicking at the tentacles that waved at their feet. Nearer the Earth Mouth, all the organic matter had died, its energy sapped and its bones sucked clean, plants and trees grayer than deep winter. Tamara helped DeWalt into the ashen ring of death. They caught up with Chester and Emerland, who were hiding behind a cold outcrop of granite.

The odor of fungus and rot hung in the air. The Earth Mouth throbbed, shaking the earth around the group. Neon pulses of light vomited from the alien throat: lime, then crimson, then indigo.

Tamara whispered loudly enough to be heard over the low rumbling wind, "It knows why we're here."

"I don't even need to read minds to know that the alien sonuvabitch is mighty pissed," Chester said. He reloaded the shotgun with trembling fingers.

"Wh-what do we do now?" Emerland's head swiveled rapidly back and forth as if he were watching a Ping-Pong match from the front row.

Chester and DeWalt looked to Tamara, silently acknowledging that she was the leader now that Chester had brought them through the woods.

"First the fungicide, then the TNT," she said. "Maybe the explosion will spread the poison to the far reaches of the thing. It's trying to dig its way to the water table. If it gets there . . ."

"And didn't you say something about sunup?" Chester looked up through the inert trees. The night was losing its grip and the moon had fallen low and weak in the sky. Dawn pinked the top of Antler Ridge in the distance.

"Wire the TNT together, just a few sticks should be enough to set off the whole batch," Tamara said, pulling the sticks from her pocket and placing them on the ground before DeWalt. She had known nothing about explosives before, but now she at least had DeWalt's vague knowledge, thanks to her invasion of his mind.

As he worked with the wires, running the electrical fuse into the blasting cap, Tamara leaned against a boulder. She tried to block *shu-shaaa* out of her mind, but now she was picking up the entire collective, the parts of the whole that were screaming across the galaxy, crunching matter and sucking the juice from stars as they grazed their way back to the beginning of time.

She wondered if she was strong enough. She closed down and focused, shutting off the Gloomies, turning down the whine that jammed the frequencies of her mind. Then, she reached, not across light-years but miles. To Robert.

As her mind swept out, past DeWalt's concentration and Chester's rage and Emerland's fear, she found Robert. She tried to tell him everything would be okay, that she would be home soon. And maybe since she was temporarily telepathic, she might just dig through his psyche and see what was bothering him. Maybe she could take advantage of this brief gift and find out his true feelings.

If God gave you a gift, you were supposed to use it.

She reached, trying to get a connection, but something was cutting in, static or a stronger signal. Had *shu-shaaa* gained power from just that little burst of sunrise?

Then she realized it was Ginger, asleep but with a vibrant mind, a mental radar dish looking for information. And she sensed what Ginger was sensing, that two creatures, the bad people, were emerging from the forest behind the house. And Robert was . . .

She saw now through his eyes, tasted his acrid cigarette, smelled the dew on the grass, felt the rough grain of the porch rail under his elbows, the throbbing raw ache in the back of his hand where he had been tainted and infected. She felt the strong urge that tugged him toward the forest, heard the strange voice that called him to go among those leaves and meet the things that would welcome him fully into the fold.

Tamara jolted Ginger, telling her to wake up and bring Daddy in, telling her to hurry hurry hurry because there wasn't much time and the orange daybreak jumped a little higher in the sky and the two creatures twitched with new hunger and they sensed Robert's bioenergy and *hurry Ginger hurry.*

The connection died, cutting off like a phone line in an electrical storm.

Because the earth moved.

* * *

Nettie was floating floating floating heart of feathers in Bill's arms only his arms were skin, strange skin. Why did she feel like she wanted to sleep but something wouldn't let her and why oh why was her throat so dry, had been ever since Ann Painter the Savior no the shu-shaaa *had planted that kiss that drowned both body and soul—and what was that light?—oh, Bill, you better put me down because now I want to kiss you and then you'll be like us everything must be us and my mouth can't tell you to put me down and save yourself but how foolish it all was, once was blind but now I see, how easy it is to surrender when nothing matters except the feeding and growing and changing and the harvest and then the end of everything.*

Oh, Bill, if I could only tell you what it's like but it's much easier to show now I see your human eyes looking at mine let's see if I can still draw your lips and your tears so warm and your skin so warm the way it was this human afternoon so long ago why are you crying, silly boy, O ye of little faith, is it because my breast is stilled but never my desire no never again that, oh, but I forgot you haven't changed, you know people never change, only things like us.

Only shu-shaaa.

Only now, my love, you said open your heart so let me in let us all in I told you there was room for forgiving it's a big room let me open the door and oh the glory.

Yes, your breath is sweet and close and I'm sorry it has to end like this but I want to give.

I can't
I love you Bill
shu-shaaa *wants*
But I can't
your light and heat forgive me
a time to embrace
forgive me my trespasses
and a time to refrain from embracing

I love you Bill
I love you shu-shaaa
I have sinned so I cannot save you
I love you too much, Bill
to make you like me
good-bye

She opened her eyes and Bill saw the green glow flickering in her retinas, something inside her trying to swell and explode. She twitched in his arms, tossed her frantic hands around his neck, drawing his head down for a final kiss. Bill yielded, helpless against the power she held over him.

Bill knew she was already gone, already infected, already like the monsters that milled outside the house. But still she lived, somehow, even without a heartbeat. And Bill couldn't resist her suddenly too-red mouth. Many things sparkled in her eyes, things beyond his simple understanding, but all were beckoning and tempting. Their lips nearly touched, but at the last moment she stiffened and pushed him away.

Bill held Nettie against his chest as the warmth faded from her body. He pressed his face near her mouth, hoping to feel the vapor of her breathing. But all he felt was the mist of his own tears as her flesh wilted in his arms.

"Bill, come on!" Sarah was at the back door, looking through the peephole. "Those things . . . whatever they are, they're not back here."

"Nettie," he said to Sarah, softly. He was holding Nettie as if she were a rag doll whose threads were unraveling.

"We've got to go now, Bill," Sarah said, coming to him and tugging at his elbow. The preacher and his congregation still battered at the front door. Sarah glanced into the living room, then shut her eyes against her own remembered horrors. "My parents—I know how you feel. But we can't give up. You wouldn't let me, and now I'm not going to let you. We've got to try to live . . . for them."

Bill looked at Sarah, then back down to Nettie.

"She's dead, Bill," Sarah said. "I'm sorry, but that won't bring her back. She's with God now."

Bill wasn't so sure about that. Whatever those monsters had planted inside her, whatever they had done to her—

"Let's go," Bill said through gritted teeth.

Sarah threw open the door and they ran across the side yard, Bill carrying Nettie. He felt naked under the moonlight, exposed to God, raw. His truck was in the parking lot, its engine still running. Whatever the creatures were, their hands seemed too clumsy to use keys. He thanked the Lord for that small blessing.

Sirens flared down the narrow street and red lights strobed across the tops of trees. Bill slipped once and saw a fluid movement out of the corner of his eye, but he regained his footing and ran without looking back. They reached the truck just as a police car skidded to a stop beside the graveyard.

"You drive," Bill yelled at Sarah. He gently lifted Nettie into the truck seat as Sarah slid behind the steering wheel.

"Take her out of here," Bill said.

Arnie McFall, the town patrolman, jumped out of the police car and ran toward Bill. Sarah backed up the truck, throwing broken asphalt as the big tires spun. Bill watched until the truck was out of sight, then turned toward the graveyard.

Arnie had his gun out and was shining a spotlight at the figures wafting among the tombstones and the cemetery trees.

"What in the holy hell *are* they?" Arnie asked Bill, not knowing whether to shoot or jump back into his cruiser and speed away.

"Hell's people," Bill said, just before the ground rumbled and the grave markers toppled and the night fell in.

*   *   *

The alien absorbed the vibrations through its altered cells. The chaotic waves emanating from the approaching specimens disrupted its feeding, disturbed its healing, scattered its focus. It signaled the outlying roots and spore-infected units, commanding them to withdraw, centralizing its energy in the heart-brain.

The symbols swarmed, broke loose, and spilled through the soup of its senses:

Tah-mah-raaa-kish.

Eyez-gwine-see.

Luv-yoo-bill.

No-fuk-eeeng-eee-vil.

Hells-pee-pull.

Gwine-see.

Sun-uv-a-hooor.

Tee-in-tee.

Poy-zun.

Poy-zun.

Kish-poy-zun.

Tah-mah-raaa.

Poy-zun.

The shock of the dark energy sent ripples through the alien, stunning it, compelling it to contract around its center. Driven by instinct into self-preservation, it huddled itself into its birth position.

Chapter Thirty-Four

Robert felt the tremor. It was slight, just enough to knock the ash off his cigarette. He knew that there were few earthquakes in the Appalachians, that the upheavals and tectonic distress that had pushed the mountains out of the crust were eons past. He wondered if the construction crews were blasting over at Sugarfoot again. It seemed too early for them to be creating such a public disturbance.

And he wondered why he wanted to go out into the woods, with his hand throbbing and his head splitting open in pain, his thoughts not quite fitting together.

The screen door creaked open, the loose glass rattling. Ginger held the door open with a small hand. Her eyes were wide and Robert looked into them. Then he shook his head. For a moment, they had looked exactly like Tamara's.

"Come in, Daddy," she said, with no sleep in her voice.

"Another bad dream, sweetheart?" Robert said, grinding his smoke into the ashtray and staring into the forest.

"No, Daddy. Mommy says come in."

Her face was so solemn that Robert almost laughed. Almost. "What is it, Ginger?"

"Mommy says the *shu . . . shu*-something"—Ginger

scrunched up her face in concentration—"the bad people are coming. Out of the woods."

"Who?" Tamara couldn't have called, or else Robert would have heard the phone ring. Ginger must have had a bad dream. And why did his head hurt so much?

"Please come in, Daddy," Ginger said, and then she was a six-year-old again, pleading and confused. "They speak for the trees."

"Like the Lorax."

"No, not like him."

"Okay, honey. I'm coming."

Robert looked around and saw nothing but the dim outlines of trees whisking faintly in the stale dawn breeze. But he stepped inside and closed the door, then locked it. He knelt and hugged Ginger. "We'll be safe now."

"Mommy thinks she hopes so."

Robert wiped at his eyes. Must have been the lack of sleep that made him confused, made him want to go under the trees and lie down in the leaves. Maybe he was dreaming right now, and had brought Ginger into it to keep away the loneliness.

"They speak for the trees," Ginger repeated.

"Mr. Sun is coming up, and he makes the boogeymen go away."

"Sometimes. But not all the times."

Her eyes were too earnest, too wise and knowledgeable for a child's. He loved her so much. He hoped that she wouldn't be cursed all her life with the Gloomies.

"I don't think so," she said, in answer to his thoughts.

Virginia Speerhorn felt the tremor in her sleep, and it woke her up without her knowing why. She thought it was the excitement of her big day that had caused her insomnia.

She rubbed her eyes and looked at the clock. It was already five. Time for her to get up anyway. She wanted to take a shower and spend a half hour on her makeup. Then a quick breakfast and she'd be downtown before most of the tourists crawled out from between the sheets at the Holiday Inn.

She turned the bathroom faucet until the water was steaming hot, then stood under the showerhead. As she vigorously lathered her skin, she rehearsed the speech she was going to give on the stage before Sammy Ray Hawkins played. She believed that visualization was the key to success. She saw the moment as if it were on film.

And she was at the microphone, looking out over a sea of tourists and voters and big spenders and community leaders and movers and shakers, and they all looked up up up at her, every head tilted, every eye fixed on their queen—no, *mayor*— waiting for her to bestow her seal of approval on the festivities. She would be in her lavender linen dress with the padded shoulders.

Virginia pictured herself addressing the crowd in her strong, amplified voice, moving the jut-jawed farmers and the tie-choked realtors with equal ease. Children would not be distracted by the smells of cotton candy and the bright balloons that bobbed on the ends of a thousand strings. The women would be unable to hide their natural jealousy. Sammy Ray himself would yield to her celebrity. Even the birds would quit their senseless chirping.

All attention would be hers. It was her favorite moment of the year, even better than when the Town Council annually approved the budget she insisted upon, even better than sitting in the lead car during the Fourth of July parade, even better than being declared the winner and still-reigning champ of the Windshake mayoral elections.

She stepped out of the shower and toweled off, running the fabric luxuriantly over her skin. The phone rang, but she knew it would stop before she had time to reach it. Then she heard the thumping at the front door. She had a reputation as an early riser, but no one would dare be so presumptuous at this hour. She slipped into her robe, shivering as she walked down the hall to the door.

Virginia turned on the porch light and squinted through the peephole, expecting either Chief Crosley with news about Emerland or one of the Blossomfest committee members with an eleventh-hour problem. At first, she wasn't sure what she was seeing. Her breath fogged the peephole glass like Vaseline over the eye of a camera. She looked again at the wide distorted froggish face and the quivering flesh, at those familiar freckled cheekbones that were so much like her own. She saw the son she had raised and treasured and diapered and suckled, the boy with those deep green eyes— no, Reggie had *brown* eyes.

And he was supposed to be in bed. Confused, she opened the door. Her baby was hurt or sick . . . her son was . . . Reggie was home.

He fell into his mother's arms as the earth shook again.

Rocks and dirt clods showered down on the group and the boulders wiggled like loose teeth. Bits of soil and thick rot spewed from the Earth Mouth.

"Sonuvawhore!" Chester shouted, falling backward and dropping his shotgun. It clattered against stone and slid to the ground.

Chester rolled over onto his hands and knees and scrabbled to the edge of the granite face that shielded them from the Earth Mouth.

"Dee-double-damn you. We're going to blow you back to hell," Chester yelled, shaking his fist in the air. The tremor eased and Chester looked back to see DeWalt sweating over the TNT. Tamara was watching DeWalt, too, but her eyes seemed focused beyond the paper-wrapped sticks.

"I wonder how stable that stuff is," Emerland said, grinning like a doped-up court jester. Chester figured Emerland was touched in the head, two pecks shy of a full bushel, nuttier than a Payday bar. Hell, they *all* were, every single goddamn thing in the ass-end-up universe.

"Don't know if we ought to wait around for the next little hiccup," Chester said.

Tamara finally spoke. "Gentlemen, I think it's time. Is the detonator ready, Herbert?"

DeWalt nodded. "As far as I can tell. May as well put the rest of the TNT into the thing. I just have to push this button. The explosion of this batch will set off the rest of it."

Tamara lifted the can of Roundup from where it had fallen on its side. She carried it to the ledge, removed the cap, and tilted the can, letting the thick concentrate glug down into the deep alien hole. The wormy tendrils inside the throat shriveled and writhed and the white roots along the stream bank began turning to jelly. Tamara tossed the empty can into the dark opening.

"Drink up, you old bastard," Chester said. He lifted the sack of Acrobat M-Z and tore the flap, ripping at the paper with his aching fingers. He tossed it over the side in a white dust storm, then emptied his pockets of the TNT and rolled the sticks gently into the hole. Emerland followed suit with the Sevin after breaking the bag open against an edge of sharp stone.

"Attaway to go, Emerland." Chester slapped the developer on the back. Chester was starting to like him a little, now that both of them had dirty knees and money didn't matter. He wondered if maybe they were all the same under the skin after all, that rich or poor or sinner or saint, they were all equal in the eyes of God when they faced a common enemy.

Naw, he thought. *Don't reckon so.*

He chomped into his tobacco and rolled it around in his mouth to collect some juice, then spat into the Earth Mouth.

He watched with satisfaction as powdery molds fell from the roof of the cave. He noticed for the first time that the light of dawn was now brighter than the neon radiance of the hole.

The ground shook again, frantically but with less force. Chester hoped that the poison was slowing it down, making it weaker. Tamara had said something about the alien becoming part of what it ate, and if it was part of the Earth now, then a generous helping of earthly poison ought to put a twist in its innards.

"Do it. The sun," he heard Tamara saying to DeWalt.

"Can't."

Chester turned and saw the tears in DeWalt's eyes.

DeWalt pushed the button again. "Must be the battery. Dead."

They looked at each other. "Then so the fuck are *we*," Chester said.

The Earth Mouth rumbled as if in agreement.

"Ginger? Honey? What did you—" Robert stopped. Then he tried an experiment.

"No, Daddy, I don't want any chocolate milk. That's only for nice times, not now," Ginger said.

"Can you—?"

"—hear Mommy? Sometimes her words just come in my head. She thinks it's sort of silly. But she's scared, too."

Anxiety ground Robert's guts between its molars. "Can you take me to Mommy?"

"No, she doesn't want me to. She wants us to stay here. Until they blow up the monster . . ."

"*They?*"

"Emerland and Chester and Herbert DeWalt. That's funny, DeWalt has a bleeding heart."

"Tell me about them."

She did.

* * *

Bill felt empty, aching from a loneliness, as if his heart had been ripped out and replaced with straw. Yet he also burned with rage at the things that had killed Nettie. He turned away from the graveyard and looked at the patrolman.

Arnie swung his two-handed grip on the gun from side to side, tracking the slow, swarming movements among the trees and monuments. His eyes were wide with fear and shock. "Do I shoot them, or what? Where the hell is the chief when a body needs him?"

Bill figured they didn't teach this situation at the police academy. "It's no sin to kill what's already dead," Bill said. "Or at least ought to be."

"Are you drunk or something?"

"No. Was blind but now I see."

Sandy Henning fell through the hedge ten feet away from them and looked up with her deep alien eyes. She ran the broadleaf of her tongue over her swollen lips. She sprayed something toward the sky, her sagging face quivering. Arnie pulled the trigger twice, and the thing that had been Sandy Henning exploded into a slick pool of miasma.

"They're juicy," Bill said. "Miracles never stop ceasing. Behold. He turns the water into wine."

"Bill?"

Bill looked at the stars and the fading moon, trying to see the face of his cruel God.

"Bill?" Arnie asked again, and Bill could actually hear the patrolman gulp.

"Yes, Arnie?" Bill smiled. His smile scared himself almost as much as it did Arnie.

"Got a shotgun in the car, if you're up to helping."

Bill followed Arnie to the cruiser, its lights oscillating against his face in a steady panic. Arnie tossed Bill the shotgun, a short-barrel pump-action. Then he reached under the dash and pulled out his radio mic. "Unit Six here, you copy, Base?"

Static squawked into the air. The hedges were coming to life, teeming with the creatures who had turned their affections toward Bill and Arnie. Bill pumped the shotgun and the clack was pure metal authority.

"10-4, Unit Six, I copy," the radio sputtered. "What's your 10-20?"

"Responding to that 10-36 at Windshake Baptist. I've got a 10-44, or, uh, a 10—hell, I don't know if this situation's even *got* a damned number."

"Come again?"

"10-33. Send backup. On the double. Got some creepers here."

"10-9, Unit Six?"

"Screw it." Arnie tossed the mic onto the seat. He turned and fired his revolver at the nearest moist hunk of plantmeat. Bill raised the shotgun and pressed the butt against his shoulder.

"We will come rejoicing, bringing in the sheaves," Bill sang in a barely recognizable melody, then sent a palmful of pellets screaming into the night.

James looked hopefully out the window as the heavy moon sagged over the horizon, its gravity towing the night along with it. The orange and red flames of dawn licked at the retreating darkness.

Maybe now he would be safe. Now he could warn people, in the daring daylight when sanity wasn't as suspect. He hadn't see any more of *them* in the last couple of hours. He'd heard no slogging or snapping, only the drumming of his beaten heart and the occasional wail of sirens. He went to check on Aunt Mayzie. He knocked on her door, softly at first. No answer.

He opened the door a crack, peered in, and saw her still

form on the bed. She would be safer there than coming with him. He let her sleep.

James went outside, smelling the air with its fragrant blossoms and lawn grass and faint trace of decomposition. It was an air he was almost afraid to breathe, a spring freshness that he'd never again be able to trust. He looked around, at the shadows of the trees and shrubs, at the fence covered with honeysuckle vines. Nothing moved along the street, as if even the wind was still in bed. He jogged toward town, his head up.

The first of the vendors were out uncovering their display tables and draping their banners. They worked like automatons, Styrofoam coffee cups steaming at their elbows as they arranged their wooden ducks and woven baskets and birdhouses and handmade quilts. Most of them were craft gypsies, in town for a fast buck and a ticket to the next one. The woman at the Petal Pushers's booth barely gave him a glance as he passed her.

A couple of long-haired men in shorts, tank tops, and big boots were running wires to the performers' stage, troubleshooting the sound system. A blond-haired woman sat behind the mixing board, arching her back as she swept her hair behind her. One of the sound men walked over to her and planted a greasy kiss on her lips. The other roadie climbed onto the stage and started speaking into a microphone.

"Testing, testing, one-two-three," his voice boomed out of the speaker stacks. A few heads turned from the booths.

James kept moving toward the stage, the dew thick under his Nikes. If he could get to the microphone, maybe he could warn them.

"Testing, testing . . . this is only a test," the roadie said.

Something stumbled from the shrubs at the edge of the Haynes House and reached for the source of the noise. James saw its dripping jaws and the unmistakable hunger in its eyes. Its *green* eyes.

The roadie at the microphone didn't notice that the band

had attracted a new groupie. He kept on with his sound check, trying to draw the attention of the snuggling couple behind the mixing board. "Had this been an actual emergency, you would have been instructed . . ."

James shouted at the roadie, but the man couldn't hear over his own amplified voice. The watery monster fell onto the stage and slid on its belly like a mutated and overgrown infant.

" . . . uh, where to tune . . . blah, blah, blah. Hey, Mick, is that all right, man?"

But Mick was too busy with the curves and tongue of the blonde to respond.

James waved his arms at the roadie and pointed to the creature.

The roadie ignored James, experienced in dealing with crazed fans and overdose cases. "Yo, Mick? That loud enough?"

The marsh-creature fell against the drum kit, knocking over a cymbal stand. Its pale skin glistened under the early sun. The roadie turned and saw the horror that was only a few feet from his ankles. A scream pealed from somewhere down the block and a table full of handmade pottery clattered onto the street.

Somebody ran behind the stage, too fast to be one of the creatures, and James heard another scream. He wouldn't have to warn them after all. Seeing was believing. Even if you weren't sure what you were looking at.

The roadie kicked at the marsh-creature and his boot stuck in the jelly of its neck. The creature reached with thorny hands and clamped onto the man's shin. His scream ripped through the microphone and across the upset morning.

"Help me, Mick—iiiiieeeee." The roadie whimpered from fear as he fell. Mick started around the mixing board, then got a better look at the thing that was attached to his buddy. He slowly backed slowly away, his eyes like cameras taking horror stills.

The blonde screamed and ran toward the Haynes House. She was up the steps and headed for the door when the nearby haystack erupted. One of the creatures fell onto her, chaff clinging to its wet skin as it hugged. It pulled her into the hay and gurgled contentedly as it sucked her face.

James jumped onto the stage and grabbed the mic cable and pulled the stand toward him. The marsh-creature crawled over the roadie, leaving a slimy trail across the man's skin. James lifted the mic stand and swung the heavy cast-iron base into the creature's back. Raw, milky fluids oozed from the wound, but the creature kept on with its mission. It pressed its wide mouth against the man's face, muffling his final scream.

James looked down from the stage and saw that a half dozen of the things had come out of the alleys and back-streets and woods.

Hell's come to the High Country, he thought. *Some hero you turned out to be. A ghetto Paul Revere with a bum horse.*

"Run, you stupid bastards!" James yelled into the micro-phone. The roadie sprawled and relaxed, staring at the sun, a stupid smile of joy crossing his face as the creature slid off of him. The roadie rolled toward James, the beginning of an unhealthy glow in the dead, eager eyes.

James jumped from the stage and ran toward Mayzie's house. He wondered what he'd hoped to accomplish in the first place. He'd seen *Night of the Living Dead*. They shot the niggers no matter what. If there was a riot, the best place to be was out of sight and out of mind.

Along Main Street, the vendors fell over one another as they tried to escape. Two elderly women were pressed against the locked door of a drugstore. A bearded man with glasses gathered up leather goods that had spilled from his table, mindless of the horror in his pursuit of commerce. James ran past him, kicked in the glass of the drugstore's door, and helped the women inside.

"Hide way back in the dark," he said, then left them heading down the aisles.

A man in a sweater-vest and headphones was tangled in electronic equipment and cords. A vinyl banner that read WRNC 1220 AM was draped across the front of his table.

He lifted a hand mic and said, "This is Melvin Patterson live at Blossomfest, and you won't believe this—I *see* it and I still don't believe it—live from WRNC, brought to you by your good friends at Bryson Feed Supply—"

A slick creature in khaki rags rose up from behind the table and clamped a hand on the announcer's shoulder. The man continued speaking into the mic: "—something's going on and it seems like a stampede of customers, so round up the family and get down here before all the good stuff's gone."

The creature yanked at the man, spun him, and the mic dropped to the ground. James ran to the table to help, but the creature had already swallowed the man's tongue and groped at his eyes with fibrous fingers.

James slipped into an alley, hoping the creatures hadn't noticed him. They hadn't.

They were too busy with the harvest.

Chapter Thirty-Five

Tamara looked into the dark maw of the *shu-shaaa*. A thick gurgling, what might have been a chuckle, arose from deep within the alien's bowels. Then she was inside DeWalt's head, attending the latest meeting of the Royal Order of the Bleeding Hearts.

Mr. Chairman, I've failed. Again.

Because you went beyond your capabilities, Oh Brother. You tried to make a difference. You tried to give a damn.

I thought . . . maybe just once—

—you'd do something for somebody besides yourself? Oh Brother of mine, Oh Bleeding Heart, pardon my laughter. After fifty-plus years of doing nothing, you thought you'd tie on a Superman cape and save the world? That's rich, Brother.

But at least I tried. I *tried.*

And failed, as usual. And do I detect an itch?

"It's okay, Herbert. It's not your fault."

"Tamara?" DeWalt wasn't sure if he'd heard her voice or imagined it.

"Yes."

In here? How—?

"I don't know. I don't know a lot of things. But I know it's

better to try. To care. It's what makes us human. It's what
separates us from the thing we're trying to kill."

*Look here, lady. I don't know what you're doing breaking
into this meeting—this is a private club, and this meeting is
members only—but the Lodge Brother is happier when he
DOESN'T care.*

Mr. Chairman, she has power. She knows about the alien.
About you.

*Oh Brother, nothing's as alien as your own inner self.
That's the truly frightening thing.*

"No, Herbert, that's not the worst thing. Numbness is.
Emptiness. Coldness. Being dead with no hope or memory
of life."

Hey, you. Get out of here. The Brother's mine.

"Herbert, I'm going to show you . . . let you feel what
shu-shaaa wants for us, for everything. This is its memory
of how the universe was *before*. And how *shu-shaaa* wants it
to be again."

Uh . . . too black . . . don't let me suffocate.

Bullshit, Brother. It's one of her tricks.

"See, Herbert? That's worse than anything. And that's the
same thing your Chairman wants, only on a lesser scale.
Nothingness."

Tamara, how can we—

"I don't know. But we can't surrender. To this Earth
Mouth *or* our fear."

But that TNT was our only hope.

"No. Hope is our only hope."

*Brother, don't listen to her. Better safe than sorry. Mr.
Chairman? Brother?*

"Herbert, what are you—"

Mr. Chairman, I would like to turn in my resignation to
the Royal Order of the Bleeding Hearts, effective immediately.

"*No,* Herbert, not that."

Yes, Tamara. It's the only way. And 'tis a far, far better thing, blah blah blah.

Brother! Hands back to balls at once.

Sorry. Meeting adjourned.

"Herbert, don't!"

Brother—

Shut the hell up, Mr. Chairman.

The alien shivered in the heat of its pulsing heart-brain. The confusing symbols raced through its pulpy flesh, sparking contractions among its tendrils.

Bleee-deeeng.

Haaart.

Tah-mah-raaa-kish.

Dee-waaalt.

Maz-zah-sun-uv-aaa.

Che-sher-sun-uv-aaa.

Sun-uv-aaa.

Ohp.

Aaar-on-lee-ohp.

Ohp-is-aaar-on-lee-ohp.

Tah-mah-raa.

"Our only hope," Tamara thought. "Hope is our only hope."

DeWalt is going to do it, and maybe I shouldn't try to stop him.

Because *su-shaaa kish* and the *shu-shaaa* was afraid and *shu-shaaa* was beautiful and loved her loved her loved her—

She put her hands over her ears but still the alien loved her.

Chester wasn't sure what was happening. First, DeWalt had frozen over the TNT, staring at the detonator switch in his hand. Tamara was looking at DeWalt strangely, as if seeing the back of his eyelids. Emerland was gaping over the ledge at the rancid pulsing throat of the alien sonovawhore.

Another tremor shook the stones loose, and after the dead trees stopped swaying, DeWalt stood up. He ripped the shotgun from Chester's hands.

"Don't do it, DeWalt," Tamara said.

Chester didn't know what she was talking about. DeWalt had fucked up the TNT in typical California Yankee fashion, or else Emerland had screwed it up by being a goddamned cheapskate who bought lousy equipment for his demo crews. It wasn't Chester's fault, no matter what. Hell, maybe it was nobody's fault but God's to make such a thing and then drop it right here on land that had been Mull property since the Revolutionary War.

He was tired and grouchy and way too sober. "Damned shotgun won't do diddly against that thing," he said to DeWalt.

"Maybe not by itself. But close enough, it might—"

"—trigger the blasting cap," Tamara said. "With enough heat and pressure. But that would be too close—"

"To survive? I thought of that."

"I know," Tamara said.

Chester thought they were both crazy, as addled as that monstrous creature that had embedded itself in the mountainside. Tamara stepped forward, raising her hand to stop DeWalt, the sickly alien light pulsing off her face. DeWalt leveled the shotgun at them.

"I suggest you folks head for the hills," DeWalt said. "Because like Bobby Zimmerman said, way back in better days, a hard rain's gonna fall."

Bill was out of ammunition. One of the things stepped toward him and he gripped the hot barrel of the shotgun and was about to swing the heavy wooden butt into its face. The face belonged to Fred Painter, fellow member of the Windshake Baptist Board of Deacons.

No, Bill told himself. *It's not Fred anymore. Now it's one of THEM.*

Old Fred had switched sides. Fred was among the armies of the Antichrist. The enemy. Evil.

"Onward, Christian soldiers," Bill yelled, swinging the gunstock into the bloated face. It exploded like a bag of soup.

Arnie shook the empty shell casings from his revolver and reloaded behind the open door of the cruiser. Now that day was breaking, Bill could see how badly Arnie trembled. Wet corpses littered the edge of the parking lot, limbs still writhing.

"Come on, Bill," Arnie yelled. "Let's get the hell out of here. There's too many of them."

Bill stepped toward a gap in the hedges.

"Bill!"

He turned and waved. God had given him a mission. He struggled through the bushes into the graveyard. He would take back the church.

Bill asked God to give him strength. Not the strength to resist the devil, but the strength to send the devil back to hell. Leaves and moist things shimmered at the corners of his vision, but he fixed his eyes on the bronze cross that caught the sunlight above the roof of the church. Golden rays poured around the cross, a sign from heaven if there ever was one.

Hope is our only hope. The thought came from nowhere. Bill smiled. That was exactly the type of message God would send in a dark moment.

"Hope is our only hope," he said aloud. He'd have to remember that one.

Bill headed for the open vestry door. Hallelujahs spilled from his lips.

James shook Mayzie, trying to wake her. She wouldn't open her eyes. She was stiff and cold.

Dead.

He was supposed to protect her. He had failed. One little job, one little purpose on earth, and he'd messed it up. How could he ever face his mother? How could he ever look in the mirror again?

He sat on the edge of the bed and the mattress springs groaned. His aunt's body shifted slightly. As he looked out the window, as he listened to the faint screams and distant sirens, he watched a honeybee lighting on a damp Easter lily.

He hated flowers.

There was a noise on the windowsill.

The glistening mailman stumbled into the flower bed outside the window. James jumped back as the creature slapped a palm against the glass. The mailman grinned, drooling fluorescent nectar. James was sickened by the sight.

This must be the monster who'd ended Mayzie's life. This sludge-faced mutant had taken away the woman who'd given him nothing but love, even when James was thinking only of his own problems. This thing was to blame for the great ache in his chest.

James lifted the window, his head dark with rage. The trembling creature reached for James as if it bore special delivery mail. Its green eyes flashed in joy. The sun was higher now, hot and red, and James wondered which side the sun would take in the coming battle.

Robert held Ginger on his lap. She'd finally fallen asleep, but Robert was afraid he'd never sleep again. Because Ginger had told him everything her mom had seen, about something called *shu-shaaa* and how it ate the trees and came from the sky and all kinds of cosmic things that weren't part of Ginger's vocabulary.

Robert had no choice but to believe. Because he'd heard Tamara briefly in his head himself, gotten a flash-frozen bolt of the black nothingness that *shu-shaaa* stored in the bowels of its long memory.

He looked out the window at the sun spilling onto the tops of the trees and sending the shadows of night fleeing toward the west. He imagined the slime-skinned people wandering through the undergrowth, foraging, digging up roots and grubs and berries, shopping for meat.

Maybe it was time to have a little faith. He couldn't pray, that would be too corny. But he could have faith in his wife. Not that he'd proven to be faithful himself, but at least she had courage. A courage that came from the family, from her belief in his love, from the foundation of the home.

The courage to hope.

And if she could somehow pick up on his thoughts, maybe it would help her in some way to know that he was behind her. That he loved her. That she was the only thing he wanted to believe in. That he'd help her make the sacrifice.

He just hoped her sacrifice wasn't the ultimate kind.

Bill found Preacher Blevins at the pulpit, standing under the vaulted ceiling. The preacher was a blasphemy, the devil, even if he was more milk white than red. The preacher was gnawing on the wooden cross that had hung from the back wall of the sanctuary. Ripe goo dribbled from his ruined lips.

Bill walked down the aisle, his feet hushed by the carpet. The thing that had once been his preacher, the leader of Windshake's flock, the living vessel of God's word, was now a slobbering hell spawn. Blevins had walked after strange gods. And those gods had delivered him unto evil.

The preacher looked up, his green eyes piercing into Bill like twenty-penny nails through flesh. Bill kept walking.

"For God so loved the world," Bill said, summoning his courage, feeling the anger settle deep inside him and give way to calmness.

The sun streamed through the plate glass, throwing beams of blue and red and yellow across his path.

"He gave his only begotten Son, so that whosoever should believeth in Him . . ."

The preacher dropped the cross onto the dais and lifted his rotten arms.

" . . . shall not perish, but have everlasting life."

Bill tossed the slime-covered shotgun into the pews and it clattered across oak. The Lord's love would be his weapon. Hope was his sword, faith was his shield. He stepped onto the dais.

Chapter Thirty-Six

DeWalt pulled in the hundred-foot fuse with one hand, stepping on the slack with each tug, pointing the shotgun with his other hand. Tamara screamed into his mind, but he was too distracted to listen, too busy toting up the plusses and minuses of his life. He wouldn't let her stop him, he wouldn't let the throbbing alien scare him away. Then he had the blasting cap in his grasp, wired inside three sticks of TNT.

"So long, Chester, Tamara. Emerland. You, too, Mr. Chairman," he said.

Tamara will understand, and maybe after it's all over, she'll be able to explain to the others.

"Better run," DeWalt said to them, stepping around the rocks to the edge of the Earth Mouth. Emerland was the first to move, taking a hesitant step, then another. Tamara started to speak, and DeWalt waved the shotgun at her. She tried once more to get inside his head, but he begged her to stay away. She followed the developer down the trail, because she knew how serious he was about not letting anyone stop him.

Chester paused to toast DeWalt with the last of his moonshine. "I guess you're not a gutless California Yankee after all."

"Screw a blue goose, Chester."

"I'll do that, partner." Chester chucked his empty liquor jar into the Earth Mouth, nodded farewell, and followed the others. Just before he turned, DeWalt saw a glint in the old man's rheumy eyes that just might have been tears.

As DeWalt watched them go, he tried to calculate the force of the coming explosion. The sun was rising fast now, its golden eye peering over the far ridges. He forced his aching knees over the lip of the putrid hole, and the creature's aroma of decomposition and decay rose around him like an otherwordly smog.

Tamara looked back once, but she was too far away for their eyes to meet. But not their minds.

"*Hope* is our only hope," he thought at her as he slid inside the Earth Mouth.

He saw the TNT scattered among the slick, wet stalagmites and fuzzy molds and wavering tendrils that licked at his skin, and he was overwhelmed with the unthinkable depth and power of *shu-shaaa*, and for the first time he thought of the alien as it really was: just another creature following its natural instinct.

Like him, it was just another parasite.

His mind connected to the *shu-shaaa*, and in that split-second link, the thing's intelligence washed over him, warm as south seas, and he could feel the alien trying to assimilate him, understand him; their minds swapped thoughts like a reflection bouncing between two mirrors, on and on to infinity.

Then he saw what he instantly knew was the heart-brain of the alien. It was a slick sac, throbbing in time to some cosmic clock, lavender colored and veined with liquid roots. The heart-brain sang to him, sending its lullabies into his tired mind, serenading him into what would be a long, endless sleep. The alien was beautiful. He loved it, loved it, as he had loved nothing on this earth.

How could he ever have wanted to destroy this wondrous miracle?

The thing tried to slide a word into his skull, a word picked from the dark depths of his brain: *Bruuu . . . thuuu- uur. Oh bruuu-ther.*

Then Tamara was in his head again and he was afraid he wouldn't be able to pull the trigger because he only wanted to join the deep blackness the sweet nothing the dark lovely emptiness but then he knew he couldn't kill it how could he ever have wanted to kill the lovely but Tamara pulled him back with her thoughts back to Herbert the Bleeding Heart and even the Chairman was on his side and he was Herbert fucking Webster DeWalt the *Third,* goddammit, and before the alien could love him and lick him into oblivion again he was wondering if the percussion from the shotgun would be enough to detonate the blasting cap that he held in his left hand.

It was.

It wasn't enough.

Tamara sensed it, even as she felt Herbert dying, tuned in as his mind screamed red and yellow pain. She felt the quick white burning in his guts, felt something sliding out into the distant night as his thoughts fell into themselves like black holes, as he became pure light then peace then chaos. Then Herbert was out among the stars, far-flung and wide and never to be reassembled.

That microsecond became frozen like an ice crystal, its many facets glistening, each facet a different possibility. Tamara searched the long corridors: *there,* the heart-brain, demanding and winning her devotion.

"Tah-mah-raaa."

It was learning. Learning to love her. Learning to let her love *it.*

So easy. As easy as falling into a warm pool.

Just go under.

But the other facets . . .

Her love.
Kevin. Ginger. Robert.
Robert?
Yes, I'm here, honey.
Robert?
Here with you. It's beautiful . . .
No.
I can't, not alone, it's too strong.
You're not alone. Never alone.
But you see how wonderful it is, Tam. What joy. Oh, what peace.
But we can't all live. Not with that thing. It will eat us all.
I want to live.
We all want to live.
WE ALL WANT TO LIVE.

Bill tugged at the hooked briars that dug into his neck. Hot blood trickled under his shirt as he fought the preacher. He remembered some of the words that Nettie had read to him, her lively eyes flicking across the pages, her voice like music, her skin as sweet as meadows. He heard the words in his head as if she were saying them now: "He that eateth my flesh and drinketh my blood hath everlasting life, and I will raise him up on the last day."

Bill grabbed the preacher's lambent head and lifted it over the dais. Fogs leaked from the preacher's gums. Bill lost his grip on the slick, sodden skull, and the wide mouth came forward.

"So he that eateth me, the same also shall live by me."

The preacher, Satan in wet flesh, grew suddenly stronger. Bill was pushed backward, the preacher's hands sawing at the meat in his neck.

"I am the bread of life. He that eateth this bread shall live forever."

The preacher's head bent low and Bill was tilted over the

pulpit. The devil was winning. Just as the disciple Thomas had done two millennia before, Bill suffered a moment of doubt.

The preacher's raw lips pressed against his own and the first whispers of eternal hellfire licked at the base of his brain. Satan murmured tenderly, lovingly, his saliva hot on Bill's cheek.

The pulpit toppled and Satan crawled onto Bill's struggling form. Bill was trying to roll over and run, flee from the church door and away from salvation and damnation and trials and tribulations and temptations. But the devil was loathe to let him.

He struggled blindly, sliding on his back across the varnished floor. The devil hounded him, wagging its pulpy tongue. Bill's hands felt splintery wood. The cross. The Lord had provided.

Bill lifted the cross, the saliva of prayer on his lips, and drove the wooden tip between the screaming green eyes.

James grabbed the arm of the creature that leaned in the window. Juice spattered on the carpet as it smiled with rotted lips. The creature tried to speak and a drop of thick saliva hit James in the eye. At the contact, he felt a jolt like lightning, and in the same throbbing split second he was rolling, flying, soaring—sweet Jeez Louise—he was flipping out. Suddenly he was a white woman and his name was Tamara and this had to be stress taking its toll, grief scrambling his senses, a hammer of the gods shattering the gray jewel of his brain, how else could he explain away these walking mushrooms and wait a second, that was the only explanation, he had to be *dying* or something, but by God he'd take one of these bastards with him, except hold on here, Mister Wallace, this creature is already *dead* and what the hell is *shu-shaaa* and who are you, Tamara?

Whoa . . . now we're in the "heart-brain," is that right,

Tamara? That must be that swollen-looking purple thing
there, inside what looks like a disease-ridden sewer pipe.

And this is your daughter, Ginger? And your husband, Robert. Son, Kevin. Pleased to meet y'all.

So this is how it feels to be white. Funny, but it's just the
same as being black, at least from the inside. Now would
you please mind telling me what the hell is going on and
why am I here dying inside your dream and why isn't time
passing?

And you? Herbert DeWalt, you say? Okay, let me get this
straight. You're dead and you're dust and energy now but
you're not going to leave until we kick this *shu-shaaa* thing's
ass back to whatever black hole it crawled out of, and, gee,
what a swell trick this is, let's all walk in your dream, Tamara.
And I thought I was crazy before, when the green eyes got
worse than white eyes ever were.

No fooling? You want me to *join* with you, Tamara?

Because we all want to *live?*

In unity, in harmony? A peoplehood of people?

Sure, why not, got nothing better to do while I'm waiting
to wake up in a straitjacket. Right fucking on and save the
whales, sister.

You think you can beat this thing?

Yes, but you need my help? *Our* help?

Sure. I need some good karma to buy my way onto the
soul train, so I might as well go for broke. Because, like you
say, hope is our only hope.

Aaar-on-lee-ohp.

"Join with us, *think* with us, because we're all one and
only one of us can win."

Tamara's thoughts were exploding, spreading bright and
white and thin just like the universe did when it got jump-
started by physics, heat, and *shu-shaaa*. She felt James in
her head, she knew him, she lived his life, all in the eye of a

needle of a heartbeat. She sensed his ambition, and also his bitterness, his pain. His guilt. And his hope.

And others crowded behind him, Sarah Blevins, a man named Bill Lemly who held a dripping cross, Chester, Emerland, more people joining in as if answering the call of a distant bell.

A scythe of doubt cut across her mind.

Would she fail Robert like she had her father? Would she fail her children? Was she too weak to handle the gift that had been granted her? Would she let them all down?

"I won't let you fail," Robert interrupted. "I won't let *us* fail."

Their minds mingled like streams. She saw his weakness, his frailty, his humanity, but all was forgiven in that moment of mutual need. All that mattered was that he loved her. And the same humanity that was his weakness was also his strength. *Their* strength.

Funny, she'd always thought of love as an invisible but real force, only now it was taking shape and texture and color and Ginger was helping, Kevin, too, only Ginger was a lightning rod, she was harnessing and directing tremendous energy without even knowing what she was doing.

Tamara knew what the energy was.

The power of love, multiplied. Herbert, Chester, James, a dozen, no, a hundred, now a thousand human minds whose dreams and hopes and consciousness were swelling into a fat golden teardrop of heat that poured out over the *shu-shaaa* heart-brain, that suffocated and scorched the poisoned, throbbing alien.

It was like the Beatles song, all you need is love, only with looser harmonies, something that sounded like lip service when you said it aloud but became the most real thing in the universe when you actually experienced it.

And the *shu-shaaa* absorbed those thoughts, that feeling and strange emotion, reflected them back and absorbed them again, an endless loop like the infinity of two facing mirrors.

The laws of nature were flexible. Laws were made to be broken. Tamara was a conduit through which the collective energy of human souls flowed. She summoned the extra foot-pound of pressure that triggered the blasting cap of their combined minds a fraction of a second after Herbert DeWalt fired the shotgun.

And she was, and they all were, Bill Lemly driving a mahogany cross into a monstrous pasty face, because love took many forms, each strange and wonderful and equally awe-inspiring.

The power of love. Something the alien had never known, not the way a human could know it. A power beyond understanding, a power that was beyond control.

It was real here in the landscape of Tamara's imagination where this cosmic war was being waged. And right now, that was the only place that mattered.

Because love was winning. Love was hope, love was mighty, love was blind, and at the moment, love was a righteous bitch that wanted to survive.

The golden teardrop exploded with a force that rocked the far corners of the conscious universe.

And the microsecond flashed forward as she screamed her mind at the exploding heart-brain, as she drew on the power of a thousand other human minds, as the force of hope ejaculated its hot combustion into *shu-shaaa,* and it collapsed and disintegrated outward.

Dirt and stones and hunks of thick sludge spewed from the Earth Mouth, and she felt it dying—no, not dying, only changing form, changing back into random atoms and space. She felt the explosion that rocked the foundations of its alien chemistry, felt the poisons blasted to the cold heart-brain of the thing, felt its spores curdle and suffocate, felt its roots spasm and sag, felt its alien consciousness take an uncomprehending waltz into the darkness that was nothing like its vision had promised, a darkness that was only darkness, without any kind of bliss or peace or bottom—darkness and darkness only.

And it was weeping.

Then she was rolling away from the falling trees and a fist-sized rock bounced off her shoulder and Chester had his arm around her and he was mentally cussing a blue streak and Emerland and Robert and Ginger dreaming of a rabbit and Kevin person everybody at the same time too many for one brief insane moment her thoughts were out among every organism in the world, an organism orgasm, every bird and bug and dandelion and crabapple and crawfish and lily and paramecium and virus, and it was blinding madness and mercifully the too-long eye blink passed and she was spitting gravel and twigs from between her teeth as the dirt rained down through the dead leaves of trees.

Then she was Tamara again, soiled and concussed and bleeding in spots, but otherwise, more or less intact.

The explosion woke up Little Mack. He'd fallen asleep under the trailer, too tired to cry any longer. When his eyes snapped open, he'd forgotten what had happened and didn't understand why he wasn't in his bunk bed with Junior snoring above him.

Then he saw his mom, and she had found him, was coming to cuddle him, was crawling across the gravel driveway on her raw hands and knees. But she was too slippery and naked and gross and pukey and her eyes were green but their glow was fading, like a flashlight whose batteries were out of juice, and her skin was getting all shrivelly and Jell-O—looking and was starting to slide off her bones.

She looked like she was in pain, but then her upper lip fell away and she looked like she was smiling again and she looked like she wanted to give Mack a good-bye kiss but then her other lip fell off along with the rest of her face and her skull collapsed like a mud balloon and then Mack was screaming and screaming and screaming and his mother was a heap of steaming slime and then she dried under the sun and flaked and lifted away as the wind cleaned up the mess but Mack was screaming and screaming and he wasn't ever going to stop.

James's eyelids flickered open as the creature slid limply away from him. It collapsed in the flower bed beneath the window, crushing the daisies and filling the air with a thick sweet smell. James watched as the creature withered wetly and dissolved. Sirens blared across the hills.

He felt as if he'd awakened from an odd dream, one of the dense kind where you were a character in somebody else's movie. Except he somehow knew that it was real. His fingers tingled and he looked at the slick stains on the window ledge. Yes, it had been real.

Because he could still *hear* Tamara in his head.

"We won," she said. "We won."

Right on, lady. United we stand. Brotherhood of man, sister-hood of woman. A peoplehood of people.

He'd seen the explosion, a bright flash of green on the slope of Bear Claw. He'd suffered that quick slice of telepathy, and something strange had dashed across the bottom of his psyche, leaving footprints. He knew he'd never understand what really happened, but that was fine by him, because he wasn't sure he wanted to.

But he wanted to know if the victory was final.

"We can always hope," Tamara said in his head.

Hope?

Yes, he hoped. Didn't someone once say that hope was the only hope?

He had seen, in that one long heartbeat, what life had to offer, and what the options were. Things could always change for the better. His aunt was gone, hopefully to a better place, but the living had a duty to live. His mind felt clear, absent of color. Maybe *he'd* been the racist one, had taken an attitude too far, had shut himself away and enslaved himself to the very prejudice he loathed.

He sensed that the nightmare was over, that whatever had caused the horror had gone to its crazy grave, that today was the first day of something, that it was time to pick up the pieces and start all over again. It was time for a change.

Maybe sometimes people *could* change.

The trees looked vigorous and revived, as they did after a spring rain. James went out into the clean morning sun to see if anyone needed help.

Bill looked down at the stain where the devil had lain dying. The Lord had come to Bill in his moment of need, come on a white horse, no, as a white cloud, no, just pure goodness, shedding Bill of sin and darkness. The Lord had triumphed. Now Satan was back in hell, where he would lick his wounds for the next thousand years or so before he got up the nerve to try again.

But Bill wasn't worried. The Lord would always find a servant to work through, would always recruit somebody to serve as the right arm of God. Might made right, and right made might.

He took off his shirt and wiped the blood away from his neck and then cleaned the slime from the scarred cross. He carried the cross to the back of the dais and hung it gently on its hook.

Then he knelt and gave thanks.

Chapter Thirty-Seven

Chester sat on his porch and watched the government trucks and research vans and men in foil suits crawling over his property. He didn't reckon their fancy meters and screens and snoop dishes would turn up much hard scientific evidence. All that was left was a damned hole in the ground. Everything else the alien had touched had flaked off and disappeared. Still, Chester knew the goddamned government liked to make a big show when it got the chance.

They'd tried to evict him and declare his farm a disaster area, but he told them in no uncertain terms that he wasn't leaving, that they'd have to send up a tank and roll over his ass before he would get out of his rocking chair. They could dig in the dirt and scrape the trees and bottle up creek water all they wanted, but Chester wasn't going to set foot outside his property for at least a couple more weeks. He just wanted to rock and stare off into space and forget. Alien invasions were rough on an old-timer.

He lifted his moonshine to his cracked lips. He still had a few jars of Don Oscar's finest stowed away in the pantry, but soon he'd have to find a new bootlegger. He was going to miss Don Oscar.

His puppy sat at his feet, grinning around some wet leather. The little guy wasn't Boomer, but Chester figured one droopy-eared gasbag hound was the same as another. Chester had let him have Junior's abandoned footwear to gnaw on, to get his young gums toughened up.

The telephone rang. Chester had moved it out on the porch in case Tamara called. He liked the sound of her voice, especially when it was *outside* his head.

"Yuh-ello," he said.

"Chester. It's Emerland. Listen. Four million, how about that?"

"I told you the first ten times, no sale. Ain't changing my mind."

Emerland had broken both legs when a tree had fallen on him during the explosion. It had taken Tamara and Chester half the morning to carry him out, with him bitching and griping and threatening to sue every step of the way. Now the greedy bastard continually rang Chester from his hospital room, upping the ante.

"Dammit, Chester," Emerland said. "Can you imagine the publicity this is going to get as soon as the story leaks? Do you know just how much cash Alienworld will rake in after I get a theme park up and running? Can you just *imagine?*"

"No, Mister Plaster Pants. Ain't never had much imagination. Just gets a feller in trouble, as far as I can see."

"Okay, four and a quarter, you old bastard. With residuals. You know, a stake in the profits."

Maybe Chester could part with the place for five mil. It was only his birthright. Only dirt and weedy fields and falling-ass-down buildings and memories, and not all the memories were good. Every man had a price. But having Emerland swinging in the breeze was almost as much fun as a shitpile of money.

"Don't reckon so. Bye, now."

"But, *Chester—*"

Chester hung up. He wanted the line free in case Tamara called. Of course, for a while there, she hadn't needed a phone. She just spoke right into his head.

And that was creepy as hell, but kind of natural once you got the hang of it. Except her "powers," as she called them, were fading, growing weaker day by day. So she'd started keeping in touch by phone. And that was okay, too.

He looked up at the thick white clouds, good solid April clouds a body could stick a pitchfork in and twirl around like cotton candy. He wondered if DeWalt was up there, part of the clouds, part of the sky.

The government men had taken his chickens. He didn't mind the least little bit. Fewer mouths to feed. He flexed his drinking arm.

He spat toward the yard but came up short. His porch had a new stain.

James was cleaning out Aunt Mayzie's things, packing them so his mother and her family could decide how to divide them up. With the funeral so fresh in everybody's mind, it wasn't a good time to dwell on material things. Still, Mom would want the saltshaker collection. She liked little knick-knacks.

James looked at Aunt Mayzie's chair. A depression in the vinyl seat cushion made it look as if her ghost were sitting there. James sat in the ghost's lap and opened the coffee table drawer. It was full of dog-eared spiral notebooks and curling legal pads.

He pulled a notebook off the top and opened it. It was Mayzie's handwriting. He read the first page.

FOR JAMES: SNOW ON FLOWERS
On hyacinth winds,
April walks a barefoot whisper across tilted
    fields

At the shore of warm green seas, she sneezes and
*   mourns*
the coming of the hummingbirds and counts the
*   tides with watered eyes*
as butterflies cut yellow trails

Her ice-blue heart melts
under the volcano-glass stare of the far fallen
*   sun*
she glistens with reluctance

As night again collects its threads
she breathes the mint of cooling hope
and pulls the fabric, winters past,
across her moondark skin

In dreams she cries the dew.

Poetry. Hundreds and hundreds of pages of poetry. And she'd never told him. He read some more, his heart pounding with excitement. Some of it was good enough to be published, as far as he could tell. Certainly better than some of the stuff he'd read in college textbooks.

Aunt Mayzie must have been writing for years, if not decades. And she'd never said a word. Here was her life, in a million syllables and fragments and broken thoughts and taped-over rips and smeary eraser marks. The symbols of her soul. He wondered if she would mind if he mailed some of it off. He had a few literary contacts from his days at Georgetown.

Maybe he could repay her in this way, by showing her work to the world. It was the least he could do. He was starting to come to terms with his guilt. Maybe he hadn't failed her. Maybe she had just been ready to go home to Uncle Theo and Oliver.

And maybe he'd stay in Windshake a while. He'd met

Sarah on the street, when the press and the scientists and the National Guard had stirred up the town and started combing through the wreckage, trying to catch some of the drying flakes of the dead. He wouldn't mind getting to know Sarah a little better, and she'd had her own losses. Maybe they could need somebody together.

And besides, the place needed a town nig—no, make that an *African-American.*

Dignity wasn't a gift given by others, and there was no easy ticket into utopia. Dignity came with consciousness and breath. Compassion was more important than life or death, or those terrible states of existence in between. And utopia had its own problems.

He started reading the rest of Mayzie's poetry.

Bill looked out over the meadows at the foot of Fool's Knob, at the Lord's great natural work. He could almost imagine the pressed place in the grass where he and Nettie had joined in the flesh.

He still had his memories, even if they were starting to fade with the passing of time. The bad memories had fallen away, the sharp edges of nightmare had dulled, the old pains were dead and buried.

But the good ones faded, too, and that made him sad. He could barely picture Nettie's eyes. He knew they were dark brown and deep, but he couldn't quite recollect how they made crescents when she smiled. He didn't remember her voice clearly, even now, here in the field with the sparrows making their songs and the breeze tickling the jack pines. He had to breathe deeply and swell his chest to catch a faint reminder of the smell of her skin.

But they would be meeting in the sweet bye-and-bye. It was just a matter of being patient until the Lord willed him home. He only wished he could have given Nettie a good Christian burial. But she had dissolved like the others.

He couldn't bury her flesh, and her soul was far gone to a better place.

He hollowed out a depression in the damp soil with his fingers, scratching at the roots of clover and dandelions. He picked a buttercup and laid it gently in the shallow grave and pressed the dirt over the bright yellow petals.

Tomorrow was Easter, a day of rebirth. But today was just another day spent sealed inside a dark cave, waiting.

He knelt in the grass and prayed, then stood in the meadow and looked a way off.

Tamara put down the magazine she'd been reading. Ginger and Kevin were playing Sorry on the living room rug. It wasn't cold, but Robert had built a fire in the fireplace anyway. The flames were loud and cheery.

Robert sat beside her on the couch and kissed her on the neck. "I'm going to kiss you every five minutes for the rest of your life."

"Can I have that in writing?"

"Hey, you know me well enough by now. After all we've been through?"

"We can get through anything as long as we stick together," she said. So maybe that was corny. She didn't care. It was true, whether dealing with otherworldly invasions or the stresses of everyday life.

"You still haven't told me about—"

"—and I will, when the time's right. There are still a lot of things I need to figure out."

"I'm sorry for the way I acted. About the—

"—Gloomies. And being selfish."

"And doubting you. And for . . . you know."

"Shhh. I know. You're only human, thank goodness." She touched him lightly on the head. "I understand. I've *been* there, remember?"

She looked at Ginger. Her face was scrunched from concentrating on the game. Kevin was too old for Sorry, but he played because Ginger asked him. He was a good brother.

Tamara had been overloaded with powers after the explosion, almost as if *shu-shaaa*'s dying spirit had jumped into her head. And she'd been able to do all kinds of odd things. Reading minds was easy, she could handle that. It was the other stuff that scared her, like being able to move objects with her thoughts and making the tree branches bend a certain way and making the clouds gather in the sky. And she believed, though she never tried, that she could make the earth move a little faster in its orbit or the moon drop down for a good-night kiss.

And Tamara had sensed Ginger's powers, somehow a miniature, immature version of her own. No person should be so cursed. Nobody should have to see the future. She didn't want Ginger to be followed around by Gloomies for the rest of her life. So she had sucked up those powers, vacuumed them out of the corners of Ginger's mind by a process she couldn't describe in a thousand psychology papers.

Ginger turned away from her game, smiled at Tamara, then took a drink of hot chocolate. Just a normal six-year-old girl. She picked up a crayon with two bare toes and put it to her mouth and bit it.

Well, maybe not TOO normal, Tamara thought.

Tamara wished she could get rid of her own powers as easily. She didn't think she had the wisdom to wield them. She didn't think any mortal did.

But the powers were fading. Nothing lasted forever, and she now knew that was a good thing. What still bothered her was the lingering memory of the *shu-shaaa*'s dying cry.

Each night when Tamara closed her eyes and hunted for sleep, the cry haunted her. The cry was one of pain, an agony brought by understanding, because at the last, it had realized the destruction it had wrought on this world. Just before the explosion, it had linked with Tamara and translated the strange pattern of human language and thought. It had finally understood the price of its own survival. And, in its alien way, it suffered regret. It had joined with Tamara and the others in that huge tidal wave of togetherness that had swept it to destruction.

The creature had accepted its death so that others might live.

In Tamara's darkest hours, when Robert snored and the sheets were damp, she wondered if perhaps the alien had been more human than any of them.

Across the cosmos, in the nibbled edges of nebulae and Oort clouds and asteroid belts and white dwarves, *shu-shaaa* paused in its star grazing. The members felt a small prick as one of their collective died. There was no pain, only an emptiness that was quickly filled and forgotten.

They resumed their feeding.

About the Author

Scott Nicholson lives in the mountains of North Carolina, where he is currently working on his third novel, *The Manor*. Look for it in September 2004! Readers can contact Scott via his Web site at www.hauntedcomputer.com.